INEVITABLE ELLA

THE TRIPLE TROUBLE SERIES - BOOK 2

VH NICOLSON

For my family

AUTHOR'S NOTES

Please note this book comes with a content warning. This book is intended for over 18s.

My books all come with the guarantee of a happily ever after but sometimes the journey to get there can be a hard fought one. The main focus of my books is love, romance and happiness.

Please keep that in mind. Also there is lots of humor too.

However, just in case you aren't sure, and if you are a sensitive reader then please proceed with caution, here's a content warning list.

Triggers: forced marriage, kidnap, marriage of convenience, extortion, blackmail, the use of high-end escorting services.

For Content Warnings & Tropes of All My Books, Please Scan the QR Code Above.

CHAPTER ONE

Ella

"Sorry, say that again, Fraser. You *love* me?" My Scottish lilt vibrates through the echoing hotel stairwell.

Either my ears are playing tricks on my brain, or I have had one too many tequilas tonight.

"Shush, Ella, someone might hear us." Fraser darts his eyes around the space.

Detecting an edge of concern, I watch as he cranes his neck upward, making sure no one is listening on the floors above.

As he wipes his dirty-blond locks from his tanned brow, he begins nervously pacing across the concrete floor in his black patent leather dress shoes.

I wish he wasn't so flipping handsome.

He's tuxedoed up to the max, wearing it like it's his second skin.

We're at the Winner's Ball.

The flagship golf tournament, The Championship Cup, takes place every four years in our historical little town of

Castleview Cove. Today was the final and this evening we're celebrating the winner. Fraser came in fourth place.

He caught me unawares when he gently cradled my elbow, then coaxed me through the heavy door leading to the hotel fire exit stairwell.

Once out of earshot from everyone, the words *I still love you* poured from his delicious lips. He repeated them a few times before I truly understood what he was saying.

Four powerful words I never thought I'd *ever* hear from him again.

"Don't shush me. You don't get to play with my feelings, Fraser," I grit out between my clenched jaw.

As he stares at me, I feel the unspoken words dancing behind his eyes all the way down into the depths of my soul.

Determined to deflect the tears I feel forming behind my eyes, I dig my nails into the delicate fabric of my black silk floor-length evening dress.

I'm so confused. What the hell is he thinking?

My sister, Eden, bumped into Fraser on the beach a few weeks ago. He begged her to speak to me, asking me to get in touch with him again.

Hesitation held me back until I finally gave in and messaged him. I've tried so hard to release him and let go. But try as I might, the feelings I have for him still surround my heart.

Not knowing what to say, it took me a full morning to form a few simple, keep-it-breezy-how-are-you sentences. Wavering to send it or not, I hovered over that button before eventually pressing send.

Our brief conversation was exactly that, brief. We both agreed we harbored no hard feelings toward each other. He apologized. Expressing how sorry he was, and asked if I could forgive him. I agreed to do so.

Through my tight jaw, I try desperately to find the right words to say next. "We've only just started speaking to one another again, for the first time in years. You haven't spoken to me since I was twenty-one. I'll be twenty-eight soon. That's a helluva long time to then spring *this* on me. When you asked Eden to ask me to message you, I only did it to help us move forward. To be civil to one another."

I thought it would help me move on, bury the hatchet, but nope, it didn't make me feel any better. Not one little bit.

And now this? I never expected *this*.

Turning away from me, he tilts his head back, looking up through the spiral stairway, and lets out a heavy breath.

"Fraser, you left Castleview Cove to pursue your dream of becoming a pro golfer. I never stopped you. You achieved what you set out to do. But we split up. You ended it with me. It's done." My breathy voice cracks as I remember the weeks that followed his departure.

When Fraser left, I was only sixteen. He was two years older than me, but I knew, even back then, that no one would ever replace him.

After five years of dating from afar, I became accustomed to the distance. Only seeing him now and again when he returned for a few brief visits between his busy schedule.

Then he broke up with me, destroying my heart in the process.

He was, and still is, my one and only true love. Not that I would ever tell him that.

Fraser swings around to face me again, determination written all over his face. "I never, for one minute, ever stopped loving you, Ella. I never wanted to split up with you. I *had* to." His voice full of painful regret.

I stumble backward in my sky-high black strappy heels.

Had to?

"I'm pretty sure that's the biggest lie you've ever told, given the fact your *wife* is sitting in the ballroom of this very hotel we're in. I shouldn't be here with you, alone. This is wrong."

So wrong.

Fraser slides his hands into the pockets of his black dress pants and drops his head to his chest. "Everything's a mess. My life is not my own."

This is news to me. His social feeds and posts certainly do not reflect his words. Fraser's life looks like one big, joyous holiday in California. Perfectly preened influencer wife and a handsome son. Carefully curated home. Posts from dozens of cities and championship golf courses from around the world. He has a picture-perfect life.

His wife's not just beautiful, she's striking. Long brunette locks, sparkling straight white teeth, endless tan, and envious legs, with boobs I would trade my mother in for. Nothing like me at all. She's from great stock. Wealthy and highly influential. Her father owns half of California, I believe. Well, I know, because I stalk their social media excessively. Her father is a sports agent; he only represents the most successful athletes, including Fraser.

Being married to that family suits Fraser.

He's living the life we always dreamed of living together.

"You're lying," I say.

In all the years I dated Fraser, he was never a liar. However, the man standing in front of me now, I no longer know. It's been so long.

"I am *not* lying. I promise." His weary, crystal-blue eyes meet mine. "Ella, you know me."

"I don't know you anymore," I whisper, shaking my head.

I really don't.

When Fraser won a golf scholarship in America, he was so excited. I was too. Excited about what it would do for our future together.

Once he left our quaint little Scottish seaside town years ago, I believed, in the beginning, we could make it work. I was too young and naïve to think otherwise.

As time passed though, *I* slid out of his heart.

"I don't know why you're doing this. This isn't a game," I say, almost inaudibly.

"I'm not *playing* with you. I'm telling you how I feel, Ella."

"This isn't fair."

"What's *not* fair is watching you tonight, dancing, having a great time with someone I know very well. Knowing that *I* should be with you. Are you with Luke?"

"No, I'm not *with* Luke; I'm his date for tonight only. Not that it's any of your goddamn business. You. Are. Married." My voice echoes through the space. "You think it's fair for me to watch you with a wife? You have a kid now. I've watched your new life play out from afar for years. So don't stand there and tell me what's fair and what isn't. *You* ended *us*. I never had a choice."

"*I* never had a choice either."

I wrinkle my brow in confusion. "What do you mean *you* never had a choice? You got married, then had a son straight away. Tell me, were you with her before you broke up with me?" Clenching my fists by my sides, I grip my dress tighter. "Did you cheat on me with her?"

"No. Never," he bellows.

"Then what happened?"

Silence.

I wait. "Speak to me," I demand.

Nothing.

Frustrated, I turn to leave, but Fraser reaches out, halting me, grasping my wrist. "Please stay."

His touch creates an instant zap of static electricity, reminding me of how magma hot we were together as sparks dance between us. It takes my breath away as I feel his touch sparkle everywhere.

I whip back around. "Please don't do this. You have to stop."

"I don't want to." He runs his calloused fingers, reminding me of his pro golfer status, upward across the smooth skin of my pale arm, up over the spaghetti straps of my dress.

"We can't do this, Fraser," I whisper.

"I know we can't. But I *want* to."

His other hand grips my waist. He pulls me in close and grinds himself into me.

Someone send help.

Being reminded of his six-foot-three stature, I tilt my head upward and we face off eye to eye.

Our weighted breaths reflecting each other.

He faintly strokes his fingertips into the nape of my neck before weaving them into my long platinum locks.

Dipping his head to mine, he fuses our foreheads and lets out a heavy sigh. My pulse picks up speed quicker than an Eminem rap.

"I miss you so much, Ella."

He pulls me in closer still, his solid athletic frame against mine. Sliding his hand down from my waist, he cups my backside, letting me know what I do to him as I feel his hot, hard length through his dress pants.

Instinctively, my body wakes up. As if it's been waiting all this time for him, my traitorous clit throbs at his closeness.

Keeping my hands firmly glued to my sides, it takes everything within me not to reach out, from fear of touching him and never wanting to stop.

But he isn't mine and I've never forgotten how he discarded me like I meant nothing. Like *we* meant nothing.

Striking hard in my chest, my heart swells with both sadness and desire.

Shallow puffs of air wisp against each other's skin as he pulls his cheek to mine.

I feel his desperation to connect once again. His tender touch flips my pulse into a frenzy.

"I meant what I said." He bows his head closer to the curve of my neck.

I close my eyes, inhaling. Delightful warmth trickles across my skin as his sandalwood and musk scent awakens all my senses.

"Tell me you feel the same," he presses.

I do feel the same.

I've longed for this moment.

I want him and only him.

I've never stopped wanting him.

I want him to kiss me, to take me.

Because no other man has ever lived up to him.

Fraser feathers his generous lips against my neck, and I can't stop the moan that escapes my throat.

His touch is all my body desires, but we shouldn't be doing this.

Realization suddenly hits hard. "The man I used to know..." I whisper. "Was not a cheater and *I* am most definitely not a home-wrecker."

I step backward, forcing myself out of his arms, and

whip around to grab the emergency door handle, instantly missing the warmth of his touch.

He stops me in my tracks when he says, "You're right, Ella. I'm not a cheater."

I spin back around to meet his icy eyes and I can't help the next question to fall from my lips.

"Is your wife cheating on you?" My voice raised in a disbelieving tone. It's the only possible explanation for his ludicrous outburst this evening.

He doesn't reply.

My perplexed heart plummets as my anger turns up a notch. "Wait a minute. Is that what this is about? Your wife is cheating on you, so you decide to cheat on her too? I thought you were better than that."

"No," he exclaims. "It's nothing like that. It's complicated."

"Then enlighten me," I push.

"I can't." He expels a long groan. Furrowing his brows, he digs the palms of his hands into his eyes.

I have to draw a line in the sand between us right now. "Since high school, I have been madly in love with you."

Moving his hands from his broad face, his hopeful eyes pop open.

"It's only recently my mom informed me that I could have trained to be a dancer anywhere. She would have let me move and study to be with you. I regret not doing that now." I tuck my lips into my mouth before continuing, ensuring I don't botch up what I want to say because there are so many words that went unspoken between us. "The girl you knew back in high school would have swooped into your arms. Your confession is something I do not take lightly and the old Fraser, the one I know, would have been careful and handled my heart with care. But the Fraser who dumped me on my twenty-first birthday, he is someone I don't recognize. I don't know what happened to you when you moved away, but you changed." I motion to the space between us. "And you and me? We are done. We were over a long time ago. You made sure of that."

"But you just said…"

"I know." My eyes glaze over. "But you married someone else. You replaced me instantly."

Ouch, that stings to say out loud. It really is time for me to move on in order to maintain my sanity. It's been too many long years since we split. I'm so pathetic for holding on to him.

He's married.

"I never stopped wanting or loving you, Ella. Never. I've thought about you. Every. Single. Day." His husky tone is thick with torment.

A lone tear rolls down my cheek. *Why is he doing this now?*

"Please stop saying that." I bow my head.

He tentatively shuffles toward me again and lifts my chin with his pointer finger.

His blue eyes hold me hostage. I love his eyes. I've dreamed of his kind, cool crystal-blue jewels I could butterfly stroke in for thousands of nights.

"Please don't be upset, Bella."

When Fraser discovered my name meant 'beautiful fairy goddess,' he started calling me Bell, short for Tinker Bell, then he combined it with my name to make Bella. I always loved it because he's the only one to call me that. It's simple but significant. I haven't heard it in such a long time.

"Don't call me that," I plead.

"You will always be Bella to me. *My* Bella. I can't explain what happened or what's going on. I want to, but I can't. I have never cheated on Anna, but I don't love her." A deep *V* forms between his brows. "And I *never* cheated on you. I love you. It's always been you. Christ, it's so fucking complicated." He shakes his head.

But he married her. None of this makes sense.

Gently strumming his rough thumb across my jaw, my stomach backflips.

"I've lost count of how many times I picked up the phone to speak to you, but I couldn't dial your number. I'm so sorry. I wanted to reach out when I came back for Chloe's funeral and saw you, but I fucked everything up. I don't blame you for not wanting to speak to me."

I still love his throaty husk. "You sound so American now. Where did your lovely Scottish accent go, Fraser?"

He scoffs. "I know. My mom says I think I'm Gerard Butler. Flipping in and out of Scots and American. I don't even know I'm doing it."

I pull a half smile.

"What's changed, Fraser? Why are you telling me this now?"

His defeated shoulders sag.

Fraser leans in, and his lips make contact with my forehead. *Oh boy.*

This feels so familiar that erratic flutters batter around my heart.

"There are things I can't tell you. My life... it's not... Anna... she's not..." He doesn't finish.

I don't know what he's trying to tell me.

We stay like this, firmly planted against one another, neither of us willing to spoil our precious trip down memory lane closeness. He feels the same, but so different, all at the same time.

"Please tell me, Fraser; you can trust me," I whisper.

"I can't. I want to explain. I want to be with you. But you're right, this is wrong." He steps back quickly with a look of utter anguish across his face. "Fuck," he mumbles. "Please know I'm not lying, and I am still in love with you, Ella. I was forced to stay away from you." Without another word, he spins on his heel, sprinting up the concrete stairs, leaping two steps at a time, until he's out of sight.

I battle the urge to run after him, but I know I have to let him go. Again. Even though I have so many questions.

Forced to stay away from me? But why?

What couldn't he tell me? If his wife isn't cheating, then what is it?

I'm dumbfounded by his words. What a surreal twist of events.

I let out an audible sigh of relief knowing he'll leave tomorrow, heading off to the next golf tournament. Hopefully, it's as far away from Castleview Cove as possible.

Who the heck would *force* him to stay away from me? What happened all those years ago? I try to recall but come up short.

My head thumps in time with my aching heart. I'm a fool for harboring the feelings I've had for him for so long.

I do have to get over Fraser. It's time for me to set sail on a new voyage, with no more Fraser fog clouding my vision. Although that crushes me, I have to do this. I've never admitted how much I still feel for Fraser, to anyone, including myself.

It's been seven long years. It's time to let go.

Relaxing my hands, I try to smooth out the clusters of my dress I've been desperately holding on to, but my efforts fail to flatten out the crushes. Screw it. It will have to stay like that.

Everyone will wonder where I am, and this dingy

staircase is making me feel drab and gloomy. *I need to get out of here.*

With luck, Fraser and his wife leave the ball early. I don't think I'll be able to look her in the eyes. Fraser and I did nothing, but what we discussed and the way Fraser held me feels deceitful.

Right, Ella, pull yourself together.

Shaking my head to straighten myself up, I comb my fingers through my icy strands. As I glance upward, a small, gray, fluffy feather floats across in front of my face and lands at my feet. Since Fraser left all those years ago, I find feathers everywhere I go. Some days I find two or three.

I started finding so many I had to Google it. Apparently, feathers are a positive omen for better things to come. But here I am, still waiting for the Universe to jump on board and deliver whatever those things are.

Head held high, I stride back through the staircase door, where I throw myself straight into the path of two of my friends, Toni and Beth.

"What have you been doing in there?" Toni quizzes.

"Eh, I was getting some fresh air."

Toni and Beth both frown.

"In there?" Beth grabs my hand, rolling her eyes. "Whatever. Eden needs us out in the parking lot."

"What's wrong?" I ask.

"No idea, but shit's going down, apparently." Beth hitches her dress up before she strides toward the back entrance of the hotel, pulling me with her.

"She won the guy. The very guy who won The Championship Cup today. What the hell is wrong with my sister now?"

Can we not have one night without drama?

CHAPTER TWO

Ella - Nine Years Ago
Ella, age 18; Fraser, age 20

"I can't believe how quickly the last few weeks have flown by and I'm leaving again tomorrow. I'm gonna miss you so much, Ella."

"Don't or you'll make me cry again." Squeezing him tight, I snuggle into his athletic, bare chest. His visit has been too short and too fast. I want to stay here forever.

Fraser and I dated throughout high school since I was thirteen. We grew up together. Our sweet relationship progressed from dates on the swings, movie nights, and dinner in the dining hall at school, to late night parties, skinny-dipping, and exploring each other's bodies—somehow managing to hold off having sex until I was legally allowed.

"We've managed two years apart already. But once I've completed my scholarship in America, we have a plan, right?" he questions.

"Yup. You continue on your path of becoming a mega-famous, rich pro golfer. A few more years and you'll be there. I'm so proud of you." He chuckles as I confirm our plan. "I complete dance school and become a magnificent dancer and dance teacher. Once I'm qualified, we'll see where we want to live. Buy an obscenely offensive big house. Get married. Have lots of beautiful babies."

"Eh, we never mentioned babies. Did we?"

"Mmm, I'm sure *I* did."

"Is that right?"

I lift my head and rest my chin on the bronzed skin of his broad chest.

He sails his fingers across my temple.

"I love you, Fraser. I want to have your babies one day."

He smiles back at me with a cheeky grin. "How do we know it won't be triplets? With you being a triplet. I cannot imagine how much work that would be. Three?" He shudders.

"It will be a lottery." I giggle.

"I'm not a gambler."

"Nope, neither am I. But I like the idea of triplets. I love being one."

"I miss you so much when I'm in America." We carefully study one another. "I really love you, Ella. You're my one and only."

A lump forms in my throat. "I love you too, Fraser Farmer. I think about you all the time."

The next few months feel like they are going to be harder than normal. He doesn't come back very often, and he's away for much longer this time around.

Fraser bops my nose.

"I have something for you." He rolls over, slides open his nightstand drawer and pulls out a gold and black box, then sits up.

I mirror his actions, dragging the dark-navy sheets upward, draping them around my body.

Fraser removes the lid of the miniature box, revealing a yellow-gold necklace. Dangling from the glinting chain is an intricately detailed gold feather.

"It's beautiful, Fraser," I gasp. "Can you put it on me?"

Leaning in, he loops the two ends around my neck, clasping them together at the back.

Out of the blue, Fraser then scoops me up and I give a little squeal with surprise. He straddles my legs around his hips, enveloping me with his hot, hard, naked body.

Pressed skin to skin, he whispers in my ear, "That little feather is a symbol of my protection. I'm your guardian angel, Ella. Think of me always. When you do, I'll know."

I squeeze him tighter as the tears form, blurring the dark walls of his bedroom in his parents' house.

"Keep me close. Right next to your heart." Fraser nuzzles his face into my neck. Gripping the back of my head with his giant hand, the other encased around my slender waist, he compression cuddles me, soldering us together.

I can't hold it in any longer. Shaking in his arms, I weep.

"My heart hurts," I blurt out.

"Mine too, Bella."

We've spoken so much about him leaving again, but I'm not prepared. I don't want him to go.

Each time, it gets more and more difficult.

I lean out of our tight embrace.

Fraser drifts his thumbs across my cheeks, wiping my tears away. I gaze into his arctic blue eyes. "Twelve months, right? One whole year and you'll be home again for a couple of weeks?"

His sensual lips break into a reassuring smile. "Yeah. We have a lifetime together; we can do twelve months. Can't we?" He nods gently and I agree with him, melting into him as he moves in and kisses me.

"Make love to me, Fraser. Make it last twelve months."

And he does, in such a way that makes it hard for me to ever forget him, leaving him imprinted in my heart forever.

It was the last time he did.

I was grief-stricken, yet again, when he left.

I missed my best friend.

I missed sharing fish and chips on the beach with him.

I missed our cuddles and kisses.

I mourned the loss of our unique love. Our friendship. The laughs we shared.

I missed sharing my day with him.

I missed everything.

It hurt every day. But I coped because it was only twelve months.

Then his schedule became even more frantic as he rose through the ranks, working toward his golf tour card and becoming a pro golfer like he'd always dreamed.

I waited for him.

I went off to dance school with my sisters.

Remained faithful.

Loved him every day from afar.

Twelve months came and went and he never came back to Castleview Cove.

The 'I love yous' stopped.

The telephone calls became less frequent.

He changed.

He withdrew.

Over time, he stopped calling altogether.

I don't know what happened. Not only did a physical ocean separate us, but an emotional crevasse divided us too, and then the space between us grew wider than the Grand Canyon.

Two years later, on my twenty-first birthday, he called out of the blue and ended us officially. Shattering my already broken heart completely.

He married someone else a few weeks after our breakup and started a family in quick succession.

The last time I saw him was at my niece Chloe's funeral.

My sister, Eden, tragically lost her baby when she was six months pregnant. It devastated our family. Fraser's brother, Jamie, was Chloe's father. On that day, Fraser tried to talk to me, but I couldn't even look at him. The raw agony of our breakup tore into every fiber of my soul. I couldn't get over us. Our lives followed different paths.

We chased our dreams separately.

I watched him become a husband and father.

All without me.

And I shut down.

Since him, I've never loved another.

He may have left Castleview Cove, but he never left my heart.

He's still there.

Tucked inside it.

CHAPTER THREE

Ella - Ten Months After the Winner's Ball

The bassy track thumps through the music system of our dance studio. Watching my students glide, then pop in time to the double-quick chorus, I count them along. "And one, two, three, four, five, six, seven, and eight. Yes, guys, you nailed it. Well done," I whoop.

T3SDS, that's what our dance school is called. We shortened it as we thought it sounded cooler than *The Three Sisters Dance School*.

I adore my triplet sisters and we have the best fun teaching and running the business together. It allows us to be creative and do what we love daily. There is no better feeling in the world than being surrounded by those who share the same passion as you.

It's remarkable considering how small our little town is, but social media has been good for us, and it's opened up some incredible business opportunities. We are now fully booked for the next twelve months.

Hip-hop is usually Eden's class, but me and the new dance instructor, Trevor, have been splitting these classes between us. This is my favorite class. As well as modern and contemporary. I'm lying. I love it all. Even tap, which I am not very good at.

Trevor has been a godsend. He's been keen to introduce several new classes. He jumped on board with us to cover Eden's maternity leave, but we decided to take him on permanently, along with another three instructors. Go big or go home is what we've decided.

We've also taken on a new administrative assistant and an accountant too, as we were struggling to keep on top of our continuing demand.

We've even had requests from all over the world to run live online classes. I've already begun my research, figuring out how we will do it. It's been fun and the possibilities for us are endless if we go global. We're even thinking about delivering evergreen dance courses on our website too, so people can dip in and out whenever they want, from the novice to the advanced dancer. My sisters and I decided we're doing it all. I'm pumped to get started.

We are on the up-and-up and business is booming. It seems our hard work over the last few years is finally paying off. It's super exciting to see us expand in ways we never thought possible.

For some people, they dance to express themselves, but for me, it's a form of meditation. Focusing on the repetition of steps, losing yourself in the music, one beat at a time, to escape the everyday humdrum of life as adrenaline flies through your body. I love it.

Being a fraternal triplet is awesome. I adore it, adore them. We are unique in our own ways. Our varying shades of blond hair make us look similar in appearance, but our height differences, eye color, and style set us apart.

Eden is the playful, fun side of our trinity, while Eva is

the serene, calm side; my grounding tool. She's thoughtful and our homemaker, loving nothing better than being surrounded by her two sons, Hamish and Archie, and she's a wonderful mother. And while Eden may not know how to switch the oven on, she is the one who brings light into all the dark areas in our lives, the one who is always there for us. She also has one of the best heads for business and finance I have ever known.

Our styles couldn't be more different either. I'm more grungy rock glam and love a good pair of leather pants paired with a distressed rock band tee—I have dozens. Eva's more boho chic and drives about in her carefully restored green metallic VW camper van. And then there is Eden, the littlest of us all. She loves a good slogan shirt—one combined with Minnie Mouse on it and she'll claim it as hers.

My eyes search around the studio.

Who would have thought only a few years ago, that we would be here now, with over two hundred students registered and an enormous waiting list to boot?

My chest fills with pride as I take it all in, grateful for how far we've come.

"Let's go through our routine one more time, then we're done for today," I call out across the room. "And I'm going to join you this time." Everyone cheers and I smile wide.

This is my last class of the day before Trevor takes over the night classes.

"From the top," I instruct, catching everyone's eyes in the wall-to-wall mirrors.

And I snap, pop, arch, point, and give it my all.

If only I could dance all day, then I wouldn't have to think about anything or anyone else.

Especially not *him*.

"Hi, it's me," I call, opening the giant gray door into Eden's hallway.

"Yay, Aunty Ella's here. Thank you, Universe. I need a break," my sister, Eden, calls back.

A small chuckle escapes my throat as I drop my overnight satchel on the floor.

Eden recently gave birth to triplet boys and it takes our entire family to care for them. Eva and I have been taking turns to help at nighttime, although I've been doing the majority, as her own boys keep her busy. My mom was hoping Eden would have at least one girl. But there was not one to be seen. We girls are now outnumbered.

It's exhausting caring for three. I have no idea how our parents managed.

Being a triplet is fun. Being the parent of triplet babies, not so much, I have discovered.

How we've all been holding down our own businesses too—Mom and Dad at their Castleview Cove Sports Retreat and mine, Eva, and Eden's dance school—I have no idea. Life is busy.

Walking around the corner into the open living space of the house, I'm welcomed by a beautiful sight. Eden and Hunter, her husband, feeding all three of my nephews on their oversized gray velvet corner sofa.

"Hi." I slip my black leather jacket off and automatically scoop a bubba and bottle off Hunter. How Hunter feeds two at the same time is beyond me. Maybe it's because of his Mr. Tickle-length arms.

Happiness bounces off Eden and Hunter. They had a roller coaster of a journey this past year. But here they are. Contentment surrounds them. Hunter King, pro golfer. He won the last Championship Cup. He's a star, and he's not just gorgeous, he's next-level demigod gorgeous. Eden and he are smitten and so deeply in love. Nothing is ever too much bother for Hunter. He adores my sister and handles her like she's a porcelain doll.

I couldn't be happier for her.

She deserves it all after everything she's been through.

My eyes bounce between the two lovebirds on the sofa as they affectionately gaze at their beautiful sons.

I dip my head and swoon into the eyes of my nephew, too.

"Which one is this I'm holding?" I move him outward to get a better look.

"Lachlan," Eden replies.

"Ah, Mr. Poopy Dooper," I smirk. I love him. I love all three of them.

"How can you not tell them apart yet?" Hunter scowls.

"I'm winding you up. Lachlan has a freckle on his nose." I rock from foot to foot gently as he sucks loudly. His cartoon-sized eyes stare back at me. He's so cute. "Lewis has a little strawberry mark on his neck and Lennox has a little cowlick that spirals upward."

"Girl's good, huh?" Eden dazzles a cheeky grin.

"She sure is. Thanks for helping us these last few weeks, Ella. Eden and I are forever grateful." His sultry American accent floats across their new home.

"That's alright. I've loved every minute of it." I really have.

"What about Callum? Does he not mind you being here all the time and sleeping over again?" Eden asks.

"Eh, no. I don't think so."

To be honest, I didn't ask him. My new boyfriend and I, well, we're good. It's fine. It's not fire and sparks and shit, but he's a nice guy. Solid. Reliable. He owns his own carpentry business, and he's good to me. *But* this is another relationship that, yet again, is not working for me.

I'm giving myself a sore head as I contemplate ending things with him.

"Do your parents have Treacle and Toffee again tonight?" Hunter looks at me.

"Yeah."

My mom and dad love having my two French bulldogs. They are *my* babies.

Eagle-eyed, I flit my gaze around this extraordinary space.

Eden and Hunter recently built this gigantic white and glass-paneled house that overlooks the cove. I patter closer toward the floor-to-ceiling wall of windows to enjoy the incredible, money-can't-buy view. Unless you're Hunter, of course. He bought it.

Everything they've built all happened so quickly. Love. A house. Marriage. A family. I'm sort of envious in a way.

I desire the level of contentment and love they have.

My heart often aches with the loneliness I feel at having no companionship with anyone. No connection. Now twenty-eight, I'm still single. I always thought I'd be married with a family by now, but clearly, that was never on my life path.

"I enjoy helping with the night shifts," I assure them. I do. Also, it means I don't have to see Callum tonight. "I'll be up and away early. I have Tartan to muck out and some of the other horses whose owners are away on vacation, so I offered to help this week. Then I have dance classes from midmorning to late afternoon to teach."

"You're a machine, Ella." Hunter peers up from his beautiful boy nestled in the crook of his arm.

"Mm-hmm." Anything to distract me from the reality of my loneliness.

"You alright, babes?" Eden's concerned brow creases.

Not really, no.

"Yeah, I'm good."

I haven't told a soul about Fraser's confession to me ten months ago. I've been feeling a little melancholy and unsettled since then. Desperately trying to bury my emotions deep. Keeping busy has been the best distraction.

I've replayed his words over and over. "*I never stopped wanting or loving you, Ella. Never. I've thought about you. Every. Single. Day.*"

They've been eating away at my thoughts day in, day out. I can't shake them. I've been tempted to contact him via his social media, but it's deceitful. Regardless of our history, he's a married man.

I also thought getting myself a boyfriend would help. It didn't. I need to end things with Callum, soon.

I'm sure there's something wrong with me. I would love to settle down with someone I love, but I can't seem to find *the one* who lights me up. Except *him*.

"I know you. You are *not* okay." Eden's blue eyes widen. "Wanna tell me about it?"

I give a one-shouldered shrug. "Nah."

"Well, I'm here when you finally decide to open up." Eden throws me a warm expression.

The three of us lose ourselves caring for our little bundles of joy.

One by one, each of them drifts off.

Enjoying this snuggle time with Lachlan, I hold on tight and let him cozy into me.

Eden shuffles toward the stairs. "Okay, I'm gonna have a

long hot bath. I feel yucky. Let's have dinner. One more feed. Then bed. Can you help me into the bath, please, Hunter?"

"Yeah. I'll be right there. Go slow on the steps, baby."

I love how tender Hunter is toward her. For me, they are power couple goals. Eden had a C-section, and she's healed well, but she's still very fragile.

"Are you happy enough here?" Hunter asks me.

"Yeah. I'm just going to enjoy my cuddles with my handsome nephew."

"Handsome like his dad?"

"Nope, like his papa," I jest.

"Piss off, you." Hunter scowls. I can't help but chuckle at how much his American dialect is becoming more and more Scottish as the months pass.

A loud *ding* from the doorbell echoes across the house. Lachlan squirms in my arms. I still. A little yawn leaves his gummy pouty mouth, then he nuzzles into me again.

Phew.

"I need to adjust the volume on the bell; it's too loud." Hunter runs barefoot across the polished concrete floor to answer the door. It's just as well they have underfloor heating. That guy never wears socks.

A muffled, low voice rumbles from the door. Like the eighth wonder of the world, visitors haven't stopped dropping in to meet the triplet King boys. The gifts never stop either. With Hunter being so famous, he's sent so many baby things to promote from all the major brands in the hope they'll appear on his enormous two point one million social media following. Eden's had me donating it to the local charity shops and the women's refuge in the next town.

I wish Chanel would send three leather bags to Eden for us triplet girls. A black and gold one for me would be awesome. I'll keep dreaming. Although Eden would make me auction those off for charity, too. *Goddamn do-gooder.*

I snuggle myself into the deep, feather-filled cushions of the sofa with Lachlan. No doubt it's Callum at the door. He said he would pop by to see me, although he normally lets himself in when he knows I'm here.

"It's awesome you're back." I hear Hunter excitedly clapping his hands together. "We've got loads to talk about. Team tournament coming up, man. First, I need to help Eden upstairs, but I'll be straight back down. Make yourself at home, Fraser."

Shit.

No way.

Fraser?

CHAPTER FOUR

Ella

"Ella might make you a cup of tea. You should stay for dinner, Fraser." Hunter catches my eye and winks over at me, then runs up the stairs, leaving me alone with him.

Like hell is Fraser staying for dinner.

Across the neckline of my black washed-out Rolling Stones tee shirt, I sweep my worn gold feather pendant left and right along the chain of my necklace. Something I do out of habit.

I slowly lift myself up from the sofa and turn my head from the corner I've nested in, revealing myself more.

Over my shoulder, I'm directly met by Fraser's chiseled face. My heart flips out at the sight of him in his simple white tee shirt and gray joggers. *Aw, man, gray joggers.*

He rubs the back of his blond, closely shaved neck, then runs his fingers through his wild, dipped in sunshine locks. With his arms raised like that, his tee shirt lifts slightly. I wonder if his Californian tan dips beyond that *V* I can now clearly see.

And he's grown a little blond goatee beard since I last saw him at the Winner's Ball. *Oh, I like that too.*

I can't stop staring.

My body deceives me as I clench, trying to stop the ache blossoming between my legs. I don't want it to react this way, but it does. *Traitor.*

"Hi." He blinks his steely blues.

I remind myself to breathe.

"Fraser, what are you doing here?"

"I came to visit Hunter, Eden and the triplets."

He lays a chic black-and-white gift bag from the local five-star spa on the mirrored console next to him and strides toward me.

Please don't come too close. Stay right there.

"That's not what I'm asking. What are you doing *here* in Castleview Cove? When did you get back?"

"Yesterday. My mom's not well, Ella."

"What's wrong with your mom?" I sit more upright.

"It's breast cancer. Don't stress." He flashes the palms of his hands up to stop me worrying. "They caught it early. Her radiotherapy finishes this week, and I wanted to be here. She's doing well, but I haven't been able to get back with all the tournament dates I was already committed to. I'm back now and have some time off to spend with her."

"Fraser, I didn't know. I'll have to pay her a visit."

I love Fraser's mom and dad, Susan and Jim. I dropped in all the time when Fraser moved away. I became their surrogate daughter. Susan was devastated when Fraser called it off between us. She always believed we would get married. I'm definitely making it a must-do this week to visit her, maybe even take her some of my homemade fudge that she loves so much.

"She'd like that. She still misses your Sunday visits and shopping trips together."

Happiness weaves through my veins, recalling how much time I spent with that lovely woman.

Then I notice exactly how close Fraser is.

"So, who's this?" He leans over my shoulder, now standing along the back of the L-shaped couch, his familiar scent encroaching on my space.

"This is Lachlan." My heart bursts with pride at how perfect he is. "I could eat him."

Reaching out, Fraser smooths his pointer finger across Lachlan's chubby cheek.

"He looks sweet enough to eat," he whispers.

"He does."

"So do you."

Fraser delicately glides his fingers down my arm and lays his hand over mine that's lovingly wrapped around Lachlan.

A mix of oxytocin, dopamine, and norepinephrine surges, making my heart beat faster.

"If my memory serves me correctly, Ella, you taste fucking delectable."

Uncharacteristically, a warm flush floods my cheeks.

"Can you remember how I taste?" he whispers against my temple.

I do. "No."

"Liar. Have you thought about me these past few months?"

Yes. I can't think of anything else. "Nope." I blink.

"You blink when you lie. I know you. You're still wearing our necklace."

Cocky twatfart.

"Who do you think about when you touch yourself, Ella?"

You, only you. "Chris Hemsworth."

"You blinked again. Another fucking lie. It's me. It's written all over your face."

Excitement expands my chest. "Stop swearing in front of Lachlan. He can still hear you, even though he's sleeping."

"He's a baby, Ella." He moistens his lips.

At an impasse, we stare at each other.

He whispers, "Isn't *this* what you always wanted? The house, triplets, a husband."

I did. I wanted it all with *him*.

I still long for those things.

Ouch, that stings. He's right. Eden is living the life I always dreamed of. It's what Fraser, and I planned *together*.

I *am* envious and it's not a feeling I'm familiar with.

Maybe that's why I've been spending so much time here. I'm sad this is not my life. My two sisters both have kids and husbands, although Eva has been having a tough time of it lately since Ewan lost his job, and then there's lonely little me with a house, two dogs, and an ill-tempered horse who hates me and likes to bite my ass at every opportunity.

Beneath his spun gold lashes, Fraser's eyes dilate with passion.

A flurry of desire flickers between us. This is what I'm missing with Callum—unparalleled connection.

I inhale as he dips closer still, a micrometer from my crimson painted lips.

"What are you doing?" I purr as pleasure burns between my thighs and I suddenly feel a rush of wetness. My body only responds to him like this.

"Reclaiming what's mine." His voice rumbles low.

Reclaiming?

My blood pumps swiftly with the need to kiss him.

Breathing roughly, he's losing his restraint. His tempting lips ghost mine.

"What the fuck's going on here?" a voice suddenly booms behind us.

I flinch. Fraser retreats at supersonic speed, revealing Callum.

"And you are?" Fraser responds confidently.

"Her boyfriend."

Just brilliant.

"Ella?" Callum quizzes.

"Eh, Fraser…" I stutter, "… was meeting Lachlan." I raise Lachlan slightly in my arms, displaying him as evidence.

"I'm so sorry, man. I thought you two were kissing." He chortles and rests his hand on his chest.

Callum is super pretty, younger than me by two years, but he's a little dim and naïve sometimes.

Man, I feel bad.

Envy. Almost cheating. Lying. I think I must have stepped into someone else's persona as I rushed through Eden's front door today.

Fraser's eyebrows fly upward. "Boyfriend? You never said, Ella. Introduce me then."

I mumble fast, "Callum, meet Fraser; Fraser, meet Callum."

Callum shakes Fraser's hand. "Wow, that's some grip you've got there, Fraser. Nice to meet you."

I'm sure his firm grip was intentional.

"Comes with the job."

Realization falls across Callum's face. "Shit, you're Fraser Farmer, *the* golfer Fraser Farmer?"

"Yeah." Fraser folds his arms across his thick chest, widening his stance.

"I thought I recognized you. You're a local legend. Wow, Hunter King *and* Fraser Farmer under one roof. Wait till I tell the lads. Eh, did you two not date back in high school?" Callum sweeps his pointer finger back and forth between us.

Oh boy. There it is.

"Yeah, for eight years, wasn't it, Ella?"

"Five," I snap back.

"It was eight."

"It was five and you know it, Fraser. When you left for the last time, we were over. You made sure of that. I was eighteen and remember it like it was yesterday. You gave up on us three years before you officially broke it off. You checked out."

"Woah, woah, woah. I'm sorry I asked." Callum holds up his palms.

I'm hopping mad. Eight years, my ass. What a joke. He's delusional.

"Evening, Callum," Hunter welcomes him as he leisurely jogs down the stairs into the open plan space. "I'm about to start dinner. Do you want to stay?"

Christ, Hunter, sense the mood in the room.

"Sorry, I can't. I need to carry out some estimates and call customers back. I have a list as long as my arm. Next time, yeah?"

Phew.

"Sure thing," Hunter replies. "Are you staying, Fraser?"

"Are you staying, Ella?" Fraser turns to ask me.

Like a dazed fish, my mouth bobs open and shut a couple of times as I attempt to reply, but Hunter answers for me. "Yeah, Ella's staying to help with the night shift." Hunter groans at the predictable night ahead—nighttime feeds and diaper changes.

Why did he tell him that?

Say no, say no, I think to myself, hoping Fraser hears my silent plea.

"Eh, yeah. That would be awesome. It would be great to catch up," Fraser replies with a cat-that-got-the-cream grin.

Damn it.

"Right. I need to head off. I just wanted to come and give you this." Callum walks toward me, leans down, and plants a firm peck on my mouth.

I feel nothing but force a smile.

Fraser's eyes narrow.

He's got no right to be mad. He's married. What am I thinking? Oh my God, I almost kissed him. Actually, scrap that. *He* almost kissed *me*.

"I miss you, Ella. When are we going to have a night out? Or in?" Callum eyes me hopefully.

I wiggle myself off the sofa, being careful not to wake my sleeping beauty. I don't want to put him down. Actually, he can act as a buffer between myself and Callum. Good plan. I hold him firm. "I'll walk you to the door."

Standing on the front doorstep, I decide this is my moment. "I've been thinking about us, Callum."

A doubtful frown furrows his brows.

"I'm really sorry but—"

"Don't say it, Ella. I think I already know."

"It's not that I don't like you, Callum. You're a great guy."

"Yeah, yeah, I know. We haven't had sex in six weeks. Do you think I'm stupid?"

"I don't know what's wrong with me. I do like you. It's, oh, I don't know."

I feel so deflated. Why can't I feel love for anyone?

"I know."

Does he?

"You're busy, married to your business, with Eden being off and juggling the upkeep of your horse and dogs and the new triplets. Maybe right now, for us, it's not the right time."

That's not it at all. "I guess so."

"Right. Well, I'll be off then. It's been fun. If things slow down, ring me, Ella. I really do like you." Before he leaves, he taps a chaste kiss on my cheek. I watch as he leaves in his white work truck and disappears down Hunter and Eden's private drive.

Yet another failed relationship. *I suck at this shit.*

Walking back into the main living area, I hear Hunter and Fraser chatting rapidly about who knows what in the kitchen. Boring golf stuff probably. I know Hunter has an upcoming tournament and they're playing in teams together. With Fraser, it would appear.

I feel Fraser watching me, following me with his gaze. I cautiously lay Lachlan in the large Moses basket Eden had custom made, right next to his brothers in the quiet, shady space in the corner of the living room. Instinctively, he reaches out and grabs Lewis's pinky. Lewis clasps Lennox's.

I marvel at them, drinking them in. I've bonded with these little dudes, sealing them in my heart forever.

"Wine." Fraser suddenly passes me a glass and I take it from him, breaking my dreamy moment. "So, you have a boyfriend?"

"So, you have a wife?" I take a large sip of the cool liquid.

"Touché." He takes a sip of his beer. "Not for much longer."

I pull my brows in. "What do you mean, not for much longer?"

My glance downward confirms he's not wearing his wedding ring.

He smirks at my action.

"Aw, that feels better." Eden teeters down the stairs, interrupting us.

Go away, Eden, I need an answer. Is he getting divorced?

"Ah, Fraser." Eden welcomes him with open arms. "Hunter said you were here. It's so nice to see you. I hope you're staying for dinner?" She gives Fraser a quick squeeze.

"I am. Although I can tell Ella's not happy about me being here."

"I never said that," I blurt out.

"I have three kids already... well, four." Eden motions toward Hunter. "I have no space for anymore. So, if it's going to be a problem for you, Ella, you're just going to have to get used to Fraser being around because he is a huge part of Hunter's life."

I roll my eyes. I've been told.

"Eden, I brought you a little gift. It's for you, though, not the babies. It's a spa day at The Sanctuary."

"Oh, my goodness. That's so kind of you, Fraser. Thank you."

Eden gazes down at her boys. "How are my boys? Aw, look at them holding hands," she coos.

"Omne trium perfectum," I chant our triplet motto.

"Everything that comes in threes is perfect," Fraser translates instantly.

Eden and I stare up at him, but he focuses his eyes on me only.

"Oh, I remember. I remember everything, Ella."

The last time I saw Fraser at the ball, he seemed deflated and unsure of himself. But the guy standing in front of me is more like my old Fraser.

But he's not yours, Ella.

"What's going on?" Eden bounces her eyes between the two of us.

"Nothing," I say.

"Something," Fraser answers in unison.

Eden laughs. "Right. Okay then. I need food before I dissect that. I am star*ving*. Bring me food, Hunter."

"Coming right up, baby. Park your hot ass at the dining table and bring those two bickering baboons with you." He and Eden chuckle.

"Hilarious, Hunter." I roll my eyes.

Throughout dinner I experience a whole heap of opposing forces, the familiar meets awkwardness. Strangely, this feels almost normal. I can't explain it. Like this is our regular clique; as if we do this all the time.

The four of us chat casually, but every time I look up, Fraser's staring directly at me, pinning me to my seat with his eyes. Like he wants me for dessert. I need a cold shower to cool down.

My emotions and urges make me squirm in my gray velvet seat.

He's unsettled me tonight, *again*.

And I'm desperate to ask him what he meant about his wife.

"Do you want another beer, Fraser?" Eden asks.

"Yes, please. I'll have to get a taxi home and get Mom's car tomorrow."

"If you don't have to get back, stay."

"You sure, Eden?"

"Yeah, yeah. You can take the end bedroom along the corridor by Ella in the guest wing. The one with the Jack and Jill bathroom. It's quiet along there. Away from little hungry tums and loud lungs, although the boys are pretty good in the night. They shouldn't wake you."

Under the same roof for the night with Fraser. *Aw, hell.*

"Alright. Thanks."

How is he able to stay over, away from his wife? He said *not for much longer* earlier. I need to know.

"So, Anna's not here?" I sound sharper than I wanted to, before sipping the last of my wine. I'm not drinking anymore after this glass. I'm on the midnight shift.

"Nope, she is not." Leaning over the table, he steeples his fingers against his temple.

"Why not?"

We can't stop staring at each other.

"Because I'm filing for a divorce or an annulment."

Excuse me? A rush of blood thumps deep in my chest.

"Oh, Hunter mentioned something, Fraser. I'm so sorry to hear your news." Eden pats his arm.

She knew?

"Annulment? Surely, it's a divorce?" I lean back in my chair in shock.

He doesn't respond.

"How is your son taking the separation?" Curiosity gets the better of Eden.

"We haven't told him yet." Fraser clears his throat. "But he's not *my* son."

I hear Eden gasp.

I glance over at Hunter. With a firm nod in my direction, Hunter confirms Fraser's telling the truth.

My wineglass slips through my fingers and implodes against the concrete floor.

CHAPTER FIVE

Fraser

Ella remains motionless as the glass splinters against the polished concrete floor.

"Oooooooh, my lovely new floor, Ella," Eden hisses quietly through clenched jaws, carefully trying not to wake the triplets.

Ella's in shock.

Trust me, all of those years ago, I was too.

Not because I didn't know Anna's boy, Ethan, wasn't mine. It was everything else surrounding my circumstances that threw me into a state of shutdown.

I took care of him, though. Because I *had* to.

"Ella?" Eden knocks on the glass dining table.

"Sorry, Eden, hang on." Her focus fixed on me. "I'll clean it up in a minute. What did you just say?" Ella shifts her trademark perfectly polished French-manicured nail my way.

"The part where I'm getting a divorce or the part about my son not being my son?" I reply.

"Both."

I want Ella to know I am getting divorced, but I need to explain the complexity of my situation one on one with her. Alone. Not here. I puff out a breath. "I don't want to talk about it."

"Well, I do." Her feline spring green gems sparkle with urgent curiosity.

She's stunning. She hasn't changed. She's lightened her hair slightly to a crisp white tone, making her appear more elfin-like. And she always wears that catlike black flicky eyeliner that's sexy as hell against her pale skin and dark cherry red lipstick I want to mess up.

"Why so curious? You have a boyfriend, remember?"

"No, I don't. I ended it tonight at the door. And we're not talking about me. I asked you a question."

"Ella," Eden gasps. "Another one? Just like that?"

So, this is a regular occurrence.

"Fucking brutal," Hunter mumbles. From the corner of my eye, I watch Hunter tip his head back, chugging down the last of his beer.

"It wasn't 'just like that.' We haven't had sex for weeks. There was no magic, sparkle, none of whatever it is you and Hunter have."

It's the connection she and I have.

Had?

Have?

Fuck knows, but it's what I remember and what I feel now.

"It wasn't there. It's been coming for weeks," she says, defending herself.

"Or *not coming*," I taunt.

Hunter sniggers.

"Oh, stop being so childish. Anyway, I don't know why I

told you that. We're not talking about me." She folds her arms across her chest.

"Let's clean up," Hunter instructs Eden, tilting his head toward the kitchen as if to say, *let's get out of here*. "I'll sort the glass. You leave the dishes on the side. Then rest, Cupcake."

"Eh, yeah. Let's." Eden and Hunter scurry around us, cleaning up. Then they make themselves scarce outside onto the deck.

Ella and I sit firmly in place. I seem to have entered a staring contest that I didn't know I was taking part in. But it gives me the opportunity to drink her in, memorizing every curve, tilt, and edge of her again.

The urge to leap across the table and crash her luscious lips to mine licks flames across my self-control.

I'm not ready for this chat. Yet. I'm kicking myself for bringing it up. I should have waited.

"I don't want to talk about it." I drag my hands down my face as thoughts of my current situation wrap around me like a coil of chains around my chest. Ella's going to hate me when all *this* comes to light, and I dread what my family and friends will think of me, too. "I do, however, need to speak to Hunter."

Pushing my seat back to remove myself from her before I say something I shouldn't, I step away from the table.

Ella stands quickly, stomping her elegant frame over to my side of the table with a look of determination written all over her beautiful face, her hair swishing as she moves.

"So, we're not going to talk about you telling me you still loved me ten months ago or that you're no longer with your wife or your mom's been sick or that you were *forced* to stay away from me? And what exactly did you mean by annulment? You don't want to talk about any of that?" Her mouth hardens. "Because there seems to be an awful lot you need to explain. You could start with the boy you have plastered all over your social media accounts not being yours. Right now. I want to know."

She checks my social media.

I move cautiously toward her, weaving her fingers into mine, giving me hope when she doesn't pull away. The love I've had for her for a lifetime pulls me in close.

Leaning in, I whisper into her ear, "I can't, Ella. I want to, but I can't. Please be patient."

I don't know where I would even begin. I'm not ready. It's all one big fucked-up shambles.

I inhale her comforting and cocooning warm scent before skimming my nose along her jawline, then focus my eyes on her mouth. She bites her deep Chianti-coated bottom lip with her teeth, then sucks in a breath.

"Please know this. I am not *with* Anna. I never have been."

"How is that possible?" she whispers, shaking her head.

"I can't tell you now."

Her eyes flit upward, drilling deep into my desire.

"Fine," she snaps, anger blotching her skin. "Have it your way." She pulls her hand out of mine. Internally, I beg her to hold on to me. I need her. I don't have anyone else.

With that, she shimmies her sassy, fine ass up the stairs. Fascinated, I watch her slender streamlined hips swish side to side, her hot ass encased in high-waisted, wet-look, black, skintight pants. That's a vision I'll save for my spank bank later.

She disappears down the brightly lit corridor of the upper level, out of sight. I want to follow her into the light. I've been living in darkness since I left Castleview Cove and her all those years ago.

"And so it begins," Hunter snickers, a hint of mockery in his voice as he drifts back through the sliding glass doors.

"Shit, this is gonna be tough. She's gonna hate me. Everyone's gonna hate me." My shoulders sag at the enormity of it all.

I can't tell her anything yet. Only Hunter, his agent, Lisa, and my new lawyer know my story and we have a plan. There's an enormous amount at stake, including my career. I could lose everything.

"It's alright, man. I'll stand by you." Hunter pats me on the back. "Let's chat tomorrow in my office, so let's get an early night now. C'mon. It's been a tough month."

It sure has. It's been a full-on month of major decision-making, paperwork, and stress.

The beginning of my end. Or the start of a new chapter.

Ella

Midnight. This feeding time is painful. I don't mind the early morning one, but this one always feels exhausting. The pull to hop back into my cozy bed is much too strong for me. In fact, I'm certain I can hear my vast bed calling my name.

Eden has just put Lewis back down. Lachlan and Lennox are next.

I hear Eden scuffling about outside the nursery door. We feed the boys in here at night, so we don't disturb each other. It's a quick lift through into this beautiful space and we have little bouncy seats for the boys. I'm sitting between them, legs crossed, a bottle in each hand, and the boys are guzzling away. Hunter is scheduled for the next shift, so we've left him to sleep.

"You go to bed, Eden," I say as she twists her head around the door. "I'll change them and pop them back in your room, honey."

"You sure?" Even with help, she looks ever so tired, with shallow rings around her eyes and pale skin. Birthing triplets is no mean feat.

"Hey, can I ask you something before you go, Eden?" I keep my voice low, being careful not to disturb the boys.

"Yeah. What's up?"

"Why didn't you tell me about Fraser divorcing his wife?"

"I've been so busy with the boys and people visiting, I genuinely forgot. I didn't know about his son, though. Or his not son. I was shocked by his confession. It seems a little crazy. He said annulment. What did he mean by that?" She screws up her face in confusion.

"It's weird, right? How is it even possible? He's been with Anna since we split up. If not before."

"Do you really think so? Fraser never seemed the cheating type, Ella. He doted on you throughout high school."

"Yeah, but afterward he forgot about me, and nothing he's said so far makes any sense." I shrug my shoulders. "Forget it. It's late, Eden. Go back to bed. I won't be here in the morning as I'm off to the stables, remember?"

"Oh yeah, and thanks for tonight and all the other nights. I don't know what I'd do without you. But I'll see you next week though, yeah? We can manage. Go out, have fun this weekend." She yawns wide and unapologetically. "Love you."

"Love you too. Now go back to bed. Night." I shoo her away.

I go back to dreamily watching the boys, with only the

sucking sounds of their little mouths now and again echoing through the nursery.

Although this shift zaps all your energy, there is nothing more meditative than the silence of the night.

I stretch out my back and neck, rolling from side to side. Bottle feeding is brutal on your shoulders. All the pregnancy books I read when Eden was pregnant talk about vaginas, cervix, and pelvic floors. Not one of them mentioned the back and arm pain from the relentless bottle feeding with triplets.

I drift my focus back to the boys. Almost finished.

Removing their bottles, I lift Lennox into my arms first, pushing myself to my feet. Time for windy pops. Swaying back and forth, I rub his little back and he snuggles into my neck. He smells like cotton candy and sweet milk.

Lachlan wails, which is most unlike him. Eden and Hunter's boys are exceptionally patient. They wait on each other like they know. They're not screamy or crying babies either. I think the mellow nature of Hunter and Eden's relationship is woven into the fabric of their DNA.

I bend down. "Hey, hey, wee fella. Aunty Ella will be two minutes. I promise."

"I couldn't sleep." Fraser startles me as he meanders into the nursery in his gray joggers. Shirtless. My annoyance at him from earlier disappears instantly. "Need a hand?" he asks.

Holy bejesus. He's filled out.

Adrenaline rushes through my bloodstream and I let out a startled cough.

"Eh, you can do, yeah. Do you know how to wind?" My eyes stare at his million-pack abs.

"I do, Ella. I have done this before."

Of course he's done this before.

"And my face is up here." He runs his hand over his rippled stomach, then points to his amused face.

I shake out my body, trying to ground myself. *Focus, Ella. Back to the babies.*

Watching Fraser, he dips and handles Lachlan carefully as he lifts him into his athletic arms. "C'mon, wee dude. Let's beat your brother. Let's see how loud you can burp."

I can't help but smile as I watch him with the baby.

We sway and pat together in silence.

Fraser is so deliciously sexy with Lachlan draped across his ripped body as he swaddles that little soul into his large, powerful arms.

I whimper.

"You alright, Ella?"

I nibble my bottom lip, trying to hide my excitement as warmth flows between my thighs. I imagine myself licking his sun-kissed skin, dipping my tongue into each divot of his stomach, like licking honey out of a jar.

My sex pulses.

Lord have mercy.

I try to force myself away. But my eyes root themselves firmly, like the Queen's military guard, on his body.

Lennox distracts me by burping, then proceeds to violently throw up all down the back of my vest top, neck, and booty shorts. "Oh, gee, thanks, Lennox."

Fraser plants a soft kiss on the top of Lachlan's fuzzy head to hide a smirk. What is it about a large, athletic, tanned guy swaddling a tiny baby?

I feel a twinge in my pelvis. I think my ovaries went into supersonic overdrive.

Lachlan burps loudly. "Attaboy," Fraser praises him before he lifts the bottle and starts giving Lachlan the last of his feed.

"C'mon. We'll walk and feed together. You need to shower. I'll finish feeding them in your room." Fraser moves back through the nursery door.

We enter my bedroom and I nest Lennox around two pillows, propping him up, then pass Fraser his bottle. As our fingers brush, the static electricity of the carpet underfoot causes an spark between us, making me jump.

"Go change, Bella."

This feels like we've done this a hundred times together. This routine. It's enjoyable and familiar and gives me a brief insight into what our lives could have been like, and I suddenly feel like I've been punched in the gut at what might have been.

But it's not your life, Ella. Stop being silly. He's not yours and neither are these babies.

"I won't be long."

I shower then change into the only clean suitable nightwear I have—tomorrow's underwear. It's this or jodhpurs and a polo neck top, and I don't want to bother Eden by scrambling about in her drawers looking for pajamas. I pull on my black lace bra top and matching Brazilian thong panties. It's typical of me not to bring extra clothing. Flinging my hair up into a messy bun, I head back into the room to discover the two tiny darlings, both fast asleep, next to Fraser, who's casually draped across the bed with his bulging muscular arms behind his head. Now there's a vision I'm storing for later.

"You have the magic touch," I praise.

In so many ways.

It's insane how much I feel for him, and how angry I am at myself for feeling attracted to him, even after all this time.

Fraser surveys my body, short-circuiting my brain momentarily. I'm riveted to the carpet as I feel his gaze bite down hard on me before he lets out a low groan deep down in his chest.

Energy ripples between us, boosting to a new level.

He gulps as if needing fresh air.

A few unbearable breaths pass before he slowly breaks our moment. "They took the last of their bottle fast. They're winded. I changed them both, and now I need to know where to put them down."

I must have been in the shower longer than I thought.

"You're good at this. Grab Lennox," I whisper, scooping Lachlan into my arms. "Follow me."

We head down the long white and glass balconied hall together to the east wing of the house.

"Nice ass."

Yup, my ass is literally hanging out for all to see. "You've seen it a hundred times before, Fraser."

"Mmm, not in a *long* time. Peachy keen, babes."

"Sh," I whisper-scold. "This is Eden and Hunter's room here."

We tiptoe in, settle the boys in their white wooden cribs, next to Lewis' then tiptoe back out across the thick gray carpeted floor, being careful not to disturb my beautiful sister and her husband who are so lovingly wrapped around one another in their grand bed.

It makes me so happy to see Eden settled. A smile breaks from my mouth.

Heading back along the corridor to my bedroom door, I whisper, "Night, Fraser. Thanks." He follows right behind me. "Where are you going?"

"Through here." He points. "Through the Jack and Jill bathroom to my bedroom."

I forgot we're sharing an adjoining bathroom. Although I would like him to follow me into my bed.

Stop it. Stop it. Stop it.

"Night, Bella."

I sneak another cheeky glimpse of Fraser's beautiful body over my shoulder before he latches the bathroom door shut.

If he was mine, I would never grow tired of the view. I'd orgasm on the spot, every day, eye-fucking him. I'm on the verge of one now.

I groan, wishing he hadn't stayed here tonight.

Tossing and turning, I see one o'clock, two o'clock, and then three. When did this giant luxury bed become so uncomfortable? Exasperated, I give up. I know the only thing to help me sleep. Internet porn. I need to relax and de-stress. I push my sleep mask up, grab my phone, and I scroll for ages.

Nope. Not doing it for me tonight. I slap my phone facedown on the nightstand, grumbling to myself.

I know the only thing that's guaranteed to work. Taking myself to the place inside my head I've been going to for years, I think about Fraser, although I have a new vision of him to focus on. Of him tonight, on my bed. All muscles, ab divots, and tanned skin.

I slip my blackout sleep mask back down over my eyes. It's necessary in this virgin white, bright house Eden has.

Shuffling down the bed to get comfy under the covers, and removing my lace underwear, I lazily sweep the pads of my fingertips, lightly brushing my skin.

Trailing a path across my neck. Drifting downward, picturing *his* hands on my nipples, I brush my fingers across my skin. Imagining Fraser massaging my breasts, I pinch my nipple, rolling it hard between my finger and thumb.

Then I glide my hands across my hips, moving closer to where I want them to be, sweeping my inner thighs, I move to my center. Wanting so desperately for my hands to be his more than ever, my breath hitches.

I press my finger to my clit, softly rubbing. My skin prickles in anticipation. Tension builds as sparkles dance in my soft folds. Diving south, I delicately stroke from my sex to the top of my clit, picking up speed with each rub, coating my tender bud with my excitement.

A deep moan leaves the back of my throat as I imagine his luscious lips on my neck, dipping lower as his muscular body encases mine, dominating me.

Rubbing harder, my core burns. I need more. Dipping my finger deep into my pussy, I envisage Fraser inside me.

Steely-blue eyes appear in my mind as I imagine Fraser fingerfucking me. I add another finger and thumb my now-swollen clit, circling it, running across it over and over.

I spread my legs wide and apply more pressure, taming my moans as I lose control.

My chest rises and falls with urgency as the tension between my legs soars.

A burst of cold air fans across me as my covers are removed at high speed.

What the hell? I quickly reach up to remove my sleep mask.

"Leave it on and don't fucking stop, Ella," Fraser commands deeply.

This isn't happening. *Am I dreaming?*

I hesitate.

"Fine. Let me." His husky voice, laced with determination, makes me squirm as I second-guess if he's an illusion of my fantasy.

Fraser lays his warm, large hand over mine, confirming he *is,* in fact, in my room, fanning the flames of us. When we spark, we light fires and I'm burning with urgency for his touch. He lifts my hand, then I feel him sucking my coated fingers into his mouth. "Sweet as candy," he mumbles around them.

Holy shit, I love how dirty he is.

Guiding my hand, he moves it back south, over my bare, wet folds. I thank the heavens above that I had a wax appointment yesterday. He moves my hand back and forth, slowly, gently, tenderly, remembering exactly what I like.

Our fingers dance across my clit. Then my fantasies come to life as his thick fingers dip lower. Circling my entrance, he plunges one deep into my hot core and I moan in ecstasy.

"Fuck. You are so wet." Hot breath sprinkles into my ear before I feel him slide his other hand behind my neck, twisting my face toward where I think his face is.

I feel him close, laying his temple next to mine.

"Who were you thinking about, Ella?" he rasps.

I can't lie. "You," I pant.

I rub my bundle of nerves with purpose as his finger fucks me desperately. I feel him add another finger. I hiss as my back curves off the bed.

"Let go. Come for me, Ella."

My orgasm gathers speed as Fraser gives me more, reaching my magical spot so deep inside. In and out, over and over.

"Call out my name; let them know who you belong to."

My muscles contract. I have no control left and I come furiously; my body shaking and humming with delight.

Fraser covers my mouth with his plump lips, swallowing my moans of ecstasy as I call out his name as commanded.

Dipping his tongue into my mouth, desire covers my body in goosebumps as our first kiss in forever becomes frenzied. We attack each other roughly, gasping, clashing tongues and teeth. Groans escape us as we breathe heavily.

"Are you not with her anymore?" I need the confirmation.

"I've never been with her. Not ever. I promise. And we are separated," he reassures me between kisses. "It's you. Only you."

I clasp his face. I want him. Now. It's so wrong of me to want him after all the hurt he caused me and the fact that he's still married. But I *need* him, my body not giving me any choice. It's overriding any rational thoughts telling me I shouldn't be doing this.

Reading my mind, I feel the bed dip between my legs.

In the dark, like this, with him, is everything I've reminisced about for so long.

Now I want to feel him again for real. I move my hands downward on an adventure of exploration. Feeling his hard muscles scatter with goosebumps as I venture south, I skate my hands across every luscious part of him, not missing an inch of his washboard physique. He's buff and huge compared to all those years ago. His body feels insane, no longer a boy, but a man, a fucking intoxicating, strapping deity.

Moving my hand farther down, my urgency takes over. I reach out in the dark and discover he's naked from the waist down. He wants *me*.

I wrap his hard cock in my hand and glide his dripping wet length through my fist. He's thick and long. I can't remember him being this big.

He hisses at my touch.

Stroking him up and down, he stops kissing me, his mouth open against mine, obviously losing control. He wants this and so do I. I've waited too long, and I'm not willing to wait any longer. I circle his waist with my lean thighs and plunge him into my hips. Unruly desires take over my body as I guide him into my wet center, letting him know my intentions.

"Condom?" he mumbles against my skin.

"I'm on the contraceptive shot. I'm clean. Always use a condom. Only ever skin on skin was with you." I can barely string a sentence.

"Aw, fuck. I'm clean too. Only ever been bare with you," he pants. "Tested last week."

In one hard thrust, Fraser fills me up, gloriously stretching me. Between his weeping cock and my wet, silky center, we drown in each other, panting between hard, open mouthed kisses.

My body comes alive with every move. He lights my body up like a bioluminescent firefly.

Clawing at each other and moaning, ferocious pent-up frustration builds as he rocks and thrusts furiously back and forth, circling in and out. It's everything I know I've been without since he left.

Not knowing where to put our hands, we continue touching, inspecting, searching for each other in the dark.

I grab his sculpted ass, slamming his thick cock into me, deep.

"Ah, Ella," he pants. Digging his hand painfully into my hips. I wrap my legs around him tighter as he drives himself deeper with every single earth-shattering thrust.

In the pitch-black, I reach out and pull the back of his head, wanting all of him, crushing his face into mine. We breathe hard, gasping against one another, mouths open as I yell into his throat to fuck me like he's never fucked me before.

Clawing, carnivorous, pawing like a hot wild animal, I

crave him.

I grip his solid body now covered in perspiration, not wanting to let him go. He's all I've hungered for. This is raw and carnal and I'm wilder than a barbarian in heat.

My body vibrates as sensations I haven't felt in forever finally crescendo. But it's never, ever felt like this; this feels new, exciting, like we're meant to be back together.

Our impending orgasms are about to burst into flames, as he fucks me double time. The giant bed bangs off the wall, neither of us caring to think about who can hear. I feel so unhinged, on the edge of explosion. Hastily, I lower my legs, digging my heels into the bed, thrusting my hips into his, urgently pulling me in closer. Sensations sparkle across my spine, through my pussy and thighs as my body begins to shudder, building and building until I can't take any more.

I need us to come. Now.

To connect us once again.

And we do.

Simultaneously, we erupt.

My core burns.

He fucks me through my orgasm.

Unabashed, into his mouth, I moan and gasp as sparks dance behind my eyes.

The words *I love you* burst from Fraser's chest, but he silences me with his mouth before I can respond because I do love him. I never stopped.

Even after all this time.

He owns my heart.

And he still loves me.

Breathlessly, clenching, grinding, and convulsing, we slowly come down from our high as he leisurely slides back and forth until he stops completely.

For the first time in forever, I feel so content and happy. Tiny bubbles of ecstasy dance across my hot, sticky skin as he trails gentle kisses across my neck and shoulder, making me melt into him like liquid.

No one else makes me feel like he does.

He's awakened the dormant beast within.

He's ruined me forever.

Again.

And I'll ask him all the unanswered questions I have for him tomorrow, but for now, I want to enjoy this moment.

Fraser

My heart won't stop bouncing in my chest. I never imagined we would connect again in this way so fast. Never truly believed she would ever trust me again.

Sex with her was never like this. It was incredible before, but this was next level uninhibited.

I want Ella. There's no way I'm letting her go again.

I told her I loved her when I poured myself into her. I hope she doesn't run, and she believes me because I do. She's been mine forever.

I slip my pointer finger under her sleep mask and flip it up. Leaning on my forearms, I pull back and search her bright eyes in the darkened room. This is where I belong.

Why did I have to fuck everything up all those years ago?

"Hi," I whisper.

She tucks her head into the crook of my neck, and I toy with a lock of her hair. Ella's either feeling shy or she's instantly regretting what we just did.

Shit.

Panic and doubt flood in at the thought of losing her

again. It would be too much for me. I won't survive, but I'm not sure she'll stand by me once she knows everything, anyway. She may consider what I have done unforgivable.

"Hey, babes, are you okay?" I ask.

Removing herself from the safety of my neck, she peeks up. A shadow of her warm smile appears, then she kisses me so tenderly it settles my heart.

Shifting out of the bed, I take her hand and lead her to the bathroom to clean up, where we shower each other tenderly in complete silence, washing the past away.

She stalls and sucks in a breath as she discovers her scripted name tattooed into the skin along my right lower hip and groin area. Delicately, she brushes over the two interlaced feathers dangling from the letters of her name representing me and her with the title of *our* song by Metallica underneath—"Nothing Else Matters."

It's the song we played over and over, made love to, and she sang to me on the phone often, when I moved away. It was our reminder that, no matter where we were in the world or how far apart we were from each other, it didn't matter because both of us knew how important we were to each other.

"It's always been you," I tell her.

Our eyes unite as she continues to smooth her fingertips over my branded skin, then she kisses me passionately.

We kiss and kiss, taking our time, remembering each other, our desperation now gone.

Once showered, we head back to bed together. Exhaustion takes over, and we both drift off in our cocoon of satisfaction and pleasure. Safe in each other's arms once again, I hold her tight, not wanting to let her go.

But when I wake in the morning, she's gone.

CHAPTER SIX

Fraser

"Morning," Hunter greets me as I park my ass in one of the black leather wingback chairs in his home office.

"Morning."

"You alright, man?"

"Had better days, months, and years."

"Hey, Lisa and I are going to do everything we can to support you. We've already started. Your lawyer is positive we have a great case. You need to focus on that. Clark Johnson is the best lawyer in the state of California, and Lisa's a phenomenal agent. We've got you, Fraser."

I lean back in my chair and stare out of the floor-to-ceiling windows.

Why couldn't I have been more like Hunter and not screwed up so badly early in my career? I certainly wouldn't be in the shitstorm of a living nightmare I'm currently in.

"Nate Miller has had it coming for years, Fraser. Now is the time to take the cockroach fucker down. To get your life back. He's a dick. We should cut his cock off and feed it to him after what he's done to you."

He's right, but I'm scared shitless.

Nate, my agent—also my father-in-law—is a ruthless sports agent. Classes himself as a purebred family and businessman.

He's far from it.

He's a scheming, dodgy-as-hell, corrupt, filthy son of a bitch agent.

He owns most of California.

Dozens of poor bastard sportsmen.

And me.

"I'm gonna lose it all."

"No way," Hunter affirms. "Lisa, Clark, and I, we're *not* gonna let that happen."

I know he means it. But it's only words. It's not real. We don't actually know what's going to happen once we start proceedings.

My fear, however, is totally real. It creeps into my thoughts, and I feel it in my body every hour. Sometimes it hits me when I least expect it and other times it slowly winds up into my lungs, squeezing them until I can't breathe.

This is harder than I thought it would be. Saying and doing are worlds apart, and the enormity of my situation has me waking up in the middle of the night covered in a cold sweat. I need out of this contract with Nate or I'm going to have a goddamn breakdown.

I'd reached my breaking point during the last Championship Cup tournament here in my hometown of Castleview Cove.

Seeing Ella again, I wanted my life back. With her.

In a moment of weakness, I poured my heart out to her at the Winner's Ball, telling her I loved her, but I couldn't get the rest of my story out to tell her what was really going on.

Plus, I was under an agreement not to speak about my situation to anyone, as I'm contractually bound by Lucifer himself, Nate, but I was so done with it all.

Sheer desperation pushed me to open up to Hunter last year, spilling my story, explaining everything. He instantly offered to help me. I was geared up. Pumped to get started. But the action part of it? It's slowly but surely killing my spirit and I've been having serious doubts. My aching heart and sanity can't take it.

The two primary goals are to win Ella back and move Anna and Ethan into a new house, one that isn't owned by her father. And my third goal is to recover some sort of normality back into my life. I crave a *normal* life again; a life I can be happy in. I haven't felt happiness or contentment for such a long time. I can't remember what that feels like. And fourthly, ensuring my mom and dad have a place to live.

Ella's my priority though, my rock. She always was until I messed it up.

I pull the back of my neck as the tension in my body builds yet again. It's been soaring for weeks. I need the gym. I need to let off some steam and stretch; get the adrenaline pumping again. Take out some pent-up frustration on the punch bag. Then refuel and find Ella.

"Can I use your gym before I go?"

"Of course. I'll join you if Eden's mom and dad have arrived to help with the boys."

"You're happy here, aren't you? Settled, in love with Eden?"

He smiles a fuck-yeah grin. "That pocket rocket of a girl rocks my goddamn world. And have you seen those beautiful boys she's given me? Man, she has me by the balls with just her giggle." He looks out toward the Cove through the window. "This place is magic. So is she."

Hunter has it all. It's what I could have had if I'd had my head sewn on straight when I first started playing golf and left for America.

My hometown of Castleview Cove feels magical. I know what he means. Our historical town may be small, but it's steeped in larger-than-life stories. I spent hours as a young boy playing in the castle that stands tall above the Cove. It watches over everything. From the nine golf courses and beaches, to the pier and the ancient stone ruins scattered throughout the town. It sees and hears it all.

The golf history it holds is what I love most about the place. Where golf originated. Where my career path began. Luckily for me, golf is in my bones and I'm really good at it. I spent hundreds of evenings after school playing, practicing, and being coached here. I was one lucky son of a bitch to win the scholarship when I did, although moving away to the States was also partly to blame for the circumstances I find myself in now. It's where I met Nate.

When I was younger, Ella always came to after-school practice. Then we'd grab fish and chips and walk to the beach. We had a special spot, a little nook around the corner of the rocks, where the golden sand met the cliffs. One day, we scaled the rocks and discovered a ledge. From that moment we spent hours together there chatting, kissing, and laughing. I miss those times.

Up on that ledge, I carved our initials into the rugged sandstone. *F & E. Fraser & Ella.* That became our thing... *Forever & Eternity.*

My bones have been aching to come home. To help my mom and dad, especially since Mom's breast cancer treatment. Now they're both getting older, I want to move back. I've spent way too long away from them. It's time.

I need to be here, especially as my brother Jamie isn't around anymore, either. Although, for now, we are better off without him. He seriously needs to sort his shit out before showing his face here again. We have enough going on right now, and I'm glad he's currently in rehab.

The last time he visited Castleview, he caused too much heartache for so many, especially Hunter and Eden.

Many years ago, Jamie was in a serious fishing accident, killing three of his crew. Jamie was the only one who survived. It did things to him I cannot even begin to imagine. A short while after his accident, he left Castleview Cove. He left Eden, his girlfriend at the time, behind at six months pregnant. Then she unexpectedly lost the baby. My parents were utterly devastated. We didn't know where Jamie disappeared to, so we couldn't tell him. I returned for the funeral. My niece's funeral. Eden named her Chloe. It was a harrowing day; one I will never forget.

I will never forgive my brother for leaving with no forwarding address. My parents were frantic with worry for years, not knowing if he was alive or not. Then he contacted me out of the blue. Money. That was all he was after. When I told him about Eden and the baby, it was like I had read him a list of groceries. He didn't even flinch. It was the weirdest thing.

We are complete opposites, Jamie and me. Not cut from the same cloth at all. My family is everything to me and I take care of them; call and check in every day, even on my most busy days. I made an oath to myself, after losing Ella, to keep in touch with my family, even when it seems impossible.

I lost the best thing that ever happened to me. I'm not losing anyone else.

Eventually, Jamie started asking for more and more money, but I finally stopped bankrolling him a few months back, after I got him checked into rehab for his PTSD, which led to his alcohol dependence. When he's released, he's been told he's not getting another penny from me. It's time he grows the hell up because the Bank of Fraser is officially closed for business. I'm done with people taking advantage of me.

Luckily Hunter and Eden found their way back to each other and I'm delighted Eden found happiness with my friend. I spent a lot of time with Eden growing up while dating Ella, and she became like a surrogate sister to me.

Hunter and Eden are perfectly matched, and he adores her. Moving here from Florida was a big step for him, but because we travel so much as pro golfers, it means we can live anywhere in the world.

And this is where I belong. It's where I want to be. Surrounded by people I love. I don't want to be in California anymore.

I haven't walked along the beach yet since I returned. It's my favorite thing to do. Fish and chips on the beach. Dipping my toes in the cold North Sea. It's grounding and there truly is no better feeling.

It's what my soul hungers for right now—normality, stability, *home*.

"You're a lucky guy. And thanks for everything, Hunter. Seriously, if this all works out, I'll be forever in your debt."

"No need for that. Playing fair, happiness above all, and living your truth. I want the best for you. We're teammates, *friends*."

Hunter's one helluva guy. I don't think I'm going to get

through this without his never-ending supply of positivity and belief in me.

"Eh, before you dash off, though..." Hunter frowns as I rise to my feet. "One question."

"Yeah?"

"Do I need to buy a new bed for the guest bedroom?"

I pull my eyebrows hard together. "No, why?"

"Well, I'm pretty sure with all the banging Eden and I heard in the night, well actually, in the early hours of this morning, we thought we may need to replace it, 'cause it definitely sounded like you and Ella were trying to break it. Either that or you were trying to kill her because she was screaming bloody murder. Really fucking loud, too."

Oh shit. I flush. I didn't think they'd hear us, considering how far away we were from their bedroom.

A wide-assed grin spreads across his face as he taps the pen in his hand against his glass desk.

"So, well, right, I, eh..."

"I'm yanking your chain, Fraser."

I sigh, a deep heavy sigh, 'cause I can't figure out why she left this morning without speaking to me. Although she barely said a word after we had sex, either. An undercurrent of worry thrums through my temples.

"This is what you wanted, right? Ella. I sense something's up. What's wrong?"

"We never spoke after, you know?" I feel like a high school asshole speaking about her like this. "And then this morning she was gone."

"She's at the stables this morning. Mucking out. She has a horse. Did you know?"

"I didn't, no."

There's so much I want to know about Ella. I want her to fill in the gaps and share it all with me. But first things first, I need to find her. Check I didn't fuck everything up last night, again, and make things right between us.

"You two need to sit down and speak to each other. You have *got* to tell her, Fraser. Everything."

"Shit, man, she barely speaks to me now and when she does, we end up bickering. How will she ever trust me again? She's gonna walk straight out of my life again if I tell her too soon. I need to build her trust." All of my confidence and bravado I felt last night has gone out of the window after I found her gone this morning.

I'm petrified of what she'll think of me.

"She trusted you enough last night. I think that speaks for itself." Hunter rolls his chair back from his desk, rises to his feet, and moves toward me.

I'm not so sure.

"Stop overthinking this. If you want her to trust you, be truthful. Talk to her. Lay it all out on the table. Everything." Hunter grabs my shoulder and gives it a reassuring squeeze. "You'll feel better once you do."

"You're right." A jolt of excitement courses through me. If she knows the truth, maybe she'll accept me back in her life. Or maybe she won't listen to a word I have to say.

"Rather you than me, Fraser. Ella makes my fucking testicles climb up into my body with one look." He shudders, making me chuckle.

"She's actually a pussycat underneath all her feistiness," I reply.

"Well, she makes me feel like a fucking pussy. I'm sure her spirit animal is a honey badger. Looks quite cute till it opens its mouth. She scares the shit out of me. You are hardcore. You need some serious amount of good luck to win that one over."

Chuckling, we head out of the office.

"C'mon, Hunter, I'm gonna whoop that pussy ass of yours in the gym."

Then I'm going to win my girl back. Because I'm not living another day without her in my life again.

Ella

Lost in my world, mucking out Tartan's stable, I'm consumed by my thoughts from last night with Fraser. It was unbelievable. The way he touched me, he quenched my decade-long thirst for him.

He breathed life into me again, taking me to a place I never knew existed. It felt new and exciting and strange, but so familiar. It's such an odd cocktail of emotions I'm feeling today about it all.

His body makes my sex ache for more. He's bigger, broader than he used to be, and fit as hell. *So sexy.* All muscles and tan. I'm also convinced he's had a penis enlargement too. He's way bigger than I remember, and he knew exactly what to do with it last night.

And the way he handled me with such care and tenderness afterward. He made me feel special.

But I can't let it happen again. It was too much too soon.

Maybe it was a good way to get it out of my system.

Or wreck me forever?

Although... he knows me and my body, and he lit me up like I was the Fourth of July.

There has been no one who fires me up like he can, and our connection is unique and something I can't even explain, even after all this time.

He hears my thoughts.

But even with so many years passing, my hurt still burns

like wildfire in my belly as all the unspoken words between us have been left unanswered. And yes, our dynamic has changed between us now that we're older, but he still drives me into a trance-like state when I'm near him that makes me feel inebriated.

My insides turn to Jello when I'm around him. It's so unfair.

My mind's in a confused state of bedlam. I keep seesawing back and forth. I want him; I don't want him. He loves me; he loves me not. Man, I'm exhausting myself.

And then there's his wife and son. Who's not his son. How does that even work? And he's getting divorced too. Does that mean there's a chance for us? Do I want a chance with him? Oh gosh, I don't know. I need coffee.

A text message *dings* from my phone, breaking through my thoughts. I slip my phone out of my side leg pocket and slide the screen open.

Eden: I'm guessing from the sound of it... by it... I mean the loudness of your bedroom antics last night... you and Fraser are back on?

Shit. I've never had sex in close proximity to my sisters before. *So not cool, Ella. Not cool at all.* It's all Fraser's fault. He makes me lose myself.

Me: I'm so sorry about that. It won't happen again and nope.
Eden: You sure?
Me: Yeah, why?
Eden: From the sounds of what Hunter and Fraser were talking about earlier, Fraser's on a mission to win you back.

A fluttering sensation dances around my heart.

Me: Is that so? He's not told me what's going on. No way can anything even remotely happen until he tells me.

Eden: Listen to him when he does. That's an order, not a request.

Me: What do you know?

Eden: Not my story to tell. Talk to him.

Me: Do you know where he is?

Eden: He was heading back to his parents for a shower after his gym session with Hunter. That was quite a show I watched this morning with the two of them working out. *Flames emoji* *Popcorn emoji*

Me: Dirty bitch. You in heat and can't do the dirty?

Eden: Yup. One week and counting.

Me: Not long.

Eden: Too long. Have you seen my husband? Although Fraser's looking pretty fit. Wow. He must work out every day to look like that. He's huge now.

Me: He feels incredible.

Eden: I bet he does! Anyway, remember, receive not transmit, Ella.

Me: Okay, bossy boots.

Eden: Have a great weekend. Hunter and I are off to oil the guest bed, you know, 'cause it sounded like it needed it last night!

Me: Stop it!

Eden: ;) Gets you back from all the ribbing you gave me when I slept with Hunter for the first time. #justsaying

I chuckle, slipping my phone back into my pocket. Eden has really started enjoying life again this last year. It's a wonderful thing to witness.

So, I need to listen to Fraser. *Okay, Eden, I will.*

I continue to muck out Tartan's stall in a state of

confusion. The morning has passed so quickly because my mind is full of Fraser.

His touch, his lips on mine, and the way he circled his hips. I think I need me some more of that. Yes, sir.

Or do I?

I may get hurt again. It feels like a risk my heart can't take.

I took the brunt of the heartbreak the first time around; I shouldn't even be considering revisiting the past.

Inhaling a deep breath, I give my neck a good stretch left and right to ease the tense thoughts and hard labor of the morning.

So far today I've fed, changed the rugs, and mucked out all the horses whose owners are on vacation this week, leaving Tartan's until the very last.

Luckily for me, Tartan likes to dine on his bedding. By the time I usually get to the stables in the morning, he's already eaten most of his straw, saving me heaps of time mucking out.

I'm short of time to exercise him this morning as I need to dash back to shower and then run to dance classes. Ivy, the owner of the stables, assured me she'll get someone to do it for me when I leave.

"Tartan, stop biting my ass." I swat the air when he yet again nips my backside.

A low, husky voice makes me jolt. "It was me."

Pivoting around on my heels, I tumble backward, but I'm caught by two strong athletic arms.

Fraser.

He circles my waist and pulls me in close.

"Hey, Bella. You are sexy as fuck in these skintight riding pants," he whispers.

It happens so fast. He covers my mouth with his and I

lose myself in his touch. His kiss scorches my skin as our tongues collide, greeting each other.

I can't resist him. I'm a fool to think otherwise.

I drop my fork into the sparse hay and run my hands up the back of his shaved, thick neck. I'm enchanted by his scent, which sticks the middle finger up to any shred of common sense I have left. Unable to stop, we grip each other tightly. Fraser skims his hands down the curve of my back, and rests them on my black Jodhpur-clad backside, pulling me into his rock-hard cock. We hum into each other's mouths in appreciation.

Excitement builds as the clip-clop of horses' hooves and voices thrum around us.

We should stop this, but he deepens the intensity of our kiss and the horny bitch in me wants more. I pop my eyes open to be met with his ocean blues. He grins against my mouth, winks, and then closes his eyes, growls softly, and loses himself in our moment. I join him.

Throbbing between my thighs drowns out everything around us, and I melt into him.

Kissing was always one of Fraser's specialties. With a little added dry humping, he could always kiss me to orgasm. I'm shocked at how my body remembers his touch. He's intoxicating.

Fucking my mouth with his tongue, he walks me backward into the dark corner of Tartan's stall. A gasp of air leaves my chest as I crash into the wooden wall behind me.

Thrilling sparks of energy dash between us. Fraser hooks my left leg around his waist and rubs his hard, cloth-covered cock against my sex.

He's relentless; grinding and kissing me, driving me wild. Glimmers of an oncoming orgasm begin.

Oh shit. What am I doing out here in the stables?

"We have to stop," I pant heavily, hearing the faint bark of a dog in the distance.

"No, we don't. You're close. I know you."

He's right. *Oh boy*.

Fraser pulls at my hips, grinds, and rubs faster. "I'm not stopping until you're shaking," he mumbles.

His words send me over the edge, and I can't stop. I tilt my hips into him, rubbing my clit through my thin pants against his impressive bulge. Sensations slide up my thighs and spine, into my hot, wet pussy as my clit pulses with pleasure, flying over the edge of ecstasy and beyond. He kisses the hell out of me to muffle my moans. Fraser catches me as my legs continue to shake, then give way.

"I've got you." He holds me up as I descend slowly.

He leaves me feeling breathless.

I lean out of our leisurely kisses.

"You're so beautiful, Ella. I've missed you so much."

Oh hell, no. What am I doing?

I push him away and, fleet-footed, I run out into the courtyard.

"Get out, Fraser." I hold the door open, instructing him to remove himself from Tartan's stable.

"What?" His brow wrinkles deeply.

"I said, get out," I say through clenched teeth, not wanting to startle Tartan. A thousand different emotions buzz everywhere. "I can't do this." I wrap my arms around myself. "Please get out so I can close the door."

Fraser moves around Tartan slowly. I close the stable door behind him.

"What's wrong, Ella?" He frowns.

"What's *wrong*?" I pound back and forth across the cobbled ground. "Everything."

"Everything?" He screws his face up.

I deliver him the facts. "Yes. Everything, Fraser. You, me, us. The past. It's all wrong." I draw an invisible line in the air. "Last night was wrong. We should never have done what we did, and now..."

He steps toward me with fear in his eyes. "Please don't say that. Last night, now, was *not* a mistake. Not for me. Never."

"I hate myself. Hate *you* for making me feel and act the way I do." I stop pacing and arch my neck toward the gray cloud-filled sky because I can't look at him. I'll cave if I do. "Why the hell did you have to come back?" My voice echoes around the stable block.

"I told you, my mom's sick."

My throat closes as a gigantic lump forms. I clasp my head in my hands. "You never came back for *me*," I whisper. I sound like a proper princess. His mom's not well and here's me, acting like a spoiled, self-centered bitch.

"Ella." He strides toward me.

I step away from him.

"Stay over there." I flash him the palms of my hands to halt him. "Last night, now. Ten months ago. You're messing with my head, Fraser." A sob leaves my throat. I close my eyes and cup my face with my hands in a rush. "I waited for you."

I hate crying. I'm usually stronger than this, but I've been holding all these emotions in for so long. "And you can't fix us with sex."

Strong, warm arms swaddle me.

"I'm so sorry, Ella." He kisses the top of my head and holds me firm.

I shake my head back and forth in disbelief. I want to be with Fraser so badly, but I can't let him hurt me again.

"My heart hurts," I whimper.

Fraser squeezes me tighter. "Baby, I know. Mine too."

What does he mean, his too? How dare he.

I thrash about and push myself out of his arms, making me stumble backward. "What do you mean? Your *wife* broke your heart too? Fucking hell, Fraser; deepen the knife, why don't you?"

I sniff furiously and wipe my tear-stained face with the back of my sleeve.

"That's not what I meant, Ella. Not even close. I mean, my heart is broken too. Because of *you*."

"Me? How exactly? What the hell did *I* do?"

He stares me down. "You did nothing. It's what I did. You don't know what I did, Ella. What I became. My *wife* is not my wife. On paper only, that's all she is. Nothing more."

He's not making any sense.

"So, you're telling me after all this time, you and she never had a relationship? No sex? Nothing. You must think I'm an imbecile. And you have a son? Were you with her before you dumped me?"

Baffled by the sequence of events surrounding our relationship, I can't work out which way is up because he said last night that his son wasn't his son, and he's never had sex with his wife, who isn't his wife. He keeps saying these things, but none of it makes any sense.

I can feel my blood pressure rising by the minute. I need a logically straight answer.

"I'm telling the truth."

"Is this the same truth about your son not being your son? Oh, but that's right, you don't want to talk to me about it. But using me for sex is okay. Have I got that right?"

"You left this morning without a word, and last night you hardly said anything to me afterward. So don't push this back on me." He scrunches his face up in pain. "And you're not listening to me. I'm flat out telling you, Anna is not my wife, not in the *real* wife sense, and Ethan is not my boy, biologically. It's a fucking marriage of convenience." He bellows his last words, his voice bouncing off the square-shaped yard.

I step back. "A what? You've lost me. Come again?"

He's so confusing. Finding it hard to catch my breath, I feel like I'm losing control.

"Fuck." He grips his hands by his sides to form fists. "I didn't want to do this here. Not now."

"You could have told me last night, and you didn't."

Trembling all over, my mind feels like it's suddenly disconnected from my body. Fraser and I have never fought. I don't like this, not one bit.

"No, I couldn't because I didn't know how to. I wanted to, but I'm so fucking ashamed and embarrassed." He drags his hands down his face and groans.

"I don't understand," I whisper, struggling to get the words out. "You implied back at the Winner's Ball that Anna cheated on you. Was that not true?"

"You assumed I meant that. I never said she did. Anna's a good person. She's as messed up as me about the whole situation."

"Marriage? A situation?" I cover my mouth. I think I might be sick.

"Yes, Ella, a situation. Anna and I, and poor little Ethan —he's Anna's son, not mine—we are *a situation*. One I wanted to explain to you properly. Not yelling at each other like *this*." He motions to the square courtyard.

It's then I realize we've drawn a crowd. At least five sets of eyes are on us.

Ivy catches my glazed eyes and sends me a knowing nod. "Everyone back to work. I'm sure you've all got enough going on in your own sad lives than to be concerned with Ella's."

"Shit," he mutters under his breath.

Oh no, what if someone heard Fraser's confession and sells it to a newspaper?

An unfamiliar sensation of unease washes over me. I started this here. I didn't mean to.

My lower lip trembles.

Fraser is so famous. Especially in our little hometown, nothing is sacred from the gossips. They love nothing better than stirring things up in the Cove. If Mrs. Mitchell catches wind of this, then we are royally screwed. She's got supersonic ears, everywhere.

Fraser grabs my hand. "Come with me."

"No." I try to yank it back.

He whips around to face me. "Yes, Ella. One minute, that's all I need."

He squeezes my hand and begs me with urgent eyes.

I agree with a gentle nod and start walking on my jelly legs.

With our hands laced together, he marches me out the arched entrance of the courtyard, around the corner, away from the stables.

Out of earshot, he stops suddenly and circles to face me again, staring at me with determination.

"Now listen to me, Ella, and listen carefully. I am picking you up tonight at six o'clock. Ready or not, you will come out with me, and I will explain everything. What you have to hear, it's not pretty, but it's my life. I would never intentionally hurt you. Ever. This was not how I wanted this to play out, but here we are. Be ready at six. I know where you live."

He leans in, kisses my forehead quickly, and with that, he stalks toward his mom's little red car.

"Fuck," he yells, kicking the graveled driveway, shooting stones everywhere. He storms into the car and slams the car door.

Watching him drive off in haste, he disappears out of view, leaving my cloudy head filled with confusion.

What a bizarre thing to say. A marriage of convenience?

I don't even know what that is. Sliding my phone out of my thigh patch pocket, I open it quickly and search *marriage of convenience*.

Words spill across my screen... *contracted, no love, personal and financial gain, political reasons, strategic purpose, no mutual affection, sham.*

Sham?

I clumsily slide down the stone wall behind me and sit on the dewy grass.

Why would Fraser marry someone out of convenience? I don't understand.

I need an explanation.

I'm going to demand one.

I'll be ready at six o'clock alright.

CHAPTER SEVEN

Fraser

My firm knock of Ella's shiny gold door knocker against her black front door sets off a multitude of mini yelps and barks.

"Oh, be quiet, you two," I hear Ella's muffled words.

As she opens the door, I'm greeted by two four-legged balls of fun who instantly weave through my legs in excitement. One jet-black and one caramel-colored, they both have little gray hoodies on.

"Toffee. Treacle. In." Ella points into the house. "You better come in, or they won't. They are friendship seekers and desperate to speak to anyone who comes to the door. Goddamn manwhores."

"Hmm, and here's me thinking I was special."

Her take-no-crap eyes bore straight through me as I set foot in the door.

"Have you calmed down since this morning?" She tips her chin upward.

Yikes. This evening may be harder than I expected.

"Yeah. I lost myself earlier. Will you forgive me?"

"We'll see." She tilts her head side to side, weighing how she sees tonight going. "Give me a couple of minutes to get the boys settled, and then we can go. I didn't eat. I assume we're eating?"

She looks incredible. Her thick platinum hair flows down against the black-and-gold leopard-print floaty shirt, leaving nothing to the imagination. Her black lace bra glimmers through the sheer chiffon, highlighting her ample cleavage peeking out from the top of her undone buttoned collar. *Hello, girls.*

Like always, her makeup is perfect, like it's permanently tattooed on. Black winged eyeliner and dark cherry red lips. She's sexy as fuck. I want those rich lips wrapped around my cock again. She always sucked me like I was the best thing she ever tasted.

"Fraser?"

"Eh, yeah." She wakes me from my daze and I clear my throat, knowing that sordid thoughts about her won't help me tonight. "Sorry, yeah, we're eating."

"Come through. Where are we dining?" She wiggles her sexy dancer hips back and forth, padding down her elegant hallway. She's tucked her shirt into high-waisted, leather, biker-style leggings and teamed them with high black strappy sandals.

I follow her sway, unable to take my eyes off her for a minute, having to adjust myself as I walk. Shit, this will be difficult. *Focus, Fraser. Focus.*

"Champs."

She stops in her tracks, then swivels on the balls of her feet against her gray-and-white diamond-checkered floor.

"Champs?" She flutters her green gems.

"Yeah."

"I think I need to change for Champs. It's a five-star restaurant, and I have leather pants on."

"We have a private room, and you look sensational, Ella."

"I'm not too hookery for a five-star, then? You sure?" She crinkles her nose.

The thing about Ella is, everyone thinks she's super confident, however, deep down lies an undercurrent of self-doubt and a little under-confidence, something she only ever let me see. Hope fills my chest as she lets me in again.

"You are beautiful. I wouldn't lie to you."

"You mean you never used to lie to me, then you did?"

I walked into that one.

"Let's not do this now. I promised you I would explain, and I will, tonight."

She rolls her head back, eyes the ceiling, and lets out a heavy sigh. "Okay. But I know you're only taking me out somewhere so I can't throw shit at you or lash out if we're in a public place."

I burst out laughing, then instantly stop as she glares my way. "Don't tempt me, Fraser. I can find something to throw at you right now."

She bends down to pick up the dog's water bowls. I flinch, but she stands tall, then leans over the sink and fills them to the brim. I thought she was serious for a second.

Bending at the waist to pop the bowls back on the floor, I'm greeted with a sublime view of her ass in those tight-as-shit pants. *Holy crap. Think of anything but her divine body.*

Time to change gears.

"Eh, why are your dogs dressed in hoodies? Do their coats not keep them warm enough? And what are they?"

"French bulldogs," she coos affectionately. "They get cold. They only have thin coats." I don't believe her for a second. I think she enjoys playing dress up. These wee fellas are her babies. "Isn't that right, boys?" She glances down at their droopy little faces.

"They look so happy." I chuckle.

"Oh, they are. You can tell."

What is she seeing that I don't?

"They have their own Instagram account. You should follow them. They have lots of clothes and we do a pic a day. Don't we? Oh yes, we do." She snuggles into them.

She's so in love with them.

"An Instagram account? For the dogs?"

"Yeah, want to see? I get sponsorship opportunities for them all the time." She reaches for her phone off the black granite kitchen countertop. Her house is small, but she's decorated it beautifully. In warm shades of charcoal, black, and white, with brief hints of gold sprinkled throughout. This is the old derelict courtyard we used to play in when we were teenagers. It's been converted into five homes recently.

She sashays toward me, head down, concentrating on her screen. Her fresh sandalwood fragrance reawakens my memories of us. It's seductive and spicy, like her.

"See." She thrusts her phone into my hands.

"Twenty-four thousand followers? That's insane." I scroll downward. Rows and rows of daily costume posts. I spot one with Treacle in a bumblebee outfit. Poor mite.

"Eh, have you seen them?" She points to the two little chubby pups sitting on the kitchen floor. "They are so cute. Who couldn't resist those wee faces?" Ella's whole face lights up.

She's right, they are cute. "They look like bats."

"They do not look like bats," she shrills. "Do you hear what Fraser is calling you boys? He's a meanie."

"Check out the size of Treacle's ears; well, I'm assuming that's Treacle since he's as black as treacle and Toffee is toffee-colored. Right?"

"You would be correct."

"Well, Treacle looks like a giant bat. And he also seems too warm in that hoodie, puffing and panting. You've turned into a crazy dog lady. Oh, and horse lady."

"That's normal for him. He's a puffer. And it's perfectly normal to be in love with two beautiful little souls who don't answer back and give me hardly any grief. They're the perfect companions. Tartan, on the other hand, likes to bite my ass and gives me no end of grief."

"It was me who pinched your ass earlier. Do I give you grief?"

"More than all the men in my life combined," she says deadpan.

She crouches down and the two little fur balls waddle their short and pudgy bodies toward her. "Right, boys. I love you. Mommy will be home soon. Okay? No barking or old Mr. Riley next door will be on Mommy's doorstep again. Do we have a deal?" They snuggle into her. "Good boys."

"Let's go." She rises to her full height, then turns to face me.

I resist the urge to lean in and kiss her.

Time stands still for a moment. I don't want to move from here. I'm putting off the inevitable, but she needs to know.

She has this extraordinary power over me. I move slightly toward her as an electric current draws me closer.

Her chest expands, and a nervous twitch flutters across her mouth. She then blinks, inhales quickly, and clears her throat. "I'll grab my purse."

I bow my head to my chest. *Fuck*. This night is going to be tough. Especially after she rocked my world last night.

Rotating to head out the door, I give a little wave to Ella's *boys*.

Treacle growls low in his chest in disapproval. I don't think he likes me.

In the car heading to the restaurant, we drive in silence. "Why did you borrow Hunter's car tonight?" she inquires.

"This is the same Range Rover I have back in the States. And tonight, Ella, I don't think my mom's little runaround would quite woo the pants off you. I'm trying to impress you."

"You don't need to impress me, Fraser. Give me answers, yes, but not impress me. And you're not getting my pants off again."

Ella's a straight-talking girl. She says what she means, and she means what she says when she says it. But sometimes she goes deep into her cave and won't let anyone in, won't speak to anyone, and won't tell anyone what's going on. I guarantee she's not told a soul about our conversation in the stairwell all those months back. It's also the reason she hasn't spoken to me for years. She wouldn't let me back in. Also, when you play with her trust, it could very well be lost and gone forever. I hope not that's not the case with us.

"Here we are." I park up at valet parking and exit quickly, running around to her side to help Ella out from the high SUV. She's five foot six, but it's still a little high.

Passing the keys to the valet and slipping him a tip, I offer my hand to Ella. She takes mine in hers, but as soon as her feet hit the curbside, she releases it like I'm contagious.

Confidently, she strides in front of me, winding up the path into the restaurant, which sits off to the side of the main hotel spa. She's not happy with me at all and I feel disappointment bouncing off her.

Once seated in our circular-shaped private room, we sit across from one another around the two-seater table, studying our menus. Nerves kick in and I can't see any of the options. It's all a jumbled mess.

I can't think of anything but her being here with me. Me, about to shatter her heart and share my shameful story.

A tap at the door signifies the waiter entering the dimly lit, dark berry-colored space. We quickly order, although I have no idea what I've ordered, and our private waiter for the evening exits, leaving us alone.

"So?" Ella leans in slowly, rests her elbows on the table, and cups her chin with her delicate hands. "I'm all ears."

CHAPTER EIGHT

Fraser

"Before I start. Will you promise not to leave tonight? Hear me out. Finish your meal with me?"

"I don't know if I can make that promise."

"Please, Ella," I beg.

Consideration flits across her face. "Okay, but if I ask to get a taxi home, I want you to respect my wishes and let me go."

"Deal."

"Also, I want the whole truth. No holding back. No lies. Everything, Fraser."

"Double deal."

A soft thrum of elegant music drifts in the background.

She anchors her attention to me.

I straighten my black dress shirt sleeves with long, nervous strokes, then take a huge gulp of water.

I think my heart is considering jumping out of my mouth and running out of the room.

"So, where to start?"

"You broke me, Fraser. All those years ago. On my twenty-first birthday. Start there."

Shit.

"I can't apologize enough about the timing. Seriously, I fucked up big-time. I know I did."

I reach my hand out for her to take it, but she doesn't respond.

"I can't accept your comfort, Fraser, because my head is swimming with the need to know what the hell actually happened all those years ago. From my perspective, I did nothing wrong. I waited for you, like some dumbass pathetic fool. Then you married someone else as soon as you dumped me. And today you speared an arrow-shaped bomb through my heart, telling me you married someone based on a contractual agreement. None of it makes sense. So, start talking because I'm about to lose my shit any moment now," she says, spitting venom.

"Okay." I shove my fingers through my hair. "When I left Castleview Cove for the last time, the time I gave you our necklace." I point to Ella's collarbone.

She reaches up and gives it a quick rub and I like knowing she draws comfort from the gift I gave her all those years ago.

"My schedule got busy because I got good at golf. Better than I was. I didn't stop calling you because I didn't care. I got distracted. And I was stupid and young. It's pathetic of me, I know. Then when I turned twenty-one, I was approached by this guy called Nate Miller."

"Your father-in-law?"

"Yeah, my *now* father-in-law and douchebag of an agent. Back then, I didn't know who he was. Well, I knew he was a shit-hot agent. But what I didn't know was he was as corrupt as they come."

Her perfectly arched brows fly up in surprise.

I continue. "He offered me fifty thousand dollars, plus he said he would pay off my mom and dad's mortgage. In return, he made me promise to let him represent me exclusively when I turned pro. I didn't know it then, but it happens all the time among sports agents, and it's highly illegal."

I close my eyes and summon a breath to keep my story flowing. I want to get it all out fast, but I don't want to miss anything out.

"I was sworn to secrecy, and he had me sign an NDA about the offer he made me, but this wasn't a full contract. He was teasing me with gifts. Luring me in. He delivered on his promise; paid off my parents' mortgage, and I received the lump sum. I was so happy, and I felt special. Like I was important. I seriously thought he believed in me, and it would be the start of something for us. Me and you. To start a fund to build or buy the home we dreamed of together, Ella."

"What's an NDA?"

"It's short for Non-Disclosure Agreement. It's a contract that basically means you can't tell anyone about anything you sign in agreement to. So, the money advance, my parents' home. All of that. It's signed and sealed and kept behind closed doors. Ninety-nine percent of the time, these contracts can't be accessed or made available to anyone. What I didn't know at the time was I had also signed my mom and dad's house over to Nate. I was too stupid to read the small print."

I take another swig of my water. Although it doesn't help; my mouth feels like freeze-dried sandpaper, but I have to get this out. I swallow the ball of dust in my throat.

"Nate continued to entertain me, took me to lots of fancy

restaurants and introduced me to what I thought was the glamorous and appealing side of my job. Within a year, I earned my golf tour card; it came naturally to me. It was then I fell down the rabbit hole of excessive drinking, dabbled in some gambling, but only when I was out with Nate. He had a game plan. Sometimes I would get into a bit of debt at casinos he'd take me to, but Nate would help me out, pay it off for me, and tell me everything was fine. But I drank more, partied a lot, then I damaged my wrist."

"I remember. You only returned my calls a couple of times that year," she whispers.

What a selfish, self-centered prick I turned into back then.

"I took prescription drugs for the pain to get me through tournaments. Then it all got out of control. Over the next couple of years, I lost myself." I clear my throat.

"One morning, I woke up in a hotel room in Vegas. I had no recollection of how I'd arrived there, checked in, nothing. I woke up alone, luckily. I was so confused. I called Nate in the morning because the last thing I remember was being out with him for a meal the night before, along with another four athletes. One was a basketball player, and the others were football players. It was a 'getting to know each other' night; that's what he said. He flew us out there, more schmoozing to make us sign with him. On that morning's phone call, Nate told me to come down to breakfast. They were all waiting for me. Dazed and woozy, I dragged my sorry, shocked ass downstairs to be welcomed by Nate, seated alone in a heavily guarded private room.

"Nate informed me over breakfast I had lost over half a million dollars the night before in the hotel casino playing blackjack. Apparently, I borrowed the money from him. Bewildered, I had no idea what he was referring to. I could only recall us all having a meal in the hotel and then... nothing. Nate produced a contract I had never seen before. But as clear as day, in black and white, scrawled along the bottom, was my signature. As I read the words, I discovered I'd finally agreed to sign with him. I'd been holding back because something felt off. My gut was right. Within the contract, it outlined the percentage he would receive from my future sponsorships, championships wins, magazine interviews, and television appearances. He would get a massive chunk of my winnings, way above average, on everything. It also stated within one clause that if I didn't keep winning and performing well at golf championships or failed to perform to his standards, then he had every right to change the terms of the contract and threatened to take a bigger percentage of all my earnings. So, in order to fulfill my end of the agreement, he planned on working me hard. He had me by the balls. He still does.

"He presented all this debt I was due him for dozens of nights out. He'd kept tabs of everything, and it wasn't just a few hundred bucks. It ran into the thousands, hundreds of thousands of dollars even, and the contract didn't stop there; there's more to tell you."

I shove my hand through my hair, rest my elbows on the table, and bow my head. "I'm an idiot."

Ella rises from her side of the table, moves her seat, setting it down on the floor by my side, and rubs my shoulder.

"Hey, you're not an idiot. You were young and naïve. Plus, you were all by yourself in a foreign country, traveling the world alone. How could you have known?"

"I should have known. I stopped calling you, kept my distance, removed myself from reality, worried that you would discover what a mess I was making of my life. I was twenty-three at this point. I was a stupid, distracted dumbass. Wrapped up with some dodgy people. I ran up colossal amounts of debt, apparently. Nate forced my hand, unwillingly. I think I was drugged that night in Las Vegas. In fact, I know in my heart I was. It's so obvious, knowing what I know now, and speaking to the guys I went out with that night, the same thing happened to them. They have no memory of the evening either, and they all signed contracts that same night, too. And I looked it up. Rohypnol. I think he drugged me with it. It all sounds so crazy when I say it out loud, but it happens, and I think it happened to me because I have no memory of that evening after our meal.

"Anyway, over breakfast that morning, the same morning he showed me the contract I had supposedly signed, he sucker punched me again. He made me call you. He sat and watched me do it."

I never felt so helpless in all my life. Nate didn't care that it was her birthday or listened to me when I begged him not to make me call her.

"He forced me to finish it with you, because he said I had to break all ties with my past, as he had a better future planned for me. His daughter." Slumping forward, I pinch the bridge of my nose. I felt used and hopeless. If I didn't say yes, my parents would lose everything. "I never intended to do that to you on your twenty-first birthday. I never wanted to hurt you. But there was a reason for the call."

I draw a breath before sharing the rest of my tortured tale.

"You're gonna hate me, Ella."

She rubs her hand down my arm. "Look at me, Fraser."

Twisting my neck, I meet her caring face.

"Please tell me everything."

"Before I called you, he revealed to me he had wiped off

the debt I borrowed from him the night before, and lost, in return for his daughter's hand in marriage. It was all in the contract. I have never been so dumbfounded in my life. It was like I was watching a movie about someone else's life. There is no way I would have agreed to marry her willingly. I was deeply in love with you. I know my actions didn't reflect that, but I was. And I still don't know why he chose me to marry Anna. Maybe it was because I was closest to her age or something, I don't know. He drugged me to get his own way and ultimately gave his daughter away. What a lowlife."

I shake my head back and forth.

"Imagine me, a switched-on guy, being fooled, duped. But I was in too deep with him, too close to see it, and I was a complete imbecile. The only consolation, I was not alone. Nate has done the same to many others, but not the forced marriage part of the deal," I hiss between my teeth, madder than ever.

I draw in a stuttered breath.

"So, you married her?"

"Yeah. Deal done. Unbeknownst to me, I had signed myself over to the devil. He would pay off my debts, which I'm still not sure I had. He agreed to buy us a house. I fucking hate that house." I sneer. "It was what he called 'a new beginning.' Nate reckoned Anna and I would fall in love and be one big, happy family. As if that wasn't bad enough, I discovered she was already three months pregnant."

"By who?" she asks, wide-eyed.

"Anna was in love with a guy named Lucas. He was the manager at Nate's nightclub, the one he uses for laundering money. Nate rules with an iron fist and informed Anna she had brought shame to the family. She needed to marry for success and social status, and Lucas didn't meet Nate's criteria. If word got out that his socialite daughter was pregnant by a 'simpleton', then the scandal would be harmful for his reputation apparently, not upholding the almighty Miller name. In the blink of an eye, Lucas disappeared. Anna still, to this day, does not know what happened to him. She was utterly devastated because she knew Lucas was in love with her and was excited about the baby. And then there I was, heartbroken about *you*. Knowing you'd never be mine ever again. We were a pair of sorry souls.

"To everyone around us, it seemed like we were the likely pair to marry, him being my agent and all. *Up and coming pro golfer marries rich socialite daughter of his wealthy agent.* It was a fucking sham. All of it. A marriage based on NDAs and contracts. What a joke.

"Back then, even before I signed that contract, I had become so dependent on him in all aspects of my life. I didn't see him blindside me. And since then, Nate has threatened to remove my parents from their home several times. He's relentless."

"Why did you not ask any of us for help?" She frowns.

"NDAs are rock-solid. And I didn't marry her to pay off my debts. I married her because my hand was forced. It was all there in the contract. And, Ella, the debt he presented me with wasn't hundreds of dollars, it was hundreds of *thousands* of dollars I owed him. My mom works in a grocery store and my dad's a plumber. Where the hell would they get that kind of money? I could never have asked them for help. And I signed that contract. It was my signature. To this day, I still don't know how he got me to do it. I don't recall a single thing. No flashbacks. Zilch." I pull the back of my neck.

Ella asks, "And there was nothing in the contract about ending your marriage to Anna? If you kept winning tournaments and landed great sponsorship deals, you couldn't have paid him off that way?"

"He had me on my knees. There was no negotiation, and ultimately my signature was my undoing."

"So, you married her." It's not a question; she's making sure she's clear on the situation.

"When the head fog of my situation finally lifted, the realization hit hard. I was so depressed. But it was too late. I was married. Contracted. I belonged to Nate. And Anna. The wedding was all kept very hush-hush—just Anna, me, her father, and his lawyer. Oh, and the minister."

My shoulders sag as I lean into the table, remembering the day that was supposed to be the happiest of my life. It didn't even come close.

"You and Anna have never had an intimate relationship? Like, nothing at all?"

"Nope. Never. No intimacy. There's nothing romantic between us. We're just friends."

"So, what do you do for sex then, Fraser? I know it's a dumbass question and there's so much I want to ask, but how does that even work? You're a man, you're still young, and you surely have needs?"

I internally cringe. "I used to use an exclusive escort agency." I can't look up from the shame I feel. "I haven't in over a year though."

A breath catches in her throat at the realization of what I am saying.

Shit.

CHAPTER NINE

Fraser

Perfectly timed, our private dining room door swooshes open, signifying the arrival of our meal.

My appetite upped and left before I even told my story tonight.

Sensing our unease, the waiter sets our food down and swiftly exits.

"I don't think I'm hungry anymore," Ella announces as she leans back in the cranberry velvet dining chair.

"Eat, Ella. Just something. I'll stay here all night to answer all of your questions. You asked for the truth. I'm giving it all to you." Despair gnaws at my stomach. I feel so raw and exposed. I've never shared using an escort with anyone. Typically, it would be Ella I tell first. *Great*.

Her questioning eyes stare at me, struggling with all the information I've laid on her. "So, *is it* a prostitute you use then?"

What an asshole I've turned out to be. Someone who pays for sex. Never did I think this is what my life would become.

"Used to use," I correct her. "They're not street-walking hookers. They're exclusive. High-end. Fully tested and security checked. I wouldn't sleep with just anyone. And I have never been with anyone else. Only two girls from the agency. And you."

Ella shakes her head, then sticks a fork full of salmon into her mouth. She's thinking while she chews.

"I suppose that's better than multiple one-night stands with people you don't know," she eventually mumbles.

I never expected her to say that. I almost snort a laugh.

"Do you like them? Have feelings for them, Fraser?"

How could she think that?

"Of course not. It's just sex. A safe and private way for me to get off. Bearing in mind, I have my '*wife's*' reputation to think about."

I turn in my seat to face her. "I'm in love with *you*, Ella. How many times do you have to hear that from me before you believe it? I love *you*. No one else. There's been no one else for me."

"Except for paid escorts," she says flatly.

"And how many boyfriends have you had since we split?"

Shit, I shouldn't have said that.

She blinks at me. A deep flush instantly floods her chest. "Hey, that's not fair," she exclaims through a tight jaw.

Pushing her chair back, her fork clatters against the ceramic plate as she throws it down. Standing on her sky-high heels, she paces back and forth around the circular table, desperately fighting back her tears as she flips her head back.

"I'm sorry, I shouldn't have said that."

She stops pacing, rests her hands on the back of her

chair next to me, and then bows her head. Silent tears free-fall onto the velvet seat pad.

"My heart is in so much pain. It has been for years," she whispers as she sways her head from side to side, her hair moving in slow waves.

She said it back at the stable today too. Her confession strikes another instant hard blow to my balls and heart.

"You wrecked me, Fraser. Destroyed what we had." She sobs as she continues to keep her face hidden from me behind the curtain of her hair. "And for all these years I've blamed myself, for not coming to visit you, for not meeting you halfway, for being too young, for staying with my sisters, for going to dance school here in Scotland. I've lived with this gnawing sense of guilt that's eaten away at me until it almost consumed me.

"My heart is breaking even more now, knowing if you'd reached out to me, told me. I can't fathom why you didn't trust us enough to help you." Ella's voice fades off into the distance.

I clumsily rise to my feet and pull her delicate frame into my arms, but she doesn't reciprocate my embrace. She stands there and allows me to swaddle her.

If I could change everything, I would.

"I know I fucked up," I mumble into her neck. "I never meant for any of this to happen."

I pull back and cup her angelic face with my hands, tilting her head to face me. The sight of her swollen glazed eyes takes my breath away, knowing I'm the one who's caused all her heartbreak.

"I live with deep cutting regret and guilt every day. Some days, I wish I was someone else. Even just for one day." I smooth my fingers across her cheek, trying to pour my feelings I have for her into her skin through my fingertips. I don't want to let her go because I'm scared I won't ever get to feel her like this again.

I brush a few lonely tears away from her swollen cheeks with the rough pads of my thumbs.

"Don't say that, Fraser." She shakes her head a little. "You have so many people around you that love you. Hunter is a good friend. He will help you. And that poor boy, whom you call your son, he needs you. He doesn't know you're not his dad, right?"

My chest feels like a ten-ton blue whale sat on it. "He doesn't. Anna and I have agreed to tell him before we announce our separation officially. I love him like my own. Anna and I have brought him up together. I did all the late-night feeds with her, the teething, weaning, crawling, walking, nursery, school runs. All of it. I think of him as my boy and he's a great kid."

Ella's eyes widen in amazement at my confession.

"You're such a good man, Fraser." She gently places her warm hand into mine. "Few men would do the same. And Anna? Does she have someone?"

I didn't expect Ella to think I was a *good man*. I don't feel it. I feel like a failure.

"No. She doesn't. She said she wouldn't until Ethan was older. She knew I used to visit escorts from time to time, though. We are very open and honest with each other, and I trust her with my life. Anna is nothing like her father."

Ella shifts slowly out of my arms, then thumps her tiny backside heavily onto the chair behind her. Lifting her wineglass, she downs the lot.

"But why now? Why are you filing for divorce? How can you break the contract you've signed?" Deep lines of confusion appear across her brow.

"Luckily, I've got some pretty damning information on

Nate. It's not enough, but I'm working on it. In addition, my lawyer reckons we can fight Nate on the grounds I signed under duress, making the contract unenforceable. It may not be a divorce we file for, but an annulment. We have to get our hands on the contract. It's kept in a safe in his home office and Anna agreed to help me retrieve it. His darling daughter is not as sweet and compliant as he thinks."

Deep in thought, she runs her fingers through her hair.

"And ultimately, I want out because of you. When I saw you again last year at the Winner's Ball, I knew I didn't want to spend any more time away from you. I've kept my distance long enough. It was painful seeing you again, seeing you with someone else, talking to you on Instagram. I wanted to tell you everything. I wanted, sorry, *want* you back in my life. I knew then I couldn't live without you. That's when I started setting the wheels in motion. I explained to Anna I wanted out.

"Anna reluctantly agreed because she fears her father. She's petrified actually, but she said if I could hire an excellent lawyer, work out how to release us from our contract, then she would support my decision. To be fair, we're both tired of keeping up the charade. It's exhausting. Fuck, Nate even has it written into our marriage contract that we have to post on social media as a family at least twice a month. Anna has to attend three tournaments a year to show face. He's a controlling psychopath. I'm not doing it anymore. Anna doesn't want to, either. I'm thirty years old and I want my life back." My breathing grows erratic as I quickly get my words out.

It feels empowering to say my thoughts out loud. "And it's not only me. There are dozens more boys on his books who lose massive chunks of money with every deal he closes for each of us. We're all pulling together to bring him down.

We're all being held against our will and we're all teetering on the edge of desperation."

"But how will you save your parents' house and what will happen to Anna and Ethan?"

I reach out and squeeze her hand. Trust Ella to worry about people she doesn't even know.

"I have savings, more money than I know what to do with now. Nate still takes a massive percentage of my winnings and deals from me, but I've been cleverly funneling off money, saving every cent I can."

Nate thinks I've become the prodigal son-in-law, playing along, clean-cut and living the American dream. I'm taking him down when he least expects it.

"I bought a new home for Anna and Ethan, in Anna's name. I'm releasing her from Nate, setting Anna and Ethan up for life because the house we live in belongs to Nate, and he will make her life miserable when this all implodes.

"And my mom and dad? I'm going to have to tell them they have to leave our family home because as soon as our divorce hits the press or when Nate discovers what we're doing, he'll have them removed from the house. It's his, after all, and there is no way he will sell it back to me. But I'm going to buy them a new one. I need to do it quickly before someone leaks our story."

Then I say something that's been troubling me since I left Ella earlier. "I just hope no one heard me today at the stables."

"Oh gosh, Fraser, I hope not too. I am sorry. I know you aren't just my Fraser anymore and the world wants a piece of you now you're famous."

Tension rises in the air as we both gather ourselves and Ella pours herself and me a glass of water before she empties her entire glass in three huge gulps. She offers me a sad smile, then she asks, "But what about you? What happens to you?"

I honestly don't know.

"Well, I imagine once Nate's informed by my lawyers that he's being sued, he'll try to leave me with nothing. He enjoys winning. Money and greed drives him. And my lawyer's bills will be astronomical if it goes to court, so I'm trying to organize everyone around me first. That way, I know they are safe and provided for and I have the best chance of ending this without a costly court case."

The thoughts have entered my head. He'll fuck me over and pull some bullshit half-assed story about me out of some unicorn's asshole in an effort to ruin my entire life, and that scares the living shit out of me. I've worked hard to get where I am as a golfer, and I deserve my place and world ranking.

"I may lose my career, too. He's unpredictable, powerful, and ruthless. Plus, I've broken his NDAs. There's no saying what he'll do."

The one thing he can't take from me is my talent for golf. That's what is keeping me focused. I will always be a skilled golfer.

She furrows her brows. "I didn't expect any of this tonight. I don't know what I expected, but not this. I've been such a fool, thinking shitty thoughts about you. I even considered making a voodoo doll of you. But I should have known, you always did like blonds, not brunettes." She smirks.

Oh, she's joking with me. This is a good sign.

"I only like one long-haired blond in particular," I try to reassure her. "I fell down a deep hole for a few years, being poisoned and easily led by a narcissist. I may have saved his daughter's reputation, but he keeps on winning because he's fucking me up the ass and he's been taking a huge cut of all my deals and winnings since I was twenty-three years old. I've lost years of my life with you, thousands of dollars of my earnings, and it's fucking messed with my confidence so bad. I won nothing from his contract. I lost my freedom and most of all, you. And I promise, none of this had anything to do with you. You can shred any guilt or blame you have."

Ella chews on the side of her lip. "Wow, this is a lot."

Tell me about it.

She drums her immaculately manicured nails against the black piano gloss tabletop. She's thinking. "We had sex last night. No condom. I know you said you were clean, but do you use a condom with your escorts?"

"Always. I haven't been with an escort in over a year and I've never had sex without a condom before, only with you. And you said you were on the pill; are you?"

"Of course I am. I would never lie to you," she gasps.

A nervous tremor of laughter escapes my lungs. "Thank Christ for that."

She narrows her eyes at me. "Why? Because having a baby with someone you're actually in love with is wrong? Or is pretending to have a child with someone you haven't even had sex with? Is that the perfect way to have a child? That's exactly how you should have a baby, right? Sounds like the perfect happily ever after to me."

Shit. She's right. I'm an asshole.

"No, that's not what I meant at all, it's just…"

"Let's not do this. I don't want to argue with you." She lets out an exasperated sigh. "And stop stressing. I have the contraceptive shot like clockwork, plus I always use condoms with any sexual partners. I told you that last night."

I growl with jealousy.

She grabs the wine bottle, fills her glass up again, then takes a sip. "You're in no position to get mad about who I've slept with, Fraser. You left me hanging. Then you cut me loose, like I meant nothing to you. Without an explanation. I was never unfaithful to you. I waited five years. You barely came back to see me a handful of times in those five years. The last three you didn't come back at all. You stopped calling. You stopped calling all of us. But we could have helped you. Clubbed together. Hired a lawyer. Found a way. I was waiting for you. I would have waited forever. I loved you so much." I barely hear her last words.

Loved.

She doesn't love me anymore.

Disbelief floods my chest. "You would have helped me? Even though I made all of those bad choices?"

"Yes." She slaps her forehead with her palm. "Nate must have messed with your head so bad for you to forget what we had. You must have known. You must still know. Feel it. This. Us." She gestures to the air between us. "It's never gone."

She's right. Our bodies speak to each in ways I can't understand; they know and crave one another.

"Of course I do," I say. "Last night was fucking incredible. It's what I've been dreaming about all these years. Me and you. Together again. I find these white feathers everywhere I go. I know you're always watching over me, even after all this time. I feel you everywhere, Bella." Excitement threads through my veins at the thought of creating the life we used to dream about.

She pulls a half smile. "That'll be me stalking your Instagram when you feel me, then."

"Oh, yeah, do you check me out?" I nudge her shoulder teasingly.

"A little." She pinches her fingers together in the air, scrunching her nose as if embarrassed at her admission. "I helicopter around your social feed sometimes."

"I fly around yours too." I wink, feeling relieved as our conversation lightens.

We sit back in our seats, lost in our own thoughts.

"Hey, are you okay? I am deeply sorry, Ella. I know I keep saying it, but it's been torturing me not being able to tell you everything."

"Honestly, I'm not sure how I feel. I'm assuming Hunter knows your *full* sordid state of affairs? Is he helping you?"

"Yeah, he is. Lisa, his agent, is going to be my new one. She's helping me alongside my new lawyer, Clark Johnson. I asked Hunter to wait and tell Eden as I wanted to speak to you first, although he probably told her today after I left their house."

"He must have. She texted me before you showed up at the stables. She told me I was to listen to you and hear you out. Not to fly off the handle." She rolls her eyes. "She kept your secret, allowing you to speak to me first. Our little trio are good secret keepers."

"You sure are."

"Hmm. You're one to talk. This is a whopper you've been keeping."

She's not wrong. However, I feel slightly lighter now that she knows, and my burden's shared. I should have told her the truth from the start.

"Where do *we* go from here?" She runs her fingers through her platinum locks.

"Honestly? I was hoping you had the answer to that one." I pause. "Can I ask you something?"

She slowly looks in my direction. "Yeah."

"Do you think there's still a chance for us?"

Her eyes blaze with emotion before she eventually answers. "Can you give me some time to think about it?"

"I wouldn't have it any other way. Take all the time you need."

I feel my stomach sink as I ask her another question.

"Do you think you'll ever trust me again?"

She pauses for a beat, thinking, before she says, "Trust has never had anything to do with us, Fraser. Disappointment and heartbreak are all I've ever felt since you ended it with me. I always trusted you. It's only recently I questioned if you'd been with Anna before we split up. Now I know that wasn't the case."

"Do you still love me?" My chest fills with anticipation.

Simultaneously, we swivel around to face one another, her knees braced between my thighs.

Reaching out, I cradle her face. Her worried eyes hold mine. "I know you need time, and I fully respect that, but do you love me, Ella?"

She dips her eyes, then flits them up a moment later. Scanning my face, time freezes as she considers my question.

"I can't say those words to you right now."

Right now. Soon maybe?

I smile brighter than sunshine as static energy buzzes across my skin and delight drums through my body. Because I know she does. I feel it, but I long to hear her say the words.

"And this is a lot to take in." She leans her elbow against the table, then rests her chin on her hand.

My heart stalls for a second.

"There are so many things I want to ask, Fraser."

"Shoot them my way. I'll answer everything."

I'll do anything for her at this point.

"Can it wait? Let me think?"

"Of course."

Doubt shadows my soul. "So, you don't hate me?" I whisper. I've caused so much unnecessary pain and grief in her life. She really should.

She fills her cheeks with air, then puffs her exhale out. "I don't hate you, Fraser. I'm mad at you, but I don't hate you. I hate the way you make me feel, though. This insane invisible thread you pull me in with."

We feel the same. I'm sure she's the one drawing me to her. I close my hand around hers and lay them on top of her slender thigh.

She brushes her thumb back and forth across my skin.

I watch her carefully.

My dazzling, enigmatic girl. She's now a captivating, beautiful woman. I'm mesmerized.

She flashes me a shiny white smile. "Were you scared I'd flee tonight? Never to be seen again?"

Shaky, nervous laughter trembles in my chest. "You have no idea."

She leans in, then runs her fingers through my hair. Moving down, she gently strokes my chin. "I like this little blond goatee."

I chuckle.

"But it gives me a terrible stubble rash. Look." She points to her own chin.

I can't see a thing. Her pale skin looks perfect to me, but I like the fact she's referred to our passionate encounters.

"I've missed my best friend for so long," she whispers.

I feel my throat constricting as I struggle to swallow my pounding heartbeat.

"I've had no one to speak to. I'm so fucking lost, Ella."

My lip quivers. Out of sheer embarrassment, I cover my face with my hands.

Shit. Shit. Shit.

Even when my life rocketed south, I never cried. It was like all my senses became blocked. I tucked them all away in a box, never to be unlocked. An influx of warmth fires across my chest.

"Oh, Fraser."

She surrounds me with her tender embrace.

"Don't. Please don't. I don't deserve your kindness. I messed *us* up. I've missed you so much."

I lean out of her embrace and arch my neck upward, heaving in and out to stop the feeling of utter humiliation coursing through my veins.

Ella moves in closer and slides her hands up the thighs of my black dress pants, and I revel in her tender touch.

I drop my chin to my chest.

"Fraser."

I'm so ashamed.

"Look at me. Or we can't do this."

Through my cloudy vision, I peek upward.

"My head currently feels like it's going to explode. And I've got no idea how to navigate *us* from here. We have so much more to talk about, but I'm done for tonight. I want to go home. Please know I'm here for you. I don't hate you. I will always be your friend. Okay?"

Friend. Has she already decided?

I don't want friendship. I want her, all of her.

"Just friends?" I quiz.

She shrugs her shoulders to her ears. "I honestly don't know."

Resting her hand in mine, I strum my thumb back and forth across the top of the soft skin of her hand.

"Thank you. For being so understanding tonight. I really needed this."

Her cheeks flush a wild pink.

"I'm not the ice queen everyone thinks I am."

"I know. It's why I love you."

Although, who knew Ella would be the calm in my storm? She's normally the eye of it. My hurricane. My blond bombshell is a revelation. I hope she's going to be my savior.

I honestly believed she would be finished with me after tonight. I prepared myself, yet again, for more disappointment. But, at worst, we'll be *friends*. Although that's not what I want.

"Such a tremendous waste of food." She motions at our uneaten meal. "I can't believe you booked us in here tonight. This private room is super fancy. I was right earlier. You *definitely* booked here, so we're on impartial ground, huh? I can see now why you were petrified I'd throw something." Her mouth curves into a knowing smile.

I made reservations here out of necessity, a neutral place for us to chat.

"How do you always do that?"

"Do what?"

"Read my mind. I was literally thinking the same thing."

"Because we're kindred spirits, you and I," she softly whispers.

Visions of me living the rest of my life with this audacious spitfire of a woman sitting in front of me flash into my subconscious as hope seeps in. It overshadows the constant years of my past self-inflicted anguish and suffering.

Craving to kiss her, I stifle the urge, not wanting to push things between us.

"C'mon, I'll take you home." I lay my palm out, inviting

her to take it. This time she does. And it fills me with so much joy, more than any kiss could.

She's not made it entirely clear if she wants to be with me and give us a shot or tell me to get lost completely.

She needs time.

Ella's in charge of our future together. If we even have one.

I hope we do.

Because I am nothing without her.

I don't know what happens after we leave this room, and if she kicks me out of her life, I'm going to show her why I should be in it.

CHAPTER TEN

Ella

We travel in silence, following the high cliff coastline road back down into Castleview Cove.

I've always wanted to dine at Champs. It's a Michelin star restaurant and all the celebrity types who come to play on the world-famous golf courses dine there. It's part of the five-star resort and spa, The Sanctuary, which I've been to many times, but never the restaurant. The Sanctuary is owned by Knox Black, one of my dad's golfing and business buddies. Tonight, however, I was too caught up in Fraser, listening to him, to be able to fully appreciate my surroundings and not how I wanted to experience Champs for the first time.

Peering down into the bowl of the beach cove, I watch as sprinkles of people enjoy walking along the sandy curve of the pale-golden beach and the ancient cobbled pier, finally welcoming the warmer spring weather. I'd be down there too with my two furry friends if I wasn't out with Fraser tonight.

Spring and summer evenings in Scotland are incredible.

The height of summer skies are my favorite and grants us around eighteen hours of daylight. We hardly ever get a truly dark evening. In winter, though, well, that's a whole different story. Dark and cold. That's it. One extreme to the other. This past winter has felt longer than normal and lonely, too.

I'm surrounded by lots of people who love me, but I never quite feel complete.

And here I am now with the man who holds my fragile heart, the man who consumes it and makes me feel whole. But Fraser's confessions at dinner were not what I expected at all. Not even close. There is no way in hell I would have guessed anything he told me tonight. It's unfathomable and has my head spinning.

My heart burst into smithereens as he broke down and confessed he's had no one to speak to. Keeping his enormous secret must be all-consuming. I've never seen Fraser so upset.

My broken boy.

He's lost.

A bit like me.

The whole time he was unraveling his story, which I can't quite believe is now his life, my head was telling me to run, but my heart was telling me to stay. To be there for him.

We're both heartbroken. Both fragmented.

But I'm so torn and mad. Really crazy-ass mad.

Madder at Nate for drugging him, duping him into signing a contract and then binding his daughter to Fraser. One thing's for sure; it would make an incredible movie.

But this is Fraser's actual life, not a screenplay.

And yes, I am mad at Fraser for being so naïve, for falling down a desolate rabbit hole of stupidity. Mad that he was overpowered by a money-crazed maniac and being mad at how much time we've lost when we could have been together.

None of it stops me from wanting him.

I do want a more simple life though, and I know the life I have here in Castleview Cove gives me what I seek. It's the complete polar opposite of Fraser's busy schedule of being a pro golfer and traveling around the world every month of the year. He's famous now, too, in newspapers and social media. Quiet and easy. I live a very simple day-to-day existence, walking my dogs, riding Tartan, instructing dance classes, and running our thriving dance school. I come and go as I please, go out with the girls on the occasional weekend, and keep myself to myself with no drama.

In the past six months, I've taken over the responsibility for all our social media. It keeps me busier than I would like to be. Content creation is mega time-consuming, although my friends have been otherwise occupied, so at least I've had the distraction to fill my time.

I'm a little bummed out because everything's changed in the past few months. My friends, Toni and Beth, have found happiness with new boyfriends and we have put the holiday we had planned to the Maldives on the back burner. Eden is wrapped up in her newly married life and the boys, and Eva, well, I actually don't know what's going on with her and Ewan. All I know is our usually bright girl hasn't been the same for months now. She's quiet and kept her distance from us all. I must try to grab her for a chat.

Everything is changing as we all approach our thirties, and while everyone seems to settling down and starting families here I am, still trying to figure out who I am and what I want for my life. I hate to admit it, but... I am lonely.

I'm going to grow old surrounded by nothing but dogs, horses, and nephews.

Although, could I grow old with Fraser?

It shouldn't even be a thought. He's not even divorced yet.

A marriage of convenience.

A stepson.

A court case.

I'm not sure I'm prepared for the fight ahead with Nate Miller and the turmoil it will bring.

And will the court case be in America? It may be too much time away from my business and my furry friends.

My stomach cartwheels at the thought. Having Fraser's name dragged through the courts and all over the newspapers.

I massage my fingertips into my temples.

I want to understand what's going to happen so I can formulate a plan. I need more information. I need answers, and this time I'm not being left in the dark. I'm going to make Fraser answer every single one of them.

Almost home now, Fraser carefully steers Hunter's black, shiny Range Rover down the narrow, cobbled street toward my little house.

They renovated the old courtyard at the end of the road a few years back into five quaint homes, and I was lucky enough to snap one up. It's at the far end of the horseshoe-shaped road. It's beautiful and so tranquil here, especially with the endless rolling fields of golden barley at the back of the properties. It's the perfect place for my morning journaling and coffee, something I've done since I started dating Fraser all those years ago. It helps me clear my head for the day and sleep better at night.

Sharing my feelings is not something I do well. Eden tells me I'm an introverted extrovert. Sassy and silent, apparently. So, *talking* to my journal works best for me. It's the place I seek comfort. There is nothing better than me, my journal, a coffee, and the fields surrounded by the morning silence of Castleview Cove.

It helps that everyone around me is retired or on the cusp of retirement, so no matter what time of day it is, it's always so peaceful, the mornings even more so.

It's me that upsets the courtyard residents as I have been known, on occasion, to wind up old Mr. Riley with my late-night parties following an evening of dancing the night away at the local nightclub, The Vault.

Although, I haven't been out for months. I'm losing my Party Girl nickname. I'm just too busy these days. I need to round the girls up for a night out. I quickly pull out my phone and text our group chat.

Me: Drinks at The Vault tomorrow?

Should I tell them about the last few days with Fraser? Nope, not now.

Eden: Not for me. I need a few more weeks to recover. My stomach and boobs still don't feel like my own. Next time for sure. Promise. :)
Beth: Count me in. Billy is going out on a stag night.
Eva: I can't make it.
Toni: Yes! I'm in. Evan left for America again yesterday :(I need drinks, my girls, and dancing.

Toni's been dating Evan, Hunter's fitness trainer, since the Championship Cup. It all seems to be going well. It's the first relationship Toni told her parents about. I think they had hoped their sweet Italian girl would marry a pure blood Italian stallion, but nope, Toni opted for the buff, blond, blue-eyed American who sends her completely daft. They see each other as often as they can and are making this long-distance relationship shit work.

Mmm... maybe Fraser and I could, too?

I text back.

Me: Perfect. Drinks at my place at eight p.m. first?

Beth: Awesome. See you then.

Toni: Cool.

Me: You sure you can't get Mom and Dad to babysit Eva?

Eva: Yeah, I don't feel like coming out. Next time maybe?

This is really worrying me now. I must ask Mom if she knows what's going on with Eva and Ewan. Something's not right. Eva loves a good night out and dancing.

Me: Okay. See you tomorrow, girls. And Eden... you'll be driving, dancing, and having sex again before you know it!

Eden: Oh, I do hope so :(It's been six weeks. A few more days then we're in the safe zone.

Beth: If it makes you feel any better, I was driving today, Eden. I'm going out dancing tomorrow, and I had sex this morning. Bahahahahaha!

Eden: Supportive as always, Beth!

Beth: Yup. Always here to help. ;)

Eden: Can we do drinks at my place in a few weeks, please?

Toni: Sounds like a plan.

Beth: Yes!

Me: I'll be there.

No reply from Eva. I make a mental note to visit her tomorrow.

"Everything okay?" Fraser questions, clearly worried about how distracted I am.

"Yeah. Just texting the girls about a night out." I pat his knee twice. "Your secret is safe with me. It's not my story to tell." I throw him a reassuring smile, and he smiles back gratefully.

Pulling up outside my house, Fraser leaps out of the Range Rover, runs around the back of the vehicle so he can open the car door for me. He holds his hand out, helping me step down from Hunter's high Range Rover. Being careful, I teeter over the cobbled street to my house in my Eiffel Tower heels.

As I turn my key, unlocking my front door, I throw caution to the East Coast wind and ask him over my shoulder, "Do you want to come in?"

His familiar deep *V* forms between his brows as he looks uncertain. "Are you sure?"

Nope, probably the stupidest thing I've asked all night.

"Yeah. But no funny business. No taking your top off or flirting those ocean blues at me, okay?"

He chuckles, his shoulders visibly relaxing.

"I can do that. Do I need to close my eyes then so you can't see them, or am I not allowed to make eye contact with you?"

"You can look at me, but not with that sizzling thing you do with them."

I won't survive if he does.

More soft laughter leaves his chest. "I'll go park the Range."

"There're spaces around the corner. Park there. I can assure you Mr. Riley's curtains are already twitching. He's ready and waiting for me to break the courtyard parking rules."

I step through the doorway to greetings by an excitable Toffee and Treacle. Crouching down to pat them both, giving them equal amounts of love, I swivel back around on the balls of my sandals to ogle Fraser's athletic frame saunter back across the cobbles. I'm in awe of how well he looks after himself. He's so easy on the eyes and I've found myself watching him a little too much tonight.

And to think *he's* attracted to *me*, actually, scratch that, loves me, freaks me out a little.

He must have met so many glamorous women throughout his career. And then there's Anna. She is stunning. I'm astounded he's never locked lips with her. Not even once.

I'm also a little shocked at myself too because in the past twenty-four hours I seem to have welcomed him back into my life, quite willingly, and he's about to spend an evening on the couch with me, in *my* house.

We're not in high school anymore, no longer kids, no goofing about, stealing kisses between classes through the high school corridors, or sneaking behind the bike sheds for a quick fumble at lunch break.

We've missed a whole intersection of each other's lives. We're older now. Adults. With mortgages, bills, and, oh, a fake kid and wife. *Superb*.

However, I don't think we've changed that much, apart from the fact Fraser's cock is definitely much, *much* bigger than I remember and that body, wow, that firm, sculpted body, and we *click*. Like popping candy, we crackle together. It's tangible.

I focus my attention back on my boys. "Hello, boys. How are my cute little cherubs?" I give them a good pat and lots of affection. If I don't, Treacle won't speak to me for days. He's needy. Toffee dances around in a circle. "Ooooh, you want out for a pee? C'mon then, out the back door." I stand and pat my leather-clad leg twice, fast, beckoning them through the hall, into the kitchen, and out the back door into the stunning spring pink-painted evening sky. Treacle and Toffee bound around the garden as if they haven't been outside for months. I can hear them singing, "Freedom," as they leap about playing together.

The front door clunks shut. and footsteps move closer toward the kitchen.

"So, the sizzling thing?" Fraser leans against the frame of the kitchen door. "Elaborate." He furrows his brows.

"Don't act all innocent and shit. You know that thing you do? Where you narrow your eyes and they go all dark and dreamy, like you're shooting molten sexuality at me. Like, you're peeling my clothes off with your eyes. That's the sizzling thing."

Fraser chuckles. "I literally have no idea what you're talking about. But whatever, babes. I promise not to do whatever the hell it is you just described."

Like heck he doesn't know. He does it all the time and I melt into a puddle each and every time.

Arching back, I reach down, and I peel my heels from my feet. *Ah, that feels better.* I stretch out my deep-red sparkly manicured toes, feeling Fraser's heated gaze on my every move.

"I know it's been quite an emotional night. How are you feeling?" I ask, genuinely concerned about him.

"I feel relieved. I've been carrying this secret around, keeping it from you for so long, but being with you also makes me feel better. Talking to you, being so close to you again, it feels nice. Right."

"I feel like that too." I smile shyly. "Would you like a drink?"

"Eh, yeah. Non-alcoholic, if you have it. I'm driving."

I may live to regret this, but I figure I'll get my answers quicker.

"Mmm, do you want to stay over? No funny business. We could talk some more in the morning. I have a spare room and I don't have any classes on tomorrow as we have two new instructors who take those now. I haven't had a day off in months from Tartan, so Ivy is mucking out and exercising him for me tomorrow. Maybe we could spend the day together? Walk the dogs on the beach. Visit your mom?" I ramble faster than normal.

"Are you sure?" His eyes question me.

Nope, not one bit. I don't trust myself around you.

"Yeah. We can chat. That's all, though."

"I'd like that. I'll need to text my mom. She worried last night when I didn't return. Oh, and Hunter to let him know I'll bring his car back tomorrow." Fraser slides his phone out of his back pocket and taps out a couple of texts. "There, done." He lifts his head and lays his phone on the kitchen countertop. I spot the image of his bright smiling son-slash-not-son on his phone wallpaper.

He continues, unaware of my phone screen stare. "It's weird staying with my parents again. Mom keeps asking me where I'm going and what I'm doing, and being back in my old bedroom, it seems so small now. Mom's never changed it. It's like walking into a time warp."

I wonder if his parents know he's with me tonight.

"Do you still have all those old photos on your corkboard of us?" I ask him.

"Yeah." He runs his fingers through his hair.

"I'd love to see them again."

He lifts his chin in acknowledgment. "I don't know how

it's possible, but you're more beautiful now than you were back in high school."

I feel myself flush.

"Thank you," I whisper.

Focus, Ella. "So, drink?"

"Yes, please. What do you have?"

I scurry about my kitchen, trying to find anything that isn't neon in color or strawberry-flavored. "You're gonna love the options, Fraser. Rhubarb and ginger-flavored gin. Or what about a strawberry margarita? Frozen, of course. I also have sex in the driveway cocktail, or melon liqueur?"

"You've never changed. It's a festival of fluorescent alcohol and what the hell is in sex in the driveway?"

I lift the glass bottle and watch the shocking bright-blue liquid sloshing about as I check the ingredients.

"Well, I haven't been shopping for ages and I wasn't expecting to be entertaining any beer drinkers this weekend. And in this—" I wave the bottle in my hand. "—Is vodka, blue curacao, peach schnapps, and lemonade. Want some?"

"I'll have a glass of that with ice if you have it. Just don't tell anyone I've been drinking Smurf juice, and did Callum not come here?"

"Hmm, only sometimes."

"How long were you with him for?"

"Four months."

"Do you have feelings for him?"

"What is this? I'm the one that should be asking the questions, Fraser."

He bobs his head and bites the inside of his mouth.

He's nervous.

"Fair point." His expression is neutral.

Eyes fixed on one another, for a moment, time ceases to

exist because we both have a deep longing for answers from one another.

I break the silence. "I don't have feelings for Callum. It was never anything more than a passing fling. I think he wanted more, but it's not something I could give him."

Or anyone, for that matter, because I'm still hung up on you, you daft fool.

I shift across to the other side of the kitchen and pull two gin glasses down from my display cabinet. I love collecting unique decorative cut glasses. No two are the same.

Once I've sorted our drinks out, Fraser and I amble through to the living room, where the two of us get comfy on my black leather and gold button-back sofa. It dominates the room, but I love it. It suits my slightly rich, luxurious style and not everyone would be daring enough to paint the back wall it leans against black but combined with my soft toffee walls, gold fixtures, and decorative elements, it works. It screams glamor and creates such a high visual impact.

Fraser casts his eyes around the room, and I can tell he's captivated by this sensational, shimmering space I've created that makes you feel you've come home to a sensual kiss and a warm embrace.

As I tuck my legs under me and scoot myself into the snug corner of my couch, my leather pants squeak against the fine soft leather fabric of my sofa.

"Is it leather pants for life now, Ella? It's all I've seen you in these last few days."

I coyly answer, "You like?"

Fraser smirks. "I do. A lot. Spank bank material right there. Those tight-as-shit pants drove me to hop into your room last night. Well, that, and your moaning."

I'd been expecting this chat. "Mmm. About that," I say. "It was—"

"Fucking incredible," Fraser rasps out quickly, repeating his words from earlier in the restaurant.

It was better than incredible. I've never had sex like it. I have to wiggle my ass cheeks a little and clench my core to relieve the pulsing that begins. What we did last night exceeds all my fantasies of him.

"I'm guessing from your silence, you don't agree. You said at the stables it was a mistake." Fraser slides his gaze away as he lets out a weighted sigh.

He slowly rests his sculpted arm along the shoulder-high armrest of the couch and spreads his thick legs wider.

His body language may emanate confidence and masculinity, but I can tell Fraser's self-assurance, in all aspects of his life, has been hit hard over the years.

How he can truly think I didn't enjoy last night is beyond me. It's all I've thought about all day.

"Don't put words in my mouth. I wasn't going to say that," I try reassuring him.

He leisurely bends his arm at his elbow and rests his head on his hand as he glances my way again. "What were you going to say?"

I clear my throat. "I was going to say it was the best sex of my life."

A glorious smile sweeps across Fraser's beautiful bee-stung lips, illuminating his face, making my heart skip a couple of beats.

Fraser shuffles in a little closer.

Sliding one arm along the back of my couch, he drums his fingertips against the leather, then takes a slow sip of his tropical blue drink.

I can almost hear his brain ticking.

"Best sex of your life?" He blinds me with another dazzling, cocky smile. "Is that so?"

"Yeah. Without a doubt." I try answering confidently as I rub my gold feather charm on my necklace.

I've no idea why I'm so anxious admitting that. I'm assuming it's because I rarely talk about the emotions I have for Fraser, if ever.

Opening up for me feels like I'm auctioning off my heart, but can I risk it being shattered again?

"And you?" Why am I even asking? I know he said it was incredible back in the restaurant, but I want to hear him say it again.

"Was it the best sex of my life? You don't even have to ask me. I've been wishing for last night for such a long time and now I've tasted you again. I don't think I ever want to stop licking you. Your pussy is delicious."

Holy hell, he's gotten dirty.

Pinning me to the couch with that cool sizzling stare that scorches my soul, he surveys my body and face.

Tantalizing me with his predatory look, a rush of heat flutters between my thighs.

"You're doing that thing with your eyes I asked you not to do."

"Oh, yeah?"

"Yeah, now stop it."

"Why? What will happen if I don't?" He inches closer.

My clothes will burn into flames; that's exactly what's going to happen. Although the devil himself may set them on fire because I slept with a married man.

"You need to forget the fact I am married to Anna. I've never slept with her. I've told you this. We're not *married* married."

Huh? He can read minds now?

"I know, but despite that, somehow, it doesn't feel right, and it makes me feel deceitful. And before you get too close." I raise my finger in the air to reinforce my point. "We are not kissing, and we aren't sleeping together again until you paint me the full picture."

"You're a shitty liar. You blinked." He smirks.

He's got me.

I push his chest back an inch or two, and he hitches a breath at my touch before his shoulders sag with defeat.

"You have my undivided attention, Ella. Ask me anything."

I don't even have to think about this question.

"Where do you sle—"

My question is cut off suddenly as Fraser's phone leaps to life from my kitchen and his synced smartwatch rings loudly across the room.

"Shit, I have to get this; it's Ethan." Fraser springs to his feet and steps hurriedly out of the living room door. "We speak every day I'm away," he calls back to me.

A little twinge of envy as I picture Anna and Fraser playing happy fake families with Ethan.

"Hey, buddy." I hear Fraser greet Ethan on the phone as a short hum sound indicates they're doing a video call. I then realize Fraser's voice is getting closer as he returns to the living room.

Shit, is he having a conversation with Ethan in my living room, with me here sitting beside him?

Noooooooo.

CHAPTER ELEVEN

Ella

"Have you had fun today?" Fraser asks Ethan.

I slide my feet to the floor and rise as Fraser lands back on the couch. I feel his wrist wrap around mine. He pulls me back down, then turns to face me. With a stern glare, he instructs me to stay.

"Yip. I have. But Mom said I've been too noisy today and I need to calm down. Mom wants peace and quiet." Ethan's little voice giggles through the phone in his cute accent.

"That's not what I said," an all-American feminine voice drawls through the phone. "I asked for a chill afternoon because we've had a busy morning."

My eyes pop out of their sockets as they burn into the side of Fraser's face, his fingers still wrapped around my wrist, keeping me stuck here, too close to his conversation with Ethan for my liking.

Mild panic settles in my chest.

What if Anna sees me here? What will she say? Who will Fraser say I am to Ethan? Does Anna know what I look like? She knows about me, but how much? Did he tell her we had sex last night?

Holy mother of God, I'm not ready for this.

I watch Fraser smiling effortlessly at the phone. "Hey, Anna," he calls out. I notice Fraser's American twang is slightly stronger as he speaks to them.

"Hi, Fraser." From this side view I can see the beautiful brunette, shuffling in beside Ethan on what I can only assume is his bed, because the headboard is bright blue with a giant red star-shaped wall light above it. She offers a wide, white smile back at Fraser.

A little jolt of pain fires in my heart. I dislike this jealousy feeling.

Fraser can feel me flinch, but he glides his thumb back and forth across my wrist in an *'everything's gonna be okay'* touch.

"Hey, I have someone special I want you to meet."

Oh, fuck to the no. Not happening. Never. Nope.

But I don't get the option to move away because the next thing I know, Fraser turns the phone to me and my face appears in the small top corner screen and I freeze.

"Hi, are you my daddy's friend?" Ethan asks cutely.

"Eh, um, yeah, I am. I'm Ella. I went to high school with your dad here in Scotland, and you must be Ethan. Your daddy's told me all about you," I stumble.

I watch the little brunette boy's eyes pop with wonder.

"You must be old like my daddy, then?"

"Yeah, really old and wrinkly," I try to jest.

Ethan giggles, but Anna's face remains motionless. She's not flinched once nor acknowledged me, but she's never taken her eyes off me either. My face must be twitching like crazy because my heart is racing faster than it took Jennifer Aniston to reach a million followers on Instagram.

I don't think I can keep this up. My mouth suddenly feels like sandpaper coated in dust. I grab my blue cocktail and take a huge gulp.

"Daddy, isn't your friend pretty?"

"She is Ethan. Very pretty. Wouldn't you agree, Anna?"

Fraser gives my hand a quick squeeze again.

"Yes, she is," Anna replies almost inaudibly.

I then flit my eyes briefly to meet Anna's stare. She's now over-the-top smiling back at me. I'm not sure it's genuine 'cause it doesn't reach her eyes, and there's no warmth there compared to how she greeted Fraser.

"Are you drinking bubblegum juice?" Ethan scrunches his nose up.

I examine my cocktail. "Nope, it's Sully juice."

Fraser snorts from my side.

"Who's Sully?" Ethan asks.

"Oh, eh, from *Monsters Inc.* That Sully."

"Ew, gross. Sully's pee? Mom, she's weird." Ethan looks up at his mom, then back at me. "Are you drinking that too, Dad?"

Fraser releases my wrist, reaches out and lifts his drink to show Ethan, then shuffles in close so we're both on camera.

"Yes, I am, Ethan. Look."

This is fucking weird.

Ethan sticks his tongue out and fakes being sick; he and Fraser laugh together.

"Right, so now we've established you two are drinking Sully's pee," Anna sighs. "It's time for you to go chill out, young man. Say goodbye to your dad, Ethan, so I can speak to him now."

"Bye, buddy. I love you." Fraser wishes him farewell, then Ethan returns a love you too.

I watch Anna swap the phone to her hand and rise from Ethan's bed. I turn to Fraser, looking for some help. Do I stay? Should I go? What do I do here?

"So, you two have spoken, then? Does she know everything, Fraser?"

She? I am sitting right here.

"Yes, I've told Ella everything. Well, almost everything. That's why we are back at Ella's, talking some more."

"Ah, okay. So, she knows you messed up all those years ago?"

Sorry, what now? You're no angel yourself, sweetheart.

"I've told Ella everything, Anna, yes." I detect his curt tone.

I don't know Anna, but she comes across as a bit of a stuck-up princess. As if Fraser doesn't already know he messed up.

"I've listened to everything Fraser had to say and we have a few things to iron out," I chime in. I'm not letting her talk to *my* Fraser that way.

He's been taken advantage of enough already, and for way too long by her family.

"You know it will not be an easy ride, Ella? My father's a cruel man." Anna quirks a brow.

"I know. I'm here for it," I pounce back in haste.

What am I saying? I haven't even told Fraser my intentions yet or made my decision, but this Anna bird is winding me up.

However, I know deep down in my soul, he's genuinely sorrowful. I think I actually just decided. And I know Fraser. He's authentic and grounded. He's fully aware of his pitfalls and past mistakes. He knows what he's done. And I truly believe he's sorry.

She stares back at me through the phone,

expressionless; all the while I can feel Fraser's stare piercing into the side of my flushed face. When I swivel my head around in his direction, I'm welcomed by the most beautiful and overwhelming smile I've ever seen. His eyes sparkle with delight at my declaration. Right now, at this moment, I want all of him. He's mine and I will be here for him. He's got me. I'm not losing him again, and certainly not to Anna, because I'm not sure Fraser knows her as well as he thinks he does or what her intentions are. That doesn't look like a woman who doesn't care or have feelings for him. I can tell Anna's not happy about me being around, and she certainly does *not* like Fraser touching me, either. Her telltale clenched jaw is a red flag if ever I saw one.

Fraser reaches out with his free hand, which no longer holds his drink, and thumbs my cheek. "Thank you, Ella." I lean into his touch, bathing in his familiar scent.

Anna clears her throat, interrupting our moment. I glance back at her on the screen.

"I'll leave you two to get acquainted again," Anna says through flared nostrils as she dons a scowl.

Dazed, I shake my head. I can't believe this is happening. And everything he's said earlier, his life story, is all true. Anna didn't deny it. She knows about me and Fraser is touching me. Here, in my living room. With his *wife* on the phone, watching.

My eyes latch back to his as Fraser reaches down and grabs my hand, squeezing it tight.

We're becoming experts in the art of staring.

"I'll speak to you tomorrow, Anna. Bye," Fraser responds, not looking her way. I hear her faint goodbye and the double disconnect hum as she hangs up. He then places his phone on my black glass top coffee table.

"Anna knows about me then. Like properly? You really

don't have a relationship at all, do you?" I can't believe it. This feels surreal.

"No, Ella. We are just friends. I've been truthful. Anna and I have never been intimate together. I don't want her. She doesn't want me. She knows I want you and only you. She knows I was taking you out for dinner tonight to tell you everything."

He pauses before he asks, "So, you're here for it?"

"Mm-hmm." I tuck my lips into my mouth.

"Really?"

I give myself a moment to think before I answer.

"Yes, but I have a whole 'interrogate Fraser' session still to have with you."

"Okay. I can do that. Now? Or tomorrow?"

"I think we should leave it until tomorrow."

I have so many things buzzing about in my head that require answers. I need to make a list.

"Why don't you write them down as you think about them, Ella, and that way we won't miss anything?"

I kid you not, Fraser lives inside my head.

"You were thinking about making a list, weren't you?" he whispers.

I chuckle. "Yeah, I was."

"You know they say soul mates share everything equally. They can communicate without words, through energy alone. Do you believe that?"

He moves in closer still as he continues to strum his thumb delicately across my wrist.

"Do you?"

"I asked you first, Ella." His focus is fully on my lips.

"I, eh..." I stumble whisper. Millimeters apart, he's so close now. "I think soul mates feel one another. Feel emotion, like an empath. They feel each other's sorrow, happiness, anger."

"Lust?" He runs his nose across my jaw. I can barely breathe as my lungs fill with his hypnotic scent.

"Yeah, lust," I pant.

"Do you feel my lust for you, Ella?" He shadows his lips against mine, places my hand over his rock-hard cock, then rubs it up and down across his dress pants.

He wants me.

I want him.

"Yes." My chest heaves heavily.

"It's never felt like this with anyone else, has it?"

"No."

The glimmer of a smirk hitches his mouth.

"Do you think we're soul mates, Ella?"

Too distracted by the waves of warmth that have spread between my thighs, my clit throbs, begging for him to claim me with his mouth. It takes me a moment to register he's waiting for an answer.

"I do."

"How do you know?" His hot breath continues to tease my lips.

He waits.

Then grows impatient. "Answer me." He's firmer with me than he has been all night.

I'm too distracted as he relentlessly rubs my hand across his ever-growing erection.

"Because you make me feel like I'm a tiny feather lost in your whirlwind, but you give me the strength to withstand it," I breathlessly say.

Stillness and silence fill the slither of space between us before Fraser whispers, "You're the better half of me, Ella."

I can't stand it anymore. I capture his mouth with mine because nothing else matters. No outside influences, contractual wives, or shitty sports agents. It's just us. Now. Here. We are two halves of the same whole. Complete once more.

Fraser smooths his tongue across the seam of my mouth, urging me to give him access. My lips part and instinctively my tongue seeks his. As they welcome each other, they twirl together, and I can't help my loud moan that escapes my throat as I clasp either side of his broad, chiseled face with my hands.

Lips locked, Fraser pulls me onto his lap with his powerful arms. Straddling me over his thighs, he grunts loudly as I rub myself against his thick, hard length.

Squeaking sounds echo across my living room as my leather pants make contact with the fine leather of my couch.

Fraser possessively entwines his large palm into my platinum hair at the base of my neck, roughly gluing our lips together. Recklessly breathing through our passionate, deep French kiss, we buck our hips together, desperate to find our own release.

With his free hand, he expertly unbuttons my shirt. Hastily pulling the cup of my lace bra down, he pinches my sensitive, pebbled nipple between his strong fingers and I moan as sheer pleasure builds. Fraser brushes his rough thumb across my skin, then circles the outer limits of my tit, spiraling inward before twisting and pinching my nipple again. He does this over and over , driving me to the edge of stupor, all the while relentlessly wrapping his tongue around mine.

"I thought we weren't kissing tonight?" He teases my lips.

"We're not," I whimper.

"Oh, yeah?"

"Yeah, no sex either."

"Is that right, Bella?"

I pant against his mouth. "Yeah."

His lips leave mine. Instantly dipping his head, he gently pulls my nipple into his mouth, licking, sucking, and nipping at my sensitive peak. Surprising myself, I beg him for more. On my demand, he delivers the most incredible hard suck to my nipple, flicks it with the tip of his tongue, then adds a teasing bite. Just as I think he's done, he flattens his rough tongue across my entire pebbled skin, sending a shock wave of goosebumps.

Everyone else I've been with in the past has been a goddamn amateur, but Fraser, he's a man, a blessed man with a blessed tongue and he knows what to do with it.

"So, we're not fucking tonight?" he whispers against my delicate skin.

"Nope, we aren't." I moan as I rock my clit against his solid cock. "Oooooh, that feels so good."

"Definitely not doing this."

"Uh-uh."

Fraser growls as I continue to grind against him. "We should cool off, take a shower." He barely gets his words out.

"I agree."

Fraser sucks my neck hard. *Shit, that's gonna leave a mark.* He sucks harder yet again, and a bolt of lightning flies down my spine and into my pelvis, sending a rush of arousal between my legs. "Don't stop, please, Fraser."

Obeying, he licks and sucks on the wicked sensitive spot behind my ear and I purr deep in my chest as his warm, hot breath floods my senses.

"Ella," he gasps.

I grind myself on him harder.

His lips find mine again. "Fuck, we should stop."

"We will."

We won't.

Our torturing tongues continue to slay one other.

"This is a terrible idea," he groans.

"Stupid."

"You'll hate me, and yourself, if we don't stop."

"We should spend the time talking. Getting to know each other again," I gasp.

I push my tongue into his hot, wet mouth, and we moan loud at our connection. Running my hands through his blond hair, I dig my long nails deep into his scalp. Fraser shivers at my touch.

He digs his shovel-sized hands into my hips and rubs me back and forth across his impossibly thick cock. My impending orgasm is on its way. But I want him inside of me. Now.

I've missed this. The rush. The pleasure. The excitement. I've missed it all. He makes me want to drink him in. I've been dehydrated all these years and I'm bloody thirsty.

"I want you," I rasp out and Fraser groans at my declaration as if a heavy weight has lifted off his broad shoulders.

"I'm yours."

In one swift movement, Fraser stands as I lock myself against him. Effortlessly, he wraps my leather-clad legs around his waist. Evidence of my red lipstick coats his beautiful full lips. I swipe my thumb across them to remove the worst.

"Where's your bedroom?" He asks.

I point up the stairs as he stomps out of the living room.

"Hold on tight."

Smoothly, he takes each step. Not once do his emerald-green eyes, full of expectation and lust, ever leave mine as I clasp on to him. He's so strong. He carries me like I'm a light petal in the wind and he's so broad, filling up the entire width of my staircase.

Dipping my head into his neck as he climbs the remaining steps, remembering what he loves, I trace my tongue along the side of his neck, then give his earlobe a little nibble. He moans loudly.

"You remember." It's not a question.

"I do." I breathe against his skin and he groans again.

Reaching the top of the stairs, I indicate for him to turn right along the narrow hall toward my bedroom.

As we enter my warm, cozy space, Fraser lowers me onto my black comforter, then takes a step backward.

"I have forgotten nothing about you, either." His voice laced with sex and sin as he confidently unbuckles his black leather belt.

"Show me."

CHAPTER TWELVE

Fraser

I'm going to show her exactly what I remember. What she likes and how I am the only man that knows her delectable body.

She looks beautiful lying there with her white hair spread out against the black sheets of her bedding. One of her erect rosy-pink nipples, still spilling out from her bra in invitation, begs me to suck it back into my mouth again.

"Let me undress you," she commands.

Unable to wait, Ella jumps to her feet. Watching her undress, in an instant, she's naked in front of me. Hell knows how she peeled those snug-as-hell pants from her breathtaking body, but my cock is now throbbing against the zip of my dress pants at the sight of her smooth skin, slender hips, and ample breasts.

For years, all I've wanted was her. Knowing she wants me still pumps my dying heart back to life.

Sex with escorts, which I've been doing all these years, sucks. It's just sex. Emotionless. But with her, it blows my mind how attuned we are. It's never gone. That connection to one another is like nothing I've ever experienced.

Like a genie in a bottle, our bond has been lying dormant all this time. We've unpopped the cork, and goddamn, she can fucking rub me any way she wants 'cause she hasn't only released my burning desire for her, but she's reignited the fire between us we can't control. And if I'm only granted one wish, then it's for her to stay with me forever.

In a trance, all I can do is watch as Ella reaches out to undress me. Urgency subsided, she takes her time before sliding my pants and black boxers down my legs. I groan as her dainty hand brushes against the tip of my now weeping cock.

Softly, she thumbs her tattooed name across my hip.

She's thinking.

Rising to her full height, her long locks shield her chest, concealing her beautiful tits. I sweep her hair back over her shoulders, unwrapping her. Brushing my calloused hand as carefully as I can across the skin of her neck and down the outer edge of her breast, I draw my thumb over her rosy pink nipple, setting off a ripple of prickles across her snowy skin. Ella arches her neck to the side and lets out a low moan, making my cock ache for her.

Leaning in, I brush kisses up and down, tracing the path of her neckline.

Ella wraps her warm hand around the head of my cock. I momentarily stop breathing and dig my fingers into the slope of her exquisite ass to steady me.

She thumbs the underside of my length, gently circling my pre-come across my crown, teasing my sensitive head before she wraps her dominant hand around my shaft and begins stroking me up and down. If I don't come on the spot, it will be a goddamn miracle.

Cradling her face in my hands, I pull her sugar-sweet mouth to mine. Our desperate tongues touch, making my cock throb with delight.

"I want to taste you," she mumbles against my mouth.

Oh, please do.

She continues stroking me before her mouth leaves mine. She falls to her knees and, without hesitation, she draws me into her mouth.

Squeezing my ass, she pulls me in closer as she takes my cock deeper until I feel my crown hit the back of her throat.

I won't last if she continues.

Weaving my hands into her hair, I grab the back of her neck, and she fucks me with her expert mouth. It feels out of this world, especially as it's *her. My Ella.*

She moans loud and deep, the vibration of her hums rippling to my balls.

Sucking me hard, she flicks the underside of my cock with her skilled tongue. I feel her gently caressing my balls, tracing light strokes round and round.

Adding her hand to the base of my shaft, she sucks and strokes simultaneously.

She performs the best mouth fuck I've ever had in my life. I've felt nothing like it.

In a desperate move not to blow my load there and then, I place my pointer finger under her chin to tilt her face, forcing her emerald eyes to mine. When she looks up, with my cock still in her mouth, she is the most beautiful woman I've ever seen and the fantasy I've had in my mind for all these years.

"C'mere," I command with a Cheshire cat grin, guiding her to her feet.

We kiss each other in one of the most meaningful kisses, knowing that we are *it* for each. sending shock waves to my heart. I dedicate my focus to this moment. I soak it all in. My hands explore her incredibly lean body as they sweep across her body, remembering. She's soft, smooth, and hot. A woman now, a goddess.

We fall onto the bed together, with her under me, skin on skin. I head south, my mouth watering, desperate to taste her on my tongue. It's been too long.

Kissing her from top to toe and back again, Ella wriggles and squirms as I drive all of her senses crazy, making goosebumps scatter across her body. She moans, begging for more, trying to grab and run her hands over my skin.

Moving lower, I slide my legs down the bed, pry her slender thighs open wider, and lean in to claim her with my mouth.

"So perfect. So pink. I own this pretty little pussy."

Delicately at first, I trace the seam of her lower lips with the tip of my tongue, then flatten it hard against her clit, causing Ella to arch her back off the bed, forcing my face harder into her wet folds

I reach up, drawing circles across her nipples as I move up her body. I instruct her to suck my fingers as they reach her mouth.

"Make them wet, baby."

She licks them, drawing them into her mouth, sucking hard,

I watch my fingers leave her pillowy, full lips; she bats her lashes as she silently flirts with me. My heart pounds hard against my chest at the realization that she's my girl. She said she's *here's for it* and she's now mine again. I can't take my eyes off her.

Guiding my hand lower, I slide my now wet fingers up

and down either side of her pussy lips, delighting all of her senses, building the tension as I tease her before spreading my fingers around her clit in a *V* shape, pinching, sliding, and closing my fingers in closer and closer. I pinch her clit, holding it tight, then flick it with my tongue frantically. Wild whimpers escape Ella's throat as words I can't even understand leave her lungs.

Gazing downward, she frantically pants, "Oh, Fraser. Give me more."

"I love this pussy. I'll love it more when you come all over my tongue."

I grin against her, slowly part her now swollen pink lips wider, gently drag my tongue down, and then insert my rigid tongue into her wet core.

She's so sexy. I can never get enough.

"Keep doing that," she demands, resting her feet on top of my broad shoulders. She grabs my hair, pushing her waxed pussy into my face.

I fuck her with my tongue, at the same time circling her clit over and over with the pads of my fingertips.

Switching it up, I then suck her bud into my mouth, gently at first, circling, licking, rubbing, then I glide two fingers into her hot, dripping core. She's really wet. Soaking in fact, causing my dick to get even harder.

Teasing her, I blow hot air across her sensitive bud, then locate that deep magical spot inside. I know this drives her fucking crazy. Blowing, then sucking, changing the pace from fast to slow, I continue sliding my fingers, now slick with her arousal, in and out repeatedly.

Remembering what drives her insane, I pinch the top of her lips together tight, then lick her clit up and down with the tip of my tongue.

Her moans become louder as her breathing heaves faster and faster.

"Oh, Fraser, I'm gonna come," her whimpered words cloud the air.

In an instant, she moans as she comes over and over again. My name rings out in her sweet voice, making my cock drip uncontrollably with pre-come. Her pussy tightens around my fingers and it's the most beautiful thing I've ever felt. I watch her come undone. She's lost in the moment, and so am I, knowing it's me who does this to her.

I lick her up from back to front, enjoying the taste of her orgasm all over my tongue. She whimpers, then curves her back off the bed, digging her fingernails deep into my scalp, pushing her pussy into my mouth again.

I can't take it anymore. I need to be inside her.

Giving her no time to recover, I launch myself up the bed and thrust my dripping cock deep inside her wet center. She yelps at the unexpected movement.

I still myself for a moment to stop my impending orgasm. She feels fucking incredible. There is no better feeling than being buried deep inside her.

Ella reaches up and pulls me to her lips, dipping her frantic tongue into my mouth, beckoning mine to hers, neither of us caring that my chin and mouth are coated with her excitement.

"Fuck me, Fraser," she begs.

Leaning back slightly, knees wide, I thrust in and out 'cause I can't fucking hold back any longer. I pound into her over and over, fast.

She digs her sharp nails into my ass, desperate for me to go deeper and harder.

The feeling I have with her is so intense, the tingling

sensation at the base of my spine begins coiling its way up, spreading into my balls and the tip of my cock.

Rocking against me, Ella's delicate hand reaches around to her clit and begins rubbing her sensitive nub. Fuck me, I can't think straight as I watch her circle her clit round and round. I'm getting my own private show as I watch her lose control. I can't take my eyes off her fingers dancing over her swollen bundle of nerves.

"Eyes up, Fraser," she says breathlessly. "Look at me when I come."

I lift my head to meet her lust-filled eyes as I continue to hammer into her, driving myself as deep as I can go with every thrust as she continues to rub her clit.

Through the intensity of our gaze, she sees me, she sees all my flaws, my desire for her, the undeniable passion that runs through us, and she accepts me for who I am and what I've done. Joy slides into my heart, something I haven't felt in a long time.

My emotions run wild, but I want to savor this moment, so I mellow my pace, driving myself slow and steady into her dripping pussy, undulating my hips in waves, enhancing each of our senses.

Emotions amplify. She whimpers as she verges on the edge of pleasure again.

I don't want to go fast like last night; I want her to know I'm here, I'm present, and I've got her.

She removes her hand, allowing me to go deeper, meeting me thrust for thrust.

Lifting one of her legs, I wrap it around my waist, aligning my pelvic bone to stimulate her clit.

She moans as I rock back and forth slowly, leaving a little space between each deep thrust, wanting nothing more than for her to come all over my cock with fierce and wild abandon, but I want her to feel this, feel us.

Never breaking our connection, she lazily blinks, and a soft purr leaves her delectable mouth as it forms in the shape of an *O*.

"Come for me, baby."

I pick up the pace, ensuring I hit every magical spot of hers, building her orgasm even higher.

A multitude of sparks spread like crazy up my spine as Ella cries out, clenching her pussy all around my cock, pulsing madly as she comes, and when she bites her lips and a wild flush of pink shoots across her chest, that's it, I'm done.

An enormous ball of fire explodes in my balls as I spill myself inside her, deep, roaring her name as I come. Euphoria sweeps into every cell of my soul as if the fog that's been shadowing me for all these years has lifted and I can finally see my bright future. With her. I feel happy. For the first time in forever, I feel like me. Like there's a future and possibility. And Ella is right here with me. By my side.

Panting heavily, I lean down, pressing our hot bodies together.

"I've missed this, you, all of it, Ella."

Slightly dazed, she blinks lazily up at me. "Me too. More than you can imagine."

We kiss softly at first, but I can't stop because I want more. Ella loops her legs tighter around my waist and kisses me hard, keeping me close to her, in a *'please don't let me go'* embrace.

I kiss her back, squeezing her hard, letting her know I'm not going anywhere. Reluctantly, I slide out of her, lifting her and carrying her to the shower, all the while kissing, because we can't stop; we don't want to.

This is us.

We shower together, taking our time before I get hard for her again because I never don't want to be inside of her.

I've got incredible stamina, and that's what I'm going to show her.

And I do.

All night.

CHAPTER THIRTEEN

Ella

I can't remember the last time I slept so well or felt so relaxed. Waking up next to Fraser this morning feels right. Like the planets have all aligned for me or something. It's weird and wonderful all at once.

But my worry continues to outweigh the wonderful because he's still married, and this does not sit well with me at all. I'm not sure how long a divorce takes, but I hope it happens quickly because I don't want to be the other woman. Even though these are exceptional circumstances, and that's not really the case here, I still don't want Anna looming over our heads now that we're back together.

Oh, my goodness. Fraser and I are back together.

Never in a million years did I ever think this would happen.

I roll onto my back, forcing my eyes shut. I try to calm my breathing as I feel my blood rush into my rapid heart. I chant internally... *in and out... in and out... in through your nose... out through your mouth*. I continue to do this until I feel it slow to a steady wave again, then I move into a sitting position, resting myself against my black velvet headboard.

Gazing down at Fraser's huge, buff body which dominates my bed as he sleeps deeply, lightly snoring away, my eyes scan up and down his sculpted, hard frame. He always did like sleeping naked and outside of the blankets, apart from a little cover draped across his hips, hiding his thick, heavy cock, because he has his own internal heating system and always burns like a furnace. I can't help flirting my eyes over his toned and powerful body because he's so beautiful to look at. He almost doesn't seem real. Like he's carved from the finest Italian marble. My nipples tighten at the thought of his skin against mine and how he made me feel last night.

And he does remember. He remembers how to wind me so tight, edging me to the point of mindlessness. The intensity between us is at an all-time high. At some point last night, I couldn't link words together and thought I was going to faint because I held my breath for too long, as I had one of the most powerful orgasms of my life.

He was definitely trying to make up for our lost time together.

We drowned in fizzy bubbles of ecstasy, and we fit perfectly together. It makes sense. *We* make sense. We're like sexual alchemy on crack, and it makes me feel like I'm the highest person in the room. These feelings are something I didn't think I would ever get to feel again.

Our attraction to one another is stronger than ever; it's never disappeared.

There were no jokes, laughter, or messing about last night. It was intense and slow, then fast and fierce, then close and passionate, and every time we made love, Fraser's piercing blue eyes bore into mine. At one point, my emotions were flying so high, I cried tears of elation. I felt so overwhelmed but thrilled that he was in my bed and my arms again. He held me so close, comforting me. Reassuring me he's mine.

But not really, not yet, because he's contracted to another woman.

I roll my head back and let out an enormous sigh as I look to the heavens above for a sign. Anything to let me know I'm making the right decision.

Still sleeping, Fraser rustles beside me, rolling over onto his side to face me. I spot his tattoo again. It took my breath away when I first laid my eyes on it the other night in the shower. My scripted name, the two entwined feathers, the symbolism not lost on me; one him, and the other is me. And then there's our song title, "Nothing Else Matters." It's a song I haven't been able to listen to since we broke up. *How long has he had the tattoo for?* I must ask him today.

Gently tiptoeing out of my cozy bed, I slip my black silk kimono-style dressing gown on, then grab my journal and phone off my mirrored nightstand before quietly padding down the stairs.

As I enter the kitchen, Treacle and Toffee lazily stretch out in their beds situated under the breakfast bar. It's their favorite place to be, cozied hard up against the warmth of the radiator. I quickly make myself a strong coffee, then feed the boys breakfast and refill their water bowls. Toffee finally stumbles to his feet, yawning and stretching as I open the back door, inviting them both to join me outside in the cool cusp of summer Scottish air, but Treacle stays put. He's not going anywhere yet; he loves his bed, and he's probably mad at me for ignoring him when I went up the stairs with Fraser last night. He doesn't share.

Coffee, journal, my favorite black velvet blanket from

the living room, and phone in hand, I weave my way down my gray Indian sandstone path toward my garden swing seat overlooking the rolling fields behind my house. Unlike my neighbors, I purposefully didn't erect high fencing for this very reason. The view down to Castleview Cove is everything. Watching the morning cornfield swishing in the wind with the gentle drone of honeybees and insects to keep me company, it washes away the heaviness of sleep. It's like therapy for me. Combined with journaling my thoughts, it always sets my intentions for the day ahead and helps to clear my head.

I lay my stuff on the outdoor wooden table, then sit back, draping my blanket across my knees. It's still fresh in the mornings. Bring on summer—soon.

Flipping through my journal, I always begin with a reflection, selecting a page from a few months back, checking in on how far I've come, or celebrate the things I've achieved since then.

A paragraph from last Christmas leaps off the creamy smooth page and captures my attention.

December 25th - Christmas Day

Well, well, well, Ella. Yet another lonely single Christmas. Okay, so I'm dramatizing, and I'll be spending it later with Mom, Dad, my sisters, and their husbands, along with my two beautiful nephews. But seriously, yet another Christmas, with no one special to spend the day with? Surrounded by happily married couples. And Eden's swollen belly as a constant reminder I am yet again the only one without kids.

What actually happened to my life? Why can't I find that special someone? Why, Universe, is it taking so long for my soul mate to find me? I have everything, a beautiful little home, my animals, a glorious business, and a family who adores me, but it's not enough.

Am I selfish and spoiled to want that? To say I want more? I want a special someone in my life. Someone to spend my days with, to share my life, to have fun, go to concerts, to dance the nights away, someone to celebrate everything with.

I want all of it. I am enough and I deserve all the happiness my sisters have.

This time next year, all I want for Christmas is to have the love of my life by my side.

I am worthy of true love.

I am allowing the flow of great things to happen to me and for me. I will focus all my intentions on feeling good and feeling joy.

Time to step up a gear, Ella, and manifest the shit out of finding that someone. He's coming—Yeah, right, what a joke. Like that's ever going to happen. Merry lonely Christmas, Ella!

I'd completely forgotten I'd written that. Did I actually manifest Fraser into my life again? For real? Is this it? If so, then why do I feel slightly rattled? Like I don't deserve any of this or that I am not worthy of him.

This is what I wanted. Him. Us. In my bed, where he should have been all this time. In my life. But I wanted simplicity, not complexity, and for someone without all the heavy baggage he has going on. *But*, it's Fraser. *My Fraser*.

I'm concerned about what happens next.

I trace my fingers across my previously written order to the Universe, then lift my head and stare into the clear blue morning. Now and then a seagull streaks across the sky, flying high, heading in the beach's direction, eager to greet the fishermen coming into the harbor with their early morning catch.

Sometimes I run in the mornings along the pier side to watch the boats float into the harbor and giggle to myself at the squabbling gulls fighting over the scraps left on the decks of the boats—they are feisty and courageous. It's a seagull gangsta paradise.

Tilting my head right back, I close my eyes, immersing myself in the morning dew. The need to journal disappears. My heavy heart won't allow any thoughts to flow now. Not after reading my extract from last Christmas. It has made me feel sad. I have to be in the right mood to journal. I've always been like that. All the blogs I've read say you should journal even when you feel shitty. It's apparently even more important to do it then, but sometimes, like today, when heavy emotion flips my off switch, I can't.

Treacle waddles down to greet us, finally joining our morning ritual.

I slowly sip my coffee as Toffee and Treacle jump up and nestle on either side of me on the seat. My thoughts turn back to Fraser and all the things I want to ask him. I flip to a blank page in my journal, flooding the pages with black ink as I furiously start writing my questions.

As I finish, I feel Fraser before I see him as he saunters casually down the path, then stands at my blanket-covered knees, in nothing but his snug-fit boxers. They hang low on his hips, my tattooed name peeking out above his waistband. Spellbound, I stare, unable to take my eyes off him.

Soaking all of Fraser's delectable frame in, I imagine this being the view I wake up to every day.

"Morning, Bella." A yawn pulls his chin. "You still journal?" His thick-with-sleep voice asks.

"I do."

I look up and greet him with a soft hi as a gentle flap of what feels like a happy hummingbird dances in my chest. He bends down and, with soft suction, greets me with his mouth. Cupping my face with tenderness, he slips his tongue between my lips and murmurs, "Mmmmm, coffee. I need some. You exhausted me last night."

I giggle. He smiles against my lips. "You know I'm right."

"I'm not arguing with you. You wore me out too," I whisper.

My nipples harden against the smooth fabric of my robe, responding to his touch. I could easily go another round with him right now.

Fraser leans back slightly, glances down at my chest, and smirks. "You want more? Is my girl still not satisfied?" He smooths his thumb over the delicate satin, then pinches my nipple hard. I inhale a fresh puff of air into my lungs.

Old Miss Kerr two houses up will no doubt be perving from her bedroom window. The neighbors take great interest in my life in our little estate 'cause they've got nothing else going on in theirs. I'm pretty sure Miss Kerr's got a thing for Mr. Riley, though. She's definitely jonesing for it, or from anyone who will give her even the slightest bit of attention. A few men come and go to her house. She tells me they're playing card games. I don't believe her for a second.

"You need to stop or Mr. Riley will be jerking himself off behind his curtain if you continue," I whisper.

"How do you know he's looking?"

"He's always watching, Fraser."

"Is that so? Maybe when we go house hunting together, we need to consider buying a house with no neighbors, then? It's no wonder he can't peel his eyes away from you; you are a hot piece of ass, Bella." He continues to rub my pebbled peak. *Ooooh, that is nice. But did I hear him correctly?*

"Eh? House hunting?" I ask, confused, but enjoying every minute of his hands on me.

Fraser trails his fingers over my cleavage, then moves up and grabs the back of my neck as he captures my lips again with his.

"Yeah, you know, for us?" he mumbles. "We need a bigger house if we're going to move in together."

What?

"We're moving in? Together?" I pull out of our kiss.

"Yes, if we're doing this, us." He gestures back and forth between us. "Then we are doing this right. I'm all in, Ella. All of me. With you." He's so confident.

A deep frown furrows my brow. "So, you're moving to Castleview Cove, then? You're not staying in California?" This was one of the many questions I wanted to ask him.

Fraser stands to his high-tower height, then shoos Treacle off the swing seat to allow him to sit down beside me. Defiantly, Treacle takes a few coaxes before he bounces down, then looks at me with a *'are you gonna let him move me?'* gaze. Treacle will not like that. I'll pay for that with stubbornness later because he thinks he's the most important man in my life.

Fraser peels back the blanket, sits flush against me, and then rests his arm along the back of the white wooden swing seat around my shoulders. Absentmindedly, he toys with a lock of my hair, twirling it around his finger.

"Do you not want to move in together, Ella? Is that not part of the *'you're here for it'* plan?" Concern is written across his face.

"No, eh, yes, well, maybe. It's just, well, it's a bit soon or presumptuous of you, don't you think? And I'm still not clear on a lot of things. I made a list of stuff I need to know." I hastily grab my journal. "I, um, I have... I have some things that have been annoying me for years and other stuff is new." I feel jittery. "I have to know everything about your situation, past and present; otherwise, it's going to consume me. If we're doing this, we need a clean slate. New opening credits for our story."

I'm normally someone who shuns away from her feelings and confrontation, but we have to do this. It's like a boiling pot of lava waiting to scald us both. So many things from our past were left unsaid. They can't wait any longer.

I look up from my journal to meet his worried stare. He rubs the back of his neck. With a deep sigh and a roll of his shoulders, he knows this conversation's been coming.

"Okay. Have at it. Shoot me all your questions. Let me grab a coffee and my shirt. I've forgotten how fresh the Scottish mornings are, and then I'm all yours."

This is it; it's happening. Relief floods my tired body, and my heart skips a beat in appreciation. Fraser's comforting hand finds mine.

"I still have a couple of your old tee shirts, Fraser. You can have one of those instead."

"Oh, you do, do you?" he teases, smiling.

"Yes. I do. I sometimes still wear them. Although they may not fit you anymore; you're much bigger than you used to be." I give his bicep a quick squeeze.

"And you are hotter and sexier than you used to be. I didn't think that was possible." He slowly slips his hand under the blanket, quickly locating the slit of my silk robe. My heart skips when he skims his fingers up across my inner thigh. In an instant, his talented fingers find my pulsing clit between my legs.

"I can't keep my hands off you, and this"—he circles my clit, then glides his thick finger down my wet flesh—"this is my new happy place." His eyes are pinned to my mouth.

It's mine too.

I spread my legs slightly, being careful not to reveal too much in case my neighbors are, in fact, watching. Fraser scooches in closer as he lightly circles my clit, causing a rush of cream in my core.

"You like?" he asks, his eyes never leaving my mouth.

I grab on to the top of his hand, urging him to move faster.

"Yes..." I pant. "I need... your fingers inside of me, Fraser."

"Oh, really?" He smirks. I feel him guide his thick finger down my swollen lips again. "Shuffle down slightly, Ella. Cover yourself with the blanket," he whispers.

As I do, Fraser moves in closer, plants soft kisses across my temple, and without warning, as I tilt my hips to get comfortable, he inserts his finger, making me almost buck off the seat in surprise.

This is a risky game we're playing, but I like it out here in the open, with the excitement of being caught, and I love the way Fraser makes me feel—free, adored, insatiable.

"Stop distracting me with sex. I know what you're doing," I huff.

"I love making you come. That's what I'm doing. Nothing more to it."

"I need answers."

"I know and I will give you them, but right now, I just want to touch you. To feel you fall apart from my touch."

"You said you wouldn't lie to me," I pant. "You are... ooooh." He goes slightly deeper, forcing my complaints to silence.

"I'm really not." He chuckles. "I'm no longer a gambling man, but I bet I can make you come lightning fast." His slow, seductive rumble drifts into my ear.

"Not a chance," I counter, now turned on, forgetting why I need to ask him questions.

He continues his gentle rhythmic fingerfucking. I'm not usually a wham, bam, thank you, ma'am kind of gal, but with him, my whole body responds quicker than normal, even to the slightest touch.

"Want to place a wager?"

I should say no. I still have questions I need answered, but having him here, touching me like this, makes me feel like nothing has changed; that our connection is as strong as ever and nothing else seems to matter. "Yes," I groan. I'm going to lose, I know it. He's too good at this.

"Okay, I bet a hundred dollars I can make you come in thirty seconds."

Fraser picks up a little speed and intensity, increasing my arousal.

"It's... pounds here... not dollars... Oh yes, right there... Fraser." I squeeze his hand harder. "Start counting now."

And he does.

His hot, heavy breaths trickle across my skin, sending shivers across the base of my neck and down my spine.

His thumb dances across my clit. Circling, stroking, all the while arching his finger inside of me, urging me to come. His large palm stimulates my entire pussy and I know I'm going to lose this bet as I feel my orgasm weave its way through my core, as tingles of sensual release take hold.

Fraser's been counting this whole time, but I haven't heard any of the numbers.

"Fifteen seconds left, Ella. Come for me now," he instructs with a deep boom into my ear.

He thrusts his finger deeper, rubbing my clit with persistent flicks and circles. I have no control left. I hand it all over to him.

"Ten seconds left."

My muscles clench around his finger over and over and I see a galaxy of shooting stars behind my eyes as I have an earth-shattering orgasm. An unfamiliar sound flies from my throat, but Fraser catches it with his mouth before it hits the morning air.

He growls into my mouth loudly, and I feel it vibrate against my lips before he suddenly peels himself away, leaving me gasping.

Fraser kisses my cheek and temple, trying to ground me, bringing me back to the present. He rasps breathlessly, "You are mine. This pussy." He wiggles his finger inside of me.

Tilting my hips, I let out a breathless sigh.

"Every orgasm. Your lips, your mouth. Your heavenly body. It's all mine."

Slowly, I open my eyes to meet his dominating, aroused stare. His chest heaves like he can't take it anymore. He needs to know I am his.

"I'm yours, Fraser. I always have been."

Without another word, painstakingly slow, he slides his finger out of me, lifts his hands from beneath the blanket, sucks his finger, lapping up my arousal, then smirks as he removes his finger from his dirty-talking mouth.

I love it when he does that.

"Fucking damn straight you are. And you lost a hundred dollars, I mean, pounds."

"Can I pay you in kind?"

"Five blow jobs should cover it."

"Is that how cheap your escorts are? Can't be very *high class.*"

As soon as my words are out, I regret them and throw my hand to my heart.

Fraser's face winces with a pained expression, turning away from me.

Great, Ella, way to spoil the mood.

"I'm sorry, I shouldn't have said that," I whisper, dipping my head in shame.

"It's fine. I deserve it." He leans away. Bending over, he places his elbows on his knees, then looks out across the view. "I will tell you how much an escort is. I'll tell you everything."

"You don't have to, Fraser. We've been separated for a very long time. You have lived your life in the best way that suits you. I have lived my life, maybe not in the way you would approve of either. I don't own you."

I actually don't. I have no right. He doesn't owe me an explanation about the escorts, but the rest, yes, he does.

He looks back at me over his shoulder.

"I don't think you realize, Ella. You *do* own me. You have every right. I want to tell you everything." Sitting up, he grabs my hand. "Let's get coffee first and I will let you board my fucked up little merry-go-round I've been living on."

"Okay." I nod in agreement.

Without another word, Fraser and I head back to the kitchen. I make a cafetière of coffee as Fraser heads up the stairs. I holler to him, instructing where to find his old tee shirts. On his return, we saunter back out to the garden. I'm happy to be spending time with him like this. It feels nice.

The hot steaming coffee I poured into our oversized mugs billows into the ether. We sit in silence, enjoying the morning together on my slatted swing seat. The sun dazzles and floods across the roaming fields. It's going to be a glorious day.

It's the moment I've been waiting for, but I'm petrified. I don't know how prepared I am for this. I'm also not sure I want to know all of it either. What if I hear something I don't like?

I pop the end cap of my pen in and out rapidly against my journal and take a sip of my coffee, my second of the many I need to get me through this.

Fraser clears his throat and drags his hands down the legs of his pants from last night. "What do you want to know, Ella?"

CHAPTER FOURTEEN

Ella

Without looking at my list, I know exactly what I want to ask first because Ethan's call interrupted us last night, and I lost my chance.

Fraser's sturdy frame turns sideways to face me, making the bench groan from his weight.

My tummy churns 'cause I don't think I truly want to know but... "Where do you sleep? Do you share a bed with Anna?"

"No, we do not share a bed. We never have. Anna wanted to, for Ethan's benefit as he got older, but I wouldn't allow it. It wouldn't feel right. And when they join me on golf tournaments, we book adjoining hotel rooms. Ethan and Anna in one, and me in the other. We've always told Ethan I have my own room because I would disturb them with my super early tee times during the championships."

Seems reasonable. She was probably hoping for more than a paperwork-based marriage. Also, Fraser must have incredible willpower because Anna is exquisite. They make a beautiful fake couple.

"I have my own quarters in the house we live in, too. I don't class it as *my* house because I told you it belongs to Nate. I fucking hate that man," he snarls. "We tell Ethan I snore too loudly and keep Anna awake if I sleep in the same bed. He's young; he's always believed what we said. He has no reason not to because he knows no different."

"So, you live in a big house then, if you have your own quarters?"

"Yeah, it has ten bedrooms. Exactly what you'd expect from Nate 'The Peacock' Miller. I have my own bathroom, bedroom, and dressing room. It's exactly the kind of house we spoke of building when we were younger. Do you remember?"

"I do." My heart pinches with jealousy. "I'm not so sure I want that anymore. I love my little house; it's cozy, all mine, and it's what I achieved all by myself."

"You've done so well for yourself, Ella. All of this." He points to my house behind us. "Your dance school, house, your dogs, and horse. You seem content."

"Hmm, I am and I'm not," I mutter as I look out over the serene landscape. My hands hug my mug, enjoying the heat.

"What does that mean?"

"I don't want to talk about it." I really don't.

"Tell me, please, Ella. If we start a fresh page for us, we *both* have to be honest."

I replay my journal entry through my head, and I shouldn't be ashamed of it. This is my life, after all, but I do feel embarrassed. I'll be thirty in a couple of years, and I still haven't had a serious relationship since Fraser and I split up.

Be brave, Ella.

"I seem incapable of having anything that remotely feels like an intimate relationship with anyone." I stop. "Since you."

He sits motionless, then finally whispers, "Please forgive me for all the damage I caused you. I'm so sorry."

Moments pass before finding the best way to articulate what I need to say.

"My life is good, Fraser, but I have no one to share it with. And I'm not saying I'm desperate or I want a relationship with just anyone; that's not it. Sometimes, I look around and realize everyone's partnered off, married, and here's me flying solo."

My insides cringe with embarrassment.

"With your dogs and horse." He tries to joke, but it leaves me with a heavy heart.

"Yeah. I suppose so." I inhale a deep breath, then let out an exasperated sigh.

I know Fraser is here right now, with me, but I'm not sure how real all this is yet.

"And me, you have me. I'm back." He tries to reassure me, threading his fingers with mine.

Surveying him, I give him an unsure smile. "Do I though? This is all new, Fraser, and it's only been a few days since we started speaking to each other properly."

"We've done more than talking. And we are together," he states firmly. "That's what I want. I thought you wanted that too? What happened to '*you're here for it*?'"

My heart stutters. "Yes, of course I do, but..." I trail off. "There are so many other moving parts to this. And all of it makes me feel uneasy. Ethan, Nate, Anna. Do you trust Anna? Really trust her?" I question.

'Cause I don't.

"I do. Why?"

"I'm not sure. My intuition kicked up a level last night. Like an inner knowing. She was not happy seeing me with you." I roll my eyes sideways to meet his. "You surely saw

her reaction, Fraser. I could tell she clearly doesn't like me."
I replay her pinched expression and clenched jaw last night
when Fraser stroked his thumb across my cheek.

"She was fine, Ella. She knew I was meeting with you
last night. You've never been a secret to her, and I talk about
you to her all the time. She knows it's you. You're the one.
And she knows what my intentions are with you. I trust her.
We can trust her. I promise."

Fear clutches my heart because I don't think we can. I'm
also a little jealous she's gained Fraser's trust when she's
from the enemy family who want to destroy Fraser's career
and life. Fraser is dancing with the devil and sleeping under
the same roof with her, too.

He continues. "And I wasn't going to share this with you
because I want to keep you safe, but Anna is the one who's
going to help me and the other athletes with their case.
She's been flirting relentlessly with Nate's bodyguard. His
name is Aaron. He and she have become *very* close. She's
been wooing him, teasing him, figuring out how the security
in Nate's house works, where the CCTV cameras are
positioned, what guards work specific shifts, where the
control room is, how to gain access, Nate's schedule. You
name it, she's on it. The contract he made me sign is in the
safe in his home office, along with our marriage certificate.
He let it slip one day. He didn't think I heard, but I heard
alright. Anna's close to gaining access."

Gosh, she really doesn't like her father. I have a sudden
thought.

"And what about Anna's mother? Does she know about
this? She surely can't be on board with this crazy setup?" I
ask, flabbergasted at my off-the-cuff question because I
never considered this before.

"Anna's mother died in a car crash when she was only

four years old. Anna was raised by nannies and staff. She had a very disjointed childhood. Anna is an object to him. There's no love there. He's a vile, heartless man."

Poor Anna. Looking back at my own upbringing, Eva, Eden, and I had an awesome home life. Our parents truly loved each other and still do. Our home was full to the brim with fun, giggles, and care for one another. I couldn't imagine it any other way.

"I'm so sorry to hear that, Fraser." I take a moment before asking my next question. "So, when you return to California, will you continue to sleep at the house?"

He runs his hands through his thick blond hair. "Yes. Until we move Ethan and Anna into their new home I've bought them. It takes six weeks for the sale to go through, although I am trying to speed it up."

"So, you're staying here, for what, another three weeks, then back to live with Anna and Ethan for another three? In the same house? Even if we're back together?" I rub my forehead rhythmically.

I do *not* want him living in that house with her. Ethan, I understand, but not her. I don't know why I don't trust her. She's got him hook, line, and sinker, and I think she knows it, but I don't think Fraser realizes it though.

"Do you not want me to sleep there anymore? If you don't, I won't, Ella. I'll do anything to make things right between us. I've fucked us up for too long, but I have Ethan to consider in all of this. He's acclimatized to me being away a lot, and I would like to spend some time with him before Anna and I separate officially. I have to see him. I love him. He's like my boy. If I move into the pool house in the garden for three weeks, would that be okay with you?" He raises his eyebrows in question.

My posture goes limp as I realize I'm going to be the

worst stepmom ever. What a selfish cow I am. Of course, he has to see Ethan.

I need to push my feelings aside for now.

"I'm being a complete bitch. Sorry, ignore me. You can't do that. It's not right for Ethan. It's wrong for you to sleep out in the pool house. Go back to the house and continue as normal."

"You have never been a bitch, Ella. This is unchartered territory for us all, but we can navigate this together—me, you, and Anna."

What a fucked-up threesome we are.

"And where are you planning to live when *you* move out?" I question him.

"I have three tournaments in the US. I'll be in and out of hotels for the best part of four weeks. Then I have a charity ball I'm speaking at in Los Angeles. My plan is to visit Ethan, then head straight back here to make sure Mom's recovering well. I'll have a week off, another championship back in California, then Bermuda, and I am hoping I get to play Georgia, but I have a feeling Nate may waylay all those plans. I don't know what his reaction will be."

Wow, he's busy. He's got it all worked out, and he's making plans to come back to see his mom. He didn't mention me.

"None of it will be perfect, Ella, but we need to make sure we don't screw up Ethan in the process. The impact that divorce can have on kids his age can be irreversible. The first year is going to be the toughest. If we can all get through it, we will get through anything."

I set my coffee cup on the wooden table and start wringing my hands. "When are you planning to tell Ethan you're divorcing and what about visitation? Have you and Anna worked it all out yet?" My questions keep on pouring out, and I feel happy he's answering and keeps filling in the blanks.

"Firstly, Ethan knows we're moving house, but we've told him it's a surprise so he doesn't tell his grandfather, should he unexpectedly drop in at the house. He doesn't visit often anyway, so it shouldn't be a problem. Anna detests her father and doesn't have much to do with him. More so since Ethan was born. He sends his heavies around when we don't toe the line, like when we don't post on social media or miss family get-togethers or when he has a mixer he wants us to attend, but as I've already told you, he likes to control us, so he visits now and again to ensure his assets are safe and well. That's all he sees us as, commodities, and I'm his biggest cash cow. Anna likes to keep him sweet by visiting him instead.

"So, when I return to California in three weeks' time, Anna and I are telling Ethan we are separating. I think I've lost more sleep over how we tell Ethan than any of the other shit I'm dealing with."

He's never mentioned losing sleep over me or worrying about what my reaction would be.

But this is a little boy we are talking about here. Shut up, Ella.

"I've expressed to Anna how I would like to have Ethan visit me here in Scotland for some of the school vacations. He adores my mom and dad, and they both adore him too. We need to work out how many weeks I have him for. And again, he's okay with me being away with all the tournament dates. It's all he's ever known since he was born. I think he'll be okay with me not being around. He's a well-adjusted kid. We will work together to ensure Ethan is looked after, emotionally and physically."

For the next hour Fraser and I ping-pong questions back

and forth where he tells me everything, sharing how much money he has set aside for lawyers. It's an astonishing amount.

He reckons the court case will last for several months. That's if it goes that far. If it does, there's a high likelihood he'll have to stop competing in golf tournaments because all his time will be consumed with the case. He listed several big sports personalities who are all in the same position as him with Nate. No contractual marriages, but lock-tight contracts, high commission percentages, and families who are on the verge of losing their homes, too. He shared very intimate details of all his finances, including how much he's set aside to purchase a house for his mom and dad.

He's taking care of everyone else first before himself. The level of selflessness he displays has left me feeling a little guilty over any of my petty problems, like worrying about Anna wanting Fraser. None of that matters because Fraser has some pretty big shit going on in his life. If he doesn't look after himself, or more to the point, if I don't look after him, he'll be on the verge of a mental breakdown within a couple of weeks.

He has plans to pack all his stuff up as soon as he gets back to California in three weeks' time. He has no plans to take anything from the house Nate bought for them. He's letting Anna have it all. He's only taking his belongings— clothes, tools, a few bits of gym equipment, but that's it. He's already sold all the cars he's collected over the years too, apart from a vintage Camaro he's faithfully restored and shipped back to Scotland. He informed me it has a special place in his heart, something he refurbished himself as an escape from his reality.

Fraser explained how he's saved the money from the sale of his cars and set it aside to pay for a new house here in

Castleview Cove for himself, or us, as he keeps referring to it. However, he can't spend it yet in case his lawyer fees spiral out of control. I'm also not sure I want to move out of my lovely home I've dedicated the last two years to decorating.

When I asked him if there was any possibility of evidence of his possible drugging that fateful evening, he informed me it would be too late now, too many years have passed.

I tell Fraser I don't need to know anything about the escort service he used, but he insists I know, so there is no stone left unturned.

He hasn't used the service in a year, confirming to me again that he's only ever been with two of the girls at the agency. Apparently, the girls don't tend to leave. No wonder. At one to two thousand dollars a session, I wouldn't leave either. "What happens if Nate finds out that you used the agency in the past?"

Fraser sighs. "I'll be honest and upfront. I'm not a liar. I'll do a tell-all interview on American television if I have to. The television networks would have a field day with my life story; they'll be fighting over me like a pack of wolves. Trust me."

Argh, I don't like the sound of that.

"Would you really sell your story, Fraser?"

"If I have to defend myself, tell the truth, clear my name. Yes, I will. I'm not hiding anymore."

As I ask question after question, Fraser fills me in on more aspects of his life with Anna. Their relationship, friends—very few from the sounds of it. Anna likes it that way, doing everything she can to protect their secret marriage contract. She's not happy. She wants out. Wants to be free. Free from her father.

I don't blame her.

Although isn't it funny how your perception of someone's life isn't actually true? The whole vibe of his and hers social feed is full of joy, love, and contentment. But like a cheap knockoff Chanel handbag, it's all fake.

It makes me question lots of other people I follow on social media too. We're all the same. Winging every day, seeking happiness and our purpose, with some of us never actually finding any of it. Including Anna, it would seem.

Although, apparently, Anna's thriving influencer Instagram account is what she will use to maintain her life with Ethan. Fraser revealed he had offered to pay child maintenance and alimony, but Anna had declined and reassured him the house was more than adequate, not wanting to inconvenience Fraser for longer than necessary. A very detailed contract has been drafted, outlining the terms of their divorce. Fraser said he will let me see it; however, I don't want to. It's a personal matter between him and Anna.

"How are you feeling, Fraser? Are you okay?" I ask, concerned about Fraser's mental well-being.

"I feel better since I spoke to you last night. Now that I'm with you, I feel better than I have in years." He leans back against the wooden swing with an easy smile.

He seems more relaxed.

"I am worried, though. I'm worried about your safety. Anna's future. Ethan's stability. And I've shared where all my money is going, worst-case scenario I may end up living back with my mom and dad, especially if I have to use the money from the sale of my cars if my lawyers' fees are more than I expect. I have to tell my parents today about the house, me, everything." He leans forward again and bows his head as if it suddenly becomes too heavy to hold up.

"But I would like to buy a house with you. That's what I want. I want to start house hunting together straightaway. Simply look. That's all." He holds his hands up.

"Okay, let's not get too excited. I think we have a few more hurdles to jump across first." I chuckle nervously. This is happening all too fast for me.

I think he should move in with me. But I don't want to suggest that yet. And my house is tiny compared to his ten-bedroom house, *with* a pool house, by the sounds of it. *Nice.* He's used to space and extravagance. My little two-bedroom home is a shoebox.

The whir of a car starts up in the distance, evidence that my neighbors are up and about.

"I can come with you to your parents. Be there when you tell them."

"You would?"

I nibble on the side of my mouth as he lifts his head in hope. "Yeah, I'll be there. I want to be."

"Thank you." He pauses. "For listening. For sticking with me." He sheepishly smirks.

"I don't think I've ever felt so at war with my feelings before. This all feels so surreal, Fraser."

"Yeah, but we're going to do the surreal together. Aren't we?"

This is so hard. I stare across the field, looking for an answer.

"Ella, look at me."

I turn to sit sideways on the bench, fold my leg under me, and tuck my silk rope between my thighs to hide my bare modesty underneath.

Fraser skims his warm, rough hand on my silk-covered knee, raising goosebumps across my cool morning breeze skin.

"For the last few years, I have lived with deep regret and sorrow over us. Over what I did to you. This is my chance to make it right. When Anna and I divorce, there is nothing or no one to keep me away from you. I have only ever loved you. Since the first day I spotted you across the dining hall in high school, with your cute braids, your striking emerald eyes and boisterous, loud laugh, you are all I have ever wanted. I knew then, and I still know. I have missed everything about you, about us. Fish and chips on the beach, our secret nook where we spent way too much time kissing." We chuckle together. "Golf lessons with you, skinny-dipping, listening to Metallica. You stole my heart when you told me you were a Metallica fan; that's when I really fell in love with you." He smiles, continuing. "Watching the sunset together, sharing your day with me. My heart can't take another day apart."

He remembers it all. So do I. I miss it all so much too. But we were kids then, and so much has changed. Will it be the same?

Fraser clasps my face. "I want to spend the rest of my life with you. I want you in my bed every night. I want you by my side when I travel to tournaments and charity events. Someone who wants to be with me. Share my success. I want to celebrate the success of your business too. I want to move in with you. Buy or build a house together. Have the family we always spoke of. I'll even get you another ten dogs if it's what you want. I want everything. But I want it all with you. We've already missed so much. And I know that's down to me. I've been foolish. I love you, Ella. I love you so fucking much."

I bow my head and sway it back and forth because this is actually happening. This *is* real. It almost feels like a dream, but it's not. I feel Fraser, here, touching me now. It's what I've been waiting for. For all these years. For him to come back to me. To explain and hold me and tell me everything's going to be okay. That he was to blame, and I did nothing wrong. I'm relieved, happy, and saddened all at the same time.

I keep my head down. "You broke my heart into a million pieces," I whisper inaudibly. "You broke me for everyone else." I feel emotionally drained, memories from the past resurfacing as I recall the days following Fraser's brutal breakup with me. I lay in bed for days sobbing into my pillow, unable to leave my room from utter heartache.

Fraser summons my face up with his pointer finger under my chin. He pins me with his warm eyes. Sliding his hand down my décolletage, gliding farther down, he stops, then splays the massive palm of his hand flat over my silk-covered heart. "Please let me fix it."

My resentment disperses into the cosmos as my empty heart fills with overwhelming love for this man sitting in front of me.

Forgiving him is necessary to heal my heart. This I know for sure. It's been shattered for too long. I want to feel whole again, cherished and loved.

I cover my hand over his. My breath hitches a little before I reply. "I won't survive another heartbreak. Please don't hurt me again," I whisper gently.

He quickly grabs me by the waist, and I squeal at his unexpected movement. He pulls me onto his lap to straddle him on the seat, wrapping the blanket around me to avoid exposing myself.

Holding my face firmly with his giant hands, he looks deep into my eyes, then tucks a loose platinum strand of hair behind my ear.

"You have my word."

"No more secrets?"

"None."

"Total honesty."

"I've nothing to hide anymore."

He moves his hands to my waist, strumming the tips of his fingers up and down my lower back playfully, across the soft fabric of my robe.

I lean into his chest and rest my hands across his heart.

"Okay."

"Okay? Does that mean we're doing this, Ella? Me and you? House hunting?"

The thought of being like this with him forever sends an involuntary smile beaming across my face and an instant bounce in my heart.

"Yes," I say breathlessly.

Mirroring my expression, Fraser grants me a dazzling smile, one that's filled with happiness and joy.

He pulls me in for a kiss. I stop him. "I have one more question though."

He groans in an '*aw shit, what is it*' kind of way. Like I'm going to swindle him at the last stroke of midnight.

"When did you get your tattoo?"

His brows fly high. He wasn't expecting my question.

"After I married Anna. I wanted to make it clear my heart still belonged to you. And I wanted you everywhere with me. You've always been with me. Here."

He places my hand on his hip.

"And here."

He places my hand over his heart again.

I can barely get my words out. "It's beautiful. Thank you."

Leaning in, I press our lips together. Not moving. Holding still. Being. I feel an invisible purr of vibration dance into my throat, then fill my body. Like I'm buzzing internally.

And it's in this moment I realize what I've known all along: he's my person. The one.

It's no wonder I have never connected with anyone else. It wasn't right.

But this is.

When I lean back slightly, confidence pours from his mouth. "We are inevitable."

I feel it too.

Let's hope we're both right.

We kiss over and over, soft, meaningful kisses, ignoring Treacle's deep growls until we can't anymore.

"Your dog hates me," Fraser chuckles against my lips.

"He doesn't like you touching me. He's so jealous. You know he's the most important man in my life?"

"Not anymore," Fraser states, and continues to hungrily kiss me into oblivion.

Nope. Not anymore.

CHAPTER FIFTEEN

Ella

For the last hour I've sat clutching Fraser's hand as his mom and dad picked apart his sad state of affairs. His contractual marriage, Anna's boy, Nate's backhanded contract signing, and the extortionate cut Nate takes from his earnings. His suspicion around Nate drugging him on the fateful night that brought him to his knees. The status of Anna and his relationship, their home life, his brother Jamie and his rehab, Jamie borrowing money from him—this was news to me. Wait until I tell Eden that one. He told them everything.

To say his parents were, or still are, in shock would be an understatement.

The look of utter bewilderment across Susan and Jim's faces as I appeared through their front door hand in hand with Fraser was the first of many shocks to come.

Quickly making fudge before we came here, I thought it would help to soften the blow, but it didn't. How could it? *Silly, Ella.*

Susan was so pleased to see me though, instantly pulling

me into a warm embrace. She's lost so much weight since I saw her last. She informed me she has no appetite because of her intensive radiotherapy treatment.

She and I managed a giggle about how pink her boob has turned with the radiotherapy. She's always been one to look on the bright side and fairly positive she'll make a quick recovery, as she's not needing chemotherapy at present. So for now, it's a waiting game.

Her new thin-as-a-drain-pipe frame can't hide how beautiful she is, though, with her steel-blue eyes and immaculate blond shoulder-length bobbed hair. And she's always loved fashion. Today she's wearing a pale-pink blouse covered in a deep-red rose pattern, tucked into her jeans, with a stunning designer gold belt and matching gold sandals.

I love the woman sitting in front of me. I would be devastated if anything should happen to her. She's my family. Jim and Susan both are. And even though we've only seen each other in passing these last few years, since Fraser and I broke up, she always stopped in town if she saw me, making time, checking in with me, asking after my sisters, the business, and my parents.

I actually wondered how I hadn't seen her about recently. Now I know why.

Susan and Jim have been married since they were nineteen. Both high school sweethearts, still crazy in love, and have lived in Castleview Cove forever. When Fraser left for America, Susan couldn't wrap her head around the fact her boy was moving to '*the other side of the world*'. She loved telling everyone how proud she was though—she still is, and she loves a good Fraser brag. Both Susan and Jim are very traditional in their beliefs and I can see Fraser is blowing their little Castleview Cove minds with every word he speaks. Fraser informed me it's only the last couple of years they've finally visited him in California. Jim persuaded Susan it was time to go see the *big world*. Bless their hearts.

Fraser's father, Jim, is a tall, lean man, over a foot taller than Susan, making me realize where Fraser gets his height. He's a gentle giant of a man. Quiet. Thoughtful. He's still very dark-haired, with not a fleck of gray to be seen. In his mid-fifties now, he's incredibly handsome. His deep-brown eyes give nothing away. He's an introverted man. I think that's why I find him so intriguing.

Sitting on Susan and Jim's brown leather sofa now, I listen to all of their queries, mainly from Susan. Regardless of how nervous Fraser is, with ease and grace, and in a very matter-of-fact manner, he explains every single little detail to them.

"And you're with Ella now? Back with Ella? Or you've always been together?" Susan's expression slides into a confused frown. "I can't get my head wrapped around this. Can you Jim?"

"I'm a little lost myself," Jim answers gruffly.

"This is all news to me too," I reassure them both. "Fraser and I broke up once he was under contract with Nate. But I didn't know this at the time. I would never go with a married man. Ever. I have too much respect for myself and for others to do that. Fraser and I have only *just* gotten back together and only since he's told me everything."

Well, that's not strictly true, but I'm hardly going to tell his parents I fucked him in the dark without all the facts the other evening.

I need to figure out how to tell my friends and family. *"Hey, so I'm going back out with Fraser. You know the guy that broke my heart, the one I cried a river over, and I couldn't leave my bed for? Yeah, him. And by the way, he's got a wife he's been contracted to since we split up. He's never had sex with her, but has a son, who's also not his. He's signed to a dodgy agent who drugged him; his signature is on a contract he doesn't remember signing, so he's taking his agent to court. Oh, and did I mention his wife is his agent's daughter? The court case is going to cost millions. He may not have a home, or job, left once the court case is over, but we're back together and I'm standing by him."*

Fucking.

Lead.

Balloon.

Susan shakes me from my daydream as I play out that scenario in my head. "That makes sense to me now. And you're okay with this *situation*, Ella? I know you. I know how much your heart broke when you split up. And I never approved of what you did to this beautiful girl, young man." Susan wags her finger in Fraser's direction. "You cannot do that again, Fraser. Ella deserves better."

Did I tell you I love this woman?

"Believe me, I know. And I never wanted to break up." He pulls the back of his neck with his free hand. "I won't hurt her again." He turns to me, lifts my hand to his mouth, and places a soft kiss on my knuckles. "I won't, I promise."

I internally swoon at his tender gesture.

He shifts his focus back to his mom and dad. "Ella and I have spoken about this at great lengths today. I'm not going anywhere this time. Ella's it for me. Mom, I'm telling you I may lose everything. Someone drugged me. You'll lose your home, and you decide to give me a lecture about Ella. I know I've screwed up. But I can't take it today, please. I'm so sorry." I feel Fraser's pain through his defeated demeanor. "I know you are worried, and entitled to be upset. I am not discrediting your feelings." He sighs. "I'm sorry I messed up."

Susan fires back, "All of this is a shock to us. I'm making sure you look after this beautiful girl. And houses, cars, those are material things." She waves her hand around. "None of it matters, Fraser. I don't care about this house because I have memories. All stored up here." She taps her temple with her thin finger. "I would like to move, anyway. Your dad and I spoke about this before my breast cancer diagnosis. I'd like a smaller garden and a house all on one level. I love the new houses they've built down by the beach. They have lots of them left. We visited the show home a couple of weeks ago. We know the exact plot we want. I fell in love with it, but I felt guilty wanting to move because you bought us this house, Fraser, but if it belongs to Nate Miller, let him have it. Moving home feels like divine timing. It's meant for us. I feel it." She gets excited at the prospect. "Your dad and I have savings. We don't need your money."

I watch as Jim gazes in admiration at his wife as she continues. "There are too many ghosts here now. After Jamie's accident, this house became tainted. We need to let the past stay in the past. It's time. Time for fresh memories to be made. Can we go today, Jim, and put our deposit down?" She reaches out, tucking her frail hand into Jim's giant one.

Jim nods a yes as Susan continues. "The saleswoman said with no mortgage we could move in within six weeks."

Her giddy grin bounces excitable energy around the room.

"Your father and I will stand by you no matter what. You know we're your biggest champions. I don't know how well I will be or if I can travel for the court case, if it gets to that stage, but hand in hand, we will unite as a family. I can't believe you never told us about the money and the marriage." She rubs her brow with her fingers. "I feel somewhat responsible for this. You left when you were so young. It was irresponsible of us letting you go to America by yourself. This is all on *us,* Fraser. We didn't visit you enough. I could have done more and been there for you."

"You couldn't, Mom. I was double-crossed. This is my responsibility, not yours. I was older, too. I should have known better. I was a careless fool," Fraser disagrees, pointing to his chest.

"We have to take part of the blame. I don't agree. And that son of a bitch, Nate Miller, we trusted him with you. And then it turns out he's a smiling knife. I don't like any of this, Fraser. And poor Ethan. Can we still call him our grandson? Will we still get to see him?" Her blue eyes plead.

"Of course you will, Mom. I plan on having him for a few weeks over summer vacation and some of the other school breaks," Fraser reassures her.

"And Anna's okay with you having him?" She frowns.

"Yeah."

"Do you think that will last? What will happen when Anna finds someone? You're not telling me you will get to see Ethan indefinitely, not if, but when, Anna takes a new husband. It will happen, Fraser."

She's so frank. I never thought about that.

He replies, "I'm guessing we will have to take one step at a time, Mom. I honestly don't know."

I give his hand a good comforting squeeze. That's going to be so painful for Fraser if that does eventually happen.

"And all this time, you've been *married*." She uses air quotes on her last word. "You've never kissed once? How have we never noticed this?"

"I'm baffled too," Jim pipes in.

"That's easy. We tilt heads toward each another for photos. Stand close together at tournaments. Position Ethan in the middle of us, one of us on either side. Or one of us dips down to Ethan's height for the press. When Ethan was younger, we used to position him on our hips in the middle of us. It's simple adjustments, really. And we never stayed here with you when we visited. We always stayed in hotels, so you wouldn't know we had separate rooms." Fraser is so matter of fact about it.

It's so obvious now.

"Huh." Susan shakes her head. "Well, I have never heard of anything like this in my life. Although do you remember, Jim? Now what was his name?" She taps her chin. "Oh yeah, Brian McDonald, that was it. He married the hussy from the next town over so they could partner their father's lawyer businesses, making them the biggest in the region. There is no way that young girl wanted to marry that podgy old fart. He was twenty years her senior. Died of a heart attack last year. She's no doubt sunning it somewhere exotic with her new boy toy. Mrs. Mitchell informed me he's fifteen years her junior. People nowadays. They have no shame."

I try to stifle a giggle.

"Oh, stop it." Fraser gives me a playful nudge to my side. "This is my life we are talking about. And stop talking about people, Mom. You don't know what she had to do or why. Unless you've been through it, you wouldn't understand."

Susan smooths her hair with her hands.

"I'm sorry, son. So, let's get back on track then. House? I would like to put a deposit on my new beach bungalow today and get the ball rolling as soon as possible. Ethan? We will get to see him still. Anna? Well, I was never sure about her anyway, and maybe this is why she was always a little cagey around us. I've never trusted her."

"Mom," Fraser warns.

Jim issues Susan with a stern scowl and a quick shake of his head, indicating for her to stop.

Interesting. Susan feels the same as I do about Anna. Or maybe Anna is nervous around his family. I can't work her out yet.

Jim and Fraser's firm warning doesn't prevent her defending herself, though; she won't be deterred. "I'm allowed to have an opinion, Jim. And Fraser." She looks straight at him. "You know she doesn't like us. Visiting our poky little home. We are hardly Hollywood glamor. I've seen the way she looks at us. It's so obvious we don't fit into her socialite life."

"She's not like that, Mom, and regardless, she's still my wife for the time being and you need to stop talking about her. She's going to help me with the case. You've got her all wrong."

Oh, stop defending her, you big nincompoop. Argh. I'm a level ten jealous bitch.

"Okay. Sorry." Susan rolls her eyes and draws a zip across her mouth. "But Ella is back in your life. You are not, I repeat, not to mess her about again. This is your lifeline. You've been given a second chance. I'm so thrilled you two are back together." She claps her hands with glee. "And the money you were going to give us for a house. Use it to buy yourself one. Not lawyers' fees, not Ethan, not on cars. But set foundations somewhere. Buy yourself a home to call your own. Where will you buy one? Are you going to continue living in LA? Will you two be able to handle long distance again?"

Fraser's parents' hopeful looks scream, '*please say you're moving back to Castleview Cove*'.

Putting the two of them out of their misery, he answers,

"I'm moving back here to Castleview. Ella and I are going to move in together."

"Eventually," I fire in.

Fraser turns to me and scowls.

"Well, we will, Fraser. Just not right away. We chatted about it this morning. And you have loads to sort out before we can consider it. You can stay with me until we find a house and while you are yo-yoing between tournaments, shipping your stuff back from California and straightening everything out."

Damn it. I didn't mean to say that out loud, but it makes sense.

"But I have the money now if I'm not buying Mom and Dad a house. I want to buy a house together. Not eventually, but now," he states.

"Oh, you are so frustrating. I already have a house, Fraser. It could take months for it to sell. Selling a house requires organization. I haven't even told my parents we are back together." *Or Eva.* I've spoken to Eden, though, and that went better than I expected.

I feel a hot flush winding up my neck and ears. I need to psych myself up for those chats. *Oh boy.*

"But we are moving in together, Ella. The sooner you get your house up for sale, the better. I am all in with you. And we need to see your parents to tell them. We'll go after we leave here. Together. But can we keep the specifics of my circumstances under wraps for the time being? Can we just tell them Anna and I are separated? You can tell them all the other details once the press release comes out."

"If that's what you want." I don't think it's right, but I'll save this discussion for when we're alone. "And it hasn't been that long since I bought my house. I don't know if I want to sell it just yet." I can't get my concerns out quick enough.

"You don't have to sell it if you don't want to. You could rent it out if you prefer?"

"This is too much to decide right now, Fraser." My breath hitches in panic.

I need to lie down.

Sensing my distress, he says, "You're right. I'm sorry I'm getting ahead of myself. I'm just keen to be with you." He squeezes my hand.

Neither of us notice until a shadow falls over us both, but Susan's made her way across to us. "You're coming home?" she softly whispers with glazed eyes.

Fraser stands to greet her.

"Yeah, Mom, I'm coming home."

"Oh, Jim, our boy's coming back." Tears stream from her eyes as she pulls Fraser into her warm embrace. "Ella." She summons me to stand, instantly pulling me in as I do. "You do not know how happy I am."

"Oh, I think I do. Are you trying to squeeze the air from me, Mom?" Fraser chuckles, struggling to get his muffled words out as his cheek is squished into hers. I know that's what she's doing because mine is pushed painfully into the other side of her face, too.

For a little thing, she's strong.

"I love you, pair," she chimes. "This is the best news we've had all year."

She leans out of our three-way embrace and wipes her tear-stained face.

"Are you getting married?" Her watery eyes light up as she speaks.

I blink. Once. Twice.

We've discussed how we want to be all in, be together, but we haven't discussed *that*.

Fraser shoves his hands in his pockets, hunching his herculean shoulders as he does.

Well, this is awkward.

I suck my lips into my mouth and watch as Fraser fills his cheeks with air, his eyes popping wide open.

I help him out. "Fraser's still married, Susan. We're taking one step at a time."

Fraser points a nervous finger at me. "Yeah, that."

I don't think he wants to marry me. He looks scared shitless.

Baby steps, Ella, baby steps.

Wrapping my arms around myself, I bow my head and intensively study the floral rug beneath my feet.

Sensing our awkwardness, Jim intervenes. "I think you two still have a lot of talking to do. Focus on each other. That's what is important now. And, Fraser, we know you're back for your mom, but you and Ella need to reconnect... re-establish what you had. And when you move back, we'll see you all the time between tournaments. For now, forget about us. Your mom is doing really well. The doctors are positive she will make a full recovery, so make the most of this valuable time while you are here in Castleview. Go from here to visit Ella's parents. Tell them you're back together. No matter how hard this will be for you, Ella, you have to trust they will forgive Fraser, trust your judgment, and respect your wishes to be together again. Whatever choice you make with your home, your parents are good people; they will understand. But this is big news, and you need to tread carefully. Be honest with them about Fraser. Tell them everything."

Wow, this is the most I've ever heard Jim speak.

Fraser stiffens beside me. Whatever Jim said has upset him. "We'll go now," Fraser confirms as he shoots out the living room door with great haste, leaving a cold puff of air behind him. "I'll be back later," he flings his gruff voice back over his shoulder. "Ella's going out with her friends tonight."

Oh, he doesn't seem happy.

"I'll see you tomorrow, maybe." I give Susan a quick squeeze and goodbye nod to Jim, then scurry out of the house.

I struggle to keep up with Fraser in my untied ribbon black biker boots as he dashes up the street to my parked black Audi TT.

I impressed Fraser with my new car I recently upgraded to. My coupe car, essentially a two-seater, is totally impractical with two miniature dogs. However, my boys don't take up much space, and the two undersized seats in the back are perfect for them.

When we dropped Hunter's Range Rover off before coming here, I pulled Eden for a quick chat, filling her in on the last crazy twenty-four hours of my life. She knew most of it already, as Hunter had filed her in.

The beautiful thing about Eden, no matter what, she always stands by me and Eva. She's stronger than the three of us combined. More than she realizes. More than any of us realized until recently.

She told me to uncage my heart, set it free, and allow Fraser to heal it, delivering a lecture about not being so closed off all the time. She informed me to let her and Eva into my cave I go into and never come out of.

That cave is where I feel most comfortable. My heart's set up a small camp there. It's warm, closed off, protecting itself from the outside world, and anyone who may hurt it.

Eden's got me all worked out. But it's time to walk out of

that dark cave without looking back, stepping back into the light where it's freeing, joyful, and full of love.

Although I think I may have leaped into the sunshine last night with Fraser. My heart beats stronger every time he tells me he loves me, and it feels unreal. As if I'm having an out-of-body experience. It's oddly unnerving and completely out of character to willingly release my caged heart, but I'm doing it.

Eden and Hunter also informed us they would help where they can. Eden promised us full access to Hunter's private jet if and when we need it. Although she's on maternity leave, she will step in if I need to go to California at a minute's notice, taking over the social media responsibility for our dance school.

Over the last year, Eva, Eden, and I have taken on more executive director roles within the business. We all love to teach the dance classes, and we do still, but it's becoming impossible as our business gets busier. The three of us discussed taking on yet another two dance teachers and extending the current dance school building or moving to new premises. I think the latter is the option we will go for. Also, Hunter's offered to become an investment partner. He wants the business to grow; anything to make his girl happy.

Our dance school sits on the back end of Eden's former barn conversion home. It's big, but too small for our unexpected growth.

The old barn rests within the grounds of my parents' sports retreat. Eden restored and converted it a few years ago, allowing us space at the gable end to start up our classes.

Since Eden moved to her new home, it's been sitting empty for months, waiting for a new beginning. None of us can decide what we want to do with it. One thing we all agree on is if we don't sell it to an understanding buyer, they will close our noisy dance lessons that are beating through the wall day in, day out, in an instant. And it's too nice to convert to a dance studio. It's a beautiful home and should live out its purpose.

Leaving us with only one option, sell the entire building, pushing us to expand.

"Hey." I sprint after Fraser. "What's up?" I ask, finally reaching him.

Spinning around on his heel, I'm greeted with Fraser's pained expression.

"You think I don't know your parents will hate me all the more when they find out the things I've done? My circumstances? Like breaking your heart wasn't bad enough. Shit. This is so much harder than I thought, and I didn't need my dad reminding me I'm a disappointment." He points back in the direction of his family home.

"Whoa, he didn't say that."

"He didn't have to, Ella. I could sense it. Will your parents forgive me? Can *you*? Because you haven't told me you can yet. Can you truly forgive me? I am scared shitless I will lose you again. What if your parents tell you to stay away from me?" He runs his hands through his hair. "And I saw the look in your eyes. Marriage? I want nothing more than to marry you."

Phew. He wants to marry me. My shoulders sag with relief.

"Ella, I would marry you today and make that happen. It kills me that I'm being held prisoner by a piece of paper."

He walks a few steps away from me in the opposite direction, stomping out his frustration.

"Eh, wait a minute," I say. "I never mentioned marriage. Those were not my words. And I do forgive you. I forgive you with every bone in my body, but I'm scared shitless, too. I'm petrified when you fly back to America you'll leave me again and never come back. Along with a life-changing court case, nasty newspaper headlines, people's opinions, and also I'm technically going to become a stepmom overnight, too."

My greatest fears roll off my tongue. I am so exhausted with all of this and it's only day one.

Fraser's eyes widen as if he hadn't given my last statement a thought. *He hadn't.*

I go on trying to justify his mom's genuine query. "Your mom is happy for us. She expects us to do the whole traditional relationship thing — the house, the wedding, babies. I want that too." There, I've said it. I want it all, the whole shebang.

"Babies?" He frowns, snapping his head back slightly.

Oh, he clearly doesn't want children with me because he already has a *son*. But I *do*. These are all the unsaid things we haven't addressed yet.

I chew the inside of my mouth to stop me saying anything else.

"You want babies? Still? With me? Even after all my shit? She wants a family with me." His last mumble is not a question.

I bob my head up and down as he looks back at me.

Fraser paces back and forth across the sidewalk, muttering words I can't make out.

This is it, this is when he runs for the hills. I've spooked him good and proper this time.

Fraser grabs his hair fiercely in his hands, growling, then suddenly stomps with determination directly for me. Like a man on fire, he grabs me and crashes his lips to mine. As if my lips lessen the intensity of the flames, he holds his still against mine.

Okay, I didn't expect that.

"You have no idea how much I want to marry you and have a family," he mumbles. "I want lots of babies. Mine. With you. And they'll be beautiful if they all look like you. Our own house. An elaborate wedding we always spoke of all those years ago. I want to do it all properly."

Gasping between dynamic kisses, my body relaxes into his. I'm a sucker for his confession. And his lips.

"I don't need any of that fancy-schmancy stuff."

"I know, but I want to give you it all, anyway. You forgiving me makes me so goddamn happy, but it kills me that I can't give you all of it now." He continues holding my face, dipping his tongue into my mouth between his desperate words. "I promise you, when this is all over, I will marry you. And we will have the best goddamn fun practicing making those babies."

Our kiss is long and passionate, making me flush all over. I feel the heat build between my thighs, setting off a small hum of pleasure from the back of my throat.

"You're my new religion, and I will worship you every single day, Ella. Especially if you keep making those noises."

As if the millimeters between us were too far for him, sheer desperation urges Fraser to wrap his almighty arms around my waist and pull me in closer.

Dominating me with his magical lips and sweeping strokes of his tongue, he stays glued to me as we become one. He pours his love into me through his touch. He moves from my mouth across to my cheek, my eyelid, and then plants a soft kiss to my temple before he rests his forehead gently against mine.

"I'm so grateful for having you in my life again, Ella. I can't believe you're mine."

"I'm here for you... always. I'm yours."

"And I'm yours. Forever and always."

I know he is. I feel it. With all my heart and soul.

"We need to stop doing this in the street. What if someone sees us?" I whisper my concern.

I lean out slightly and blink my worried eyes up to meet his.

"No one will see us here." He looks around the empty narrow street.

He goes quiet, thinking. "I'm desperate for Anna and me to make our separation announcement. It doesn't matter about Mom and Dad's house now, not now that they've decided they want to buy one of the beach bungalows. I can help pack up their house quickly."

"How soon do you think you can make your official announcement, Fraser? Can it be quicker than three weeks?"

He starts his verbal list. "I need to speak with my lawyer first. We have a lot of details to iron out. Speak with Lisa, my new agent. She and I need to slightly tweak the statement we've prepared, and then we can go public. And the biggest thing of all, we need to tell Ethan. But I need to be there, in person."

He's mentally calculating. "A week? I can go back to California next week. That way, Anna and I can tell Ethan together. Make our statement across our social media, announce to the press, and we take it from there. My lawyer is ready to serve the papers to Nate. We can do it in one big blitz. This is all happening faster than I expected, but I want to be with you so bad." He hugs me tight, like he's trying to imprint his feelings on me. "Ooooh, that gives me heart squeezes," he says. "Feel my heart."

"I can already feel it booming against mychest." It's so strong, I'm certain people five blocks away can hear it. "You're going to be fine. You have a great team around you. Your family. Me. Are you okay?" I'm really worried about Fraser having to be strong by himself but he gives me a quiet I'm fine in response.

Firmly, I bolster my support. "Talk to me all the time. Share everything with me. Your feelings, what you're thinking, especially on your shittiest of days. I'm here for it. Remember that."

He closes his eyes. "Yeah, give me a minute." He clears his throats. "This is all becoming so real now."

"A week?" I sound desperate to finally make him mine.

"Yeah, a week. I don't want to wait any longer. Fuck it. I'm so over Nate Miller holding me hostage. I'm going to call the realtor too this afternoon, see if we can move the new house purchase along for Anna. I want to be with you. But I need to return to Los Angeles, unfortunately."

"That's okay. If you promise me you'll come back this time." A nervous twitch forces my mouth sideways.

"I'm not leaving you again, Ella. I promised you."

"When you're away, I want you to check in with me every day. When you have a dip in mood, when even more crap hits the fan. Anything. I'm the pillar that will hold you up."

I watch his Adam's apple bob up and down.

"God, Ella, I don't deserve you."

"Yes, you do. You're a great man. A saint. So, you've made some bad choices, but we're moving on. The past is staying in the past. The choices you make from here on in, these are the ones that matter." I rest my hand on his heart. "Your heart is big, beautiful, and strong. Determined. And you love unconditionally. My goodness, you've loved me from afar for all this time. You've looked after a little boy who isn't yours and supported Anna, too. You are deserving. This is your time now. Time to be happy. Time to be free and time for us to be together. I'm ready."

"I don't know what to say. You keep surprising me."

I keep surprising myself. I'm not sure where my strength and words keep coming from.

"Well, what I'm about to tell you next is not a surprise, Fraser."

His eyes crease with worry.

"We need to go see my parents now."

He sighs. "We do. C'mon, let's get this over with."

"You need to tell them the whole truth, though, Fraser. No holding back."

He stands motionless, considering, his eyes searching mine. "Okay, you're right."

We eventually walk the few steps to my car hand in hand.

From the corner of my eye, I spot a familiar silver vehicle. The exact same one was parked outside my house earlier. It's not a car I recognize; it's definitely not local, so it's most likely lost tourists. It looks like one of the cars for hire I see around town. It's very easy to lose your bearings through the narrow network of roads in Castleview Cove. Every road looks the same.

As I pull out from my parking space, heading toward my mom and dad's sports retreat, the silver car behind disappears out of sight as I drift slowly around the corner.

Nothing could have prepared me for all the surprises lurking around *our* corner.

Absolutely.

Nothing.

CHAPTER SIXTEEN

Ella

Surprisingly, the impromptu meeting with my mom and dad went better than I expected.

My parents had already spoken with Fraser at Eden's house the other morning, so they knew he was back in Scotland visiting his family.

They weren't overly shocked to see Fraser and me together, either. I suspect Eden had something to do with that. *Sneaky little imp.*

Although I've never been more grateful. They were expecting us, so the conversation flowed with ease from the moment we stepped in the door. And my father welcomed Fraser back into the family with a firm double pat on the back.

Fraser was open and honest as he explained everything with precision.

As with his own parents, mine also had heaps of questions. But Fraser stood strong throughout, answering everything they fired at him, and was deeply apologetic about how he previously treated me, making promises to never repeat the hurt.

Hearing the personal details of Fraser's circumstances over and over normalized everything.

We've both agreed to focus on our future, and although we may have to revisit the past throughout Fraser's case, we have to leave the past where it belongs.

As we left the retreat, my mom pulled me aside to have a private word with me. She informed me she was shocked by Fraser's news and a little confused, but what she said afterward will stay with me forever.

"Ella, it's rare we get a second chance. If ever. Fraser's being honest with you; he's opened up. And you've been wearing this self-sabotaging armor for so long now, you wear it like it's normal. Let him love you. Really let him in. Throw down that armor, be vulnerable. I've watched every boyfriend come and go since Fraser. I know now it's him you love. But you have to give him a winning chance. Even when things get rough, crossing those unpredictable seas. Because of Fraser's circumstance, those rough seas are inevitable. But if you want him, push through. Start imagining what your life will be like on the other side when the storm clears. Because it will come; you're not there yet. But you will be. I want to see my strong girl kick ass when she has to stand her ground and go for what she wants. Be the couple you long to be. There's no great mystery to love, sweetheart; you simply have to let it in."

Every word she spoke hammered away my hard armadillo exterior, smashing through it one word at a time. She held my hand so tenderly, and as she did, I cried yet more tears. I've cried more in the last three days than I have in years. I knew she was right.

Fraser's face turned gray when he spotted our huddle from across the parking lot. Deep concern showered across his face, worried my mom would talk me out of his life.

If anything, she made me even more determined.

I'm telling myself a new story. It's one of truth, freedom, and love. After all the lies I've told myself over the years, it's not that I am unlovable or can't love. It's because I love him and only him. Not that I've said those actual words to him. I'm not ready. Yet.

Looking back at what seems like the longest day on record, and it's not even three o'clock in the afternoon yet, Fraser and I walk silently along the soft sand of Castleview Cove with Tartan and Treacle chasing the naughty seagulls in front of us. I begin to imagine our life together, just like Mom said. And I like it.

I begin to panic as he threads his hand into mine, knowing how well we go together like quill and ink. "Someone might see." I say, looking around.

Fraser examines the beach, lifting his head to peer through the brim of his baseball cap. "There are only a handful of people on the beach. We're safe."

I hope so, as he gives my hand a squeeze, making me feel happy. Which is an odd sensation for me. Contentment bubbles away and it feels wonderful.

The pair of us smile as we watch my two miniature furballs braving a dip in the cold inky sea.

"This is the first opportunity I've had to visit the beach. I really miss home. I miss you." He looks my way.

"Not for much longer. This will be your new normal soon."

"Mmm." He stops walking, twisting around to face me, and continues his thoughts out loud. "Announcement, move in with you once Anna and Ethan are settled in the new house. I have a couple of tournaments, but," he stalls. "As soon as they're done, I would like to take you away on vacation before the madness of a court case ensues."

My cheesy grin gives my delight away.

"Oh, Ella likes the sound of that," he notices.

"She does. Where?"

"Well, a little birdie told me." He leans forward and whispers in my ear, "Eden." Then he faces me again. "Your friends changed your vacation plans this year because everyone now has boyfriends." He rolls his eyes. "Don't you just hate when they do that?" He scrunches his nose.

A small, nervous giggle leaves my throat.

"So, I thought why not take Ella to the place she was supposed to go?"

"The Maldives?" I gasp in surprise.

"Yes," he says through an excited-looking smile.

"You don't have to spend your money on me or shower me with gifts and things. I only want you, Fraser."

"That's not what taking you on vacation is about, Ella. We need a holiday for us. Away from everything. My dad's right. To reconnect. Discover each other again. And I'm desperate to see you in that tiny leopard print bikini you used to wear when we were teenagers." His eyes twinkle with mischief.

"I don't have it anymore," I smirk.

"Well, you'll have to buy a new one then. The smaller the better, although I don't think we'll be wearing any clothes. Not for what I have planned."

"We have a lot of making up to do."

"Yes, we do."

Fraser's hooded gaze zooms in on my mouth. "I've missed these." He thumbs my bottom lip with his rough thumb.

"You don't have to miss them anymore. They're yours."

"I prefer them when they're wrapped firmly around my cock. And the way your red lipstick always leaves a band around it, branding me as yours."

My mouth salivates at the very mention of it. In agreement, my nipples tighten.

I moan in satisfaction when Fraser pulls me in for an illicit kiss. His hard, rigid tongue dives deep, seeking mine. He then sucks, making my panties instantly wet with my arousal.

"You love my lips," I mumble. "I love your tongue."

"That right, Bella?"

He continues to attack my mouth.

"You have to stop." It doesn't matter that Fraser has pulled his black baseball cap down low in an effort to hide his identity, his tall and bulky frame stands out like pink thong panties on a gray elephant.

"Am I making you wet?"

I lift my eyes to meet his. "Yeah, *that* and we are out in public. We should be more careful." My clit disagrees, pulsing for his attention. I lean out of our kiss slightly. "We need to stop. Plus, you're ruining my lipstick." I pull my sunglasses off, using the lenses as a mirror as I try fixing it. *Argh, what a mess.* Then I pop them back on when I'm finished.

He sighs. "You're right. But I can't get enough. My fucking cock is dripping for you." *Oh Lord.*

"Feel how hard I am. It's all because of you." He discreetly rubs his thick cock against my hip. Although he didn't have to. I could already feel it.

"Not long now and you'll be mine officially," he growls.

My heart does a little celebration dance. His announcement can't come quick enough.

"Until then, let's round up your two little precious bats, Meghan and Kate?"

"They are not bats; they are dogs. Stop calling them that. And they're both boys," I exclaim.

"Treacle's a princess if I ever I saw one."

A giggle escapes my throat. He really is a princess.

He continues joshing with me. "What about yippy and yappy? That better? Or grumpy and frumpy, and you know which one of them is grumpy," he states.

We both say, "Treacle."

I step out of our embrace, attempting to move away.

"Ah, stay there a moment until Fraser Junior calms down." He spins me around. My back meets his front as he hooks his thumbs into the belt loops of my black skinny jeans.

"Fraser Junior?" I chuckle.

"Got a better name for him?"

"Yeah, Ella's Anaconda."

He scoffs. "I'm not calling him that, but he is yours."

"Pleased to hear it."

Moments pass, then I feel Fraser kissing the wicked spot behind my ear, sending a hot shiver down my spine, whispering into my skin that I'm now clear to move.

"We should live on the beach. It's the only way your dogs, well Treacle, will let me near you. It's the best distraction." Fraser's gaze drifts to the frolicking pair.

"That's a great idea. But why don't you try rounding them both up? You need to build Treacle's trust. Toffee already loves you; he's such a tart."

"Okay, I can try."

I pass Fraser their leads. "I'll stay here."

Sauntering off down the sand, I watch his broad, towering frame move toward my fur babies. I can't take my eyes off him and that tight ass. *Man, does he have a great ass in those jeans.* He is the eighth wonder of my world. Maybe his ass is the ninth.

Pulled from swooning, my phone chimes indicating a text.

The text preview across the screen makes me cover my loud gasp with my hand. I swipe my phone open, confirming the words I've read.

Unknown Number: He'll never be yours.

What. The. Hell.

Me: Who is this?
Unknown Number: None of your business. Know this. Your days with him are numbered. Make them count.

My happy heart floods with panic. This is the last thing Fraser needs. Or me.

Me: How did you get my number?
Unknown Number: I have my ways. Enjoy him while it lasts. It won't be for long.
Me: Who are you talking about?

I know it's Fraser this stranger is talking about, but I need confirmation.

Unknown Number: Fraser Farmer.
Me: Who is this?

Unknown Number: That, Bella, is a secret.

Bella? No one calls me Bella but Fraser.

Is it Anna? Surely not. Fraser's made it blatantly clear she's not interested. Although by the look on Anna's face last night. It could be her. Maybe she's jealous. Jealous Fraser has someone, and she doesn't. And I can't blame her for having feelings for him if it is her. She's lived with him for the last seven years, brought her child up with him. It would make sense. But I don't think she's the type to send threatening text messages. She came across as someone who stood her ground; forthright and upfront. Although, then again, I don't know her. And while I trust Fraser's character assessment of her, his track record isn't solid grounds to go on. Nate is living proof. I type a message back.

Me: I guarantee I will find out who you are.

I do not know if that's true, but I need to show I'm not willing to be intimidated. I watch intently as the three dots on my screen indicate the person is responding.

Unknown Number: We'll see. Like I said, have fun while it lasts.

Crap. Everything's already getting so complicated. Fraser was right. This will be full on for us all.

My heart pumps faster, causing it to jump about in my chest.

I can do this. I want him. And we can do this together. It's just a text. Nothing more.

Argh. I hate this feeling of uselessness already. I would

give anything for a magic wand right now. I'd wave it about in an effort to make Fraser's troubles disappear.

I lift my head from my phone in time to welcome Fraser back.

All thoughts pushed aside, I watch as he confidently walks toward me. "Everything okay? You look worried."

"Yeah, I'm fine," I lie.

Ignoring the text, I lock my phone and slide it into the back pocket of my tight, black jeans. I'm not telling Fraser about it. He's got enough on his plate.

However, I may call Hunter for a quick chat; he always knows what to do.

Fraser's concern shifts instantly, looking pleased as punch with himself, and he dons a confident grin.

"Look who listened when I called. Treacle, my man." He looks down at Treacle and offers him a high five. "C'mon, princess, don't leave me hanging. Aren't you a good boy? Yes, you are," Fraser coos. "I think he's warming to me."

I'm not sure he is.

"Shall we see if he'll let me kiss you, Ella? Test my theory?"

Fraser tilts his head downward and raises his eyebrows. "What do you think, handsome? Can I kiss your mommy?" Treacle's deadpan, downturned face stares back at Fraser.

"I think that's a yes," Fraser speaks for Treacle.

I can't help but giggle. These two boys are giving me so much life right now.

Carefully Fraser leans in, with Treacle and Toffee's leads still in his hand.

Tentatively, I reach out to Fraser, closing the small gap. Fraser's hopeful eyes say I think we're good. He subtly bobs his head with the grin of a conspirator.

We lock lips. No growls yet. *Okay, this is progress.*

Fraser whispers, "I think we're good."

As he finishes what he's saying, Treacle becomes territorial. A slow, low growl leaves his throat, ending on a sharp bark that leads to more high-pitched yelps.

"Oh, dear," I mock.

Disappointment flickers across Fraser's dazzling face. "I want that wee fella to like me."

I can't stop giggling.

"Don't you start. Everyone likes me. I'm a likeable kind of guy," Fraser jests, pulling me closer to him.

As my laughter becomes louder, Toffee joins in Treacle's yapping choir. The next thing I know, my excitable boys circle around us in quick time, tangling themselves around the bottom of our ankles.

"Shit, what are they doing?" Fraser panics.

They've done this to me before. I know what comes next.

I firmly command them to stop, but it's too late. Their retractable leads wrap even tighter as they chase each other round and round, like it's the best game of Ring Around the Rosie ever. They're past the point of listening to me. There's no coming back from this.

"Brace yourself," I command, looping my arms firmly around Fraser.

His eyes pop wide. "What the hell do you mean, brace myself? For wh—"

Too late. Treacle's strong, stocky body takes off at high-speed, gunning for the shoreline, with Toffee chasing after him. Pulled to their capacity, the leads tighten, instantly whipping our legs from beneath us. With a loud thud, we hit the glittering sand with force.

Landing flat on his back, winding Fraser, I fall on top of his chest with my full weight. He's been hit with both barrels.

Realizing we're now lying on the ground, Toffee thinks we're playing a game. He runs back to us, jumps on Fraser's head, and begins licking his face repeatedly.

Gasping for breath, Fraser groans out loud, squeezing his eyes shut. "I fucking love your dogs. Such angels." He wheezes, then wipes his face, trying to stop Toffee from licking him to death. All the while, Treacle barks his head off at us, bouncing up and down like a kangaroo on his hind legs.

"Oh my God, I'm so sorry. Stop it, Toffee." I gently push him off Fraser, desperately trying to stifle my chuckle.

"Oh, you think this is funny, do you? Tied up together?" he teases.

Without warning, he grabs my waist, flips me over, and presses his hot, hard body flush against mine. Running his fingers up my ribs, he pushes my arms above my head, pinning me to the dusty sand as he clasps our hands together.

"Would you like me to tie you up, Ella?" His eyes grow dark with curiosity.

That's not something we ever tried together. We were too young and naïve back then. Yeah, we had sex, lots of it when he was back visiting, but nothing risky or experimental.

"We're already halfway there. I'm game if you are," I tease back.

"Oh, I'm game. Have you done anything like that before?"

"Nope." I shake my head from side to side.

"Good."

"Have you?" I ask, testing him.

"Yes.

"With the girls from the agency?"

"Yes, with them. I haven't been with anyone else but you and them. Remember?" He says, wide-eyed.

He's not ashamed of his sexual history; it's all the other crap he's ashamed of.

"It's fun and a big fucking turn-on, Ella. Knowing you can't move. Under my control."

Sparks fly between us as Fraser tries nudging his knee between my tied legs, urging me to give him access. I hope no one we know is around. It doesn't matter if the beach is quiet today, we're taking a gamble.

"I like the sound of that." I feel a rush of excitement in my core at the thought of Fraser controlling me with his big, beautiful body.

"I do too, but you know what's even better?" He breathes gruffly.

"What?"

"Freedom, being untied. Your hands roaming every inch of my body. Because I adore your touch. I've missed it so much. No one touches me like you do. And when you touch me, I feel it everywhere. It's incomparable. I want your hands on me all the time. Dripping your feelings into my skin with your touch. It's a feeling I can't get enough of."

I never expected him to say that. I thought he was going deep and dirty, telling me he wanted to fuck me seven ways to Sunday, but he went left field.

Imagining his touch is something I've done often.

"I would like to touch you all over now," I say, teasing my thumb against his in our clenched hands. "But we can't do that here, Fraser."

"You certainly *cannot*," a voice from behind startles us.

Aw, crap.

CHAPTER SEVENTEEN

Ella

It's a firm but soft, delicate voice.

One I would recognize anywhere.

I cheekily grin at Fraser as his face pales. He recognizes it too because we sound the same. It's one of our triplet quirks. We're not identical, but our voices are. It freaks my dad out and we like to have fun with him pretending to be each other on the phone sometimes.

"Hey, Eva," I call shyly over his shoulder.

Fraser bows his head quickly. "Shit," he whispers into the crook of my neck. A nervous laugh leaves my throat.

Shit is right. I haven't had the chance to inform Eva about Fraser and me.

"He swore, Mom; he said shit. You're not allowed to say shit. Shit is a swear word." My seven-year-old nephew, Archie, starts his lecture. I think he's going to be a politician when he grows up. He's book smart, acts like a twenty-year-old, and can talk himself out of any run-in with his brother. It's never his fault. Believe me, I know. I've witnessed it hundreds of times.

"Archie, stop saying shit," Eva cautions him.

"But he said shit. And if I'm not allowed to say shit, then neither is he. And who is he, anyway? Why is he on top of Aunty Ella?"

Fraser's eyes widen above me as leans back, inhaling a sharp breath with worry, sounding more like a growl.

"Is he a bear? He's the size of one. He's huge, Mom, and he sounds like one."

"Archie, be quiet. Stop being rude," Eva scolds.

Fraser slowly peels himself off me awkwardly, our ankles still bound, my dogs yipping away as he reveals himself to Eva.

"Fraser?" Eva takes a step back in shock. "Sorry, have I missed something?" Her bright eyes meet mine. "And what exactly are you two doing?" She looks at our ankles.

I bend my knees, pull myself into a sitting position, dust the sand off my washed-out Paramore tee shirt, then untangle the dog leads.

"Treacle and Toffee think they're cowboys today and rounded Fraser and me up. I'm guessing you spotted them. That's how you knew it was me?" Eva bobs her head in confirmation.

"My dogs have taken their crazy pills today," I say nervously. I wanted to tell Eva directly about Fraser. I'm mad at myself for not going earlier. This is not how I wanted her to find out.

Mom instructed me to head straight to Eva's after I left the retreat, but I headed back to my house to let my dogs out and the beach sounded so appealing when Fraser proposed we go for a walk. It had already been a tough talking day. The beach sounded uncomplicated. I crave uncomplicated.

"I'm sorry I was coming to see you straight after here."

"It's okay. So, you two?" She wags her finger back and

forth between us, jangling her statement mile-long length of golden bangles.

"Yeah," Fraser confirms.

Eva quizzes Fraser. "Still married?"

"Separated. Getting divorced."

I watch their private conversation unfold.

"Moving back here?" Eva asks.

I know she's only asking for selfish reasons. She loves me and doesn't want me to leave Castleview Cove. Maybe a long time ago she wouldn't have minded, but us triplets are stronger than ever.

"Yes. Buying a house here. With Ella. Eventually."

Eva's eyebrows leap up.

I quietly watch Eva consider her next question as the wind swooshes her long black boho style skirt against her shiny black Doc Marten boots. Holding on to her toffee-colored Fedora hat, her caramel locks float in the wind. She looks like a bohemian angel, as I admire her beauty. She's so goddamn cool. I wish I could pull off her custom style. She's unique and naturally beautiful.

"Wow," she simply responds, then turns to me. "You forgive him?"

"Eva," I exclaim.

"It's okay," Fraser informs Eva, as I squirm beside him. "Now is not the time, but Ella will explain everything to you. In private. The beach is too public."

"But dry humping Ella is acceptable?" she says deadpan.

Oh, yikes, Eva may be the tough one to win over. I didn't expect this level of coldness from her. She's so different lately.

"What's dry humping?" Archie screws up his face.

"Oh my God, Archie, go play with your brother. Why

don't you and Hamish try to untangle Treacle and Toffee from one another once Aunty Ella unties her ankles."

"But Mom, I want to know what dry humping is."

"Archie. Not today," she raises her stern voice as she replies.

I don't know what's gotten into Eva recently, but she doesn't seem like herself. She's our homely family maker. Our warm embrace. Today she's cold, pissed off, and clearly past her boiling point. And she never speaks to Archie or Hamish with a fierce tongue.

Unaffected, Archie rolls his eyes, then turns his attention toward my dogs.

"Hey, are you okay?"

"Nope." Her eyes glaze.

"Wanna talk about it?" I finally release mine and Fraser's ankles, allowing us to stand. Now free, Treacle and Toffee take off at high speed, with Archie and Hamish blazing a trail after them.

"Nope. Tomorrow maybe, but not today, Ella."

I fold my arms in front of me and wait for Eva to have more questions.

Fraser clears his throat, dusting himself down. "I'll help the boys and give you two some space. It's nice to see you again, Eva. I'm sorry we didn't visit you earlier. It was never our intention for you to find out about us like this. I have more respect for you than that."

She sighs. "It's fine, Fraser. Sorry. I'm not feeling myself. But, hey." She taps his upper arm. "I'm happy for you. Ella's missed you something wicked." She smirks.

How embarrassing. My cheeks flush.

Fraser gives a small wave and a cheeky wink my way, then heads over to sort out the carnage I watch unfolding farther down the beach where Treacle and Toffee have dashed off to.

Little Hamish, who's only three, is being pulled along the sand by my dogs on their leads, his legs dragging behind him. I swear to God those furry dudes are out of control today.

Eva and I stare in shock, then burst out laughing as Fraser chases the dogs, arms flapping wildly. Poor Hamish is still being dragged, but he won't let go. Fraser's begging him to do so, with Archie on his heels, screaming and laughing behind them all.

All it does is spur Treacle and Toffee on, and they take off at high speed, as if they're competing in a dogsled race.

They clearly think this is another game.

"Your dogs are mental."

They are.

"I think I need wine. It's been some day." I try rubbing the tension away in my forehead that's been building.

"Me too."

"Still not joining us tonight for drinks?"

"Nah. I'm going to skip it. Next time, maybe. So, Fraser, huh?" She changes the subject.

"Mm-hmm."

"He's filled out. Wow. What does *that* feel like? I'm assuming you've done the dirty?" she asks coyly.

"You know me so well. And I'm not telling you how it feels. Anyway, you have Ewan; he's well built."

Us Wallace triplets do like buff, athletic guys.

"I wouldn't know. It's been a very long time since we've had any kind of intimacy."

"Eh, what?"

She shakes her head, begging me not to pry. "Are you free tomorrow? I have so much to tell you. And it looks like you do, too." She tilts her hat-covered head in Fraser's direction, who has somehow wrangled my two nephews and the dogs. *Good job.*

"He's a keeper. Look at how natural he is with my boys." Eva looks on in admiration.

I continue to watch him playing across the beach, chasing and tickling the boys, making them laugh.

"He's certainly something. He gives me heart flutters."

"That's never changed, huh? Must be the real deal, Ella. I used to feel the same about Ewan."

"Used to?"

"Mmm, things have changed."

She looks out at the sparkling sea, watching the ferocious waves in the distance crash against the high sandstone walls of the cove.

Deep in thought, we stand together in comfortable silence, watching the boats far out at sea glide along the horizon with the odd shriek of a seagull singing through the salt-thick air.

"Hey, ladies," a deep velvet voice interrupts our daydream.

Spinning around, we come face-to-face with the aloof and mysterious Knox Black. It's very rare to see him outside of his five-star resort, The Sanctuary, or his grand gated estate.

"Hey, Mr. Black," I say.

"It's Knox, Ella. How many times do I have to tell you that?" he scolds me.

I flush. "I know, but it feels weird. Dad always told us to address you as Mr. Black," I giggle nervously. Wow, Knox is gorgeous, but he has this knack of always making me feel uneasy. His stern scowl and commanding presence are incredibly powerful.

Today is no different. Even dressed down in indigo jeans and a crisp white polo shirt, walking barefoot along the sand with his black Labrador dog, Sam, his stature still demands attention. He's enchanting.

Jet-black hair mixed with dark, brooding eyes makes him a dangerous cocktail. You can feel it.

"Eva." He nods a curt welcome, stretching out her short name.

I watch Eva give a faint shiver.

Hmm, interesting.

Knox's gaze grows darker as he drops his eyes up and down Eva's incredible dancer figure. Their eyes then lock for a second. And I feel like I'm looking in on something I shouldn't be.

I interrupt their moment. Well, I think it's a moment. It sure as hell feels like one. "Have you been golfing with my dad recently?"

"Not for a few weeks. We're refurbishing the spa at the hotel." He pushes a little dangling strand of his black hair back off his forehead, his eyes stay fixed on Eva.

He rubs his broad, scruff-covered chin. "I actually have a proposal for you girls. Well, the dance school. And how we could work together. I would like to discuss that with you sometime, if possible." He looks directly at Eva again.

Well, this is new. Or have I just never noticed the way Knox looks at Eva before?

I speak for us both. "Eden's on maternity leave at present. I have a slammed schedule coming up, which I need to speak to you about, Eva," I address her, then turn back to Knox, "but you could deal with Eva directly and she can run your idea past us."

Eva dips her head, hiding her face with the rim of her

wide-brimmed hat, and begins playing with the metal buttons on her vintage, black leather jacket.

Knox and I look in Eva's direction, waiting for an answer.

As she lifts her head back up, their eyes meet again, and I'm sure I can hear the crackle of attraction bouncing between them.

What is going on?

"Okay," Eva softly whispers.

"Great," Knox responds stiffly. "Call reception, inform them we spoke, and they'll book you in for an appointment."

Eva chews the inside of her mouth as she bobs her head in agreement.

"I had better be going. Goodbye, Ella." He cocks his head. "Eva."

On a last-minute glance, he rests his gaze on Eva's lean thigh that's now peeking out of her long split of her floaty skirt. With a shake of his head, he turns on his heel and stomps off into the distance.

Both of us ogle his strong, broad back.

"Do you mind explaining? What the hell was *that*?" I ask with a gaping mouth.

"What do you mean?" Eva answers sheepishly.

"That, with him." I point in Knox's direction. "I could feel it, like you both wanted to rip each other's clothes off or something. That's what I mean by *that*."

"Hardly, Ella. I don't know what you're talking about. He is dad's friend. And he's way too old for me. His son, Lincoln, is only a few years younger than us. He's divorced. A gazillionnaire, no less. And I'm married—well, for now— for goodness' sake, with two kids. We are worlds apart. How the hell would that work?"

Married, for now? I'll circle back to that in a minute.

"Eva, there is no way you didn't feel that. I felt it. And he's hardly old; he's only forty-three. And he's fucking hot. Did you see his ass in those designer jeans? He's delicious," I tease, seeing if I can pull a reaction from her.

"Ella, keep your voice down."

I look around. Screw it, no one is paying attention to us and there are people way off in the distance.

"There's no one here. So, tell me then, Knox Black?"

"Oh my God, there is nothing to tell, Ella." She pauses. "Apart from..."

I lean in.

She continues. "...the time at the Charity Spring Fling Ball. Remember at the Sanctuary last year?"

I nod my head, remembering.

"Well, Knox asked me for a dance." I remember. He asks no one to dance. He barely speaks to anyone. Eva pulls her hat off and starts fanning herself as if she's replaying the memory. It's not even hot today. I thought it was going to be a glorious day, but the Scottish sun can be so deceiving, sunshine and cold air all at once. "Annndddd, when we were dancing," she continues, "he told me I was the most beautiful woman in the room. But I was forbidden fruit. Fruit he desired to taste."

My eyes widen. Eva pops her pointer finger in the air.

"Don't say a thing, Ella."

"Him?"

"Stop talking."

"You?"

"Stop it."

"Knox Black likes you?"

"Enough."

"Wants to taste you?"

"Shut up, Ella."

"Oh my God." I rest my hand over my shocked mouth. "What the hell did you say when he told you that?"

Eva places her hat back on her head, then wraps her toned golden arms around herself. "I told him I was married."

"And...?"

"He said if I was his, he wouldn't let me go to a ball by myself. He'd make sure everyone knew who I belonged to. His. Well, actually, he said mine, referring to himself." Eva plays with the sand beneath her chunky boots. "And then he said he wanted to... you know?"

"No, I don't know." I'm making her give me all the details.

"Well, you know, peel my dress off and stuff."

"And stuff?" I really am making her deeply uncomfortable.

Eva peels off her jacket.

"Man, it's boiling today."

It's not. Warmish? Yes. Boiling? No.

"So?"

"Well, he said he wanted me. And he'd been thinking about me."

"Holy shit, girl. And then what happened?"

"He instantly apologized, said he'd spoken out of turn, and promptly ended our dance."

"Why have you never told me this before, or the girls? Wait until I tell them." I clap my hands.

"Don't you dare tell Toni and Beth. Seriously, if that got back to Ewan. Not that it matters now, but seriously, Ella. No. Don't tell them. Or Eden."

"Okay, okay." I hold my hands up.

"Let's chat tomorrow. I have so much to share with you.

And you to share with me." Eva tilts her head in Fraser's direction.

We really do. Wait until she hears my news. Mind-blowing clusterfucks all around.

"Come to my house tomorrow. I'll make us lunch. Wanna drop the boys off first at Mom and Dad's so we can talk uninterrupted?" I ask.

"Yeah. I'll call Eden too. I'd like to speak with you both at the same time."

Must be big news. *Damn. I don't like the sound of this.* "Perfect." I fake a smile. "Shall we retrieve our boys?"

The waves fizz along the shoreline as we walk arm in arm, enjoying the fresh salty air, kicking the odd seashell as we walk lazily together toward the giggles, barks, and joy-filled air.

"It's so peaceful here today." Eva flicks her head back, her eyes closed as she bathes her freckled face in the sea air.

She looks more relaxed than I've seen her in weeks.

I hope her and Ewan are going to be okay.

We say our goodbyes and head off our separate ways. Unbeknownst to us, there was a shark lurking along the shore, but it wasn't in the water.

CHAPTER EIGHTEEN

Ella

A festival of cackles, whoops, and clattering heels burst through my front door, disrupting the obscene French kiss Fraser and I are lip-locked in. Thankfully, I haven't applied my lipstick yet.

"Oops, sorry." Beth abruptly stops in her tracks, hugging her bottle of wine.

"Mama mia, *merda*," Toni gasps a *shit* in Italian as she stumbles and smacks her face into Beth's back. "Beth, I almost kissed the back of your white silk top with my red lipstick," she giggles.

Toni glances upward, her mouth instantly drops open.

"Hey, girls. It's nice to see you again," Fraser rolls off his charming tongue as smooth as Casanova.

"Eh, you too," Beth says, her frown growing.

Biting my lip to stop my nervous giggle from escaping, I indicate for the girls to head through to the kitchen. "I'll be there in a mo."

"Mm-hmm," Toni hums, flirting her deep Italian hazelnut eyes up and down Fraser's colossal frame. "You kept this one quiet." She eyeballs me next as she drifts past Beth, Fraser, and me on her way to the kitchen, flicking her long brunette locks over her shoulder as she goes.

"How are the golf tournaments going, Fraser? Should you not be in California? Are you not competing this year?" inquires a confused Beth as she smooths down her immaculate super shiny, fiery-red shoulder-length locks.

The thing about Beth is she is genuinely interested in golf. Me? I only watch it to ogle Fraser. I've done so for years. But for Beth, this is her career.

As the CEO of The Scotland Golf Association, she oversees everything golf related. Luckily for her, the association's head office is in Castleview Cove, and she's built an incredible support team around her to manage and maintain the high standards of golf in Scotland. She's inspiring, a leader, and she appeared on the cover of *Majestic* magazine last month, only the biggest selling women's magazine in the world. I feel honored to be her friend.

"Nope, I had to dip out of this one. My mom's not well, Beth."

"Oh gosh, Fraser. I'm so sorry to hear that. Is she going to be okay?"

"Yeah, yeah. She will be. I'll let Ella fill you in."

"She's got a lot more to fill us in on," Toni mumbles, leaning against the doorframe of the kitchen. "Sorry, ignore me. I'm sorry to hear that, Fraser. Do send on my family's regards. Tell your mom and dad to pop in for an ice cream on me. They still come in every week for their date night, you know? My mama said they've been coming to Castle Cones Ice Cream Parlor every Wednesday since they were eighteen years old, when my Nonna and Nonno used to run the business."

Toni now runs Castle Cones. Her parents handed over

the ice cream parlor two years ago now. She's renovated every inch of the tourist attraction, and this year she won the title of Best in Flavor at the Ice Cream Awards for their Coconut Orange Crunch. It's dreamy and I imagine it's what drinking a tropical island would taste like.

"I'll let them know. They will love that." He grins boyishly. "Now, I'm off. Have a great night, girls. And we will catch up before I go, Beth. I'd like to speak to you about some opportunities to work with the association. I'm only here for another week. But could we meet up?"

"One hundred percent, sounds intriguing. Let me give you my phone number." Beth pulls her phone from her black patent clutch, and the pair of them exchange numbers. "Done. Cool. I'll leave you two to say your farewells. And we'll speak later. Bye, Fraser." Beth wiggles her hips down my hallway.

Low whispering begins in the kitchen between Toni and Beth, making Fraser and I laugh.

"They will want to know everything. You know that, right?" I smirk.

"Oh, I know." A spontaneous laugh breaks from his chest. "Tell them I'm fucking ah-ma-zing in the sack."

"We left high school a very long time ago. We don't talk about stuff like that anymore."

Yeah, right.

"I wish you did." His eyes gleam with mischief. "On a serious note, I know you trust those girls with your life. You can tell them. I need to stop worrying about what other people think of me. But can you let them know to keep mum until it's all officially out in the open?"

"Oh, they won't say anything. The girl code pact we made when we were fourteen still stands strong."

He chuckles. "You still have that?"

"Yes." I raise my hand, pointing to my fingers as I run through our five very simple pact rules. "No sharing each other's secrets, no dating ex-boyfriends, no lies, no talking about each other behind each other's backs, and most importantly." I point to my thumb. "If your outfit looks like shit, be honest and tell the person to change it. Simple," I finish with a straight face.

"I think the last one should be changed to no sexy dresses allowed and passed as a law." Fraser tries to hide his smirk. "Because I would quite like you to change into something less revealing. You're making my cock twitch seeing you in this sheer black mesh dress. And I like those leopard print heels you have on. Save them for me one day."

"I have a crop top and shorts on underneath. You can't see anything." I exhale, smoothing out my figure-hugging dress that's kissing my curves.

"I don't have to see. I know what's under this dress, and it's fucking wicked." Fraser leans in, planting a lusty kiss to my magic spot behind my ear, licking as he does, then he blows hot breaths against it. He accurately hits the spot every time. I could have him do this for hours. It feels incredible. I reckon I could have an orgasm from this alone. A gentle sprinkle of sparkles waves down my spine into my core.

Leaning back suddenly, he says. "I need to go, Bella."

"You're such a tease."

"I'm leaving a reminder of what you can look forward to tomorrow. Plus, you have a blow job bet to pay off from this morning. Four left. I can't wait to fuck your mouth again." He thumbs my swollen bottom lip, remembering what we did a mere hour ago in my bedroom. He sucks in a breath. "But I need to leave now before I tear this sexy-ass dress off your body and have my wicked way with you right here in front of your friends."

I would let him, too.

I eventually wave Fraser goodbye. Shaking myself out to drum some sensibility back into my head, I clatter my front door shut.

Time to face the music. Turning around in the hall, I'm greeted by full-on fiendish grins from Toni and Beth.

"Tell. Us. Everything." Beth shuffles from side to side on her feet excitedly.

"Now." Toni thrusts a full glass of wine into my hand.

I'm going to need this.

"Let's go into the living room. You two will never believe this."

Fraser

"She's over there." Beth points to Ella as she casually takes a sip of her cocktail.

From across the nightclub, I spot Ella, full of liquid spirit, sandwiched between two guys, both grinding front and back on the dance floor. A ball of fire burns in the pit of my stomach as I spot their hands on her. I'm about to fucking lose it.

"What the fuck is she playing at?" I yell over the thumping music of The Vault as my blood boils.

Managed by my old high school buddy and Beth's brother, Roman, The Vault is the only nightclub in town, and as always, it's jumping.

Formerly an old bank, they have converted the teller booths into a fifty-foot-long bar along one side of the club. Gold and black interior throughout, it's a sparkling metallic extravaganza of light and shade. The entire back wall behind the deejay booth sparkles with recessed lighting, making it look like one giant velvet button-back sofa.

"She's been on a mission since we arrived, and now she's out of control. She said she wanted to forget about everything tonight," Beth explains.

I know how she feels.

"Hence the reason I called you," Beth confirms.

As I watch, Ella trails her hands up her waist, over her glorious tits, and splays her hands through her hair, all the while weaving her hips from side to side.

The glowing spotlight shining above her lights her platinum-white hair up like a halo. She's my angel. Except she's not right now.

My muscles tighten as the guy to her front suddenly grabs her hip into his and starts grinding against her rougher now.

"Fuck this."

"Go give 'em hell," Beth laughs from behind me.

Winding my way through the thick sea of dancers, I eventually reach Ella and her two new sleazy dance partners.

"Excuse me, mate," I say to the guy positioned at her front. Eyes closed, lost in the music and one hundred percent three sheets to wind on cocktails, Ella hasn't noticed me.

Flattening my arm out to place a barrier between him and Ella, I say, "Do you mind taking your hands off my girlfriend?"

The guy behind pops his head up, spotting me instantly. Callum.

Shit.

"Girlfriend? The last time I checked, you were fucking

married, Fraser Farmer," he punctuates my name with a snarl.

Aw hell. I don't want to cause a scene.

"Fray-zurr?" Ella slurs, responding to Callum. She giggles. "Come join us." She flaps her wrist about, beckoning me to her.

She really is stupidly drunk, barely able to hold her head up as it rolls about.

"I don't want any trouble," I try reasoning with Callum. "But I'm taking Ella home now."

"The fuck you are. She's staying here with me." Callum curls his lips, smirking, then snakes his arm around her waist.

I flex my fingers, then draw them into fists. "Let go of her or I won't be held responsible for what I do next."

Callum, full of liquid courage, shouts back, "I don't think so." He shakes his head cockily. "You are married. Ella is not with you. She is certainly *not* your girlfriend."

"Frayzurrrr has a wife. A wife whooze not a wife." She laughs uncontrollably. "We are a reallllly fuckt-up threesomeness." She hiccups.

"See. You have a wife. Ella is not your girlfriend," Callum confidently reiterates his point. "Because she was with me until a few days ago."

I'm done with this prick. "From what I've heard, you couldn't keep her satisfied, and you hadn't had sex for *six* weeks, Callum. She was definitely *not* with you. And you want to know how I know? Because she was with me the night she dumped you."

"Fuck you, Fraser." He pushes Ella out of his arms like a rag doll into mine.

"What the fuck is wrong with you? You do not treat her

like that. Do you hear me? Fucking pushing a woman," I rage, stroking Ella's back tenderly.

"Mmm, you smell nice." She nestles in.

"Hey, calm down, Fraser. Everyone's looking," Beth yells from behind me.

With Ella firmly planted against my chest, I look around and sure enough, I have drawn an audience. I think the table in the corner has heated popcorn, preparing themselves to watch the show unfold.

"Fucking have her. She's a fucking whore, anyway," Callum spits with indignation.

Trying not to lose my cool, I slowly pass Ella over to Beth and Toni, who has now appeared. "We've got her." On either side of Ella, they hold her upright. "Please don't do anything stupid," Toni begs.

I don't answer.

Closing the distance between Callum and me. I stride forward with purpose. Callum takes a couple of steps backward as I bring myself to my full six-foot-three height. I'm double his width too, but I spread myself out more to create the desired effect I'm after. As I lean in, he leans farther back. *Not so cocky now, are we?*

"Here's what we're going to do, Callum. We're going to pretend this conversation never happened. I'm going to pretend you're a true fucking gentleman of epic proportions and you didn't just call my girlfriend, because, yes, she is my girlfriend, a fucking whore. Because you and I know Ella has more respect for herself than to fling herself at every dumbass with a hard-on, otherwise, you never would have dated her. Am I correct?"

"Ye— yeah," he stutters.

Going in for the kill, I reach for his hands, curling my strong fingers around his.

"You will never speak to a woman or handle a woman the way you did tonight ever again, or I will fucking break these pretty little paws of yours." Callum flinches as I squeeze his hands harder. "And we'll see how many bespoke fucking kitchens you can make then, shall we? Understand?"

I squeeze tighter. "Do you?"

"Yes," he squeals.

"Great. Good man." I wink before I give him another threatening clench. He winces before I release his hands.

Fuck me, if I haven't given everyone a full show this evening, as well as telling a full nightclub that Ella Wallace from Castleview Cove is my girlfriend, and I'm fucking married. *Nice one, Fraser*. I need to call my lawyer and Anna, stat.

I watch Callum cradle his hands, rubbing out the pain, anguish written all over his face. "See you around, Callum. Remember to be a good boy now."

Confidently, I turn around, walk toward the girls, hoist a completely inebriated Ella into my arms, bride over the threshold style, and like a caveman on steroids, I walk straight out the nightclub door.

Way to go keeping a low profile, Fraser.

Back at Ella's house, I lay her down gently on her bed. She's going to have one helluva headache in the morning.

"Ooooh, I don't feel so good," she mumbles.

"You're alright, Ella. Fraser's got you," Beth reassures her from where her and Toni stand in the doorway, having helped me get her home.

"Frayyzurrr?"

She pops her eyes open. "Ooooh, phantom Frayzur is here," she coos.

"Phantom? What is she talking about?" I ask Beth, confused.

Beth laughs. "Well, since you and she split up all those years ago, Ella has these imaginary conversations with what she calls *Phantom Fraser*, but only when she's drunk. It's quite something to hear and watch."

Huh? I raise my top lip in an Elvis curl and frown.

"Oh yeah. Watch," Beth instructs. "Hey, Ella, what would you like to tell Phantom Fraser tonight, babes?"

I perch myself on the edge of the bed next to Ella.

"What wouldn't I tell him?" She rolls her head from side to side. "For a stra, nope, sta, no, starrrters, I would tell him I don't trust his wifey. She is beyoouutifool. I'm not as pretty. Look at this kink in my nose." She clumsily draws a line down it; her eyes follow her finger, making them go inward and goofy-like. There's no kink. "But me no trusty her." She waves her hand about limply. "I think she wants to jump Frayzur's bones. How could she not? He's so beautiful and he belongs to her. It makes sense. Maybe they should stay together as a family. Make it work. That would be sooooo much easier," she rambles, rolling her eyes, expelling what she's been holding back from telling me.

My heart aches at her confession.

She cups her hands around her mouth in an oval shape and whispers at me. "I don't think she likes me. Mmmm, mmmm, nopy de dopey."

I shake my head in disagreement.

"She will literally have a full-on conversation with Phantom Fraser." Beth folds her arms in front of her. "But for now, I'm leaving before this gets any weirder." Beth grins.

"If you want to ask her anything, now's your chance. Alcohol is Ella's truth juice."

"Beth! I love you, Beth. Badass bossy bitch Beth. She's so cool. Isn't she so cool, Frayzurr?"

Beth giggles. "That's my cue to go. Love you too, babes." Beth leans down, kisses Ella's smooth forehead, and then exits the bedroom. "See you later this week, Fraser. And, eh, good luck!" Beth cheers back up the stairs as she leaves the house with a loud clatter.

Ella hiccups, making me smirk at her ridiculousness.

"You feeling okay?"

"Nopeeey. It's beyun a realllly looonnnnngggggg day."

"Want to tell me about it?"

"Nope." She closes her eyes, then pops them open, wildly looking at me like a mad woman, as if she's had a new thought. "Well, Frayzur, the real one, not you, Phantom Frayzur we had sex." She whispers the word sex. "Loads of the jiggy stuff."

"Really?" I tuck my lips into my mouth, trying hard not to laugh.

"Mmmm-hmmm and it was fuck-ing epic. He's really good with his hips and he does this magic flicky thing with his tongue, you know, down there." She points downward, making a face. "He has a magical tongue." She starts singing. "Oh yeah, Frayzurr has a magic tongue." She dances her fingers in the air and shrugs her shoulders.

She really has lost the plot. I let out a little nervous laughter and I feel terrible for taking advantage, but I can't help laughing at the same time, wanting to know what she's thinking.

"Tell me the things you don't want the real Fraser to know."

"Do you not like my singing?" She knits her brows together. "Ocht, well, okay, one." She points her finger shakily in the air. "I do not, nope, not at all, wanna be a stepmom. Stepmoms suck. Andddd I'm gonna suck more than any other stepping mommy. I shouldn't say this." She looks around the room, then cups her hands around her mouth to conceal what she's about to say. "Frayzur said today he's lost more sleep over telling Ethan about him and Anna splitting up. I know he's a little boy, but he's not his son. I don't think I could bring up someone else's child knowing they weren't mine. I don't know if he's stoooopid or a saint."

She removes her hands from her mouth, then rubs her tired eyes.

"Do you think he lost sleep over me? Don't answer that. I think he has a heart of gold, but I want my own kids, you know? Did you know Frayzur has a wife? A fuck-ing wife. Of course, woo, I mean, you know. We've had these conversations—did I say that right?—before." She pours out her scrambled thoughts.

She pouts. "I wanted to be his first wife. Life is so unfairrrrr," she moans.

Her rambling honesty penetrates my heart because I will do everything within my power to keep Ethan in my life.

She's thrown me for a loop with her inner doubts. She's clearly not happy about everything like she said and that makes me feel terrible. The last thing I want to do is cause her anymore pain. I want Ella and Ethan in my life, I know it's possible, she needs to give me the opportunity to show her that it is."And another thing," she shouts, fucking scaring me out of my wits. "I'm scared he won't come back for me. He nev-ver does."

"What do you mean, Ella?" I scowl, rubbing the scruff on my chin.

"Well, you know already, he comes back for his mom, back for family, back for funerals, back for golf championships. Golf is sooooo boring." She blows a raspberry. "But he never comes back for me. Nope. Never me. And he looks after a wife and son." She uses inverted air quotes around the words. "But he doesn't look after me. I would like to be looked after. Cared for. Someone he comes back for. But in all the time he was away, he never came back for me. No sir-ee, he did not. I don't know why I'm telling you all this again, Phantom Frayzurr." She trails off as she shuffles herself onto her side to face me. Even heavily intoxicated, she's incredibly captivating, but she's wrong about my intentions. I did come back for her this time. I just couldn't see a way out before. "I feel dizzy. Is the room doing a spinny thing? I feel like I'm on the spinning teacups," she whispers.

"Go to sleep, Ella."

Eyes still closed, she says, "I have something new to tell you, Phantom Frayzurr."

"Oh, yeah?"

"Yeah, Frayzurr signed a contract. He's a stoopid bumhead."

I'm more than a stupid bumhead, Bella.

"But you know the best thing I really like about the silly contract?" She doesn't give me a chance to reply. "Is he didn't marry her because he loved her, he did it because he had to. Do you think he really loves me?" She tucks her clenched fist under her chin as she begins to drift off.

How could she doubt me?

"I am one hundred percent certain he does. Every inch of you. You are a beautiful girl with a beautiful heart, and

Fraser loves you with his everything. He'd move heaven and earth to be with you if he could straightaway." I smooth my hand down her toned arms, comforting her.

"Do you think so, Phantom Frayzurr?" Her woozy eyes open slightly, smiling lazily as she does.

"I know so."

"Thank you." She rests her hand on my thigh. "You feel so real tonight, Phantom Frayzurrrrr."

I sweep the hair off her forehead, then thumb her soft cheek. There's no way I can spend another month or year without her.

Just as I think she's drifted off, she mumbles, "I love him, you know."

I'm rendered speechless for a couple of heartbeats at the words she's been holding back from saying.

"I know. You should tell him."

"I'm scared. If I tell him, he could break my heart again." She sighs heavily. "He broke it once. I think I'd die if he broke it again."

Well, fuck me sideways if this night just became my longest night ever. Time to fix this shit. Time to show her I mean what I say. It's time for action.

With that, she curls herself up into a ball, like a sleepy little kitten, and falls into a deep slumber. Tucking her in, I surround her delicate body in the soft black comforter.

I love Anna as a friend, but I've sat back, allowed too much time to pass, and allowed her family to dominate my life. I will do everything to protect Ethan, but I've reached my boiling point. Time to bring the game plan forward. Fuck it, it's time to be selfish. I don't think there will ever be a right time to do this, anyway.

It's time to prove my love for Ella, to show her I am coming back for her.

I'm a man on a ledge and I'm more than prepared to jump off. For her.

I slide my phone out of my pocket, locate the contact I'm after, and hit 'call.'

"Clark, are you ready to pull an all-nighter? Good. I'm ready. Get Lisa on the call, too. And Anna. We're doing this now."

I set the wheels in motion.

But nothing could have prepared me for what happened as dawn broke.

CHAPTER NINETEEN

Ella

"Uaaahhhh." I muffle a groan, my face planted heavily into the soft blanket of my bed. Well, I hope it's my bed. I can't bring myself to open my eyes. However, the familiar scent surrounding me confirms I'm home.

All I can do is lie here like a dead weight.

I can hear scrapes and small shuffling sounds. I can only assume it's one of my dogs eating a chew toy.

But again, I don't want to move to check. Everything aches. The only thing I can bring myself to do is peel my dry tongue from the roof of my mouth.

Argh, that is so disgusting, and I'm sure I've been drooling too. The edges of my mouth feel dry and crusty. *Beautiful.*

I lie here for another good few minutes before I cautiously move onto my side. Even this slight movement causes my head to pound fiercely. *What the hell happened last night? I remember nothing after my fourth, fifth, or maybe it was my sixth tequila shot.*

Man, do I feel bad? I am *never* drinking again.

I peel one eye open to check where I am, instantly coming eye to eye with Eden sitting sideways on my gray velvet dressing table stool as she rakes through my makeup drawer. It wasn't the dog making the noise after all.

"Morning, sleeping beauty." She waves her hand dismissively. "Although it is almost noon."

"How did I get home?" I grumble, glancing quickly down to check my clothing status. Relief washes over me, witnessing I'm still in last night's dress. *Thank Christ for that.*

"Fraser brought you home. Beth called him. You put on quite a performance last night, sandwiched between two men, one of them being Callum." Eden drops the lipstick she's been considering swiping back into my drawer, then eyeballs me accusingly.

"Aw, man." I roll over onto my back, rubbing my fingers deep into my temples.

I'm alerted to Eva's presence as she jumps in with her two cents from my bedroom window seat. "And apparently you told Callum and whoever else you were with that Fraser's wife wasn't his wife, and you, he, and she were a clusterfuck."

Oh, crap.

Worry envelops me as I feel a full-on flush wave across my skin, making my hands clammy as my heart races.

"And I know everything about Fraser's circumstances. Eden filled me in, as has Fraser," Eva says deadpan. "You need to get up. Shower, take last night's makeup off, wipe the slobber off your chin—'cause you've been drooling worse than your dogs do—get your shit together, and get down the stairs. Now. Fraser needs you."

Eva drops her legs off the ledge of the window seat, then promptly walks out of my bedroom, leaving her unique cedar wood scent everywhere. *Oh, that's pungent and is making me feel nauseous, although candy floss could make me feel sick today, I reckon.* "You have ten minutes," she calls back as she moves down the stairs.

"What's crawled up her ass?" I look to Eden for an answer.

She flicks her head, quickly motioning to my adjoining bathroom. "Go on. In the shower. I'll meet you downstairs. You smell bad, like brewery bad. I reckon I could sniff myself drunk from your fumes," she jests softly.

Eden stands, then leaves my bedroom, too.

For the life of me, I can't recall what the hell happened last night. *Have I jeopardized everything between Fraser and me? I sure as hell hope not.*

I had better get a move on. Eva's on marching order duty and she sure looks pissed. We had lunch plans today. Maybe she's annoyed at me for messing up our day and me not making her my priority again. She's been super prickly recently; well, I say recently, but the last eleven months with her have been an emotional roller-coaster. Our normal sunshine girl has a permanent dark cloud hanging over her at the moment.

And what did I do in that nightclub? It must be bad. *Yikes.*

As I tentatively make my way to my bathroom, I catch a glimpse of myself in the wardrobe mirror.

Remnants of my red lipstick stains my lips and the surrounding skin. Last night's mascara lines not only my eyes but it's smudged my cheeks. And don't get me started on my nest of hair. It looks like an angry bird made camp, then set fire to it. Holy shit, I look as hellish as I feel.

I take forever to get showered and ready. I'm on the verge of being sick, sweating buckets, or passing out—maybe all three.

I choose loose black sweatpants and a crop top; I can't bear anything encroaching on my rolling stomach today. It's definitely a no makeup and hair flung up kind of day, too.

Precariously, I trudge down the stairs, holding on to the walls on either side to steady me.

Rounding the corner, I slowly shuffle my sorry hungover backside from my hallway to my kitchen. I hope my dogs don't bark as soon as they see me. It already feels like a kennel of howling wolves has taken up residency in my brain.

As I enter my kitchen doorway, I find Eden and Eva leaning against the units. Concern shadows their faces.

"I need water," I say groggily, rubbing my hand across my forehead.

Unexpectedly, Hunter's here too, his bulging arms folded tightly across his body with his ankles crossed. At six foot four, he looks out of place in my little kitchen as his head almost touches the ceiling.

"What are you doing here? Aren't we were supposed to be having a girly lunch today?" I frown, although I think the only things I could stomach are a chocolate bar and fizzy juice. "Christ, has someone died?" That sudden thought bounces in. "Is that why you're all here?"

Hunter raises his eyebrows, then motions with his head to the corner of the kitchen.

On the floor, sits Fraser in yesterday's clothes. His head slumped with his baseball cap down as far as it can go. And he's pulled his tall legs into himself, his forearms resting on the tops of his bent knees.

My hand goes to my heart.

Dropping my knees to the floor, I crawl over to him.

"Fraser? What's going on?" I coax.

Apart from his head shaking back and forth slowly, Fraser doesn't move.

I place my hand on his knee.

"Please don't, Ella," Fraser says, pushing my hands off him.

Don't?

I snap my head around quickly, causing a wave of nausea to course through my body.

"Will someone please tell me what is wrong? What has happened? Did I do something wrong last night?"

Hunter flashes the palms of his hands in my direction. "Now, you're not to freak out," he says calmly, looking down.

I sit back on my heels.

'Well, now that you've said that, Hunter, I'm clearly going to freak out. Will someone please tell me what is wrong?" I shrill, as I pat my stomach gently, feeling the urge to be sick.

"Calm down, Ella," Eden says as she shoves her finger into her mouth and begins biting her nails.

Why is she so nervous? I bounce my eyes between them all.

My heart races out of control. "I swear if someone doesn't tell me what's going on now, I'm really going to lose my shit."

"It's easier if I show you," Hunter says.

As he steps sideways, he reveals a tower of newspapers behind him.

He passes me one.

I sit next to Fraser and lean back against the kitchen unit.

"Oh my God." My mouth hangs open in shame.

There in full color, splashed across the front page of the *National News*, are pictures of Fraser lying on top of me at the beach, laughing, with the headline, *Farmer Caught Cheating.*

"No, no, no," I whisper.

Hunter places a different national newspaper on top, then another and another. We're on the front of every Sunday newspaper and with each one Hunter stacks into my arms, the headlines become worse.

Farmer Rekindles Old Flame.

Horny Farmer Scores a Hole in One.

Fraser Farmer: Cheating Scandal.

Farmer's Highland Fling.

Sex Escorts: Farmer Paid Me.

Farmer Scores Himself a New Birdie.

Farmer's Secret Mistress.

Farmer's Affair with High School Sweetheart.

And the images become more sordid and taken out of context as they stack up.

Fraser and I outside his parents' house yesterday, where it looks like we're fighting and we weren't. Photos of us holding hands, then kissing.

Photos of me in the nightclub last night sandwiched between two guys, one I recognize as Callum. *I don't remember dancing with him.*

There are photos of Fraser coming out of a private entryway. Apparently, it's the escort agency he used to frequent.

Ones of us leaving my house, entering my house, us leaving Champs restaurant the other night. They're relentless.

And the last one Hunter places on top of the ever-growing pile is one of Fraser threatening Callum in the nightclub last night with an inset picture of me being held up by Toni and Beth with the headline, *Farmer Fights for*

Punch Drunk First Love.

This is bad. Super bad.

And I look like a drunk deranged tart in my see through dress and inebriated state.

My stomach lurches.

I look sideways to Fraser still crouched in the corner; he hasn't lifted his head to face me yet.

Skim reading the newspaper on my lap, the words *mistress, cheat, escort,* and *liar* jump off the page.

I drop the lot on the floor with a loud thump, the pages slide across the floor, then I cover my face in horror. I can't even bring myself to look my sisters in the eye.

Lightheadedness takes over.

This is worse than anything I possibly ever could have imagined and not exactly how we planned this to go.

Moving to lie down, I lay myself flat across the cool black floor.

I'm the girl who stays away from scandal, keeps to herself, lives a mediocre, uneventful life.

These images are not an accurate reflection of me. Not even close. Last night was my first night out in months, and I'll admit I drank to get drunk. I wanted to lose myself. Escape. Just for a short while.

For the last year, I've been doing all I can to support everyone when they need me. My social life has been next to nonexistent because I've been way too busy... too tired. Before then I was your number one party girl, but things changed, my life changed and so did my responsibilities.

And poor Fraser. He was trying to make everything right in the next few weeks for everyone concerned. Trying to fix everything so we could be together.

He doesn't deserve this.

My hands still covering my face, I whisper into them. "I

never wanted this." I shake my head lightly. It's already pounding and getting worse by the minute. "Why has this happened?"

"Because you were careless," Eva hisses savagely.

In shock, I move my hands and tilt my head to look up at her.

"Yesterday, you two were cavorting all over the beach. Not thinking about the consequences. You've been playing a risky game with no thought behind your actions. You two aren't in high school anymore. This is real life," she says firmly, with her arms folded tightly across her denim-clad chest.

Not knowing what to say, I keep my mouth shut and let Eva continue.

"To the outside world, Fraser is married with a son. And you look like the whore who broke them up. Did you seriously think you could flaunt yourselves all over town the way you have been without being seen or photographed together? Fraser isn't some random guy anymore; he's a pro athlete. Admired and followed everywhere. You two asked for this, Ella. So, when you say you didn't and ask why it happened, it's because of your careless behavior. Did you even think about Anna in all of this, Ella? She's been made to look like a complete fool," Eva finishes her lecture on an exasperated breath, like she's been desperate to get it all out of her system.

Awkwardness hangs in the air.

She's not on my side.

The only thing I hear are the sounds from Fraser's phone vibrating and pinging repeatedly.

I can only imagine the notifications, texts, emails, and calls he's been screening since the early hours of the morning.

"Right," I whisper, utterly at a loss for what to say.

Neither Hunter nor Eden say anything either, showing they both agree.

Eva continues again. "Today was supposed to be me coming here to let you both know Ewan and I have separated. I've asked him for a divorce." Startled by the sudden confession, Eden snaps her head in Eva's direction. "I needed to speak with you both, properly, explain everything." Eva bites her lips, desperately trying to hold back her tears. "And now, well, it's turned into the Ella and Fraser show. When I needed *you* today, not the other way around. So, I'm mad at you for stealing my thunder. Mad at you for being careless. Mad at you for taking risks these past few days. I needed you both to be here for *me* today. I've been psyching myself up for weeks to tell you both. Today was *that* day. The scandalous newspaper headlines are bigger than you and Fraser. This will have serious repercussions for our business, too. Did you even think about that? Trevor called me from the studio this morning. We've already had five moms cancel their kids' dance lessons. You are such a self-centered brat."

What? I've been holding up the entire business for the last year while she and Eden sorted their own dramas out.

Eva quickly flicks her tears away as they escape down her cheeks.

"I'm so sorry." I don't know who I'm apologizing to. All of them, I think.

Shame tightens around my heart as Eva's words sink in. She called me a whore.

And Fraser pushed me away.

Deep humiliation swamps my soul.

I drag myself up to stand.

Looking around the room, I don't know what I'm

supposed to do. Never one to be lost for words, my hangover is clouding my normally pin-sharp judgment and smart tongue. I'm completely out of my depth here today. I can't think straight.

In a few short days, I've shrugged off my iron-clad, feisty, cocksure cloak to expose the person I really am underneath—vulnerable, weak, and unsure about everything.

And Fraser still hasn't spoken to me properly. I think he's mad at me too, as I feel him closing up his cave. I'm sure he's currently erecting a giant *Stay Out, Ella* sign because he can't even bear to look at me.

Eden slides sideways toward Eva and wraps her hand around her head, bringing it down to kiss her temple.

"You're alright, Eva. We're here for you. Regardless of this today. We can tackle anything together, no matter what's thrown at us or how many things at a time. This newspaper stuff will blow over. We've got you, babes, you matter too," Eden says.

And what about me? It's a selfish thought, but who's got me?
No one.

And Eden's wrong. This fiasco will *not* blow over. It's only just begun. I know what the paparazzi are like. They will pick every morsel of meat off the bone until there is nothing left.

Eva needs me right now and I feel terrible for not being here for her today. I knew something was escalating between Ewan and her. I never figured it would lead them to divorce. But she hasn't spoken with us for a while now. She's clearly been trying to cope with it all by herself, so I've been kept in the dark as much as Eden has.

Leaning in, I offer Eva a hug, but she raises her hands up to stop me.

My stomach swishes about like a washing machine on full spin.

Eva has never been this hostile toward me. She's obviously really hurt by my actions. But I'm hurt by her words too.

Heading to the fridge, I grab a bottle of water, take a brief sip, and place it on the counter.

Deep sighs sound across the room from them all.

"Have Mom and Dad got Treacle and Toffee?" I ask no one in particular.

"Yeah," Hunter replies. "And I called Ivy at the stables to let her know you wouldn't be in to muck out Tartan."

I take one last glance down at Fraser. My chest tightens as every piece of joy escapes my heart.

"Okay. I'm going to nip to the bathroom," I announce, with no intention of going there. If no one wants me here, then why am I still standing in a room full of people who think I'm a *whore* and a *self-centered brat*?

I close the kitchen door behind me with a heavy heart, enter my hall, slip my sneakers on, and quietly head out the front door.

Double-checking there are no photographers lurking around, I run.

And run.

Away from my home, my responsibilities, the newspapers, the headlines, my embarrassed and angry sisters, and my beautifully broken Fraser, who doesn't need me either. He made that very clear in the kitchen, not touching or reaching out to me.

This is all my fault. I let this happen. If I had stood my ground, told Fraser to stay with his wife, told him I didn't want to be with him anymore, not given him hope and not listened to him when he told me he loved me, we wouldn't be in this position now. I wish I could press reset on the last few days.

With tears streaming down my cheeks, I race across the dirt track behind my home, over the fields, and I keep on running. With every heavy step I pound, the words I've heard today echo through my head. *Cheat, slut, escort, mistress, scandal, brat, liar.*

Whore.

In an instant someone pulled the pin, then launched a destructive grenade into my calm pond, killing all my hopes, the possibility of happiness, and a life full of love with Fraser.

We couldn't even face our first hurdle together.

Or make a start to the new life we dreamed of.

We are *not* inevitable.

CHAPTER TWENTY

Ella

Watching the sunset from the concealed nook in the cove, I shiver as the warmth of the rays disappear behind the dancing waves of the sparkling, dark sea.

Without my phone or watch, I've lost all concept of time, but it must be around seven o'clock if the sun is going down for the day.

I'm lost in my solitary thoughts with only the crashing sounds of the sea below licking against the edge of the high cliffs of the cove to keep me company.

Now and again the wind carries the faint echoes of laughter and shrieks around the corner as happy sun seekers catch the last of the day's rays.

Fraser and I used to sneak away to spend every minute of every hour we could together here. Sheltered by the rocks, you have to go treasure hunting to find this place. It's my sacred space I've never shared with anyone other than Fraser. And because it's slightly higher up, the ebb and flow of the tide doesn't interfere with its access. It's a twenty-four, seven viewing point, and boy, is the view spectacular.

We shared our dreams here together, firing each other up, excited about the possibilities of us building a home, Fraser becoming a pro golfer, me becoming a dance instructor. And we kissed here, so much kissing. Everything seemed so simple back then.

But we were foolish. *I* was stupid.

And childish.

Delusional.

Over the past few days, I've been living in la-la land thinking it was all going to be sunshine and rainbows, but today has been the wake-up call of all wake-up calls.

I've sat here for hours, watching as the boats along the horizon come and go, skimming across the freezing sea.

Pondering, revisiting, and trying to remember last night's events. Going over everything I can think of as well as reliving Eva's hurtful outburst and those horrific headlines.

I never imagined this to be our story. Part of me doesn't want to be woven into it anymore.

What I would do to go back to those carefree days of high school before everything became so complex.

Adulting sucks. Big-time. And my life, a couple of years off approaching thirty, is not unfolding how I would like it to.

Not knowing what to do, I've simply sat here, praying the Universe will help me out. But yet again, I'm still waiting. I don't think me sitting here in my deepest and darkest trench of self-pity is helping. It's repressing my ability to connect.

Physical pain thrums through my heart, knowing I have to face the music soon.

Heading back home should be my only option because I'm tired, cold, hungry, and I really need to pee; however, I don't want to face the world. Or face Eva. Then there's

Anna and Ethan. That poor family, ripped apart by our stupidity.

We were so careless and unthoughtful.

I know now the silver car I spotted several times yesterday must have been following us; it wasn't tourists after all.

I was in my happy bubble of contentment. But like always, even with the smallest of pinpricks, *boom*, my happiness bursts in a flash.

Fraser's reputation is well and truly in tatters, and the public now knows who I am. *Mistress*.

Never in my life have I felt so cheap and disgusted with myself.

Crying on and off all day has made my head pound, reminding me of my recklessness, and every thumping beat feels like the whomping bass of a subwoofer.

Cowering into the corner, I huddle myself in and wrap my arms around my bent legs as I lean into the crevasse of the rock not ready to make a move home yet.

Swollen and dry, even though I've cried buckets today, I close my tired, gritty eyes. There can't possibly be any more tears left in me to cry. I can only imagine my face is puffy and red. I must look like I've had a fight with a poison oak plantation because it feels extremely swollen and tight.

I lean my head against the uneven sandstone brick. Our brick. The one our initials are engraved into. *F & E. Forever & Eternity. What a joke.*

Dozing off, I think about nothing but the hunger pangs from not eating all day and the heaviness of my weary bones.

I'll stay up here to hide away from the world for a bit longer and shelve my problems where no one can find them or me.

Fraser

As I round the apex of our secret hideout, along the path of rocks, a little higher than the tide comes up, being careful with my foot placement as dusk sets, relief washes over me having finally found my beautiful girl nestled into the corner of our nook.

We've been frantically searching for hours. Eden and Eva have been beside themselves, and there's been more tears shed today than I've ever witnessed. We were on the verge of calling the police to file a missing person's report, but as a last resort, I suddenly had an epiphany to come here.

It's not somewhere I thought Ella would come without me, but apparently this is still her place to escape.

"I've found her," I bellow as loud as I can to everyone standing around the corner along the shoreline and pop my thumb up in the air, hoping they see me gesturing to them everything's going to be alright.

I watch as Ella's parents, her sisters, and my parents hug each other in relief. Hunter stayed back at Ella's place, looking after the children and the dogs, in case she returned home.

Moving swiftly across the ledge toward Ella, I'm desperate to make sure she's okay. Bending down, I reach out to rouse her from her sleep, and I discover she's freezing.

I panic. *Please let her be okay*, I silently beg.

"Hey, baby," I coo. "C'mon, Bella, baby. Wake up." I run my hands down her arms.

She moans. *Thank Christ.*

"Hey, wake up, sleepyhead," I urge her again.

Please wake up.

I thumb her swollen red cheek. She's clearly been crying for a substantial amount of time because her eyes are puffy and her cheeks blotchy.

I don't blame her. Today's been a fucking shocker of a day.

My poor girl. This is all on me. She's my responsibility, and I did a shitty job not preparing her for what's unfolded.

If I'd had more time, I would have sought professional media training for her. Part of my job is to always be prepared for the media. However, no amount of planning equipped me for today either.

Blindsided, I couldn't entertain conversation or confrontation earlier; I needed some space, pushing Ella away when I should have pulled her in, supported her when she needed me the most.

I have craved her all day. More than anyone, I need her.

I needed time to think. Clarity. To reorganize my plan of attack, *again*. I don't know what I was thinking, not reaching out to Ella.

Then Eva speared some pretty grim words toward her. She felt under attack. I'm not surprised Ella did a Houdini act after that. All day Eva has beaten herself up about how she dealt with her emotional outburst. She's cried a river, panic-stricken she'd overstepped the mark with her out-of-character, venomous tongue.

"Hey, baby, please open your eyes," I beg Ella. "I'm here now."

Ella's quivering breaths become shallow. If I don't move her from here, she's at risk of getting hypothermia in only her thin short top and sweatpants.

"Ella. It's time to leave. C'mon, we can't stay here; it's getting cold and dark."

Pressing my hands together, I rub them back and forth

quickly to warm them up, then smooth them firmly up and down her arms, enticing her to awaken.

"So cold," she chatters, moving her head to center.

Lazily, she half opens her lifeless eyes.

Thank fuck.

Quickly, I take my hoodie off and begin dressing her with it. "Here we go. This will keep you warm." With apathy, she tries to help. "Attagirl."

I pull her fatigued, shivering figure into my arms, surrounding her with my body heat.

"I'm so sorry," she barely whispers.

"Hey, you have nothing to be sorry for. It's me who should be apologizing. I acted like a prick today. *I'm* sorry. I did not handle things well. God, Ella, you've had us all so worried. I would hate myself if anything happened to you. You're my girl. Always. I'm here for you."

Ella nestles deeper into my chest. I feel her shoulders shake.

"Hey, hey. No more tears." I comfort kiss the top of her head.

"But I thought..." she says, "I thought you were pulling away from me. I thought you'd changed your mind. All of this is my fault."

"No way. None of this is your fault," I reassure her. "We're in this together. I just needed some space. I'm so sorry for pushing you away. I didn't mean it, Bella."

"I've been so inconsiderate, not thinking of Anna. And we've been careless." Her teeth chatter noisily. "You should be a family with Ethan and Anna. It would be so much easier for us all."

Not this again.

"Who would it be easier for? For her and Ethan? And what about me? When do I get a shot at happiness? To love freely? It would be easier for the Miller family, maybe, but not for me or us. And maybe we were careless, but part of me feels relieved I can finally share my truth." There's defiance in my tone, not believing what she's suggesting.

I want to be with Ella.

My soul longs for freedom. Without Nate Miller, I could be more than I am.

"You still want to be with me?" Her shaky voice is full of doubt.

"Yes! That shouldn't even be a question you have to ask me. I want you, always. Forever and more."

"I'm sorry."

"Will you stop apologizing, Ella. It's all my fault. I dragged you into my situation. And the papers are brutal. Those headlines and stories sold to the newspapers are all part of someone's greater plan. Whoever did this knows exactly what they are doing. I'll give you three guesses who did it."

"Anna."

"Anna? What makes you say that?" I scowl. "It's not Anna. She never wanted her name dragged through the mud like this. We had a strategic press release prepared."

We all agreed to bring it forward and release it at midday today. Anna only agreed as I promised I would do everything to protect her and Ethan. This gives me a week to sort the loose ends here, spend time with my parents and Ella, and then back to Los Angeles to break the news to Ethan.

But then we had to pull our statement because of the headlines. We are now announcing tomorrow instead, with plans still for me to go back to California by the end of the week.

"Was it Nate then?" she whispers.

"It's gotta be. He hasn't been in touch with me at all today. That speaks volumes. He has eyes and ears everywhere. He's always one step ahead of everyone. Blowing our press release to pieces before we could announce it was clever. Calculated. But I don't know what he gains from doing that."

I haven't figured out his MO yet.

"They called me your mistress. They know everything about me. Eva called me a whore," she says through shivering breaths, anguished.

"Ignore the papers. They don't know jack shit. And sweet Jesus, Ella, Eva didn't call you a whore. She said that's how the *public* will see you. She never said you were one. I was there. I heard it all."

"She said I was a selfish brat," she stutters.

As I rock her back and forth, I say, "Granted, she said that, but Eden wiped the floor with her when you left to go to the bathroom. You should have heard her. Man, for a little thing, she's sure got some fire in her belly. She defended you good and proper. Enlightening Eva and reminding her of all the hard work you've put into the business, the social media, helping with the triplets, running extra dance classes while you still have a life of your own. You're a phenomenal woman, Ella. And if it makes you feel any better, Eva has been beside herself since you went missing. She's blaming herself for this debacle."

"I don't feel any better. I'm so tired and hungry, and I need to wee," she whispers croakily. "And what about you and Anna and little Ethan?" She groans slowly and shakes her head in worry, nuzzling deeper into me. "And your career and everything? Oh God, Fraser, this is a mess."

"We will not talk anymore about that tonight," I deflect. There's too much to tell her now.

I lost three sponsorship contracts today via email. *Great.* As soon as any brand gets even the faintest whiff of scandal, then it's bye-bye. But to be fair, it's no great loss. They weren't even that great. Nate's deals are frankly fucking boring and lack anything substantial for me to get excited about, especially when he takes such a large cut. I've made it abundantly clear that I am interested in modeling for either a fitness or a fragrance brand. I've got the right look for that, but nope, Nate still refuses to pursue them for me.

"We'll chat in the morning. The most important thing is to get you down off this ledge, back home in your cozy bed, and we'll order some pizza. Okay?"

"Okay," she says slowly. "And a trip to the bathroom."

I chuckle. "Yeah, and that, too. C'mon. You've not eaten all day. You need to drink something, or you'll get dehydrated; that's if you aren't already."

"My throat's drier than a popcorn fart."

"There's my girl." I laugh at her joke, kissing the top of her head as I do, knowing she's going to be okay. "Your boys have missed you today, Ella. They're waiting for you back at the house. Treacle has been whining all afternoon for you at your parents' house. They had to bring him back. He knew there was something wrong. He's such a smart cookie." I try lightening the mood.

"I didn't mean to worry you. You have enough going on in your life without worrying about me."

How could she think that?

"You are my priority. My future. You're my everything. And if you think this little hiccup, we encountered today—" Well, it's a fucking giant-sized hiccup. "—will halt our plans to be together, you are wrong. But we've got to stand strong together." I stroke her back up and down lightly, squeezing her tight. "We may get pulled in two different directions, either choosing to do the simple thing or do the thing we have to fight for, but I'm choosing to fight for us, Ella. We both need to work toward the same target together. I'm choosing the thing I really want. I choose you. Us."

I sound stronger than I feel. If I could pluck any word out of the dictionary, bravado is the word I am leading with. My bravado has gotten me through today, as well as the last several years of my life.

Ella tips her heavy head backward, hooking me in with her watery emerald eyes.

She rests her icy hand on my cheek.

"I love you, Fraser. I have never stopped loving you."

I suck in a breath as she finally says the words I've been desperate to hear when she's not inebriated.

A hundred-megawatt grin curves my mouth. With her by my side, I can conquer anything.

"I love you, with all my heart, Ella."

With barely any energy left, she faintly smiles.

Dipping my head, I cradle her face and press a soft kiss to her trembling lips.

"Your lips are freezing. We need to go before you turn into a block of ice. Can you walk the few steps around the corner? I can't carry you; it's too dangerous at this time of the night."

It's not dark, but not light either, making visibility difficult.

"Yeah, Fraser, I can. Oh, my heart is racing. I'm so worried about us, you, and everything." She looks at me with a pained frown. "I enjoy being here, away from the world. But I don't feel brave enough to face my family yet, down there." She gestures down to the beach. "I'm not sure I can go."

Summoning her to her feet, I pull her into my arms.

"You are the most remarkable, tenacious, and strong woman I have ever met in my life. This spiral you feel you're going down right now. Fuck yeah, it's out of control. But I'm right here with you, through every loop. And I have a game plan, which we'll talk about tomorrow. We are in this together. Do not let them win. Let's show them all."

"Oooooooh, Mrs. Mitchell's going to have a field day," Ella groans.

I laugh, remembering the earlier events Ella is not privy to. "You don't have to worry about gossipy old Mrs. Mitchell. Eden's been busy today. She also had a run-in with her too when we were up by the castle earlier looking for you. Mrs. Mitchell grabbed Eden, asking hundreds of questions about you and me. Eden lost it. Oh man, you should have heard her. She actually told Mrs. Mitchell to mind her own business and to focus on her own affairs. She called Mr. Mitchell a dirty old pervert, informing her she should have him on a leash. She also told Mrs. Mitchell to watch where he goes at midday on Tuesdays and Thursdays. According to Eden, it isn't at the bowling club where he should be."

"Oh dear. He visits old Miss Kerr's beside me at those times," she grumbles. "The gossiper has become the gossipee," she joshes.

To keep Ella relaxed, I inform her, "Eden's been on the warpath today. Calling back all the dance moms who canceled classes, and they all reinstated their memberships. She set them straight. I'm not a cheater. You're not my mistress and I'm separated from my wife. The ball is well and truly officially rolling. I think I should hire your sister as my spokesperson. She's been incredible. God help the triplets. She won't take any shit from them as they get older. She could wrestle an ocean of piranhas."

Ella snuggles into my chest again. "She's my spirit animal."

She's mine too.

"No more getting comfy. Let's go, Bella."

"Time to face the music."

"Yup, let's dance." I muster all the enthusiasm I can.

"What a disastrous day."

"Oh yeah, it's been one big fat glorious train wreck of a day." I try casually brushing it off to keep her calm. "There's no denying it. But we're not sidestepping it, we're facing this together."

"Okay," she says softly, leaning out of our embrace. "Let's go."

"Hey, before we go, you've to promise me something."

"What's that?" she says through heavy, swollen, red-lined eyes.

"Please don't bail on me again. I need you."

"I promise," she wisps out.

I think we're going to be okay.

CHAPTER TWENTY-ONE

Fraser

Following Ella's great escape yesterday, I awaken to my ultimate fantasy come true. I've been dreaming about this moment.

Ella's leg is draped across my thighs, her hand wrapped around my bicep, and her lips rest on my shoulder. She's holding me firmly, anchoring me here, not wanting me to leave her.

Little does she know I'm not going anywhere.

I spent most of yesterday on calls to Anna, my lawyers, and my new agent in between looking for Ella all day. I have never been so frantic. My poor heart can't take any more surprises. If I lose her, I have nothing to fight for.

As we all pulled together yesterday, our families were a pillar of strength, providing me with confidence and belief everything would work out.

The urge to give Ella a good shake and lose my shit at her for running away from me was overpowered by the overwhelming need to scoop her into my arms and never let her go. The sight of her cold, slender frame up there on our ledge almost broke my heart.

I'm trying to be strong, but I'm barely holding it together.

Once her sisters and parents checked her over last night, there was lots of hugging, kissing, apologizing, and general reassurance. We returned to her cozy home to be greeted by three camped-out paparazzi pricks.

Ushering her quickly through the door, I made swift plans with Hunter to hire the bodyguards he uses when he's touring. They are flying in from Florida today.

The police removed our unwanted guests, and Mr. Riley from next door, who is the Chair of the Residents Committee, helped me organize the security of the courtyard. The heavy electric security gates, that have never been used, are now activated and locked tight.

I must thank him again today for his support. I actually think he enjoyed being part of all the 'excitement,' as he put it. It's far from exciting. Scary as shit, yes. Exciting? Nope, not a bit. He was so full of importance, I'm surprised he didn't have a clipboard and checklist to hand out when he was dishing out his firm instructions.

I feel awful inflicting this level of security on the other quiet homeowners, especially as this is all my fault, and I don't even live here. However, it now means Ella is protected and secure.

Last night I showered her under the hot water, washing away her fears and doubts, dressed her like she was a child, then tucked her into bed where I fed her pizza before she dozed off..

She looked the way I feel this morning—embarrassed, shameful, and humiliated.

Exposing my use of sex escorts was the worst part. I

haven't even been there in over a year, so whoever it was, has been standing by, just waiting to strike. Ella and Anna are the only two people I have ever shared that with, so maybe I am being followed, or it was Anna, like Ella said. It made me look like a sex addict. I'm still clueless who they spoke to at the agency, but I'm going to find out. I pay a fuck-ton of money to keep my identity under wraps, but the tabloids knew everything. I'm mortified. More so for my poor family. My mom and dad were horrified at those headlines in particular. I couldn't bring myself to look my mother in the eye as I apologized. I never intended to bring shame on my parents.

My lawyer is already on the ball and raised all the paperwork to sue the agency on the grounds of data protection breach. He reckons they'll settle out of court. I just want the truth. I want to know who asked for my details and who gave them out so freely. Any compensation money I receive will be given to charity. I don't want the money. I just want the information.

I'm so tired. Tired of all this shit and it's only just begun. I'm mad at myself for making Ella feel the way she does. Honestly, I can't believe she still wants me after all this.

Interrupting my thoughts, a gentle *ting* from Ella's phone sings across her bedroom.

Just in case it's her family checking in on her, being careful not to wake her, I lean over to grab her phone from the nightstand.

I read the text preview. Confused, I reread the text on her screen again.

Unknown Number: Told you, Bella, your time with Fraser is up. It was never going to last.

My blood turns stone cold.

Internally praying she doesn't have a password on her phone, I tap the message to open it, and as if by magic, it does.

I scroll through the previous messages from this unknown number. There's only a couple from Saturday afternoon.

He'll never be yours.
Your days are numbered with him. Make them count,
sweetheart.
Have fun while it lasts.

Who is this? And they mention me by name and use my childhood name for her? What the actual fuck?

I pull my hand down my face and sigh.

Yet more shit. How much can one man take?

And Ella never told me about the messages.

She knows I have a shitload of crap going on, but she should have told me. My job is to protect her, but I can't protect her if she doesn't tell me.

Gently slipping out from under the bedcovers, I pull on my boxers, fly out of the bedroom with her phone, and zip down the stairs. My heart races double time with each step.

Treacle and Toffee eye me as I move around the kitchen. Not interested in me. After all, I'm not the provider of food. They'll wait on Ella for that.

Psyching myself up, I absentmindedly watch the kettle rumble away, billowing hot steam into the kitchen while I debate if I should leave the mystery caller well alone. Cyberbullying is a police matter, but I want them to stop harassing my girl. And this person seems to know us intimately.

Putting off the inevitable, making coffee the exact way Ella likes it, I pour myself and Ella a mug of amber liquid.

As soon as I'm in the living room, I use the caffeine to flood my veins to give me a much-needed boost of energy and courage. Yet another bravado day.

Unknown number, what piece of shit does this?

I hit the call button, then the speaker button on Ella's phone.

Not expecting it to ring, it does, then connects.

"Ah, Bella, Bella, Bella. I wasn't expecting you to have the courage to hit the call button. You're braver than I thought. And it's a little early in the morning for me here, but when I saw it was you, I knew I simply had to take your call."

What.

The.

Fuck?

Anger seeps into my soul.

"Nate?" I gasp in horror as I hear his American accent drawl down the phone.

"Ah, even better. Flaky *fucking* Fraser Farmer. Although I wish it was Ella purring through the line. I believe the Scottish accent is one of the sexiest in the world. What I wouldn't give to hear her scream my name. She is one tasty piece of hot ass. Oh, and how is the man who is bailing on me, huh? Fucking hell. Fraser Farmer. Who would have thought?" He explodes into a maniacal laugh. "The man who has finally grown a backbone and wants to fight me. The man who is cheating on my *beautiful* daughter with his whore." His falsified sweet voice dramatically emphasizes every word.

"Fuck you, Nate!"

"Oh, now, now, c'mon, Fraser. You know it's all true."

"The fuck it is, and you know it. Did you sell me out?"

"Me?" He laughs casually. He's enjoying every minute of this. "Oh, you know I would never do such a thing. Why would I make Anna look like a fool in front of the entire world? You did this to her, not me. I can assure you, it wasn't me. Remember, when you lose sponsorships, I lose out too. You've got the wrong man."

I burn with rage and an instant wave of heat takes over my body.

"Oh, Fraser, you sure did screw everything up, didn't you? You couldn't leave it alone. Not happy with a million-dollar home, a beautiful wife, and the perfect son who excels at everything. Fucking around behind your wife's back, an affair no less, sex escorts. Gosh, you have been a naughty boy," he tuts through honeyed words.

"I never wanted Anna, the house, and the instant family. None of them are mine. You forced your daughter on me. You lied to me, and I will fucking bring you down. You know the truth. You're a lying piece of shit. You and I are done," I say defiantly.

His strident tone bitterly rasps, "Oh, but Fraser, it doesn't work like that. You signed a contract, remember?"

Looking out the window across the courtyard, I shake my head at his audacity.

"I never signed your contract, and you know it. You lured me in, drugged me that night, and forced me into a life and marriage with Anna that I never wanted."

"Oh, come now. Drugged? Fake marriage? That's one helluva screenplay story you made up there, Fraser."

I roughly push my hands through my hair. "Is that so? Why is it I am currently living in that storyline? And it's a nightmare, Nate. With you as the puppet master from the hellhole of horror town. And you know for a fact your daughter is unhappy too. If you love her, why did you contract her off? Like some goddamn piece of property. Do you even care about Anna at all?"

Something I can still never understand to this very day is why he used Anna as a pawn.

"Now you listen here, Fraser." His now taut tone snarls. "Anna was always going to be someone I married off. The right to make her own choices disappeared as soon as her whore of a mother died. And I never wanted *her* brat in my life."

Whore of a mother? Her brat?

I listen in disgust as he talks with complete disdain for his dead wife and Anna. I've really pissed him off and without thinking, he continues to spew his truth.

"I was always going to pick someone with stature, money, and fame for Anna. Keep the pretense up for her mother's little princess. You just so happened to fit the bill at the time Anna was letting me down. You were in the right place, at the right time for me. You were fast becoming a success, rising effortlessly through the world rankings. I could see how much you wanted the success, but you were naïve, which left you vulnerable. And Anna, the silly little orphan bitch, did everything to bring shame to my family's name. I wouldn't expect any less from the daughter of a low-life criminal and a whore. Expelled from school after school, fooling around with her tutor, falling pregnant to one of my staff. Pah. Out of wedlock? How dare she tarnish my reputation? Her bastard child will receive none of my estate. Or Anna. That's why I brought you in. To take care of her. She is not my responsibility anymore. She's your fucking problem." His cold, vicious voice pants heavily through the phone.

"Anna's not your biological daughter?" I'm stunned. I drop into the seat behind me, then stand back up again, not sure what I'm supposed to do with that unexpected news.

"Why does that come as a surprise to you? Come on, Fraser, keep up. My own daughter would never have disrespected me the way Anna did. And her dead mother is exactly where she belongs. Six feet under. Along with her deadbeat lover. Funny how history has a way of repeating itself. Like mother, like daughter. He was one of my staff too. He used to do all my dirty work for me, including my wife, it would seem. I never loved her. Her snake of a father only married her off to me to bolster his importing business. Stupid asshole never saw me coming. It's all mine now. My father would be so proud of me. She married rich, I married richer."

A sense of unease takes over.

"So, marriages of convenience and using women as a bargaining tool run deep throughout your family, does it? You don't marry for love? You marry for money, power, and politics?"

Nate lives in an underworld where I truly don't belong, where feelings don't matter and people are simply objects. We hold different family values, him and I.

"Keeps them in their place, Fraser. Look at Anna now. She turned a corner once she married you, had that kid, and settled down. I'm always right."

No, he's not. He wasn't there when Anna suffered the deepest of heartbreaks. I watched as she fell apart. Took care of her when she stayed in bed for days after he forced her to marry me, a complete stranger, and crying an ocean of tears at the disappearance of her baby's father, Lucas.

"What happened to Lucas?" I bow my head, clenching my eyes closed as if preparing for the worst.

"In my world, people come and go and if you dangle

enough money in their faces, people tend to go in the direction you want them to. Just like Lucas."

Well, color me curious.

According to Nate, Lucas simply disappeared. He made out Lucas wanted nothing to do with Anna or the baby. There was no mention of a payoff.

Giving my tense forehead a rub, I ask, "This makes little sense. Why do you care about us coming to all your family mixers, our social media posts, Anna attending golf tournaments, if she's been such a burden?"

"I'm a very well-respected man in the state of California, Fraser. A poor widower with a motherless daughter. Oh, boo-hoo. Don't we make a sad pair? But what a wonderful family man I am. Hasn't that little girl turned out well now? Perfect little family, wealthy husband who's a famous pro golfer, and handsome little son. It's all been helping me lay the foundations to become the Governor of California next year. I must thank you for the part you played. I've been using your percentage money to fund my new advertising campaign. It's pennies really, but it's helping."

The way he flippantly implies the percentage he takes from my earnings and sponsorships is mediocre insults my intelligence. It insults my hard work and skill as a pro athlete. It's hundreds of thousands of dollars, not pennies.

His backhanded compliments over the years have slowly stripped and chipped away at my confidence like a stonemason chisels sandstone.

But I'm done with his shit.

I'm now seeing him in a new light. A lonely old man with no love, family, or happiness in his life. Money perhaps, yes, but nothing else, and no one to spend the copious amounts of money with. What a sad, pathetic man.

Anna's mother never stood a chance with him. Poor woman. Poor Anna.

As Nate continues his delusional reasoning, I listen to him with the sudden thought that I'm richer in my life than him in so many ways.

"I'm an exemplary family man, Fraser. Beautiful family. No criminal records. Just wonderful. Bravo. Although you did kind of derail my campaign trail plans with this whole visiting high-class hookers and cheating on your wife scandal. That was something I never accounted for."

Nate's not a control freak, he's a megalomaniac.

And if he plans to become the Governor of California, the last thing he would want is a scandal.

If he didn't sell my story, who did?

"You're fucking crazy."

"Not crazy, Fraser, clever. A businessman. I'm always thinking ahead. Have you been thinking ahead? Planning for the future? Don't fucking answer. I know you have. I know all the shit you've been planning behind my back. I have eyes and ears everywhere. I'm no fool." He titters again. "You tried. You gave it a shot. But it's time to come home now. Come back. We'll get you the help you need, you know, for all the sex therapy you require after paying for escorts and the cheating on your wife stuff. We'll pull together as a family. Do a press conference, a few prime-time interviews, tell the world your sad story, your wife forgives you, the usual bullshit the public and your fans will buy. Because you're the clean-cut Fraser Framer." His villainous laugh cackles through the air, causing my skin to crawl. "Get your ass back to LA now"

"Fuck you."

"No, Fraser. I am *fucking* you. I have been for years. You are mine still. You belong to me. Your contractual marriage to the orphan girl is also not up for discussion. Be back by Friday or my cut from your earnings goes up another twenty percent."

"You can't do that." I panic.

"Oh yes, I can."

Why am I panicking? Screw him.

"Eh, I think you'll find you can't, actually. Because as of today, you're fired!"

"You can't fire me," he scoffs.

"I just did."

"You still have your obligations to uphold."

"Nate. You drugged me. When I signed your contract, I was not aware of my actions. I was barely conscious."

"You have no proof. Difficult to prove after all this time. And Rohypnol leaves no trace."

He confessed without knowing he did.

"I never mentioned Rohypnol, Nate. You walked yourself into that one."

Silence.

I've maybe got the upper hand here. "I am no longer playing your game of cat and mouse. I am done with you. I have looked after Anna and her beautiful boy for the past seven years. She deserves better than you. I'm so relieved she's not your daughter. You want to know why?"

"Why?"

"Because she was never yours to bargain with in the first place. She was never yours to sell off. She's not your flesh and blood. She does not belong to me or you. She's her own woman. A free one. She deserves happiness."

I need to get a DNA test on Anna. Stat. I don't trust Nate's confession until I have proof.

"You're wrong, Fraser. My house, my rules."

"Yeah, maybe according to you, but that's not how the

law works, Nate. If you're looking to play hardball, then bring it on. I'm ready."

"You'll regret this."

"Not as much as I already do. Meeting you was the worst thing to happen to me. You may be a bitter, twisted son of a bitch, but I will not allow your messed-up family ties of deceit, extortion, and blackmailing to poison me, Anna, or Ethan. It stops now. I'll see you in court. Game on."

With shaking hands, I hit the end call button and drag my fingers through my hair.

"Shit."

Having to suppress the deep scream within, my blood boils in my veins. I let out a low, deep groan from my quivering chest.

I may have blown everything. And I need to call Anna, make sure she and Ethan are safe. What do I tell her? Anna will be devastated to learn that Nate knows we had a plan. Will she be shocked to learn Nate isn't her father? Unlikely. She hates him. I'm hoping this may put a new slant on my case, too. If they aren't related, he can't dictate her life. He has no ownership, no guardianship means no marriage consent either. Now that gives me a buzz of hopeful energy.

I guarantee if Anna had known, she would have emancipated herself legally from him years ago.

"So that's the famous Nate Miller?"

My head whips around. Standing in the doorway is Ella, in the tiniest pair of black lace panties and matching bralette.

My girl.

She's the sexiest woman on the planet who fragments my normal thought path every time I lay eyes on her. She makes me forget all my worries.

"Yeah," I confirm. "He's your anonymous text number?"

Her mouth drops open.

"I'm sorry for dragging you into this, Ella."

"Don't be. I'm not."

I watch her in wonder, trying to detect if she's lying, but she's not. She really is here for it all.

"Why didn't you tell me about the text messages?"

"I didn't want to stress you out. There are other more important things to be concerned with. I was going to tell Hunter, but I forgot, and then I went out, and well, you know the drill after that."

"Tell me if anything like this happens again though, Ella, anything, everything. No one gets to threaten you, especially Nate Miller. He's dangerous."

"Okay."

"I don't know what will happen now. I think I messed up," I wince.

"No, you didn't. You tell your lawyer everything. The lies, deception, socialite climbing, marriage to improve his public image, Anna not biologically being his daughter. Contractual marriage. Extortion. Tell them everything he told you."

"But it's my word against his."

Ella pulls my phone out from behind her back.

"It's not. I recorded your conversation."

"How?" I ask, confused.

"I smelled coffee. I'm like a homing pigeon for the stuff. I thought you'd muddled up our phones. So, I came down here to swap with you. Or I would have expected coffee in bed. I've never had that before."

I make a mental note to make coffee for her every morning from now on. I'm making it my life's mission to take care of her.

"As soon as I heard you talking, I swiped left on your

phone, opened the video, and started recording. You don't need your password to open your camera. I've been standing here since Nate said the words, 'Bella, Bella, Bella.' I don't like how he says my name. He gives me the creeps." She shudders. "I'm glad you put him on speakerphone though. We got him."

"You got it all?"

"I got it all." She looks tired, but she's wearing a glorious smile.

"Holy shit. *You're* my spirit animal. I am definitely marrying you when all of this is over."

"I can't wait."

Liquid love fills my heart, my shoulders feeling lighter with solace.

At least now she knows everything I said back at the restaurant is true. She heard it all. I wasn't making it up. This is my truth. My life. Every fucked-up piece of it.

Moving toward me, she lays my phone on the table. We stand toe to toe. She leisurely laces her arms around my neck and pulls me in for a full-on luscious soft kiss. As if wrapping me with her blanket of calm, I breathe out a sigh of relief.

She leans back slightly. "You can't let Nate get away with this. Forget yesterday. Forget the papers. We know *our* truth. Let's summon your team. Pull rank and take the bastard down." Her piercing greens lock with my crystal blues and I couldn't love her more.

Chuckling at her confidence, I say, "I made a start yesterday when you weren't here, but you're right. I need everyone around a table today. Let's fuck shit up together. And we need to find out who sold our story to the press."

"We do," she says, with a hint of mischief in her eyes. "But first..."

"Fucking?"

"No, Fraser. Coffee," she scolds me playfully. "The dogs need to be let out, then they need their breakfast, and theeeennnn... lovemaking, not fucking." She wiggles her eyebrows.

She said *lovemaking* because she loves me.

"Your dogs *are* princesses. They get serviced before I do?"

"Yeah, but I will service you in ways no one else can."

She's not wrong.

"I'm on a promise?"

"Mm-hmm." She tucks her lips into her mouth.

"I like it. I'll make you a promise." I tuck a little hair strand behind her ear. Leaning in, I whisper, "I promise to fuck you with my tongue as you ride my face."

She wiggles her hips into mine, making me instantly hard for her.

"And that's just the warm-up. You and I are going to work out together this morning. Hard. Fast. And you're going to grind that little clit of yours all over my face as I lap up every last drop of you as you come."

Her lips part slightly.

"And we're going to forget all about our problems because my lawyer in America is still asleep now with the time difference and we have time. So, for now, we're gonna head back to that warm bed of yours and I'm gonna watch you fuck me while you squeeze my cock with that tight little pussy of yours. How does that sound?"

"Yes," she gasps.

I chuckle. "That's not an answer."

"Eh, sounds good."

"Better get those boys fed then, huh?" I lean out from our embrace, whiz around her, and then give her ass a firm slap before leaving her standing dazed and confused, panting, needing, wanting more, in the middle of the living room.

"I'll be waiting," I call back as I take the stairs two by two. "And you still have your blow job debt to pay back."

Picturing my days starting this way every single day for the rest of my life with her gives me the lifeblood I need to keep on fighting for us.

Even if it means living with two princess pups.

I'll even buy her a castle to put them in, if I can afford it.

For the next few hours, though, I'll cocoon her away, protect her from the evil agents and paparazzi that lurk in the dark, threatening to blow apart our one shot at living in harmony together. Because come midday, we start a whole new phase when Anna and I announce our separation.

Let the show begin, for real.

CHAPTER TWENTY-TWO

Ella

To say the last week has been the craziest of my life would be an understatement of epic proportions.

As soon as Fraser and Anna announced their separation, it was like the all-star circus swooped into town with me and Fraser as the headline act.

Castleview Cove became a hive of activity. Besides the golf tournaments, I'd never seen so many paparazzi around. We even spotted a local television network van staked out around the corner. *Have they got nothing better to do?*

Their announcement was simple and to the point.

Anna, Ethan, and Fraser were pictured together in black and white across their social media platforms, and it simply said, ***Almost eight years ago we met each other. We have laughed together. Traveled together. Stood strong together. Six months ago, we parted ways. We will continue to be friends. Co-parent together. Stand in our truth and live life to the fullest.***

No mention of love or loving each other. But the poignant words *six months ago* were purposeful. To protect me. Telling the world that I was never his mistress. It was loud and clear. And if the phrase *stand in our truth* didn't shoot a fireball through Nate's heart, I don't know what will. It was a direct message to him. I hope he listened.

I've sat in dozens of video call meetings between Fraser and his lawyer, Clark Johnson, this week.

Sat and listened to Clark's strategy plan dozens of times. So much so, I could recite his worst and best-case scenario plans word for word.

In a nutshell, in the best-case scenario we play the signed a contract under duress, nonconsensual marriage, undue influence card, which essentially means Fraser was forced to sign the contract with Nate and therefore the contract will be invalid. And because of exceptional circumstances, mainly coercion and forced marriage, they will annul his marriage. It's settled out of court. Fraser and Anna get their freedom. Done deal.

In the worst-case scenario, Nate denies everything, which is the way Clark reckons Nate will swing. Nate will raise criminal charges against Fraser for breaking his NDA, defamation of Nate's character, slander, and repudiatory breach. If Nate files for repudiatory breach, which means Nate can either choose to end the contract or enforce it, then he will also claim damages against Fraser, which will lead to a long-ass court case. Overall, Fraser loses a lot of money and his sponsorships, has lots of time off so no earnings, has to go through the full divorce process and there is the possibility of a criminal record. *Great.* And he still may never be free from Nate.

Clark did, however, make a very good argument for Nate not wanting to go down the court case path, as it will damage his reputation, especially if Anna, his own daughter, testifies against him, meaning he'll never get the Governor of California title he's after.

In amongst the media shit show and legal meetings all week, I've attempted to journal daily, repeatedly writing the best-case scenario out in full. Reaffirming in my mind what a positive outcome will look like.

Lisa, Fraser's new agent, has also been a star this week. She hasn't made Fraser sign a contract yet. She wants to let the legal proceedings begin and Fraser's contract with Nate to be terminated before he signs with her. Fraser has her contract. He's holding on to it for now. Her terms are like night and day compared to Nate's. The percentages she takes will mean Fraser's monies are mainly his, with no clauses to change the goalposts every five minutes. The expectations of Fraser performing and winning tournaments don't even come into the contract like Nate's does either.

It's a breathe-easy contract, and Fraser is champing at the bit to sign, but patience is required. Something we are running out of.

Through every meeting this week, Anna has been present, and I would like to say it's been easier now that they have announced their separation, but it's not. It's felt peculiar all week, like I'm a clown sitting at a funeral; I don't belong.

I've felt Anna's eyes on me throughout every meeting. She pulled out the pleasantries card many times, but I can see it as she glares at me through the camera. She's desperate to ask me something or blurt something out. She's holding her tongue. I'm pretty sure she doesn't want me included in any of the divorce settlement discussions. Which has to be done, unfortunately. Even if they do get an annulment, there are still separation terms to agree to, specifically around Ethan.

Fraser insists he wants me by his side every step of the

way. He wants me to know all the details. It's proving really helpful for me to know what's going on, and it's helping Fraser as he sometimes forgets some of the intricacies.

In addition, we've had to turn off all commenting across all social media platforms for the dance school, mine and Fraser's accounts, and Anna's. Before doing that, all of our accounts received some pretty damning comments and direct messages. Some so disgusting and threatening, we had to direct them to the police.

I didn't account for any of this. Being in the public eye is not fun. I've always been eager to grow the dance school's following across social media. Going viral and being insta-famous were goals. Now, though, having experienced the flip side, I'm not so keen. It's a hard pass for me.

But I'm in the thick of it now, and I'm riding the waves into unknown territory.

Do I still want to do this? Yes.

Do I still want to be with Fraser? One hundred percent, yes.

Do I feel out of my depth? Yes.

Do I love him and want to fight for him, with him? With every bone in my body.

For one entire day this week, I undertook one-to-one media training with a public relations specialist. It blew my crazy little mind. Who knew depending on what way I moved my eyes, sat a certain way, or said something in a particular tone of voice might make or break my personal brand? Me? A personal brand. I almost fell about laughing.

But hey, this is now my life. The girlfriend of a pro golfer. Fraser Farmer. My ultimate love. My tummy dances with butterflies every time he steps into the room. I can't quite believe he's mine.

Throughout the media training, I sat, absorbed

everything like a sponge from interviewing skills, how to answer on-the-spot questions, eye contact, facial expressions, how to bolster your confidence, what to say, what *not* to say. It was an exhausting day, but I did it. The course instructor informed me I was a natural, and I came across as approachable and friendly. I think I'm ready.

Currently sitting at the swanky glass desk in Hunter's office, Fraser and I wrap up our video call meeting with Clark, who meets with Fraser in two days' time at his office in Los Angeles. They have some paperwork requiring Fraser's signature in order for them to produce the subpoena for Nate.

"Thanks for your time, Clark. I'll see you in a couple of days," confirms Fraser.

"Looking forward to it. Have a safe flight, Fraser. And who knows, we may get to meet in person soon, Ella. I don't like this e-meeting malarkey."

"I promise I have legs, Clark," I jest from behind the desk.

He chuckles softly.

"Good to know. Thanks, guys. Speak soon."

With that, Clark leaves the video call.

"Right now, that's sorted. I need to eat. I am starving." Fraser's stomach grumbles.

Fraser is a tank. He never stops eating. I've had shopping delivered three times this week, and it's still not enough. He's eating me out of house and home. He's hardly been to the gym this week and yet his abs still look photoshopped. I don't know how he does it.

"I made dinner for us earlier. I need to grab it from my fridge, then we can head to your mom and dad's house."

Every night this week, we've spent it at Fraser's parents', squeezing in as much time as possible with them before

Fraser leaves earlier than planned. Fraser hired a moving company to pack up the contents of Susan and Jim's house. They are moving into rented accommodation in a couple of days, where they will stay until their new beach house is ready. They only have five weeks to wait, but Fraser wants them out of their old house before Nate kicks them out.

I've made dinner for the four of us every day and taken it to their house to save Susan cooking for us all. And hey, what's the problem with adding yet another thing to my never-ending to do list?

I'm being kept on my toes, that's for sure.

Under the strict orders of my sisters, I took the past week off.

I needed it, but it's been anything but a relaxing break.

Fraser and I have spent every moment together. In between all the calls and paperwork, we've made love. I don't know how many times now. So much sex and we still can't get enough. It's official, I have a Fraser Farmer addiction. He's the catalyst that's increasing my sex drive.

We have laughed, shared, dreamed, hugged, kissed, ambled along the beaches, and I even took him on a riding lesson. We confirmed what we already knew; Fraser is not a lover of horses.

I've never heard a grown man squeal so high like he did when Tartan made a sharp turn, then galloped at full speed across the field. I was laughing too much to inform Fraser that Tartan was being playful.

Having fun, enjoying *being* together has been awesome. Even the simplest of things, like sharing our morning coffee in the garden, have brought deep contentment into my heart.

My clouded worry has been slowly dissipating and I'm feeling like me again. All the vulnerability I have felt is being washed away as the days go by. The more we gain reassurance from Clark, combined with the separation statement, I feel like we have an actual shot at this now. In fact, I'm confident we do.

Fuck Nate, he's not holding Fraser prisoner anymore.

We're fighting together for his freedom.

Next week, it's back to normal, whatever that looks like, seeing as I now have a couple of temporary bodyguards, Liam and Noah. The best way to describe them is walls of muscle; that's it, pure and simple. Liam's nickname is The Fridge. I think that says it all, icy and enormous. Fraser assures me when the dust settles, I won't need them anymore. Thank God, as they are a little intimidating. I'm guessing that's the point.

With Fraser gone next week, I'll be chauffeured around, which I feel is totally unnecessary, but Fraser has insisted. His protection and thoughtfulness toward me melts my heart. He's so considerate and caring.

In the week ahead, without Fraser, I will be back mucking out Tartan daily, taking dance classes again, and helping Eden with the triplets. I have to resume my normal life.

I wonder if I can get Liam and Noah to walk my two boys from time to time. When I'm instructing dance classes, it would save me so much time.

I gaze around the immaculately tidy office, a chuckle leaving my throat.

"What are you laughing at?" Fraser asks.

"Oh, I was imagining how silly Liam and Noah would look walking my two dinky-sized dogs. Like two BFGs walking a pair of hamsters."

Fraser laughs at that mental picture, too.

"I love how your mind works. I want to spend every

minute of every day with you and that funny brain of yours. The past week has been like a dream come true for me."

My heart swoons.

"I don't want to go back to California, Ella. I don't want to leave you."

I've thought about this myself. Fraser going back to Los Angeles triggers memories of old. Of us driving to the airport, all the unsaid words that used to hang in the tense air between us. The feeling of emptiness as I waved goodbye.

These feelings are already resurfacing when I think about us doing the same again tomorrow.

I'm not prepared.

Fraser shuts my thoughts down. "You can erase your deep, concerned frown right now. We are not doing what we used to do. There is no sadness. You are flying out to LA in four weeks' time for the house move. We have video calls now and smartphones and seventeen billion ways to chat with each other. We'll even watch Netflix together over video call. And you are going to sit in on all the meetings I have with the lawyers and be involved with everything. I want you all up in my shit. Every day."

His reassurance makes me feel better.

I reach out to clasp his hand. Fraser changes the pace, pulling me with intent onto his lap. Hunter's hydraulic office chair hisses under the strain.

Straddling me across his sculpted thighs, he presses me flat against him.

He leans in, kisses me, and forces the seam of my mouth open. We kiss deep as our tongues dance together, gripping on to each other's hair, as if wanting to crawl inside each other's bodies if we could.

As always, our kisses turn desperate, our soft moans and gasps blend together, like watercolors on fine grain paper.

My hips have a mind of their own as they rock back and forth across Fraser's thick, hard length.

"I need you," he breathes.

Oh, this man and what he does to me.

And we're in Hunter's office with all of my family outside.

I can hear faint voices in Eden's home swirling around in the distance, with a hint of my older nephews squealing now and again.

We shouldn't be doing this, but as always, Fraser and I can't help it. We're drawn to each other by an electromagnetic current.

"Come for me, Bella."

"I want you to come too," I pant.

I arch back slightly to remove my black and gold buckle chunky boots. "Stop. Leave them on," Fraser instructs.

My kinky man likes short skirts and boots. Even better, he enjoys fucking me in both, too.

Rising, allowing me to free his glistening cock from his sweatpants, he pushes my skirt up, slipping my panties to the side. In one fluid motion, I slide down his impossibly beautiful, big cock.

Thank God I wore my flared black leather mini skirt today. *Yes.*

Fraser bites at my neck in reverence. "Oh, you are so wet for me," he whispers.

"I'm soaked for you, Fraser."

In this position, he instantly hits my sweet spot. I struggle to contain my moans as I quickly feel pleasure building in my core. Corkscrewing its way through my body, I feel the deep ache ripple in my stomach. Suddenly hot all over, it all becomes too much to bear and I need to come.

Fraser's hands grip my ass as he pushes me up and down every hard inch of his cock, digging his rough hands into my flesh as he moves me faster.

"Don't stop, Bella. Fuck me."

I grind my hips to his, sucking him into my body, over and over.

I feel so full; full of him inside me. I love this feeling. I can never get enough. Without warning, I arch my back, digging my nails into his mighty shoulders and neck as I come, clenching, milking him.

"Aw, sweet Jesus, baby." He slams me down on his cock as we both climax together.

The sense of euphoric release from us both hangs heavy in the air.

His eyes closed, he arches his neck back on the headrest of the office chair, gasping for breath as we come down together slowly.

His softening erection twitches inside me. I love this man and I'm sure he has a magical cock because no other man has ever gotten me off this quickly in my life.

Popping his heavy eyes open, his mouth explodes into a lovestruck smile.

With his arms pressed against my back, he pulls me in, capturing my lips, and delivers a soft, tender kiss. "I'll never stop loving this. Or you. Ever."

"Me neither, Fraser."

He presses his forehead to mine.

"You are my one and only."

"I know. You're mine too."

I want to stay here forever, but this is our last night together.

"We need to clean up and head to my parents' now."

"I know."

But we don't move. We sit here holding each other. Enjoying the afterglow. The peace and quiet. Just the two of us. Because there has been little of that this week.

"This was just the warm-up. We can resume this later," Fraser says. "I intend to leave my mark on you, so the weeks don't feel so long once I go."

This conversation reminds me of all those years ago when he left, too.

He didn't come back.

I want new memories to replace the old. "You don't have to because I'll be flying into LA before you know it. This is the beginning. And we can have video sex together. I've never done that before." He chuckles at my suggestion. "We don't have to make up for lost time or make it last anymore. We have forever."

Suddenly, a voice appears from the laptop. "Eh, I hate to interrupt, but could you take your forever elsewhere, please? You two are very cute together and all, but I have a meeting in this video room with my next client and it would be great if they weren't greeted with a live sex show," Clark's sarcastic tone sings across the office.

I shriek and hide my face in the crook of Fraser's neck.

Fraser reaches out and slams Hunter's laptop shut, then bursts out laughing. "What a week."

"Did you not leave the video room? I can't believe your lawyer saw my ass, Fraser," I squeal.

"He saw more than your ass," he teases.

My eyes bug out.

"I'm joking. Don't worry. Your skirt is covering your behind."

I cringe.

What a week, alright.

"Well, at least he now knows you weren't lying. You have

legs. Sexy ones, and a tasty ass. I love this ass." He gives it a firm squeeze. "It's mighty fine. And *that's* what NDAs are for: confidential shit."

Mortifying.

"Don't worry about Clark, baby. He won't say anything. I pay him enough to keep his mouth shut."

I'll never be able to look that man in the eyes again.

"C'mon. I need to say goodbye to your family, then head to my mom and dad's before I fly out on the red-eye."

My heart sinks.

"Only four weeks," he reassures me.

Sounds like forever.

CHAPTER TWENTY-THREE

Ella

Together, hand in hand, we head toward the first-class departure lounge. It's late at night, but the airport is a hive of activity. Red-eye flights are more popular than I thought.

My heart is racing with expectant grief at him leaving.

I keep reminding myself. Four weeks. Just four simple weeks.

Fraser stops suddenly.

"Before I go, I have something to give you," he says.

From the kangaroo pocket of his black hoodie, he produces a tiny black gift box adorned with a dainty rose-gold bow.

"What is it?" I ask with excitement.

"Open it and find out." He hands me the gift.

Untying the elegant bow, I slowly uncover the surprise within.

"It's a gold feather," I gasp.

"To add to your necklace."

The gold feather is slightly bigger than the one Fraser

bought all those years ago. And very shiny compared to my worn feather.

"The one you wear now is you, and this one,"—he pulls the gold necklace charm from its box—"represents me."

Oh, he's so sweet.

"I want to put it on my necklace, Fraser."

I quickly take it off and thread the super shiny feather through the delicate gold chain. Turning around, I sweep my hair to one side and wait for Fraser to hook it back on for me.

From behind, he snuggles into my neck, then whispers, "I love you." Then leaves a trail of molten hot kisses down my neck. An instant wave of goosebumps covers my skin.

Turning in his bear hug arms, I cup his face, thumbing the scruff of his goatee.

Pinning him with my eyes, I say, "I love you more than you can ever imagine."

"We can do this."

"This time feels different." I feel hopeful.

"It does." He runs his nose down the slope of mine.

We *can* do this.

We kiss slowly, passionately, deeply as the busy airport continues around us.

"I don't want to go, but I have to, Ella. Security takes forever."

"Okay. Will you call me as soon as you land?"

"Yes."

"And call me when you feel down or blue. Or if you're missing me. Or if Nate pisses you off or when you feel you want to punch something."

"Or someone, most likely."

"That too. Please don't shut me out. I'm here for you."

"Always. I promise."

He thumbs my deep frown.

"I'll require Botox after all of this," I nervously laugh.

"You need nothing of the sort. You are beautiful the way you are."

"Thank you." I bat my eyes, flirting with him. "And thank you for my charm."

"We're reunited. Together always."

I give my head a little bob.

Fraser threads his hands into my hair, pulling me farther to him for a predatory kiss. We stay like this, breathing against one another. Not moving.

He lets out a soft moan.

With one last gentle kiss to my lips, we finally separate.

Fraser walks backwards, our fingertips drifting apart, then falling away.

"Bye," he says softly.

"Bye." I wave.

Hold it together, Ella. Don't cry.

"Stay with Noah and Liam. You're my most prized possession." He gives me a sexy wink.

I nod my head in agreement. "I will."

With a final dazzling smile, Fraser slowly turns around, then walks a few steps through departures and out of sight.

"See you soon," I whisper to myself.

With a deep sigh, I head out of the airport to be greeted by Noah and Liam.

I can feel myself welling up with every step toward the car.

He's not here with me. Two minutes apart and I already miss him.

"Take me home, guys."

"Yes, ma'am." Liam opens the rear door for me.

Barely holding it together, I slide into the enormous SUV.

A deep vibration in my pocket startles me from my sad thoughts.

I quickly pull it out. Fraser's name lights up across the screen. Smiling, I press accept.

"I couldn't wait until I landed. I miss you already," he says, sounding melancholy.

The threatened tears waiting to spill, slide down my cheeks.

"Oh, thank God. I miss you too," I sniff.

"Hey, Bella, don't be upset. It's temporary, and this is the only time we have to do this."

"Until your next championship tournament," I retort.

"You'll be coming with me when I tour. Well, as much as you can. But I will always come back to you. Back *for* you. I can't wait for those days."

I feel the same. His words cause a whirlwind of butterflies in my stomach. I'm excited about our future.

"They can't come soon enough."

"We have to be patient, Bella."

"Yeah."

Silence.

"I have to go this time. I'll call you again when I land."

"Okay." I can't say much through my choked throat.

"Four weeks. Countdown begins now," Fraser reassures me.

"I know."

"I love you, Ella."

"Love you."

Only four weeks; I can do this.

"Oh my God, I can't do this," I whisper.

"Shut up or you'll spoil the surprise," Hunter whisper scolds me.

"I think I'm going to pee myself," Eden wisps out.

"You need to work on your pelvic floor muscles then," I jest.

"Piss off, it's not from the triplets. It's exciting," Eden says as she hops about.

It is.

Whipping his head around, Hunter puts his hands on his hips. "Will you two shut up or he'll hear you when he comes in and you'll spoil everything."

Eden and I silently giggle like we used to do when we were little girls.

"Children. I'm surrounded by children," Hunter mutters as he turns back around to peek out of the door crack.

Milking the opportunity, I spill some water on the floor under Eden's feet. Eden catches on to what I'm up to.

"Oh my God," she whispers.

"What now?" Hunter's patience is wearing thin. We've been hiding inside the restroom of Fraser's dressing room for the last thirty minutes. Our usually playful Hunter has officially left the building.

"I peed myself." She points to the floor.

Openmouthed, shock shoots across Hunter's face.

"You did not just wet yourself. You're a fucking grown woman. Well, all five foot two of you. What the hell, Eden? There's a toilet right there." He points, disgusted.

I hold up the water bottle and shake it about.

"You are too easy to punk, Hunter." I grin widely.

"Oh, you are so lucky we have to be quiet, or I would pour that bottle of water down your pants." He grits his teeth.

Cupping our hands to our mouths, Eden and I muffle our chuckles.

"And you, Cupcake." He points to Eden. "Will be getting a right good spanking when we get back to the house."

"Oh, goody," Eden replies, batting her turquoise eyes at her handsome husband.

"I can do that right now," he threatens, stepping toward her. Although I don't think it's a threat, more like a promise.

"Oh yes, please," Eden giggles, then covers her mouth.

I roll my eyes. "Oh, fuck off. Please stop, you two. I don't want to know what you get up to in the bedroom."

"The same shit you and Fraser got up to in my office, Ella. Oh, and the spare bedroom," Hunter says as his eyes bore through me.

"Oh," is all I can say as a wild flush spreads across my face.

"Yes, oh." He turns back around to his watch position. "I hear him. Sh."

We flew into LA last night, three days earlier than planned, to surprise Fraser. He's currently on a test photoshoot for a new designer fragrance. What I would give to be a fly on the wall. Abs for days. *Yummy*. I'm getting wet thinking about us reuniting and all the fun we're going to have.

Four weeks have dragged like a bitch. I realize now how mundane my life is without Fraser in it.

Although the phone sex has been pretty epic. He informed me my new pink glass dildo, which I've named the 'magical unicorn horn,' is getting thrown out when he returns to Scotland. I've become addicted to it, apparently. Or a-dick-ted is how Fraser put it.

He's not wrong. I can't go a day without it, but the whole time, I'm imagining it's him.

We've chatted every day, sometimes up to four or five times. Sharing silly things or video chatting as I muck Tartan out. Fraser gets up early to speak to me and with every call I know we are getting closer to being together fully.

As soon as Fraser left for the States, Callum showed up outside my gates, accusing me of cheating on him with Fraser. What a twat. I have never cheated on anyone in my life. I'm a one-on-one kind of gal. Asshole. Anyway, I set him straight, then sent him packing.

The media circus has finally calmed down, meaning Noah and Liam are no longer standing guard outside my dance classes, Castle Cones, or Cupcakes & Castles. Or the stables or the restroom. *Thank God.* I will never get used to it if we have to hire them again.

Nate was served. However, we have heard nothing back yet. I can only imagine what he's doing behind the scenes. He's getting ready for war; I feel it. We all do. The silence at his end is unsettling.

He's brewing something. Reviewing every single detail of the paperwork. I can sense a storm coming.

When Anna and Fraser broke the news of their separation to Ethan, Ethan informed them both he already knew, but didn't want to say anything. *Stupid social media.*

One of his friend's moms told her son, then her son told Ethan. *Just perfect.* We can't protect our kids from anything these days.

Anna and Fraser told him about me. Dad's new girlfriend. *Dear Lord.*

Now that came as a surprise. I wasn't expecting them to be so open.

But they made me official.

Fraser said Ethan was more excited about the fact he

gets two houses, two Christmases, and two of everything now. And more vacations in Scotland. Plus, he can't wait to ride Tartan and play with my two doggies.

We made it. Four weeks.

Lisa, Hunter's agent, shared Fraser's calendar with us so we could work out when would be best to surprise him.

Which brings us here. The three of us stuffed inside Fraser's private restroom.

My stomach somersaults with excitement. I'm utterly beside myself, but not to the point where I could pee myself like Eden.

"Here he comes," Hunter whispers. We begin to hear two muffled voices. One male, one female. "Shit, I think Anna is with him."

Damn. I didn't want to meet Anna for the first time like this. I never accounted for this scenario.

In fact, I actually don't think there is any good time for our first meet and greet. "Oh, hi, so you're the wife; pleased to meet you. I'm the girlfriend." *Great. Not.*

"What are they saying?" I ask.

"I don't know. Be quiet," Hunter whispers back.

We listen in, waiting for the right time to make our appearance.

Fraser

"Oh man, that was fun today. Thanks for coming at the last minute, Anna. I don't know what's wrong with my Range Rover. I need to call the garage, stat. I had plans to sell it within the next week to a dealership. It's never let me down. Just typical."

One more thing for me to sort out.

"That's okay. I had nothing planned other than moving some of the last of the boxes from the office to the new house, anyway. It's great we got in earlier than planned into the new house," Anna chimes happily.

"Yeah, it's amazing what happens when you offer a cash sale their way," I chuckle.

"Thank you for the house, Fraser."

"You're more than welcome. You're free from that prison we've lived in for too long. The new house is yours. Your father can never take that away from you. You're set for life."

"Thank you." She's very grateful. She didn't have to tell me. I know, as she's been much more chipper lately.

"I enjoyed today," Anna catches my eyes.

Today's been epic. They called me to do a test shoot for a new designer fragrance. They were specifically looking for athletes from across many sports. There are six new fragrances in the range, so they require six models. I hope I get it.

I've modeled for a couple of brands before, but this is bigger than anything I've ever done. Hunter's modeled before and he loves it. Nate has been keeping me small. On the other hand, Lisa is finding me golden opportunities everywhere, and I haven't even signed with her yet. She's my savior in shining armor.

I'm bronzed and oiled up within an inch of my life, standing in only a towel in my dressing room of a huge studio in downtown LA.

I catch Anna checking me out. I need to get dressed. I don't enjoy being around her half-naked. It's not what we do.

When we first got married, she came on to me a few times. She even suggested we share the same bed, for

Ethan's sake, but I have never seen Anna in a romantic way. Ella's my girl.

On the advice of Clark, I'm still yet to tell Anna about Nate's paternity. Clark helped me hire a private detective to help us figure out if Nate was telling the truth. I also snagged a hair or two of Anna's to test the DNA. How the hell the PI I hired acquired Nate's sample, I couldn't care less about; as long as he got it for testing, that's all that matters. We need that proof and I'm hopeful in a few days' time we'll have those results. I'm spewing money for fun at the moment.

In addition, the PI is doing something else for me, too. I hope he finds what I'm looking for, and quickly.

"Would you like me to wipe the excess oil off first? It's quite difficult to get off in the shower sometimes," Anna asks as she bats her eyelashes at me.

Is she flirting with me?

Before I can answer, she grabs another towel draped across the chair and begins wiping my front.

"I can do it." I try to take the towel off her.

"It's fine, let me," she purrs.

Eh, well, this is new.

"You have a beautiful body," she coos as she slowly drags the towel from my chest to my stomach.

"Thanks," I audibly gulp.

What is she doing?

"You and I, you know, we could have been something special together."

"I'm in love with Ella."

She's way too close, making me feel ridiculously uncomfortable.

"Could you love me?" She flirts her honey eyes upward

and before I know what's happening, she grabs my face and covers her lips with mine.

Too startled to move, I spread my arms out wide like a startled crab and stand there, unable to comprehend what she's doing.

"What the hell is going on?" I hear a familiar voice bellow from across the room.

Anna immediately pulls back, leaving me speechless. An audible gasp leaves her lips as she recognizes who it is.

My head snaps toward the sweet voice.

I know exactly who that belongs to.

Ella.

CHAPTER TWENTY-FOUR

Fraser

Aw, shit. This *cannot* be happening.

"No, no, no," I chant. "I... she..." I can't speak.

My heart pounds in my chest like a tribal drum.

And what is Ella doing standing in my dressing room, here in LA?

And why did she have to show up now?

Really?

What the hell are you doing up there, Universe?

Fuck. Right. Off.

To make matters worse, Eden and Hunter witnessed the kiss, too.

What did I do in my former life to deserve this level of shit?

Even though the AC is on, I start sweating buckets.

Aw, man, you have got to be kidding me.

"I never touched her," I gasp out quickly and point at Anna. "She grabbed me. I've never cheated on you. I nev—"

"I know. I saw and heard it all." Ella narrows her stare in Anna's direction.

Thank fuck for that, but poor Anna being humiliated in front of my friends and Ella.

"I'm so sorry, Ella." Shaking her head back and forth, Anna hides her embarrassed face with her hand. "I should go. I'm sorry, Fraser."

Head down, Anna rushes past me at full speed. "Please forgive me," she bursts out as she sweeps past Ella and out of the room.

"Aw, shit." My heart sinks. "I have to go get her."

Ella commands quick instructions my way. "You get dressed. Although I like you like this." Smirking, she draws an invisible line up and down my body. "I'm off to speak to Anna."

Huh? That's not the reaction I was expecting.

Ella jogs toward me, plants a fast, rough kiss to my lips. "Hi." She throws a wide white grin my way.

I shake my head, confused. She didn't lose the plot. Go off one or freak out. She's as calm as the Serengeti before sunrise.

"Hi?" I say unsure if I'm reading the signals correctly. She's being too cool.

"I'll be back." Then she reassures me with a smile.

"Be kind. And don't let her drive when she's upset," I call as Ella runs out of the room.

"Trust me." She looks back over her shoulder, her voice echoing through the warehouse corridor.

"It could only happen to you, Fraser." Hunter laughs.

"What the hell are you doing here? You could have warned me."

"Eh, surprise?" Eden splays her jazz hands up, wiggling her fingers.

"I have to speak to Anna. How did you know I was here?"

"Lisa told us. Ella wanted to surprise you. We planned it

ahead with security to let us in," Hunter confirms their plan. "And leave Ella to speak to Anna."

I dart for the bathroom door. "I've got to wash this oily shit off."

"Leave the oil on; you look like a Magic Mike stripper," Eden pipes up.

Hunter swivels around on his six-foot-four heels toward Eden. "You, young lady, should not be looking at his abs. Mine are way more defined than his. See?" He pulls up his white shirt.

In every level of his life, Hunter is competitive.

"You're so insecure. I only have eyes for you, Hunter," she teases.

"Yup, whatever. You win." I roll my eyes. "But I have far more pressing problems than your goddamn abs."

"Facts. Not your stereotypical ménage et trois. You need to chill out. Ella only wants to talk to Anna. Did she look bothered to you?" Hunter casually sits on the sofa across the room as he pulls Eden onto his lap. "Hey, baby, wanna fool around?"

Those two are worse than Ella and me; they're like a pair of horny teenagers.

Why is everyone so relaxed? And no, Ella didn't look upset about the kiss, but she could be bitch-slapping Anna into oblivion right now.

Oh God. I need to get in the shower.

Ella

"Anna," I holler across the parking lot. "Hold up."

But she keeps running toward what I assume is her black truck.

I really need to work on my cardio. The last few weeks, I've mainly worked with my dance students on their flexibility, physical strength, and isolation of body movements. And I haven't been out running either as I've been too busy. Cardio needs to be added into the timetable as soon as I return. I'm pooped. And it's unbearably hot here. Bad choice wearing leather skinny jeans; however, I wasn't planning on running in them.

"Anna, stop running. I only want to talk to you," I puff and pant. "I'm not mad."

I'm not at all. I want to fix this. Be friends. For Fraser's sake. Over the last four weeks, I had lots of time to think things through clearly. I decided to give Anna a chance, not make any assumptions, and believe Fraser when he says he trusts her.

I have to trust his judgment.

"Oh, please stop. I'm getting a stitch in my side."

And she does. Then she turns toward me.

I hold my hands up. "If I had a white flag, I would wave it," I wheeze, fanning my face with my hand. "I don't want to fight with you. I certainly didn't want to meet you like this for the first time. And I don't want any arguments. I promise."

I stare at her tear-stained face. Even crying, she looks beautiful. Fraser must have the willpower of Bear Grylls scaling a rock face.

Even I wouldn't be able to resist her, and I don't even swing that way.

"I'm not mad at you," I say.

Her chest heaves up and down. "Please don't be nice to me."

"Why would I not be nice to you? I hold nothing against you, Anna. I know nothing about you."

Other than the fact you're a top influencer on social media; your son is another man's; your marriage is fake; your father isn't your father; your mother had an affair with Nate's right-hand man and I know who your real father is. Yeah, other than that, nothing.

"Don't make me like you, Ella. I hate you."

"Hate me? Why?" My breathing calms to its normal pace.

"Because you get to have Fraser." She points in the direction of the warehouse, her long brunette locks swishing around in the wind.

"I don't get to *have* him. He loves me and I love him. I am not making him do anything he doesn't want to. I would never do that."

"Just stop."

"Stop what?"

"Stop being so nice."

I laugh.

"You're impossible," she scowls.

"Me? Impossible how?"

"I was expecting you to slap me back there. I would have, if he was mine." She puts her head in her hands. "I'm so sorry. I don't know what I was thinking about kissing him. I don't want him, not really, not like *that* anyway. My head's been pounding for days. My father hasn't been in touch yet. He's gearing up for something; I can feel it. I don't know what, but his silence screams alarm bells. I'm so stressed and scared," she whispers almost inaudibly.

Rushing in, I wrap my arms around her.

"Oh, Anna."

"I don't want your sympathy," she muffles beneath our hug, but she doesn't try to move.

"I'm so sorry, Anna."

"Being alone scares me. Without Fraser, I will be alone. He's been my best friend for years. Helped me bring up Ethan. He's a beautiful man. In all our time together, he's never tried it on with me. He's a gentleman and loyal to the core."

Her only family is being ripped apart; it's no wonder she's scared. Poor girl.

"If it helps, I'm jealous of the time you've had with him. All the time I've lost."

She shakes in my arms as she continues. "You have nothing to be jealous of. My life is not all it's cracked up to be. I've distanced myself from everyone for so many years. I barely have any friends because of all the lies and secrets. I only have Fraser. I was with Lucas for three years before I fell pregnant with Ethan. I loved him. Part of me still does. He was the same as Fraser—funny, smart, kind. Every day, I look at Ethan and see him. He's a carbon copy of his father. Then he disappeared. And now Fraser is leaving me here in California, too. It's like starting all over again for me."

I think we've opened a can of worms. She's spilling her heart out to me as a way of therapy.

She leans out of our hug, and I rub my hands up and down her arms. When she catches my gaze, a wave of bright red flashes across her chest, neck, and cheeks. "I'm sorry. I'm making a fool of myself."

"You are not. Let it all out. You can't bottle this up or it will eat you alive. Emotions can poison you if you don't speak about them, Anna. Talk to me."

Boy, does she let go and I'm not prepared for anything she tells me.

"Ella, my father is a cruel man. He threw me out like I was a donation for the thrift store. I have never felt so worthless. Throughout my childhood, he treated me like a second-class citizen. I don't ever remember him telling me he loved me, not once. When my mom died, I was raised by the house and kitchen staff. They became my family. Then when I was old enough, I was sent to boarding school. Poor little rich girl." She gives a fruitless laugh and wipes the back of her hand across her nose. Yup, even snotty she's still gorgeous.

"And I did everything to try to get my father's attention. I even had a relationship with one of my tutors to get a reaction from him. But he didn't care. He was too concerned about his reputation and how it made him look. All he did was send me to an even stricter school. It was my cry for help. For attention. I wanted someone to see me." She points at her chest. "See me as a person, not an object. I wanted him to speak to me as he passed me in the halls of the house he called a home. But he never did. We lived like strangers in his loveless fortress. And when boarding school was over, I met Lucas. He was the manager at my father's nightclub. Lucas saw me. Really saw me. And for the first time in my life, I felt alive and happy. I miss him. So much. And my poor boy never got to meet his father. I know my father is behind that, too. Somehow. I don't know how to find him. Or even know if he's still alive."

I see it all as clear as day now. Anna's been searching for someone who sees her and makes her important. Fraser hasn't told her yet about the private detective and that's not my news to share.

"I always hoped Fraser and I would connect, or he'd change his mind about you. Or over time, he would grow to love me. But he never did. The way Fraser looks at you, Lucas used to look at me like that too."

"I'm sorry, Anna."

"You should *not* be apologizing. I am the one here who

nearly screwed everything up for us all. I wasn't testing him. I know he doesn't like me romantically. God, I'm such an idiot. I actually don't know what I was doing. I'm just—"

"Scared." I finish her sentence.

"Yeah." She bows her head.

Stuffing her hands into her jean pockets, she lifts her head. "Please forgive me. I'm sorry for saying I hate you. I don't." She shakes her head. "I didn't mean it. Fraser worships the ground you walk on. He's loved you from afar, for years. I'm guessing you must be pretty special." She half smiles. "And you're beautiful."

"Well, if it's any consolation, I can't work out how Fraser has kept his hands off you because you are one of the most beautiful women I have ever met in my life. You are a class A broad. The all-American girl next door from where I'm standing."

"Oh, shut up," she blushes.

"And those boobs. Wow! Are they real?"

A burst of laughter from her chest echoes across the parking lot. "Yeah. Lucas always loved my boobs," she confirms.

"I can see why. I'm impressed. And those dimples. I can barely resist you," I josh.

"Oh, behave."

The beautiful woman standing in front of me now is a shadow of the persona she presents on her social media. Her confidence has been well and truly shattered over time.

"Please don't take this the wrong way, but I think you should seek the help of a therapist, Anna. My sister Eden's ex-boyfriend walked out on her, then she lost her unborn baby. Therapy helped her massively. Eden was the one in the dressing room. You should have a chat with her. She will tell you how it helped her and what it did for her confidence. It transformed her life."

"Thank you. I do think I need to speak to someone."

"You're welcome."

"So, two thirds of your whole are here in LA. Is Eva holding down the fort back home?"

"Yeah. We even have staff now. We need to source a new building. Our dance school is growing quicker than we expected. As you know, social media works great for little businesses like us."

"It does. I love it. And I get so many paid sponsorship opportunities. Your dance videos on TikTok are great. Your sister did one the other day with Hunter and the boys."

"Ha. My nephews are more famous than our school. People love them."

"They are very cute."

"They are. You must come and visit us at the house we've rented down on Santa Monica beach. I'm looking forward to meeting Ethan in person. Virtually is never the same. Fraser tells me he's super smart."

"He is. He takes after his dad. His real one. My father said Lucas was a lowlife. But he was smart. He had a business degree from Harvard."

"Ethan is desperate to meet you. In fact, scratch that, desperate to meet your two dogs. He has me following them on Instagram. He keeps calling them his new brothers."

Oh, that is super cute and makes me feel so much better.

"Fight for him, Ella," Anna blurts out.

"Only if you agree to spend vacations in Scotland and Christmas with us all."

A grateful smile spreads across her sun-kissed face. "Okay."

"You're family. Fraser loves you and Ethan. Never forget that."

"How can I? Have you seen the house he's bought us? And how he looks after my boy? He's special."

"He is."

"Hey, is everything okay?" Fraser appears, calling out as he jogs across the parking lot, his face full of concern.

Fully dressed. Damn it.

"We're great," I reassure him, and nod in Anna's direction, instructing him to give her some comfort.

Fraser swoops in, embracing her, and landing a kiss on her temple.

"I'm so sorry, Fraser."

"Hey, that's alright. We're all emotionally charged at the moment. We're in unknown territory. It's normal to feel confused, Anna. And you know I love you, but just not in *that* way."

She groans. "I know. I'm having a bad day. I'm sorry. I don't know what I was thinking."

"C'mere." Fraser reaches out, beckoning me to them. And our messed-up threesome doesn't feel so abnormal now as he embraces us together, wrapping us in his gigantic warm arms. I breathe in Fraser's infamous smell, the scent I can't get enough of. Him.

"Do you want to talk about what happened back there, Anna?" Fraser asks.

"Nope, I'll let Ella fill you in," she replies firmly.

"Anna is going to join us for Christmas and some vacations in Scotland," I inform him.

"Why didn't I think of that?" he groans.

"'Cause you're a man," Anna chuckles.

"I knew this would happen. You two are gonna gang up on me now, aren't you? I'll never win against you both. I don't stand a chance. One feisty woman in my life is more than enough, but now two!"

"You're already a step behind us," I say, and we all chuckle.

Snuggling into Fraser's chest with another woman, I can't help but wonder why I don't feel threatened by her, not even one bit.

I was jealous before, but not anymore. I know I am Fraser's and he's mine.

Anna was born into a life she doesn't want. Born into a family she shouldn't be part of. Nate doesn't deserve her.

The divorce couldn't come quick enough for us all. She deserves to be happy. I see what Fraser meant when he said that before.

"My girls," Fraser mumbles. "We good?"

"Yeah," Anna says, leaning out of our three-way embrace. "I feel better. Thank you, Ella."

I give her a quick hug. "Us girls have to stick together."

"Threesome?" Fraser wiggles his eyebrows, his face full of mischief.

At the same time, Anna and I quickly swipe his shoulders, and he flinches, grinning.

"Not a chance."

"No way."

We both say in unison.

"Too soon? Ah, it was worth a shot," Fraser jokes, pulling me into his arms. "Hi, Bella. I've missed you."

"Me too." My starstruck gaze meets his.

Anna clears her throat. "I'm going to leave you two."

"Hold that thought." Fraser turns his gaze to Anna. "Are you okay with driving?"

"Yeah," she says.

"I'll see you tomorrow. Come to the beach house where

Ella is staying. I'll send you the details. I want Ethan to meet Ella," he informs her.

Calmness settles in my bones.

"Perfect. And leave your Range Rover for me to sort out. I'll call the garage now and get them to pick it up," she replies.

"Thanks, Anna."

"Do you guys all need a lift somewhere?" she offers.

"Hunter has an eight-seater SUV hired for the week," I inform her. "We're good. Thank you, though."

"Eight-seater? What the hell does he need one of those for?" Fraser screws his nose up.

"Yup, you know Hunter." I drop my voice trying to mimic Hunter's deep voice. "But we have three baby seats. We need a big car." Making Anna and Fraser laugh.

"Your sister must get no sleep," Anna scoffs.

"Not much."

"I can't wait to meet everyone. Now, I'll be off. Have a great night." With a soft wave, Anna jumps into her gigantic shiny black truck and glides out of the parking lot.

"Hi," I breathe.

"Hey, beautiful." He cups my face. When his lips kiss mine, in an instant the jet lag I've been feeling and the worries of meeting Anna and Ethan suddenly vaporize into thin air.

It's all working out how we planned so far. Better than expected. Apart from Anna's kiss; that was not in the plan.

"So, you met Anna."

"Yeah."

"Not ideal."

"Nope. But I understand. She's scared, Fraser. She doesn't want to be alone. And you're her best friend. Her confidant."

"I know she is. She's been holding it all in. Did she speak to you?"

"Yeah, I'll tell you all about it later."

He scatters a path of soft kisses down my neck. "Bedroom?" he mumbles. "I need you naked now. It's been four weeks. My cock is aching for you."

The butterflies in my belly take flight as a sudden throb between my thighs begins. My pussy is such a whore. She wants him.

"I need food," I smirk.

"I have the perfect thing to feed you with."

My sex-mad man.

I giggle. "Food first. Although my parents are with us to help with the triplets. We may not get a chance."

"You're killing me."

"We have the whole top floor of the rental house to ourselves, though."

"I'll have to gag you to stifle your moans."

"Mine? You're louder than me," I tease. "Do you have any of that oil you had on?"

"It's already in my bag. I have plans for you." His eyes turn dark.

Oh goodie.

"I can't wait."

CHAPTER TWENTY-FIVE

Ella

Stretching out in the most comfortable bed I've ever slept in with the dazzling sun peeking through the curtains, I can't remember ever feeling this relaxed.

The quintessential beach house we rented along the heart of the Santa Monica beachfront is what holidays are made of and waking every morning to the fresh fragrance of the Pacific Ocean fills my beach bum heart with giddy joy.

The glass-fronted house gives us a view of the entire spectacular length of the beach and the golden sunrises and warm sunsets.

I let out a gigantic sigh of contentment as I give my toes a quick wiggle and shake out the rest of my body.

It's been the perfect week of fun, laughter, sunshine, walks on the beach, night swimming, and so much touristy stuff. The Hollywood sign was amazing to see in the flesh, but the best thing I've loved here are the hours I've spent with Fraser, Anna, and Ethan. It saddens me Fraser won't be here for Anna and her boy. Fraser is a doting father. It's been a beautiful thing to watch, and we're now firmly knitted together. It was exactly what we all needed.

We put a pin in any conversations about Nate Miller. We decided we are going to wait to see what he does. Talking about it doesn't help change anything at this point.

Meeting Fraser's lawyer, in the flesh for the first time was a little awkward. Even though I'd spoken to him several times since the video sex slip up, it didn't stop the deep flush sweeping across my entire body. *World, swallow me up.*

I pat the bed next to me to discover I'm alone.

The house is ghostly quiet, too. With three newborns, my parents, Hunter, Eden, and guests visiting, it's been far from peaceful. But it's been brilliant, and I wouldn't change a thing.

The bedroom door glides open and, like every time I catch a glimpse of Fraser, I gasp at the sight of his magnificent body.

"Morning, Bella." He passes me a billowing hot cup of coffee, then steals a kiss.

Sitting up, I reach for it, inhaling the nutty aroma. *Heaven.*

This has become our morning ritual, Fraser bringing me coffee. He's so considerate and caring. I love all the little things he does for me.

Fraser shuffles in beside me.

"Where is everyone?" I inquire.

"They've just left. Hunter and Eden have a photoshoot with that fancy fashion magazine today."

"Ah, yeah. I forgot."

Excitement buzzes in my tummy. My sister and Hunter are going to be on the cover of the world's top selling fashion magazine. So cool.

"Your mom and dad are helping to wrangle the boys for them today. Three is hard work, right?"

"Understatement of the year." All week Fraser has watched in wonder as we've all chipped in babysitting, feeding, changing. It's like a merry-go-round. Luckily Lachlan and Lennox have started sleeping through at nighttime, so things are easing up for Eden and Hunter a little. Two down, one to go. My mom said it was only a week or two after Eva and I slept through as babies, then Eden quickly followed suit. Eden's holding on to her statistic.

"We're not having three at once."

"You don't get to decide, Fraser," I chuckle.

"Yeah, but Eva had two sons separately. That's what I want."

"Again, we may not have a choice," I tease. "Did you go downstairs with only your boxers on?"

"Yeah, why?"

"You're going to give my mom a heart attack. She was eyeing you and Hunter up on the beach yesterday." She didn't know I could see her checking them out behind her sunglasses. At least I know where us girls get our taste in men from. My father is super handsome, even if I do say so myself. He's all white-gray hair and matching beard with a deep tan and muscles from working around their sports retreat all year long. He adores my mom and can never keep his hands off her. But their level of PDA doesn't make me feel squeamish. It fills me with hope. A love that lasts forever.

"It's the same as having my swim shorts on." He looks down at himself.

"It's not. I can see the outline of, well, everything in those. It's too big to conceal. They are so tight."

"Want a better look?" I don't get a chance to reply. He

places his coffee on the nightstand, then whips his snug-fit navy trunks off.

Oh, glory be.

"He's ready for your inspection." He quirks a brow.

This man can never get enough. We've been at it at least two or three times a day since I got here.

"From what I can see from here, he's a grower, not a shower, clearly," I jest.

"Shut up, woman. Hop on."

"Last day. No one here. Time to scream down the house, Fraser." I throw a teasing look his way.

Prowling down the bed and without another word, I slide myself between his thick thighs, then slowly begin licking and kissing a trail up each of his athletic inner legs, caressing them as I venture north. He lets out a low moan as his eager cock becomes hard and ready for me.

I don't know what he's doing, but he fumbles about with his phone.

"You're not filming me or taking pictures." I sit back on my heels in a panic.

"That's a great idea." He grins. "But I'm not doing that."

His phone springs to life as a soft strum of guitar strings thrum from his phone.

It's "Nothing Else Matters" by Metallica. *Our song.*

I never knew there could be such a thing as second chances or to experience love as powerful and deep as ours. We found each other again. He's my true north, guiding me back home, where I belong. With him.

I quickly remove my red lace bralette and panties, then lean down again and lick his thick, hot length from base to tip, making him flinch.

"Oh, baby," he gasps.

Running my wet tongue up and down his shaft, I plant

soft kisses over the head of his cock before swiping my tongue down his thick pulsing sensitive vein on the underside of his shaft, making his cock involuntarily twitch under my control.

"Suck me," he commands with heated anticipation.

Not. Yet.

I grab the edible lube from the nightstand drawer quickly and smother his cock to make the ride I'm about to give him a smooth one.

Making a slight adjustment to my position, I then slide his cock between my breasts. Squeezing them together, I move up and down.

"Fuuuckkkkkk." He bucks his hips, pushing, thrusting, and begging for more, and he watches every single move.

Dipping my head, I stick my tongue out and lavish his tip with every forward thrust.

All the while, the soft thrum and the words of our song pour into my soul.

"Holy shit," he hisses.

I let go of my tits and unexpectedly suck him deep all the way into my mouth.

A guttural moan rumbles from his throat.

"Oh, you have to stop, baby," he whispers.

He's on the edge of no return.

He quickly pulls me up on top of him as the song changes rhythm.

"You're a she-devil with that sinful mouth." Kissing me, he slowly sits us both up, then he slips his fingers into my wet sex.

"Oh, she's ready."

I'm desperate for him. All of him will never be enough.

Circling his thumb over my clit, he slides his thick fingers in and out with intention.

"You like that Bella?" he hisses as I rock my hips and fuck his fingers.

"I want more."

He kneels up, then moves around behind me, my back to his front, and I ready myself for what's coming.

On all fours, he hoists my hips in the air, then cups my whole pussy from behind. I feel him dip. He pulls my ass cheeks apart, then licks my soft folds front to back. His rigid tongue plunges inside of me. He loves doing this. And I love him doing it.

Holy shit.

Warmth spreads across my body at all the sensations he's giving me.

A soft shuffle behind me alerts me to him moving position. I feel his strong hand across my shoulder blades, urging me to dip down. Sliding my arms up the bed, I arch my back, ass in the air, giving myself to him.

He pushes in from behind and I suck him into my body.

"You are so fucking tight like this," he whispers.

Digging his fingers painfully into my hips and ass, he thrusts slowly at first, then his pace quickens, as if fucking me to the beat of our song.

I meet him thrust for thrust pushing myself back onto his cock, as the sun shines through the window. I'm in paradise.

I tilt my head around. He's mesmerized, watching his cock move in and out of my body.

On repeat, the melody of the music swirls around us.

Removing his hand from my hip, he finds my clit quickly and rubs me over and over until I can't take anymore. He suddenly pinches and I shudder as my orgasm hits me like a ten-ton truck, bursting into a shower of gold stars through my entire body.

Fraser slaps my ass hard, his thrusts becoming deeper and harder with desperation.

Through the space between my legs, I reach back, cup his balls in the palm of my hand and gently squeeze them upward, knowing this increases the intensity of his pleasure.

Fraser moans loudly. Taking my shot, I move my finger back slightly again, applying a little pressure to his taint, which I know is one of his sweet spots.

He growls, and in an instant, he pours himself inside of me, twitching and pulsing.

"Holy shit," he hisses.

He takes a few moments to come back down to earth before he slowly slides himself out of me. Leaning over to kiss my back softly, he startles me by giving my ass another quick sharp slap.

"Ouch," I laugh.

From behind, he lies on top of me with his body pressing me firmly into the mattress as he nuzzles into my back and neck.

"I think I went blind for a second. That was incredible."

"Did I make you dizzy?"

"Yeah. Fuck knows what you did with my balls down there, but holy shit, girl, you know my body like no one else."

"Could I make you squeal like a piggy, you reckon?"

"Probably," he chuckles.

He moves to the side and I turn to face him. We stare at each other, drinking each other in.

"Last day today, then flying back tomorrow," he says softly, tucking my hair behind my ear.

"Yeah. I don't want to go."

"I have three golf championships to play, then I'll be back here. So, another five weeks until I see you next."

"I did four weeks with no problems."

I'm lying. It dragged.

"Then we can do five easily."

"And you're going to fly in here for the charity ball?"

"Yup." I need to get a dress. It's a super fancy celebrity ball. I'm not prepared for this new glamorous lifestyle.

"We'll sort my schedule out and you can meet me in Bermuda or Georgia if you like, too. You pick."

"Oh, Bermuda sounds amazing." I get excited. "You have such a cool job."

"I do. Very cool."

Fraser pulls me in close. "I love you."

"I know you do. And I love you."

"Thank you for being in my world. I couldn't face Nate Miller without you."

He runs his thumb across my bottom lip, back and forth.

"I can't face the world without you." I pull his thumb into my mouth and suck it hard.

He gasps.

"Fancy taking a shower?" he whispers. Mesmerized, his hooded eyes never leave my lips.

I bat my eyes at him, then bite his thumb.

"Oh, baby. You're making me hard for you again."

His thumb leaves my mouth with a pop.

"You need a shower, dirty boy."

"And you need a full-on power wash, you filthy girl."

I roll my eyes. "Let's go."

Discovering each other again feels like I found the shiniest treasure chest. Once opened, it was full of greatness and gems.

He's my golden boy.

We're meant to grow and evolve together. I know he's meant to be in my life. He kept his promise.

He's healed my broken heart forever.

"Anna's here." Fraser eyes Anna's black truck parked in front of his old house.

I have to bend my neck back to gaze up high to take in the vast structure. Wow. It's a hotel. Not a home.

As we scale the steps to the grand wooden and black wrought iron front door, he captures my hand with his, entwining them together.

"She must be doing a last sweep of the house, like you Fraser. She had the same idea."

It feels weird being here with Fraser. Like peering through the binoculars of someone across the street, witnessing something you shouldn't.

Fraser wanted to do a final last check of the house, making sure he has missed nothing. Part of me is curious, wanting to see where he's been living, and the other half of me doesn't want to be here. I want to leave this place exactly where it belongs. In the past.

Fraser and I have a new future together, one that doesn't involve unhappy memories, and this place is a huge journal entry for Fraser.

Eden and Hunter jump up the steps behind us. We decided for our last night, the four of us would have a meal out together. The sun is setting; there's little to no breeze, and it's still warm out. It couldn't be a more perfect evening for dinner down by the beach. I'm going to have one of those lush pink cocktails I had the other night.

"Wow, this is some house, Fraser." Hunter whistles from behind us.

"It's not mine. This house has bad vibes," Fraser says deadpan.

A shiver spreads through my body. *Oh, what was that?*

Fraser pushes the heavy wooden doors open, creaking. It echoes loudly through the empty house.

Chandeliers hang from every ceiling I can see, marble staircases on either side of the enormous hall with a wide corridor leading to immense glass windows lining the back of the house.

Wow.

He's leaving all this behind to live with me in my doll-sized house.

"Anna," Fraser calls. "Where are you?"

Silence.

"I'm through here," she bellows back eventually.

We follow the voice along the large echoing hallway.

We enter the vast kitchen area to be greeted by the man I know haunts Fraser's dreams.

Nate Miller.

I audibly gasp as all the blood floods to my feet.

Alongside him stands Anna, who is situated between two rhinoceros-sized men, wearing black suits and malicious faces.

Fraser's big, but these guys are bigger.

Anna looks petrified.

"What's going on?" Fraser frowns.

"Ah, Fraser, you're just in time," Nate taunts.

Oh, this is not good, not good at all. Instant tension whirls through the air.

Numerous images of Nate Miller across the internet are clearly digitally enhanced because the rotund, greasy man standing in front of me now doesn't resemble any pictures

I've ever seen of him. And he's much shorter than I imagined him to be.

"In time for what?" Fraser says through a pinched jaw.

"My darling daughter was about to sign custody of Ethan over to me."

"You were doing what?" Fraser's raised voice booms, scrunching his face up in disbelief at Anna. "Why?"

Silent floods of tears slide down Anna's red face. She shakes her head, pulling her lips into her mouth.

Nate pipes up. "You see, Fraser. I've made a deal with Anna here. If you continue with your charges and allegations against me, I will take custody, legally, of her bastard son. But if you drop all the charges against me, she gets to keep him." He waves a piece of paper in the air, which I can only assume is adoption papers.

"You can't do this." Fraser moves forward. "Please tell me you haven't signed, Anna. You can't let him have our boy," he pleads with her.

"He's not your boy, Fraser. You have no say in the matter," Nate laughs, sending shivers down my spine.

It's official. Nate's a psychopath.

"So, this can go one of two ways." Nate walks around the kitchen island toward us. He stuffs his hands in his pockets before continuing. "You drop the charges, keep the boy. Stay married. Move in with Anna in the house you bought her. I never liked this fucking house anyway, and we go about our business as usual. And Ella goes back to her pathetic, mundane life. Or you fight me, I take Ethan, we go to court. I present the most damning career-ruining evidence because, at this point, your talent is all you have left. You lose Anna, Ethan, and Ella because you'll end up in prison on match fixing charges and extortion. You lose either way."

"You're fucking deranged," Fraser spits. "You can't take Ethan."

"Oh, but I can. I have all the paperwork here. See?" Nate summons one of his bodyguards over with the paperwork and passes it to Fraser.

"I'm a powerful man, Fraser. I have many friends in high places. It's all legal, aboveboard. All Anna has to do is sign. She was trying to save your ass."

Looking down at the papers, Fraser shuffles through them. "Don't you dare sign these, Anna. He is not laying a hand on Ethan. Do you hear me?"

Anna can't bear to look at anyone as her unstoppable tears flow. The urge to run into her arms to console her runs deep in my veins.

Hunter shoots in, "You're a fucking sports agent and businessman, Nate, not fucking God."

Nate bursts out laughing. What a prick this man is. "In the state of California, I am a fucking God, Hunter. I'm the king around these parts." He displays himself, arms wide.

Fraser paces back and forth. "What evidence do you have that would ruin my career? You have nothing."

Nate sighs. "Again, with all the dramatics, Fraser. Pass me the envelope, would you?" He rolls his eyes as his bodyguard passes Fraser the envelope. "Open it," he instructs.

Fraser tears it open at high speed, pulling out a dozen sheets of papers.

Walking toward the granite-topped kitchen island, Fraser lays it all down. "I don't understand. What is this I'm looking at? Why is my name at the top of all these emails and call registers?"

"This is the email trail from all the match fixing you planned."

"What?" Fraser stands back. "This is all lies," he rages. "You're setting me up!"

Darkness sweeps across Fraser's face.

"You fucking scumbag."

"I'm not setting you up." Nate winks at me.

Is this guy for real?

"It's all there," he continues. "Every word in black and white. Missing putts, missing shots. Playing bad form for an entire week, the next week winning by a mile at other championships. Sharing money with other players no matter what your result. Conceding holes. Oh, and then, of course, there's all the drugs and drink you took and the sex escorts. Gosh, the list goes on." Nate flaps his arms about in the air. "This looks bad, doesn't it, Ella? Wouldn't you say?"

We don't stand a chance against this man.

Boiling with fury, Fraser's nostrils flare wildly.

He'll never be free.

Hunter moves in, skimming over the paperwork, his eyes darting, shifting quickly from one piece of paper to the next. "You won't get away with this, Nate."

"Ha, watch me," he says coolly.

Watching on, detached as if in one of the time frames that appear in the *Dr. Strange* movie, my world free-falls below me.

Fraser's hands clench tight around the edge of the granite. He growls, his head bowed. "So let me get this straight. You've planted emails, text messages, and telephone conversations. You're going to set me up with all this fake evidence? To say I fixed golfing tournaments and if I don't drop all the charges against you, you'll take Ethan? Tell me I've fucking picked you up wrong."

Nate leisurely leans against the kitchen units. "It's all legal."

"I'll lose everything if you expose this," Fraser whispers. "Why are you doing this to me?" Fraser shakes his head back and forth in shock.

"Because I can. So, what will it be, Fraser?" he asks, emotionless. Nate moves his hands out to his sides as if he's a set of balancing scales. "Ethan or Ella, Ella or Ethan." He rocks back and forth. "That's a tough one, huh?" He scrunches his nose, smiling.

This man should be committed and currently residing in a mental asylum. He's like The Joker on crack, multiplied by one hundred.

We are powerless.

Either way, Fraser loses one of us. And possibly his entire career.

The decision is as clear as day. There is no way in the world I will stand back and watch Ethan being ripped from his family.

"No, no, no, no," Fraser mutters repeatedly.

"Anna, sign the papers," Nate growls.

"Don't fucking sign those papers," Fraser fires back at her.

"Do it, Anna. Give Ethan to me. Try to save Fraser. So he can live with his perfect whore in perfect harmony in perfect Scotland with her perfect dogs and sisters." He spurs her on. All the while, his eyes never leave Fraser's stooped body.

"You are playing with fire of the worst kind, Nate, talking about my family like that," Hunter's jagged voice blares.

"Whatever, Hunter. You have no power here," Nate smirks, flipping him off.

I hear a gasped sob and realize it's coming from Fraser. With his head bowed down still, unable to lift it, the weight of his problems is too much to bear. He's broken.

"Please don't do this," he begs through a barely there whisper.

"Sign the fucking papers." I jump and gasp as Nate bellows, spitting his command. It bounces through the empty house.

I look back at Eden over my shoulder, both our eyes full of tears. With a gentle nod from her, that's all I needed. The permission to make Fraser's decision for him. There's a child involved. I can't stand back and let this happen. Not because of me. I won't be the blockade that allows a sociopathic man to take a child that is not his to take.

"Don't sign the papers, Anna," I whisper.

"No, no, no, please don't, Ella," Fraser's voice strains. "Please don't say what I think you're going to say."

With heavy feet, I drag myself to him for the last time.

Cupping his face, I pull his red-rimmed eyes upward to meet mine, puncturing bullets of pain through my heart, knowing this will be the last time I ever meet his crystal blues. They look darker than I've ever seen them before, full of sadness, failure, and despair.

"Fraser, it's the right thing to do. I have to let you go." Tears flow down our cheeks. "We lost."

"This can't be happening. Please, don't do this." He gasps, pulling me into a fierce embrace.

"I have loved every minute of being back together. But it's time to let go of us, Fraser. We gave it a really good shot. Ethan needs you and Anna. Don't let him take Ethan."

"Don't say that; there has to be a way." He shakes in my arms, squeezing me until I can't breathe.

"There's not. You should be with Anna. Fall in love with her. Finally be a family."

"No, Bella, please," he whispers.

Over Fraser's shoulder, Anna's sobs become

uncontrollable. I watch as she grips her throat as if the sound is strangling her.

This is worse than anything I have ever witnessed in my entire life.

Utterly heartbroken, I try to sound stronger than I feel. "We will get our shot in another lifetime, maybe, huh? But our time together is not in this one," I whisper, moving backward out of our embrace.

"No, please stop. Don't go. No, Ella. Pleeeeeesssseeee," he claws at me with haunted eyes.

"Don't make this worse, Fraser. It's time. Be brave." I shake my head, biting my lip to suppress my anguish.

Synchronized, we inhale deep tortured, unbearable breaths.

Letting the tears flow, I can't stop them. "I'm sorry, Fraser. We tried. I will love you. Always." I give him one last sad smile.

Nate's bodyguards swoop in behind Fraser, pulling him toward them, away from me.

Realization floods across Fraser's beautiful face, and he knows this is final. His eyes bounce around the room, searching for help. He grabs his head as if in sudden pain. He's crushed, and I can't bear to look at him anymore.

I turn on my heel.

"Noooooooooooooooooooooooo," Fraser roars. "Don't leave me!" His screams slice the air.

"Let the girl go, Fraser," Nate drawls as I stomp past him. "Excellent choice, Ella. Good girl."

I don't look his way. I hate the bastard.

He's the devil in the flesh who's destroyed Fraser's life.

With one last glance, I look over my shoulder, only to witness the two bodyguards holding Fraser back, ripping his tee shirt as he cries like an injured wild animal, clawing at them to let him go, trying to launch himself toward me so he can run after me.

His cries vibrate through the large tomb of a home.

In one swift move, I clasp my necklace, tear it from around my neck, and throw it away.

And I run as my heart breaks into a million and one pieces.

Carelessly fleeing down the stone steps outside, I lose my footing, stumbling into the gravel, skinning my knees and hands.

I stay there, kneeling, bawling, my chest tightening with every breath I can't seem to catch. Fat sorrow-filled tears free-fall and I can't stop them.

I shake my head furiously, clutching my chest. "This can't be happening," I whisper to myself.

Stabbing barbs of pains shoot through my heart, splitting it in two.

We didn't get to rewrite our story.

It was never meant to be.

With every tear, despair slides into my soul. Every part of my body hurting.

From behind, a powerful set of arms lift me up. Hunter. "Come on, sweetheart. You're alright. I've got you."

All hope is lost. There's nothing we can do.

Memories of us are all we have left. Hunter tucks me inside the safety of the truck. Warmth surrounds me as Eden encases me with her little body as she tries desperately to pour comfort into my soul.

"Oh, Ella." She sobs along with me. As a triplet, we connect deeply. We feel each other's joy, love, and pain, and she's right here with me, feeling it all. "There was nothing else you could have done. He gave you no choice."

I stay silent. Unable to move, breathe, speak, live.

Hunter circles the car around in the driveway and with one last peek over Eden's arm, I spot the man I love scrambling down the stairs toward us, furiously screaming my name.

My heart implodes, blowing apart all our dreams and wishes.

Burying my head, I cry into Eden's shoulder, feeling morbid sadness flood into my bones.

We never stood a chance.

We had an expiration date.

Today was that day.

CHAPTER TWENTY-SIX

Fraser

"You have to get up today, Fraser," Anna gently coaxes me when she sits down on the edge of the bed.

"I will," I sigh.

"You said that yesterday and the day before that and the day before that. You've been in this room for over four weeks. It's unsettling for Ethan."

She's right.

"I'm sorry."

"And will you please eat, Fraser? You haven't eaten properly for days. And you need a shower."

Anna lifts herself from the bed, moving over to the window as she spreads the curtains wide, pouring sunshine into the room.

Dragging the covers up over my head, I groan, moving down the bed.

She whips the comforter away from me. "Get up, Fraser. You are not lying here festering for another day."

"Please leave me alone."

"No. Get up," she raises her voice.

I sit up, trying to grab the cover back, but Anna flings it across the room.

I throw myself back on the mattress. "You are so annoying." I drag my hands down my face.

"I am trying to save you, Fraser. It's bad enough my father has destroyed your happiness, but *I* will not allow you to starve yourself to death or die of a broken heart. Also, you are making our beautiful new home smell bad. You are wafting out into the hallway. It smells like someone has already died in here." She rubs her nose back and forth.

"This house is not mine. It's yours."

"Oh, would you shut up with all that shit?"

I tilt my head in her direction.

"You did not just say that. Way to hit a man when he's down. Please leave me alone to wallow in my pit of pain."

"Yes, I did just say that because you won't listen to me. And this is your house. You bought it. And here we are again. Back to square one." She puts her hands on her waist and pops a hip. "The weight of your self-pity is clouding your judgment, self-worth, and perspective. You are still alive. You are here. You have a life to live. Even if it doesn't feel like that yet, it will. And we need to figure out how we fix our situation we're in or we go back to the way things were. Your choice."

Anna waits for me to move.

My body feels dead. Part of me wishes it was the end of the world as pain soars through my body like hot barbs, making me clench in anguish.

I will never forgive Nate Miller.

I watched the love of my life run out on me. She left that very same night on the next flight out of LA. When I frantically showed up at the beach house to see her, she'd already left. Hunter talked me down from my epic meltdown as she flew out of my life, and then he delivered the final brutal blow, confirming to me that we lost and it was over.

Concentrated pain flooded into my body four weeks ago and it's never drained away. It's being held tight, like a dam.

We didn't have a choice. She was right. Nate won.

Being kicked in the balls at high speed would hurt less than the heartbreak I'm feeling right now. Worse than the first time. Worse than anything, ever. There's no cure for it. Time. That's all I need, Anna keeps telling me.

I could stay here for one thousand years, and time still wouldn't heal my shattered heart.

We examined all the paperwork with my lawyer, the adoption papers, the fake match fixing documentation, and there was nothing Clark could do to help me. The evidence was too strong, and the paperwork seemed kosher. It was hopeless.

Anna's been trying to take care of me. I appreciate her kindness, but it feels wrong to accept it.

How Ella could ask me to fall in love with Anna is beyond all my comprehension.

All I want is *her*. Ella.

I've heard Anna crying at night. That poor girl needs me, but I can't find it in myself to reach out to give her the much-needed comfort to support her. I failed trying to save us all from the paper prison we are living in. Three pieces of paper that lock us together.

An NDA, a contract that binds me to Nate, and a marriage certificate.

When I look at her, I see the pain I feel reflected in her eyes that cuts me deep. I've rejected her so many times. She must feel so alone.

I'm such a self-centered douche canoe.

I can't even look at myself in the mirror anymore, either.

I'm Fraser 'fuckup' Farmer.

Knowing I will never hold, kiss, or touch Ella ever again. Never breathe her heady scent she wears that makes me feel giddy with joy. Never get to experience her tender heart and kisses that blow my senses to pieces. It tears me apart.

When I'm with her, I feel like me. Like home. But she's gone and I feel it.

"You have ten minutes to get up, get in the shower, and get dressed."

"Okay," I whisper, but continue to lie here.

I can tell you exactly how many tiny imperfections are on the ceiling. I've gazed at them for days, weeks, desperately trying to work out what my next move is.

Four weeks and I've not had one idea how to release myself from Nate's control.

A deep sigh escapes my lungs.

My phone gives a soft *ding* from the nightstand. It's probably Hunter checking in on me for the hundredth time this week. I don't care who it is. I don't care about anyone. Unless it's her. But she won't pick up my calls. It's gone straight to voicemail every time I've tried.

Nate published a stupid statement announcing I was taking a sabbatical for 'personal reasons.' Screw him. I'm never golfing again if I have to give that man another cent of my money.

Picking up my phone, Anna checks the notification. "You have dozens of missed calls from my father, Fraser. You will have to answer him, eventually."

"Fuck him." I'm tired of being reasonable.

"And your mom. She's worried about you."

"I'll call her back later."

"Have you spoken to Ella yet?"

"No."

"Me neither. She won't pick up. I hope she's going to be okay. My heart hurts for you two," she whispers, deep in thought.

"And mine for all of us."

She nods in agreement.

Anna inhales a deep breath. "One new text message from someone called Frank Rossi." She frowns. "His message says, *Found him*." She looks up.

My stomach cartwheels with hope.

"Pass me that." I reach out.

"Who did he find?" she queries.

"Oh, his dog," I lie.

"Oh, that's lovely news." She slaps the phone into my hand.

"I'm going to call Frank. Can you give me a minute?"

"Yeah, but as soon as you're off that call, you need to go in the shower. You have chocolate on your chin and potato chips in your beard from three days ago. You are disgusting. That long shaggy beard has to go; it doesn't suit you."

I screw my face up, but she's right.

"I promise."

"You have five minutes before I come in here again and drag your ass into the shower or I'll take a picture of you looking like Fat Thor from *End Game* and post it all over social media. You're not fat; you're the opposite, in fact, but you look unkempt and scruffy. It's not becoming."

I don't look that bad, do I?

I look down, rubbing my chin. *Shit. I do.*

"Okay. Deal."

With that, she bounces out of the room, taking the comforter with her. She's serious about me leaving this room today.

I press *call* on Frank's number.

Consumed by grief these past few weeks, I had completely forgotten Frank emailed me the DNA results the week Ella was here, confirming Nate is not Anna's biological father.

I need to work out exactly how I tell her that sensitive piece of information.

He instantly picks up. "Fraser. How are you?"

"I've been better," I sigh and rub my tense forehead.

"Clark called me and filled me in. Nate Miller is a filthy son of a bitch."

"Yeah, I don't wanna talk about it. You found *him*?"

"Yeah. Along with eighty percent of everything else you've been looking for."

I spring up out of the bed. "You're kidding me?"

"Nope, and it's even better than we expected, but we need *him* to help us with the rest."

Not wanting to get too excited, I let a tiny sliver of hope run into my veins because my life has never gone to plan, and I certainly have had no luck on my side in what feels like forever.

"What did you find?"

"I'll meet you at my office downtown in an hour."

"Can you give me two?" It'll take me at least an hour to shave this fuzzy bear beard I've amassed.

"See you then."

Shit, things might very well be looking up.

Ella

"I think it's broken."

"It's not broken. Here, let me see."

"It is. Look at that bit there."

"It's not; you flip that part over like this."

I groan from beneath my bed covers. "Will you two get out of my bedroom, please? Now. You're seriously getting on my nerves."

I feel the bed dip on either side of me. Then nothing. The mattress jolts suddenly, over and over again. Then it registers Eden and Eva are now bouncing up and down on my bed.

I swiftly flip the cover down from my head to my waist. "Will you two piss off and leave me alone?"

"Nope, can't do that." Eden continues to bounce.

Eva twirls around, jumping up and down, her long caramel-blond locks flying everywhere.

"Woo-hoo." Eden does a cheerleading jump in the air.

Lying here, I continue to get jolted and rustled about over and over.

"Oh, that's not great, jumping about after you've had babies, Eva," Eden puffs.

"You need to do more pelvic floor exercises. Clench, baby, clench," Eva sings out across the room.

Screw this. I fly out of my bed.

"Well, that worked." I spot Eva in the mirror, giving Eden a high five.

I whip around. "Only because my almost thirty-year-old sisters are bouncing about on my bed, acting like five-year-olds at the fair," I say through gritted teeth.

"Oh, she's testy."

"And aggressive, Eva."

"Will you please go?" I beg.

I don't want to face the world yet, and Eva confirms my worst fear. "Nope, no can do. We made a promise to Mom.

Today is the day we peel you out of this cesspit and make sure you walk the dogs."

I spread my arms wide. "Great, well, you achieved what you needed to do. Now go away and get on with your perfect lives with your boys."

Jealousy has reached new heights in the last four weeks. It's overpowering all my senses.

Eva has her two boys.

Eden has her husband and three new sons.

Anna. She got Fraser.

My Fraser.

Everyone has their patch of happiness.

Apart from me.

"Hey, this isn't a competition," says Eden. "You do not have to be mean. We are trying to help you. Do you think we don't feel your heartbreak?"

She and Eva climb off the bed.

Eva backs Eden up. "We feel it all. We are right here suffering with you. And me and Ewan are miles away from ever coming to any type of divorce agreement; my life is far from perfect. His drinking has reached new heights. He didn't pick the boys up on Saturday to take them to the cinema and I'm barely holding it together for them," Eva sighs.

I'm so selfish.

"Forgive me. I'm sorry. I don't know who I've become recently."

I actually don't. My normal sarcastic tongue isn't just sharp, it's become a razor. It cuts deep, and it's downright vicious.

"I'm a mess." Holding my head in my hands, I break down again for the fifty millionth time. I've cried every day. I can barely eat without feeling sick to my stomach and my hormones are all over the place.

My sisters swoop in, encasing me with their warm arms. "You did the right thing," Eden whispers.

"You did, baby girl." Eva kisses the top of my head. "Using a child as a weapon for Nate to get his own way was mean and downright cruel. You had no other option. But you have us. We are here for you. Always."

"That's what Fraser told me too, and that turned out to be a lie. I miss him so much." I coat Eva's shoulder in tears, and she squeezes me gently. "I thought we would finally get our chance. My heart," I stutter. "My heart, it feels so bad. I, I can't…"

Eva and Eden swaddle me in their arms. Shushing and cooing me.

I haven't danced in weeks, but my muscles ache like I've instructed forty classes.

Dance always fills me with so much joy. The thrill of moving to music and drowning your soul in the words has always been a magical feeling.

But there's no magic or elation in any inch of my body.

I feel lost.

Hollow.

Hurt and so goddamn heartbroken.

Fraser has left me dozens upon dozens of voice messages. I haven't listened to any of them. I can't. If he's with Anna now, he should *be* with Anna. It's all levels of wrong if I speak to him again.

Three days ago, a letter from him caught me unawares. Mindlessly, I opened the mail. In my zombified state, I tore the envelope open, failing to spot the overseas postal stamp.

My beautiful Bella,

I've tried calling you and I understand why you won't pick up.

It's been weeks.

Weeks of pain.

Weeks without you.

I miss your voice. Your face. Your smile. I miss everything.

They say what doesn't kill you makes you stronger, but I don't believe that's true. I am dead inside without you in my life, and I feel anything but strong.

I've been searching for a solution. For us to get our new beginning, trying to work it out, but I don't have any answers.

For a while there, it felt like we were teenagers again and I will treasure every minute of every day I spent with you.

I'm so sorry for the hurt and pain I have caused in your life. Not just this time, but for everything that has gone before. I never meant to hurt you or give you false hope. That was never my intention.

I hope over time you will find it in your heart to forgive me.

Until our next lifetime.

F+E - Forever and eternity,

Fraser x

His letter floored me and I haven't left my bed since then.

I tried to figure out a way for us to be together, too. Played out so many different scenarios and plans in my head, but nothing made any sense. As I reread his letter, his last words were final. He drew a line under us. *Until our next lifetime.*

It really is the end of us.

"You smell really bad," Eden whispers.

I snort, blowing bubbles of snot out of my nose.

"You're so attractive. If Chris Hemsworth stepped through your door, I bet he'd leave his wife for you," Eva chuckles. "So sexy."

I laugh. An actual genuine laugh. I don't remember when I last laughed.

In fact, I do. It was the last day in California, with Fraser.

At least Fraser got the attractive-looking girl, Anna. Whereas I look—I lean out of our embrace and turn to the mirror. I gasp—really fucking terrible.

"I have spots." I gape at myself. I've never had spots in my life, and I look scrawny, pale with blotchy red patches dotting my skin. How is that look possible? I have deep puffy circles under my eyes and spilled coffee down the front of my pale-pink pajamas. "And what is *that*?" I pull up the giant knot of God knows what tangled in my hair.

"I think it's dog snot." Eden squints to get a better look.

"Or your own." Eva scrunches her nose up.

"Or both," we all say in unison.

Looking at them both in the mirror across each of my shoulders, I say, "So, shower, huh?"

They nod their heads, confirming.

"You'll be okay." Eva squeezes my shoulder.

I suck my lips into my mouth, begging my brain not to

trigger any more tears. I'm so tired of crying. Tired of feeling tired.

"I'm no use to anyone. I'm sorry I haven't been able to teach," I mumble.

"Hey, that's what we have staff for. Check us out, all grown-up big-time businesswomen." Eden tries to lighten the mood.

"We can get through this together," Eva says with confidence.

"Omne trium perfectum," we chant.

Everything that comes in threes is perfect.

I have to start building my life again without him.

Our rough sea my mom spoke of all those weeks back was too strong for us to cross together. Too unpredictable. The tide did change, but not for the better, and it never flowed my way.

Fraser was right; we were inevitable—inevitable to fail.

On the other side of the world, eleven hours away, lives the other half of my heart, where it will stay forever.

Out of habit, I reach up to thumb my necklace, forgetting it's not there anymore.

Like him.

Gone.

CHAPTER TWENTY-SEVEN

Fraser

"Are you sure this is the one?" I stare across at the Cape Cod-style house from the safety of Frank's black SUV.

We're in San Diego. Only a couple of hours away from Los Angeles.

He's been so close all along.

Frank Rossi, the private investigator I hired, outdid himself. He found the information, photos, and paper trails we were looking for. Even information we weren't searching for. But we need more.

"One of my guys has been following him for weeks; this is the one," Frank reassures me.

I'd become so deeply woven into the fabric of my anguish that I'd forgotten all about him. Frank's text message a week ago saved me from another day stuck in that bedroom, in a house I never thought I would live in.

"Do you want me to come with you?" Frank gazes at the house.

"I think I should go by myself."

"I'm here if you need me, alright? And do everything you can; we need him."

"Cheers, man." Clicking the door of Frank's black Jeep open, I step out and run across the street.

Fuck, if this is him and if what Frank says about what he does for a living is true, this guy could be my savior.

Nerves sweep in as I raise my hand and give the dazzling white door a firm tap.

With a few shuffles and clicks on the other side, it's pulled open, revealing the man I've been trying to find for months.

Lucas.

Ethan's father.

"What the hell do you want?" he barks.

"I just want to talk." I hold my hands up.

"Well, I don't want to talk to you."

I take in the guy who's been a complete enigma to me. From Frank's files, I've discovered he's clever, really clever. He's used his business degree from Harvard and is now a strategic criminal intelligence analyst for the government. I sweep my eyes up and down; he's exactly how I imagined him to be. Broad, ripped, chiseled jaw, clean-shaven. With floppy brown hair and deep-brown eyes, Ethan is his spitting image.

"Please, all I want is ten minutes of your time," I beg, desperately trying to make him listen to me.

"All you want? You've taken everything that was mine, and yet you still want more?"

"I didn't. I haven't. I promise. It's not how it looks."

"What the fuck ever. Fraser Farmer seems to get everything."

I try a different tack. "I know it was you who sold the story to the press about me. I know you've been following me. I know you spoke to the escort agency. You know everything about me. And all of that tells me you are still in love with Anna."

He narrows his eyes at me. "How do you know that?"

"I hired a private investigator. He's sitting across the street in the black Jeep." I point to it. "We both want to talk to you about something."

"I don't want to talk to you." He then slams the door in my face, making me jolt at his unexpected reaction.

I'm not backing down on this.

I knock on the door again.

"Fuck off, Fraser." his voice muffled behind the white barricade of the door.

I know what will get a reaction. "I'm not in love with Anna."

Sure enough, he bursts through the door, and I think he's going to throw a punch my way as he launches himself at me out the doorway. I have to take at least five quick steps backward, arching my back as he towers over me.

He points his finger at me, red-hot anger flashing across his face, his veins popping out of his neck. *Oh shit, he's built like a bear.* I'm big, but he's bigger.

"You are a low-ass piece of shit who doesn't deserve Anna or my boy. You took everything away from me. Anna, Ethan. My own fucking flesh and blood. And you fucking cheated on her with that Scottish girl you can't seem to keep your dick out of," he spits.

He doesn't stop. "You're a shitty father figure. Visiting sex escorts and having affairs. You're a pathetic excuse for a man. I exposed you to show the world you are *not* who you say you are. And even then, it didn't fucking stop you sinking to new lows. Releasing a statement to say you were separated. You hadn't been separated for six months.

Believe me, I know everything about your fucked-up persona."

He doesn't know everything.

He continues. "And yet, you two are back together again. In a new home. For a new start again, is it? Buy Anna a new house to fix your sex addiction and adulterous behavior to sweeten her up." He continues. "My poor boy. Why Anna is still with you I will never know? You're a phony. And your social media is a sham, perfect fucking family, my ass. Anna deserves better."

I think I wet myself. He's one scary-ass mother.

Everything he's said is true. From the outside looking in, that's exactly how it all looks. But he doesn't know.

I gulp. "Would it help if I told you our marriage is a sham, too?"

"What the fuck do you mean?" he hisses, his American accent thick.

"Anna and I have never had sex. We have no relationship. Nate Miller drugged me. He duped me into signing a contract. He also made me sign an NDA and forced me to marry her. He's ruined my life. *Our* lives. It's a marriage of convenience. I'm not *in* love with Anna. I love her as a friend. Nothing more. Anna still loves you. And Ella isn't just any girl; she's the love of my life." It all spills out in quick-fire succession.

Eyes wide, he inhales. "I'm sorry, say that again." Deep creases form across his brow.

And I do.

"I need your help, Lucas."

He stands back from me, then turns around.

My shoulders sag in defeat.

He's my only shot.

As he's about to walk back into his house, he twists his head over his shoulder. "Tell your PI to come in."

Thwack.

My golf ball fizzes through the air.

"That was a shit shot. How long has it been since you hit a ball?"

"Screw you, Hunter. It's only been six weeks."

Six long weeks with no Ella in my life.

"I didn't call you so you could insult my swing. And it was at least a one-hundred-and-twenty-mile-an-hour shot." I stare off into the distance across the driving range. *Not bad.*

Looking back at my precariously propped up phone against the wall of my driving range stall, Hunter stares at me through the camera.

"It's good to see you out of bed though, and not looking like you belong in some creepy cabin in the woods. That beard had to go."

"Yeah," I agree.

"Your posture and footing are a little off too, but those'll come back again," he notes, watching my form.

My swing is way off. He's being too kind. "Yeah. I've been finding it difficult to focus."

All I can think about is Ella.

"How is she?" I need to know.

"Not great," he sighs. "She's lost all her moxie. But she started teaching again last week, and she even got her roots done, eyebrows waxed, and she shaved her legs, which, according to Eden, is a big deal when you're a heartbroken woman. Eden and Eva are concerned about her. She's barely left the house for weeks. She's lost a lot of weight and she's a shadow of her former self. She's not the same Ella."

The guilt I feel knowing I'm the one who has caused her the pain and misery snaps my heart again.

Unconsciously, my hand clutches my chest as if I can feel her suffering.

"You alright, man?" Hunter asks, his voice full of concern.

"Not really, no." I shake my head.

"I'm always here if you need to talk."

Hunter's such a great guy. He wears his heart on his sleeve, and he's never one to shy away from his emotions. He's a superb listener, and he's been there for me every step of my festival of drama.

"I don't wanna talk about it now."

"Okay, so what did you call me for?"

"I sent you an email about ten minutes ago. Have you opened it yet?" I ask him.

"Nope, not yet. Let me check my inbox."

I whack another ball, allowing Hunter to locate and read what I've sent over. I wait with bated breath for his reaction.

"You are fucking kidding me?" he gasps, then bursts into laughter.

And there it is, exactly how I reacted, too. "Nope. Not kidding. I need your help, Hunter."

"What do you need?"

I walk closer to the phone. Using my golf club for support, I lean against it with one hand.

"It's a huge ask." My tired eyes plead into the camera. "Could you leave the boys and Eden for a couple of days? Fly out to LA? Do you think you could fly Noah and Liam in from Florida too? I'll pay for all your flights."

Without hesitation he responds, "Not required, Fraser, I've got it covered. When do you need me?"

"In a couple of days. The sooner the better, but I know you have Eden to ask first."

"For you, she won't mind. Consider me there."

"Can you keep what I've shown you under wraps? For now, please? Don't tell Eden."

"My lips are sealed. I'll tell her I'm concerned about you, checking in on a friend. I'll sort my jet out and organize Liam and Noah."

"Great, I appreciate this, Hunter. I owe you big-time."

"Anytime. Now, I gotta go butter up Eden and break the news. See you in two days."

I smirk. "Flash her one of your famous swoon-worthy grins the tabloids are always writing about."

"I'll be flashing more than my grin," he winks at me.

I roll my eyes.

"I don't wanna know."

I really don't. His happy family shines a giant light on the empty hole I feel inside.

It sucks why I can't find it in me to be happy and satisfied with Anna and Ethan. But little Ethan deserves to know who his rightful father is, and Anna deserves to be with the man she loves.

And they were selected for me. I didn't pick that family.

I chose Ella.

She's the one I want.

They say to trust and believe in miracles.

I'm expecting one.

CHAPTER TWENTY-EIGHT

Fraser

"Get your fucking hands off me." I hear Nate's muffled bellows across the damp dockside warehouse.

He's here.

I look over at Hunter, standing with arms crossed against his chest, legs spread wide, waiting for the fun to begin. He's been a power of strength to me and has become more of a brother to me than Jamie, my actual brother, ever was.

Liam and Noah manhandle Nate toward us in the middle of the derelict building.

Heaven knows how Frank found this place, but I'm guessing when you're a PI, you need somewhere to tie up a man or two, spook them a little and bring them to a place that looks like a slaughterhouse to get the information you need.

A shiver runs down my spine. Time to step up, Fraser, and play this man at his own game.

I'm being forced to step outside my comfort zone. I'm a normal run-of-the-mill guy who loves to play golf. It's all I've ever wanted to do, but since Nate Miller entered my life, I've been on a downward spiral.

I want to end this. Today.

Noah throws Nate down onto the chair in front of Hunter, Frank, and me. He grunts when his ass hits the chair as Noah proceeds to pull the burlap sack off his head.

"Keep his hands tied," Frank instructs firmly.

Blinking rapidly, trying to focus, Nate takes some time to adjust to the light. A sardonic sneer pulls at his mouth, his nostrils flaring.

He's angry.

Noah pushes his shoulders back, forcing Nate to sit up straighter.

"Get your hands off me. This is a two-thousand-dollar suit. You wouldn't know what one of them looked like if it jumped up and bit you on the balls." He continues to wrestle himself out of their hands.

Give him his due. Nate *has* balls. Giant-sized balls of steel. He's showing no signs of fear.

"I might have known it would be you." He looks directly at me.

"You have hundreds of enemies, Nate. It could have been anyone," I throw back.

"Gotta give it to ya, Fraser. I never thought you'd have the guts to have me kidnapped from my home. You're lucky my bodyguards and staff have the day off today."

"Not lucky, Nate. Planned. I know they don't work today. Because I know more about you than you think. I know *everything.*"

"Whatever. Tell me what you want," he sighs.

Fear isn't in Nate's vocabulary. He thinks he's invincible.

"I want my contract dissolved, which will allow me to

file for the marriage to be annulled. I can do that because the contract was signed under duress, therefore making it not legally binding. Clark has had several of his team investigating my case. It's mitigating circumstances. As soon as you dissolve my contract with you, my marriage to Anna becomes void."

"You're not getting it," he spits my way.

"You *will* give me it, but I'm not finished. I want the extra cuts from my income you stole from me returned. You took what didn't belong to you. I also want you to terminate the NDA I signed."

His red-hot anger pierces the thick air.

"You already told your whore, your lawyer, and this son of bitch here..." He points his head in Hunter's direction. Hunter shakes with laughter, making Nate even angrier. "...about the NDA. You breached your NDA. It's me who should have you sitting in this fucking chair, Fraser. You've no idea what I'm capable of."

"That's where you're wrong. I know this warehouse is two over from where you import and export 'coffee.'" I use air quotes on my last word. "That's code for cocaine, right?" I muster all the confidence I can.

Hunter and Frank assured me they had my back if I lost my confidence or forgot what we've rehearsed, but I continue with my script. "I also know you pay a lot of money to the local authorities to turn a blind eye. There's also the sizable 'donation'..." Again, with the air quotes, I've become some sort of caricature of myself. "...you made to the senator's office back in January. What was that for, exactly?" Nate starts to answer. I raise my pointer finger in the air to stop him. "Ah, no need to tell me. It was to guarantee your Governor of California position. I'm good, right?" I smirk.

Tiny dots of perspiration ooze from Nate's brow. I've got him.

"Oh, and what else? Oh yeah, you sent a beautiful bunch of flowers, underwear, and was it a Fuck Master 5000 dildo to Senator Wilson's wife last month? How thoughtful of you, wanting to spice up their sex life. Unusual, I might add, but thoughtful. Or was it to use for your rendezvous you have with her every Tuesday evening at the hotel on Lake Hill?"

Nate suddenly pales. "I know you need to keep Senator Wilson sweet. I'm not sure fucking his wife is what he had in mind."

I hear Hunter trying to keep it together. He's worse than a child. But he's been laughing sporadically since I showed him *the* photo via email the other day during my swing practice.

"Do you want me to go on? I have more. Much more."

He huffs. "You'll have to do better than that. You've got nothing. I see no evidence," Nate says, biting his lip.

"Oh, but that's where you're wrong, Nate. Let me introduce you to someone."

Perfectly timed, a tall hooded figure walks out from the shadows of the warehouse.

All six of us watch, mesmerized, as the stranger keeps his head bowed low. He places the laptop in his hand on top of the table behind us, casually takes a seat on the chair behind it, then opens the lid, where it springs to life.

"Who the hell are you?" Nate jerks his contempt, his loud voice echoing through the vast space.

The figure slowly reaches up, pushes the hood of his dark sweatshirt down, then lifts his head.

"Nate, I *really* want to say it's nice to see you again, but it's not," Lucas' voice hardens ruthlessly, unable to disguise his hatred.

"You were told to stay away, Lucas. I paid you a lot of money to fuck off out of my daughter's life," he spits with a venomous tone.

Through a clenched jaw, Lucas tries desperately to stifle his reactions. We've agreed to no violence. That's not our end game today. "You're a lying piece of shit, Nate. I left because you made me. You knew my family was desperate for money when my father was diagnosed with cancer. Between me trying to pay back my college debt and my dad out of work with no insurance, we were out of options. You struck when I was at my lowest. You removed me from my son's life. I missed everything. And you're not Anna's biological father, so stop calling her your daughter. It's no wonder I fell in love with her. She is *nothing* like you."

"Oh, but your father's alive; see, I *am* a family man at heart. I saved his life, and you have no loans or debts to worry about. I did you a favor," Nate replies sarcastically.

There's something clearly wrong with Nate. He's not wired right. I actually feel sorry for him. He does not know what's coming.

"He worked as a bar manager for me. What evidence does this asshole have?" Nate looks at me again.

What a cocky twat.

From Frank's inside pocket, he pulls out an envelope and hands it to Lucas.

"Oooooh, is this your scary master plan? What's inside that?" Nate taunts, trying to get a reaction from me.

"My bank details. Lucas here is about to wire all the money you're due back to me."

"You can't do that," he roars.

"Oh, he can. Lucas is not some dumb lowlife like you made out. Lucas is a strategic intelligence analyst with a degree from Harvard. Lucas protects us from assholes like you. His key role for the government is preventing organized crime and drug trafficking. He found some pretty damning information about you whilst he was working for you, and more recently, too. Overseas bank accounts, money laundering, exports and imports, email trails worth their weight in gold to lots of corrupt government workers, some further down the chain, but lots of them are way up there with the best of them. And I don't think it would please them to know your firewall was actually a wet wall, highly penetrable and soggy as fuck. We have everything on you. Your IT team needs firing. Lucas has access to all your overseas accounts. He's about to wire my money back to me."

Lucas chuckles with glee from behind me. "This is the best day of my life so far."

Lucas is an incredible guy. Someone I would want to spend holidays with, shooting hoops or kicking back with. He's smart, funny, geeky as shit, but we've bonded for life. When I told him my story, he agreed to help me straightaway. He knew exactly what and how to get the proof we needed.

I'm putting Anna's little family back together again. And I know she will understand the reasons Lucas took the money—to save his father and his family's home.

Ethan deserves his father; Anna deserves a bountiful amount of love, and Lucas deserves to be a father. He's already missed so much. Lucas is desperate to meet Ethan and reunite with Anna. He's been heartbroken for too long. He's never been with anyone since Anna and he's fighting alongside me to win her back. But we need to climb this mountain first before we hit the summit.

"You should have hired Lucas here. He's the man for the job. He hacked into your systems in less than ten minutes. He's good. I can vouch for him." I thumb over my shoulder.

"You won't get away with this." Like a ravaged dog, Nate launches himself at me. But Noah and Liam grab him, holding him back.

I move, bending down to meet him eye to eye. I feel bile rising as I can't stand this man's snake-like face.

I say calmer than I feel, "Oh I will because here's how this is going to go. You're returning my money. Ending all contracts between us. Setting me, Anna, and Ethan free. You're also giving back Anna what belongs to her from her mother's inheritance and you're going to fuck off out of our lives for good. I never want to see you again."

"You can't make me."

"Oh, I can. Could you give me the file, please?" I summon Hunter.

Passing the brown envelope which holds the key to everything, I instruct Liam to untie Nate's hands.

"Here, have a look at this."

Nate snatches it out of my hand.

As he pulls the contents from the envelope, Nate draws a breath, and his hands begin to shake.

Hunter leans in and whispers, "Is that Senator Green in this photograph with you? I can't tell. He looks different with his dick up your ass. Ironic, given you've been fucking everyone else up the ass. No one likes it when you do it to them, though, screwing them over for their money and freedom. But you seem to enjoy being fucked up the ass." Hunter's lips move in a grin.

Hunter has known Nate longer than I have. He's been a pro golfer for a few more years than me and he's always given Nate a wide berth. Hunter knew that photo would end all my problems, well that, along with everything else we have, but that photo is the beginning of the end.

"Who knew Nate swung both ways like us, Fraser?" Hunter laughs. "But we stick to swinging of the golf club type, not men. You're a coward for not coming out and owning your sexuality. Your whole life is a lie."

Frank's men worked around the clock, notating Nate's schedule. Who he saw, when, why, photographing everything, including Nate's sexual relationships with Senator Green and Senator Wilson's wife. Nate appears to have a preference for government officials.

Nate flips through photo after damning photo, emails, call registers, overseas bank transfers, bank statements, text conversations, evidence of his entire web of lies and deceit. It's all real, unlike the evidence he handed me back in LA.

"The evidence regarding you drugging me the night my contract was signed. An email confirming who would administer that in my drink. That's all in there, too. You should make hiring an organized personal assistant a priority. Your email folders are a disaster waiting to happen. Filing them under *Archive* doesn't hide them from anyone. And that's a fraction of evidence we have on you." I point to the documents and photos in his hands. "Import consignments. More photos of you with women and men in compromising positions. Text messages to the head of the biggest drugs cartel in the state of California. Lucas found it all. You've been sloppy. Exactly what will Pablo Blanco do to you when he finds out?"

As a small-town boy, I have no idea who Pablo Blanco is exactly, but Frank filled me in, and let's just say burning in hell sounds more pleasant than being caught by him.

Frank strikes a few harsh words of reality in Nate's direction. "I've seen what Pablo Blanco's boys do to sloppy businessmen like yourself, Nate. It's torture of the worst kind. Pain you can't even imagine. Remember Old Jon Taylor? He was delivered to his family in pieces for two weeks. The autopsy showed he was still alive when they started chopping him up."

Bile rises in my throat.

Nate's breathing becomes heavy, his eyes bouncing between us. Like a scared rabbit in the headlights, he knows he's been caught, and he knows Pablo will end his life if he discovers Nate was hacked so easily, exposing his secrets and dodgy dealings.

"Where do I sign?" Nate's eyes beg.

Woah.

He's gonna sign?

Is this it?

I try to steady my nerves, trying not to get prematurely excited.

"I have all the paperwork here," Lucas says, still with his head down, deeply engrossed in his laptop, tapping lightly on the keyboard. He unzips his top, pulls out an envelope, and slides the paperwork across the table. "There's a pen inside."

A few pieces of paper that will set me free forever.

My heart races.

I take out the contract Clark has drawn up, exonerating me from Nate.

"Sign along the bottom of the last two pages, Nate. You're lucky you didn't want me to take you to court. We have enough evidence to put you away for the rest of your life. You're signing to end my contract with you as well as the dozens of other athletes you screwed over, too. I have all the

NDAs here." I pull the paperwork from the back pocket of my jeans. "And all of their contracts. You should consider hiring better quality staff and security systems. Your safe is far from *safe*. All Anna had to do was bat her eyelashes at Aaron to gain access to your office. And using your date of birth as your code to your safe isn't advised, eh, no, Lucas?"

"Nope, first rule in the book," Lucas chimes in.

"And then Lucas accessed your security system with the same code to wipe the footage of Anna accessing your office. Schoolboy error, Nate. You need to have multiple passwords to protect you from people accessing your personal shit."

"I'm not dissolving the other guys' contracts, Fraser." He clenches his jaw.

"You will. Or I will inform Anna you organized for her father, her real one, and her mother to be killed in a car crash when she was four. My lawyer opened the police files. Exactly how many corrupt police officers and detectives did you pay off to look the other way? That first act was the one to send you on a path of self-destruction. Power, deceit, lies, murder, extortion, but you got sloppy forgetting to tie up loose ends and secure your assets. You deprived poor Anna of her mother. Her mother wasn't a whore; she was unhappy. *You* made her unhappy, so she turned to the man who looked at her like she was a fucking princess. Your right-hand man. And he adored her. Your old staff sure do like to talk. They knew what you did; they knew they were in love and you broke that little girl's heart when she lost her mother."

I circle around him, Nate watching every move I make. "You deprived her of a happy childhood, murdered the one person who showed her the true meaning of love. Forced marriages may be common practice in your family, but they're not where I come from. So yes, you will sign the papers and you're also signing over one hundred percent of her mother's importing business back over to her, too. It was never a failing business. It bolstered your family's business, not the other way around. It belongs to her and her family. Not you. Sign this one too." I pass him another piece of paper.

I go in for the kill. "The board of directors at AJN Holdings, you know that business that *belonged* to Anna's mother and now rightly *belongs* to Anna, not you, received an anonymous tip this morning, involving you and an obvious case of embezzlement. You've been stealing from shareholders. Vast quantities of money over many years. An emergency board meeting was arranged. They voted to kick you from the board. Frank here has eyes and ears everywhere." I repeat the same words he said back to me in Ella's front room. "They are coming after you. I suggest you find an excellent lawyer."

With the help of Lucas, he's going to help Anna legitimize her mother's importing business Nate took control of. She doesn't know it yet, but she's a millionaire.

I nod my head, confirming everything I said to him is true. *Sign the fucking papers,* I internally beg.

Nate's eyes bore through my skull. He's imagining how many ways he wants to kill me; I can feel it.

"Transfer complete." Lucas looks up with a smile.

"How much did you take?" Nate asks through a pursed mouth.

"Everything owed to me plus interest, and then there's the slight matter of holding me back from living my life. It's the right amount. I didn't take anything I'm not entitled to. I'm not a thief like you. Nate Miller, stealer of dreams."

I pause. Silence screams through the warehouse before I urge him on. "Sign the paperwork."

I think about the last time I watched Nate dish out instructions in the kitchen, shouting at Anna to sign Ethan over to him.

"My, how the tables have turned," I smirk.

Never breaking eye contact, we reach an impasse. Eventually, he looks away and I know I've won.

He signs everything. Giving it all up. Control of the importing business, which was never his to take. Termination of my contract, abolition of the NDAs, including everyone else he has shackled to him.

We set them free.

From this day forward we are no longer under his control.

The tightness in my chest and shoulders I've been feeling for all these years slowly dissipates.

"Are we done?" Nate throws the documents at me.

"Yeah, we are done." I clear my throat. "You know, Nate, a long time ago I admired you, and thought you believed in me. I thought you were going to be the one person who would change my world. And you did, but for the worse. I will learn to forgive you eventually, but I will never forget. I kind of feel sorry for you. To have never experienced love or deep connection with people regardless of who they are—friends, family, associates, your daughter. You use people for your own benefit. You're an emotional vampire, sucking the life, hopes, and dreams from people, and for what? Money? And who do you have in your life to spend it with? The people in those photos in your sad rendezvous and secret trysts in the dark. They don't care about you. You're their dirty little secret. You spend your life in the shadows because deep down you're a sad, lonely, unlikeable old man."

Realization strikes across Nate's crestfallen face. Not

moving, not blinking, saying nothing. He stands, straightens out his suit, pushes his shoulders back, then turns around to walk out of the building. "I'll see myself out."

"We are miles away from your home," Frank informs him.

"I need the walk," he mumbles, defeated.

"Before you go, I forgot to mention one more thing," I call out.

Nate stops in his tracks but doesn't turn.

"Well, two actually. This whole thing was filmed. I have a body cam on. And brace yourself. I'm appearing on prime-time national television next week in a tell-all interview about how you screwed me over, how I never cheated on Anna, and how you made me marry her. I'm clearing my name. It's all coming out, but you signed the paperwork giving me your consent, so we're all legit. It was in the small print, and I know how much you love small print. Clark, my lawyer, will send you a copy of the documents for your records."

We wait for his response, but it doesn't come.

"Anything else?" he asks.

"Oh crap, yeah, I almost forgot. The fake match fixing emails, conversations, text messages, the ones you tried to set me up with? All gone. Lucas used his best men to prove they were forged, but we destroyed them anyway. You're finished, Nate."

"Not so much of a God around here now, are you, Nate?" Hunter mocks him.

My eyes bug out in his direction in a *will you stop it, we got him, enough* look.

Silently he mouths a confused *what*? Then flashes his trademark grin. Hunter has loved helping me, but most of all, he's been waiting for Nate to fall from grace for years. There's no love lost between them, nor me.

Watching Nate finally walk out of my life, elation soars in, and without warning, I fall onto my knees and break down.

I'm free.

CHAPTER TWENTY-NINE

Fraser

"Etttthaaaaan." I wait at the bottom of the stairs of Anna and Ethan's new home.

"Yeah, Dad?" he calls back.

"Can you come down into the living room, please? I have someone I want you to meet."

"Is Mom back?"

"Maaayyyyybe." I nervously call back.

Since Nate's downfall over a week ago, I've been incredibly busy piecing together the parts of my life I didn't have control over before.

I set up a new bank account, paid all of my lawyers' fees, sorted all of my paperwork out, checked up on my car I shipped weeks ago. Picked up our annulment certificate which triggered the cancelation of my green card and my US passport.

I'm saddened because I'm closing the door on what has been my life for so many years, but I feel like I can breathe again.

I finally signed my new contract with Lisa, and she is

officially my new agent. I also won the fragrance brand contract I test shot for, and I'll be one of the new faces for their new campaign. I need to get my ass back in the gym. Stat.

The day after we cornered Nate, I'd arranged for Ethan to go on a playdate with his friends, leaving Anna and me alone in the house.

Then I informed Anna about the previous day's revelations, minus the details about her mother's death.

Producing the paternity certificate was not something I felt comfortable with either, but it was necessary. I can't imagine how awful it would be to live with a man who kept you small for years, showing no love or affection, controlling your entire life, to then discover he was never your father to begin with. With no idea how Anna would react, I tentatively passed her the certificate.

Confusion surrounded her for what seemed like forever, and then she did something most unexpected. She laughed.

Full-on belly aching laughter.

And I joined her.

But then the tears came.

And once she learned our marriage was annulled, she hugged me so tight I thought I might pass out. I'll miss her. I know I will.

She's the kindhearted gentle woman who stood by me through all the years, watching me rise and fall, and I'll miss my happy, clever boy too. So damn much.

I informed Anna that I had some help taking Nate down.

When Lucas appeared through the door, the look of utter confusion and surprise at seeing him made her faint.

Shocked with her reaction, I stood back and could only watch when Lucas ran to her rescue, scooping her up into his arms. And it was at that moment I knew those two were meant to be together. He loves her. He never stopped.

As Anna regained consciousness, she cupped his face and presented him with the biggest smile. The first genuine smile I think I had ever seen from her.

Lucas quickly blurted the truth out and told her how Nate had kept him away, why he took the money he offered him.

For the first time in my life, I witnessed tears of relief, love, happiness, and sadness all rolled into one from Anna, then I left the room so Lucas could explain her newfound millionairess status. I also left it for Lucas to decide whether to tell Anna about her mother and biological father's deaths. It's no longer my place anymore to decide what's right and wrong for her.

They arrested Nate the next day for embezzlement. AJN Holdings are taking him to the cleaners. And I hope Anna gets everything she so rightly deserves.

Which leads us here. I talked Anna and Lucas into going away for a few days together to reconnect, but today, on their return, we agreed for Ethan to finally meet his real father.

I'm so nervous, I've had to change my shirt three times. Little Ethan's been through so much. We're not together, then together, then this today.

Oh boy.

Our happy-go-lucky boy runs down the stairs, jumps into my arms, and I swing him around the hallway.

"You're getting too heavy for this. You're so big now." My muscles contract, lifting his heavy frame.

"Can we have pizza tonight, Dad? I'm starrrrvin'."

"We'll see. Let's ask Mom first."

Hand in hand, we enter the front room where Anna awaits.

"Mom." Ethan runs into her open arms.

"Have you missed me?"

"Nope. Dad let me stay up late last night and we had a midnight feast."

"Fraser," Anna scolds me.

When Ethan looks away, I hold up nine fingers to show nine o'clock, and she rolls her eyes. "Gosh, you'll have to have an early night then, huh?"

"No way, I'm not tired," Ethan says.

"Your dad and I have someone we want you to meet."

Striding across the room, I kneel and look Ethan straight in the eye. "You know I love you, right?"

"And I love you." Ethan bops my nose.

A lump forms in my throat. "Well, I have a secret."

Ethan's eyes widen. "Oh yeah? Can you tell me?"

"Yes. Can I let you meet someone first?"

"Yeah." He nods his head eagerly.

Slowly, Lucas enters the room. Worry is etched across his brow at the fear of not being accepted by Ethan, something Lucas has shared with me several times. He's petrified he won't be able to bond with him.

"Ethan, I want you to meet someone very special," Anna says. "This is Lucas."

Ethan waves. "Hi, Lucas. I have a friend called Lucas in my class at school. It's a cool name. Could I change my name to Lucas, Mom?" He looks back at her.

Our smiles dance across the room at how carefree and playful Ethan is. He's a beautiful boy.

"That's something we might chat about later, but we have something to tell you," she nervously replies.

Lucas saunters toward us carefully, almost not wanting to disturb the pile on the carpet. Sensing his nervousness, I urge him to kneel with me.

"Can I?" I look at Anna for approval before I say anything else.

She nods a soft yes for me to take the lead.

"Soooooo, Lucas is a super special person. He's been away since you were a baby on a top-secret mission," I whisper.

"Wow," Ethan says in awe, looking at Lucas. "What has he been doing?" he whispers back.

"He's been helping to save us from bad people doing bad things on a top-secret mission he can't discuss." I tap the side of my nose. "You can't tell anyone."

Ethan's face lights up. No way is he keeping that a secret, exactly the same as he can't keep a fart in.

"They sent Lucas away to make sure those bad people didn't cause harm to anyone, and he left me in charge to take care of you and your mom." I clear my throat. "My secret is that I'm not your dad, Ethan. Lucas is your real daddy."

"I assigned Fraser on a special mission, too. To protect you because I love you and your mom very much," Lucas says softly.

Ethan looks at Anna, then me, then finally Lucas.

"Do I call you dad now?" He blinks.

Lucas shakes his head. "Not if you don't want to."

Ethan takes a minute to consider his options.

Then he puts his hands on his hips. "Are you kidding? My dad's a superhero and I want to call you dad. And does that mean Mom and you will kiss and stuff? If so, that's so gross." He mimics retching.

Me, Anna, and Lucas let out an audible sigh of relief.

"Is that why you and my mom never kiss?" Ethan turns back to me.

He's noticed.

"Yeah, my mission was to take care of you both for Lucas."

"Oh, are you like Batman, then?" he asks Lucas. "And is Dad, Robin, like your sidekick?"

Lucas chuckles. "Yeah, you could say that."

"Wow." He looks at Lucas in wonder. "I'm Ethan." He puts his hand out for Lucas to shake.

And I cover my mouth to stifle my combined lump and laugh in my throat.

"Wow, that's a strong handshake, Ethan. I have been waiting so long to meet you. Your mom tells me you love gaming and computer programming?"

"I do. It's awesome."

"Me too."

"Really?"

"Yeah."

"Maybe you're more like Iron Man; he's so cool and knows all the computer stuff."

"Or Thor, you look more like Thor," Anna butts in. She puts her hands out wide to signify how broad Lucas is.

"What is it with everyone and Thor?" I scowl. Ella is obsessed with Chris Hemsworth. *Ella.* I shake my head, not allowing thoughts of her to enter my head. I need to focus on Ethan.

"Thor is handsome and big, super buff." Anna swoons across at Lucas. She never looked at me like that. It's how I know they belong.

"Mom likes the Marvel movies. Do you like them?" Ethan directs his question at Lucas.

"Yeah, I do."

"Wanna watch one tonight with us?" Ethan's hopeful eyes sparkle.

"I would love to," Lucas beams.

"I can't stay, Ethan. I'm being interviewed for a television show tonight. But maybe another night?" I say.

"Two dads to watch Marvel movies with. This is so cool," Ethan singsongs.

Lucas eases in with his next question for Ethan. "I know this is a lot to take in and I am *so* excited about watching movies with you, but I have something to ask you. Now that I'm back from my top-secret mission, how would you feel if I moved in here with Mom and you?"

"You're a superhero, right?" Ethan double-checks he understood his status.

"Yeah," Lucas answers.

"Can you move in tonight?"

He's so goddamn cute.

"I would love to," Lucas responds with a gigantic expression of relief.

"Yes." Ethan punches the air.

I know he's going to be alright and that calms me to my core.

"Ethan," I say, grabbing his attention. "Do you remember when Mom and I told you we were going to be living in different houses and we were splitting up?"

"Yeah."

"Well, now that Lucas is back, he's going to take care of you both. The only reason we stayed together was because Lucas was delayed from his mission, and we had to wait for him to return. But it's time for me to leave."

"Are you moving to a new house?" he whispers.

This is the moment I've been dreading.

"Yeah."

He looks down at the carpet. "Can we chat on video like we do at bedtime every night, the same as when you go away golfing?"

"Yeah, I would love to."

This is much *much* harder than I thought.

"Can I come stay with you sometimes?"

"Anytime." I choke up. "You will see me whenever you want. I plan on calling you all of the time. Take you to the movies. I will visit you when I can and come to as many of your football games as I can."

"I will miss you." Ethan throws himself around my neck.

"And I will miss you, buddy. I love you."

"I love you too."

And I cry yet again, like a fucking baby, 'cause that's all I seem to do these days. My emotions are all over the place. I can't think straight and my body feels like a lead weight, hence why I've taken a year's sabbatical from golf. I can't hold myself together long enough. I need to sort my shit out and work out exactly what I want to do with my life. I stopped setting goals for myself, knowing it was impossible to smash them with Nate representing me, but now I want to take time out to work out exactly who *I* am and what *I* want to do with my career going forward. For now, I'm going to focus on modeling, but that's all.

Leaning out of our tight hug, I cradle Ethan's little head in my hands. "Will you look after Mom for me?"

"Yeah. We have Lucas now." He gently says, then looks at Lucas. "You did a good job picking Fraser to look after us. He's been an awesome sidekick, Dad. Can I still call him Dad?" Oh, the mind of a seven going on eight-year-old.

"Of course you can," Lucas assures him. "There are lots of little boys and girls all over the world with two dads."

Ethan frowns. "I'm not little. I'm big, look at me. I'll be eight soon." He stands up tall.

"You're right. What am I saying? You're such a big boy." Lucas puffs out his chest.

"Do you want to come see my game console?" Ethan holds his hand out for Lucas to take it.

"Yeah, I would love to."

I watch as that beautiful boy who stole my heart walks in his rightful place beside his father.

I hear Ethan whispering as they head up the stairs. "Will you tell me about your secret mission? I can keep a secret. I cross my heart. I won't tell anyone."

While I don't like this feeling of yet more heartbreak for me, I know I'm doing the right thing by everyone. They deserve to be happy and together as a family. Even if it leaves me alone.

"He'll be okay." Anna lays her hand on my shoulder.

"I know."

"Are you sure you don't want me to come to the television station with you?"

"Lisa's meeting me there. Spend time with your boys. You three have lots of lost time to make up for. Lucas is a great man, Anna."

"And so are you. C'mere." She pulls me into a hug. "I don't want to make you cry again 'cause I know how emotional you are lately, but you're a great man and I will never forget what you did for us. I love you, Fraser."

I give her a squeeze. "I love you too."

"I hope you get everything you want in life, and I hope things work out with Ella."

I wipe my face, trying to clean myself up.

"I think that ship has sailed. She'll never take me back after all the heartache I have caused."

"You fought for your freedom; now it's time to fight for her. You can't give up."

"Mmmmm." I can't think about her now. "I have to go do this tell-all interview with Meghan Spears."

"Don't take any shit. Fight your corner and don't you dare hold back."

"I won't."

"Time to take care of you now. You've been taking care of us for so long. You deserve to be happy and you just hit the reset button on your life, Fraser."

She's right. Fresh new beginnings.

"Can I call Ethan later?"

"You can call him anytime you want."

"Thank you."

"No, thank *you* for everything, Fraser. You deserve everything your heart desires."

"I know I do, but I don't think what I want is mine anymore."

"In that case, you'll have to pull something pretty spectacular out of the bag. Show her."

She's right.

Ella

"Hey, it's me," I call out and sigh as I enter Eden's hallway.

Walking around the corner into the living area, I dump my purse and drop my tired, heavy body onto the sofa.

It's quiet in here today.

Eden gently walks down the stairs.

"Hey, you," she beams.

"Hi. Where is everyone?"

"Mom and Dad took the boys and Hunter's just out the shower."

I know exactly what those two have been up to.

"I didn't have to come for dinner, you know. You could have canceled."

Eden flaps her hand dismissively. "No way. Food's ready and you need a nourishing home-cooked meal. You're not looking after yourself and you look tired."

Great, I've become the one we all feel sorry for in the family. The one who needs to be monitored, fed, and looked after.

"I'm fine."

I'm not. I'm exhausted all the time. It takes all my energy to teach and dance. My body is completely zapped. I looked it up. Apparently, heartbreak causes some sort of chemical imbalance where your love hormones are replaced with stress ones. Whatever is happening to my body, I don't like it and I feel like shit.

"Dammit, I forgot my phone." Eden races back up the stairs.

I reach for the television remote. Mindless viewing is what I need. Although I haven't been able to concentrate. My television hasn't been on for months. I can't even be bothered scrolling social media, and I can barely hold a conversation for longer than two minutes.

Hunter has some fancy television that takes forever to boot up. Christ knows why it needs to update software every time it switches on.

Waiting for it to load, I quickly grab a bottle of water from the kitchen and have a sniff about the fridge. I don't know what I fancy to nibble. Everything tastes like sawdust to me lately.

Waking up, a dreamy feminine American voice over from the television announces, *"Coming up next on America News Daily. Stay tuned for another chance to hear the explosive and exclusive tell-all Fraser Farmer interview."*

I slam the fridge door, turning my attention to the television screen.

I feel the air being slapped out of me, inhaling on a back step at the image of Fraser's handsome face across the gigantic screen. *He sold his story? How?*

Unable to move, I'm rooted to the spot. I watch in a detached-like state as the commercial break comes and goes, and then there *he* is.

Aimlessly, like I'm floating on air across the room, I stand in front of the television.

I listen intently to every word as he unwraps his life story. All of it, in great detail.

He looks thin and tired. We are the perfect disastrous mirror image of one another.

"Fraser," I whisper at my broken man.

I don't know how long I stand there, but suddenly Hunter's voice pulls me out of my daze. "Are you okay?"

"Hmm?" I look up at him.

"You're crying, Ella. Are you okay?"

I reach up and pat my cheek. I didn't realize I was. I'm on an emotional knife edge.

"I don't know," I whisper.

Hunter wraps his arm around my shoulders as we stand watching together.

No headline goes untouched as Fraser sits explaining everything from his fake marriage, being drugged, why he visited a paid escort service, Ethan not being his, Nate's control and taking his money. He shone a light on it all, setting the record straight. He comes across as the genuine boy next door I fell in love with all those years ago, but was pulled over the coals by a power and money crazed agent.

"And you never cheated on Anna, because you were never married in the true sense?" the show host asks.

365

"That's correct. I'll admit to paying a high-class escort agency. But I used that because Anna and I never had a sexual relationship."

"And the girl in the tabloid photos?"

"She was the love of my life. Someone I was forced to stay away from."

"And now? Can you be with her?"

"I can't answer that. Can we move on?"

"Fair enough. I believe you signed with Lisa Spitery, the same agent as Hunter King?"

"Yes, now I am no longer signed to Nate Miller. Lisa is my new agent and she's like night and day compared to him. She's on my side and brilliant at what she does."

"Let's be honest, Fraser, after this, and given the enormity of what Nate Miller did to the other athletes, he will never work as a sports agent again."

"No, highly unlikely from prison anyway if you read what the tabloids exposed regarding his dealings with AJN Holdings. I'm hoping all younger athletes watch this and don't fall for false promises and lies like I did."

"So, what's next for Fraser Farmer?"

"I'm taking a break from golfing for the next year to reframe *and focus on what I want to do with my life. I've lost years. Most of it was decided for me. I was trapped. But now I'm taking a step back to decide what I want my life to look like. Nothing else matters to me."*

"And on that note, I can't thank you enough for sharing your truly unbelievable story with me..."

Nothing else matters. Was that meant for me? Is he saying he's starting a new life without me? Did he say I was the love of his life.

"I wish you hadn't seen this." Hunter pulls me from my thoughts.

"Why not?"

"Because he needs time."

"Time?" My throat feels like it's closing up. "We've been desperately trying to work out how to be together. Has he decided he doesn't want me now that he's free?"

"It's not anything like that, Ella. I promise you."

"So, you've spoken to him, then?"

"Yeah." He puffs out a long breath.

I look at Eden across the room. "You knew?"

She dips her head, not willing to make eye contact with me.

She knew.

"When was this?" I ask Hunter quickly.

"What do you mean? It's a replay, Ella."

"I know that. When was this recorded?" I stutter and point at the television like a madwoman.

Hunter doesn't answer.

"When?" I beg him. I need to know.

"About six weeks ago."

"He did this six weeks ago?" Exasperated, I push my fingers into my hair and pull it. "Why didn't you tell me?

And why didn't he call me?" I look at Hunter for an answer. "In fact, don't answer I already know why."

He didn't want me after all. I guess he liked the idea of us being together. In reality, though, leaving America, Ethan, and his life behind was probably too difficult for him.

He chose them again over me.

"I have to go." I wipe the tears from my face.

"You can't drive when you're upset," Eden calls out to me.

I don't answer.

Swiping my purse off the couch, I dash out of their house.

He's had six weeks to contact me, longer if he's been free of Nate before his interview.

He never came back for me.

CHAPTER THIRTY

Ella

I've made a cozy nest for myself along the window seat in my bedroom as I watch the rain pouring down in sheets against the windows.

I've always loved the sound of rain and love nothing better than studying the rain-streaked panes. It's calming and meditative.

My thoughts have been flip-flopping between acceptance and anger. The two polar extremes of how I feel, with nothing in between.

I tried calling Fraser last night, but the number no longer exists.

No matter how hard I try, I can't work out why he never came back for me. It makes little sense.

No call.

No message.

Nothing.

I'm guessing he never wanted to fight for us after all.

He's free to have anyone he wants now.

I am not the one.

And I'm done crying. I decided when I carried my heavy bones out of bed this morning. No more tears, although I'm not sure I have any left.

I tuck my legs into me, cross them, and let out a large audible sigh. Something my mom has been telling me I do all too often recently.

Lifting my journal off the cushion next to me, I begin my morning ritual.

Dear whoever... because I know I'm not writing to you, Universe, you are never on my side.

I don't know what to write.

I don't know who I am anymore.

Where did Ella go?

Where is the girl with the appetite for fun, laughter, and free spirit?

Bring her back, please.

I don't want to feel heavy and blue anymore.

Because this girl right here hasn't smiled or felt joy in such a long time.

I felt happy when I was with him. Deep down undeniable happiness. He felt the same; I know he did.

What made him change his mind about us?

Where is he?

I must not have mattered as much as I thought I did.

But it felt real.
For a moment there, I believed he could be mine.
Believed destiny was on our side.

A roaring lorry brings me out of my musings. Peering out of the window into the courtyard, I spot an enormous moving truck lazily rocking over the cobbles. *Hmm. Someone must be moving today.* I know Mr. and Mrs. Murphy across the way were talking about selling last month, but I never saw the house up for sale, unless they sold privately. To be honest, I've been too wrapped up in my web of self-pity that I've probably missed the signs going up. Focusing my attention back to my journal, I begin writing again.

I want to feel better.
Need to for my right-mindedness.
My fresh beginning starts today and my heart will heal with time. I've done it before; I'll do it again.
Universe, what's my first step?
Give me a sign.

When my pen finishes writing the last word, a loud knock at my front door forces me from my thoughts. Peering down out of the window, I spot a guy from the moving company waiting for me to answer. He must have the wrong house.

I'm not used to having silence in the house. Usually, a firm knock to my door would trigger a choir of yelps and mini barks, but last night, Eva appeared and took my dogs away for the night. She does that from time to time as her boys love them and today, which is a Saturday, she is having them all day for me.

I'm not scheduled to teach dance classes today and no Tartan to muck out either as they are training new staff at the stables, so I have nothing to do and all lonely day to do it. *How pathetic.* I might give Beth a call to see if she wants to go for an ice cream later and walk up to the castle.

Grabbing my silk robe, I lace the tie around me and knot a bow in it as I run down the stairs.

Upon opening the door, I'm greeted by a super cheerful guy, all fuzzy beard and tangible glee.

"Morning, Ms. Wallace." He looks at the clipboard in his hands.

"Hi?"

"Moving day. Are you excited?"

"I'm sorry, what?"

"Moving day. Best day of the week." This guy is way too enthusiastic for my liking at this time of the morning *and* on a Saturday. "Ignore the rain. It's supposed to ease off in an hour."

Is this dude for real?

"I think you must have the wrong house. My house was never up for sale, and I haven't bought a new one."

"You sure?" He looks down while I look up at the large red and gray moving truck sitting outside my door with half a dozen guys all busy unloading flat pack boxes and packaging.

"It says here, Ms. Wallace. With today's date, moving to Featherie House." He looks at me again and grins.

I laugh at his absurdity. "I'm sorry you definitely have

the wrong house. I think I would know if I had sold my house and if I was supposed to be moving today."

"I promise you I don't. This is the correct address, and it was organized by a"—he flips the piece of paper over—"Hunter King."

"Eh? Can you give me a minute to grab my phone? I think there's been some sort of mix-up," I call back over my shoulder as I run up the stairs.

I tap the call button on Hunter's name, then Eden's with no success. I head back down the stairs yet again to discover the guys are packing up my kitchen.

"What the hell are you doing? Can you please stop? I don't know if this is some sort of joke, but I'm not moving house today." I shake my head in utter disbelief.

I look at shaggy beard dude again. "Okay, but we are moving you to this house today. It says so here. Full packing service and removal," he reaffirms, presenting me with the paperwork again.

"Okay, you can keep on saying it, but I can't get ahold of my brother-in-law. He may have bought a new house and filled out the paperwork incorrectly. He buys lots of property." I hold my hands up. "Stop what you're doing. Make yourself a coffee or something. But don't touch anything else. Let me get dressed quickly and I'll nip down to this house. Is it here in Castleview Cove? I don't recognize the name."

Shaggy beard guy explains where it is. It's apparently one of the old, traditional houses off the side road leading to the golf course. I've never been down there before because it's private. The houses are like an enigma. Each is secluded, luxurious, and way out of my price range.

Scurrying around in my bedroom, I hop about at high speed, pulling on my leggings and black hoodie, my phone wedged between my shoulder and ear, trying to get Hunter or Eden to pick up. I give up after trying several times.

Scooping my blond locks into a messy bun, I check myself over. Pale, dark eyes, and lackluster... I look like a shadow of my former self as I'm off to meet a millionaire down his or her private road.

First impressions count normally, but not today.

Curving around the narrow private road of Featherie House, I stare up at the canopy of trees lining the driveway as the enormous house comes into view.

"Wow."

There are no cars around. It's peaceful here, with heaps of grass stretching far and wide, with rows of luscious multicolored flowers everywhere.

I look for a sign before getting out of my car and sure enough, to the right of the door, is a tiny wall plaque with Featherie House engraved into it.

"How the other half live."

Running across the gravel, I give the shiny brass feather knocker a good rap against the door. It's sitting slightly ajar, so someone must be in.

There's no reply.

As I look around at the beautifully manicured lawns, I imagine myself living here. I bet the winters are stunning, and it's only a short walk to the beach. It's picture postcard perfect. Turning back around to face the door, I admire the oversized black gloss front door. It's exactly what I would have picked too.

Taking my chance, I push the door open. "Hello... anyone home?"

Craning my neck further around the edge of the door, I push it farther open to reveal a fully refurbished and modern interior in golds and toffees, all accented with black, forest greens, and navy blues.

From floors to ceilings, everything is designed in bold and extravagant rich and bold colors, Art Deco style; it's glamourous and wild.

"This place is epic," I whisper to myself, looking around in wonder.

Curiosity gets the better of me and I'm suddenly in the heart of the house. "Hello... anybody here? My name is Ella Wallace." I tentatively move along the corridor, flitting my eyes around the decadent space as my voice echoes through the enormous cavern corridor. "I think there's been some kind of mix-up today with your moving truck." Or maybe it's Hunter I should be finding.

"Hunter? Are you here?"

Still, no one appears.

There has to be someone here. The door was unlocked and this house must be worth at least a cool million.

I drift through the doorway at the end of the long hall, entering the most magnificent room I've ever seen in my life. It stops me in my tracks as I take in the endless geometric black-and-white flooring, black gloss furniture, and dark navy-blue walls with giant oversized gold framed prints. And that oversized navy-and-gold velvet-trimmed sofa is everything my heart desires. I think I have love hearts in my eyes.

I'm in awe. This is how I want to decorate my little house. Although it's very similar to mine.

I've said it before but, "Wow."

Forgetting I'm supposed to be finding someone to sort out my bizarre day, I suddenly hear a faint light tapping sound of pitter patter footsteps. I know that sound. When I turn around, a little, dumpy, blue fawn French bulldog who can only be around four months old, is bounding toward me.

Instinctively, I bend down. "Hello, wee guy. Or girl. What are you?" I check. "Oh, you're a boy. Hey, gorgeous boy." I give him a good rub. "Where did you come from, huh? Is your mommy or daddy around?" He whizzes around with glee at the attention.

"Oh, you are so excited. Look at you, you're so cute. What's your name? Let me have a look." I lift him up and check out his name tag. "It's Trey. Now that is a cool name."

"It means three." A low voice startles me from across the far side of the room, forcing my head to snap up.

In shock, I almost drop the puppy.

Casually leaning against the doorway across the other side of the room leans Fraser with his hands tucked into the front pockets of his jeans, looking all buff and beautiful.

I suck in a breath.

Am I imagining this?

He walks across the room in my direction.

"Do you like him?" he grins.

"Am I having a Phantom Fraser moment?" I scrunch my face up.

He chuckles, shaking his head.

"Do you like him?"

"Eh, um, what, you, is this, are you..."

I think my brain's short-circuited.

Only two feet apart now, I reach out to stroke his face to check he's real.

He covers my hand with his, then slowly glides them both down over his heart. Like always, at his touch, electric sparkles fizz between us.

"You're here?"

"I'm here." His blue gems never leave mine. "I came back for you."

I bite my bottom lip to stop it wobbling.

He came back for me.

I feel like I'm in a dream.

"Wife?" I ask.

"Annulled."

"Nate?"

"No contract. Dissolved."

"You're free?"

"Yes." He grins.

"Son?"

"I found Ethan's father, Lucas. Ethan loves him. He's a great guy and Lucas and Anna are getting married."

My eyebrows shoot up. "Wow. Quick."

"Yeah, wow." He hasn't stopped smiling.

"So, stepdad?"

"Kind of, yeah." He nods his head up and down.

"America?"

"I live here now."

"Here?"

"Yes, here."

"In this house?"

"Yeah, in this house."

"Yours?"

"No."

"Oh, rental?"

"No."

"Huh?"

"*Ours*, Ella. Not mine. Ours."

"Ours?" I gasp. He doesn't give me a moment to absorb that.

"Yes. Do you like the name of the house?"

"Featherie House? Yeah." I frown, shaking my head, not understanding.

"A featherie is a nineteenth century golf ball that was made with white feathers."

I smile wide, unable to contain it. It signifies us both, golf combined with feathers.

Smiling still, I say, "I love it."

Still clutching my hand in his over his heart, Fraser moves closer to me, and my breathing gains momentum.

"Do you like Trey?"

"I love him."

"I know how you love the whole alliteration thing. Treacle, Toffee…"

"Trey." My smile grows wider again. I can't help it.

"And I also know how you like everything in threes, Ella."

"He's perfect," I whisper.

"Omne trium perfectum." *Everything in threes is perfect.*

"You came back for me?" I feel a small tear trickle down my cheek.

"Third time lucky. Again with the threes."

Millimeters away, Fraser pulls me in with our arms and hands linked between our bodies. I can feel his heart racing. I can feel my own too.

"Watch the puppy," I whisper.

Never letting me go, he scoops Trey out of my arms and plops him onto the shiny floor, then stands closer still. Unclasping my hand, he cradles my face.

His eyes stay fixed on mine. With the pad of his thumb, he gently smooths it back and forth across my cheek. "I've missed you. You look beautiful."

"I'm a mess." I break our gaze.

"Hey, look at me," he coos.

And I do.

"You, Ella Wallace, are the most beautiful and precious person in my life. I'm sorry for all the pain I've caused, but I am here for you now. Forever."

"Forever?"

"Forever and eternity."

This feels surreal, but this is all I've ever wanted.

Him.

A tilt my head to slowly meet his lips, melting into him, silently begging him to hold me. Fraser loops his free arm around my waist, and we kiss like we've never kissed before. It's the kiss of ultimate kisses. A kiss full of promise, hope, and pure love. And with every soft and gentle touch, it dissolves my pain, knitting my heart back together as our tongues dance in perfect slow and sultry rhythm.

Tasting him again, feeling him as the buzz of possibility flows through us. I've missed his unique fragrance, his touch and flavor.

He's exquisite, sensual, and finally, after all this time, he's mine.

My hummingbird of joy which stopped flying all those weeks ago in my heart takes flight again as I feel a strong familiar flutter.

I open my eyes and he's looking right at me, holding me with his powerful gaze. He threads his fingers into the hair on the back of my neck, gluing us firmly back together, where we always should have been.

"I'm so sorry it's taken me so long to do all of this," he mumbles between kisses.

"I didn't think you were coming back for me," I breathe.

"I would never let that happen. But I was scared you wouldn't have me back. I'm nothing without you."

"Please don't leave me again."

"Never."

Our kiss turns hot and heavy, but we never break eye contact. In this pure form of intimacy, I feel connected to him like no other person in my life and he's mine forever. Unexpectedly, he bites my bottom lip, sucking it into his mouth, becoming rougher as a promise of what's to come.

Our soul-kiss shreds the heaviness I've been carrying around with me from my body, allowing love and sheer joy to trickle back into my heart.

Unrushed, we finally come apart. Fraser plants soft kisses across my cheek, leaving a trail down my nape before he buries his head into me, gently biting, then squeezes me tight. I finally catch my breath.

"I love you, Ella," he breathes against my skin.

"I love you so much. I've missed you. I didn't think *we* would ever be possible. But you found a way." I let my tears of happiness and relief flow.

We hold each other firmly, not wanting to let go.

From across the room the door *clicks* open and a happy Treacle and Toffee bound through it, jingling and jangling their collars as they skip across the room. "I'm not here; I'm just the door opener," Eva calls.

"Peace ruined," Fraser chuckles.

I lean back slightly from our embrace. "What are they doing here?"

"They stayed with me last night so they could bond with their new brother. Treacle loves me now."

I don't believe that's true.

"And Eva was in on this?"

"Everyone is in on this."

"I'm mad at you for letting me believe you'd forgotten about me."

"I'm so sorry. I wanted all of this to be a surprise. I'm sorry if I caused you unnecessary pain. We couldn't do it any quicker. Everyone's been helping me out for the last six weeks. The builders and interior designers have worked tirelessly. We only finished last night. You were *not* meant to watch that interview of me. That was not supposed to happen. The last thing I ever wanted you to believe is that I would never come back for you. I almost came to your house last night. Hunter said you were so upset. But everyone said this was too big of a surprise to spoil." He motions to the surrounding room.

This is *big*. And it would have spoiled everything. This is the most romantic thing anyone has ever done for me.

"You've been here all of this time?"

"I've been hiding here. I did a fragrance campaign first before I left LA, but I've been busy remodeling this house for you, sorting my life out, bank accounts, new car, insurances, telephone contracts. You name it, I have done it." He raises his eyebrows. "I'm now in control."

"You won the fragrance brand contract to model?"

"Yeah. I've been signed to a modeling agency too. I'm an older model, but apparently that's what brands are looking for."

"That's crazy."

"I'm crazy about you," he says, kissing my forehead. "I'll do anything for you, Bella. I've worked my ass off getting our house ready. I had to do something really amazing to prove to you I am serious about us, to prove this is our forever. I did this for us. Do you know what date it is today?"

"No." I shake my head.

"Today is the day we discovered our little hideout by the beach. Welcome to our new hideout." He spreads his arms wide.

He's sentimental. I don't remember the dates, but he does. *Wow.*

"This house must have cost you a fortune. Is this really yours?"

He rolls his eyes. "It's *ours*. And I don't want you to worry about the money. It's all bought and paid for."

I'll have to remember to circle back around and ask him about that later.

"And while this is lovely and all, it's moving day for you. Time to make this house a home. I've managed to buy the basics, but Katherine, our designer, is coming back next week so you can finish it to your specifications."

I'm getting my own interior designer? This day keeps getting better and better.

"Aw, man, I told those guys to stop packing," I gasp.

"And they called me to tell me you were on your way here. I told them to pack and load up the truck. Hunter's name on the paperwork was a ruse."

Fraser entwines our hands together. "Quick tour, then back to your house. I don't want the movers packing your underwear drawer. Quick, c'mon, boys." Fraser whistles, beckoning our three fluff balls to follow us through the grand house. My house. Holy wow. And three doggies too.

"Yeah, I don't want them packing my personal stuff either. My vibrators are in that drawer. Along with my magical unicorn horn," I smirk.

Fraser's eye bug out. "Vibrators? Plural? You'll not be needing any of them anymore. They're going straight in the bin. Come on, this house is incredible. Wait until you see the bathroom and the master bedroom," he says excitedly. "I have so much to tell you, but today's going to be a crazy busy day." He rushes me out of the living room.

"Up here. Look," he says to the dogs as he points up the

sweeping stone and wrought iron staircase. "Well, don't just stand there, boys; let's show mommy her new home. C'mon."

I cover my mouth to stifle a giggle.

I love this man.

Room after room, my guided tour reveals the most luxurious home I have ever had the pleasure of being in, and it's mine.

"And this is the master bedroom." Fraser slowly glides the heavy, dark oak door open, proudly revealing a gigantic room with black oak paneling and wall-to-wall windows overlooking the grounds. On the far side of the room sits a black, ornate four-poster bed.

"This can't be real? Can it?"

"Oh, this is real, Ella, and it's all ours." Fraser runs toward the bed and flings himself onto it. "Come test it. Look at the view from here. It's incredible." He's like a kid in a sweet shop.

Staring at him on the bed, with his tee shirt hitched up slightly, I can't help but admire *my* view. Yup, he's right. The view from here is incredible.

He pulls me down onto the bed, his eyes full of worry. "Do you like the house, Ella? And the decor? I did all this for you. I want you to be happy."

I cup his face and plant a soft kiss on his lips that I adore so much. "I love the house. I'm kind of in shock. It's going to take a while to get used to."

"Important question… is it obnoxious enough?" He grins.

"More obnoxious than I ever imagined. You did great." I laugh at his absurdity. It's huge and over the top.

"Yes." He punches the air. "Do you like the bed? It's cool, right?"

"It's out of this world. Did you buy a four-poster bed so you could tie me to it?"

Without hesitation, he says, "Yes. But later." He wiggles his eyebrows and throws me a sexy wink. "Look, I have something else to show you."

"More?"

"More." His excitement is palpable. He pulls me from the bed, hand in hand, as he leads me over to the window. "See down there?" He points through the trees. "Do you see the building?"

"Yeah."

"That's Tartan's new home."

"What?" I ask in disbelief.

"Tartan is already here. I had him moved yesterday. We have stables," he says matter-of-factly. "You'll be able to ride him along the beach in the mornings."

I'm speechless.

"I'm making good on my promises I made to you when you were eighteen. It's taken me too long to give you everything you wanted."

"All I wanted was you," I whisper.

Squeezing my hand tightly with reassurance, he says, "You have me."

"I do."

"I have something that belongs to you." He pulls the neckline of his tee shirt.

A sparkle of light catches the long strand of gold hanging between Fraser's pinched forefinger and thumb. Our two feathers twist and turn in the air like mini wind chimes.

He's wearing my necklace.

"You found it?" I cup my hands over my mouth.

"I had to replace the chain because you broke it. I've

been wearing it every day. But let's put it back where it belongs."

I turn, and like the last two times, I let him clasp it back around my neck. I feel his hot breath tickle my skin and familiar goosebumps only he can summon dance across my body. He cocoons me in his enormous arms, making me feel safe and happy for the first time in what feels like forever.

I reach up to give my two feathers a rub. Fraser covers my hands with his. "Reunited," he whispers.

"I'm never letting you go again."

"I'm counting on it. You won't get rid of me now."

From behind us, our three little fluff balls scuffle about, chasing one another, yelping and panting as they do. Happy in their new home.

I think I'm gonna like it here.

"They're gonna ruin our new home, aren't they?" Fraser mumbles against the skin of my neck.

And I giggle with glee.

"Yeah, they are."

Our new home.

CHAPTER THIRTY-ONE

Ella - Eight Weeks Later

"As soon as this first dance is over, we are leaving," Fraser whispers in my ear.

I will never get enough of this man. *My husband.*

"Shush, someone will hear you." I giggle.

"I don't care. Screw 'em. I need you naked. I want to officially consummate this marriage and claim you as mine." He gives my ass a firm squeeze. "Goddamn churches and photos and speeches. I've been waiting all day to get you alone. Who wanted this big wedding, anyway?" He loosens his tartan tie slightly and rolls his neck.

"That would be you."

"I'm a fool. We should have eloped. I would have had you by now."

This guy.

Three days after the 'welcome to your new home' surprise, Fraser and I took a stroll along the beach. Living only a stone's throw away, we celebrated the unpacking of the last box inside our secret nook with an ice-cold bottle of champagne. We watched the waves crash against the rocks as the sun poured over the curves of the ocean. Instantly, happiness flooded my soul. I felt it; it was as if someone had filled a jug of happy hormones and poured it in from the soles of my feet to the top of my head. Deep, unapologetic contentment.

I was too exhausted having just made the quickest house move on record, and too distracted with how sore my back was from all the unpacking, when Fraser revealed a whopping emerald-cut diamond engagement ring asking me to marry him, I was yet again taken by surprise. He had everything planned.

I've been glowing ever since, and I can't stop smiling.

Unable to wait, he gave me eight weeks to plan our wedding, but everywhere was booked up solid.

On a whim, I begged Eva to speak to Knox Black for us. She's been giving him private dance lessons he won at the charity ball.

I instructed her to give him a dirty dance if she had to, so we could have our reception at his luxury spa and hotel, The Sanctuary. She finally gave in and asked him for us. And I don't know what she had to do to make him find a date for us, but here we are. Knox has been hovering the entire night, managing the staff. All the while, he's never taken his eyes off Eva. I must ask her about *that*.

"You know, we both have skirts on. It would be easy enough to slip away to the cloakroom in the hotel." My eyes light up.

"Don't call it a skirt; it's a kilt."

"And you wear it very well."

"I'm a true Scotsman today." He winks.

And I giggle. I've been giggling for weeks. I can't help it.

Fraser surprised me by wearing a kilt to get married in. I expected him to wear a tux, but nope, full-on kilt with a twist, black with Black Watch Tartan peeking out from the pleats. The green and blue tartan was a gentle nod in recognition to his great grandfather, who served in the Army in the Royal Regiment of Scotland. He even made Hunter wear one, too. I can't say Hunter isn't happy about that; I'm sure he and Eden disappeared for a reason earlier.

"I need to get it off and this dress off you, too. You look beautiful, Ella."

"I feel like I'm living in a fairy tale." I look around.

Not having much time, and running out of options, I ended up taking a quick trip to Edinburgh to buy my dress from a specialist vintage wedding shop. My figure-hugging lace dress is elegant, and it fits like a glove. I fell in love with it and made it mine.

As we stand on the side of the dance floor, the host finally calls us forward for our first dance.

Fingers entwined, Fraser leads me into the center of the dance floor and when the first note is played from our string quartet of "Nothing Else Matters".

Fraser pulls me in close to him. Our heartbeats pressed together.

"I love you, Bella."

"I feel it. I know, Fraser. I love you with all my heart."

"Always and forever," he whispers, and I nod.

Fraser plants a soft, delicate, dreamy kiss to my lips. I know this is where I belong.

Slowly, the rest of the bridal party joins us.

Swaying to the gentle music, I look around at my friends and family. I'm truly not alone. I never was. I've been surrounded by love, with Fraser loving me from afar all along.

As I look across at Fraser's mom and dad and my parents snuggled into each other, I appreciate what finding true love looks like; it's them. And for a moment there we weren't sure if Fraser's mom, Susan, was going to be okay, but she responded well to her treatment and she is currently in remission. For now, we can breathe a little more freely.

Mom was right when she said, *fight for him*, but I almost gave up on him completely. My mom's a fighter. She fought for my dad and her to be together. With an age gap of ten years between him and her, they were bold and brave to fight hard for one another. She knew what she wanted at nineteen and she never wavered. Thirty plus years later and there they are, still in love, still together and happy.

As we expected, Fraser's brother Jamie didn't appear today, no RSVP, no text, not a thing.

Part of us was relieved; it may have made for an uncomfortable situation for Eden and Hunter. But I'm saddened he didn't come to share our special day. On the plus side, there was no drama.

My eyes find Anna's across the dance floor, and she gives me the biggest 'we won' smile before resting her head on Lucas's shoulder. Choosing a small wedding, they were married at city hall in LA with only me, Ethan, and Fraser as witnesses. It was a moment I will treasure forever.

As my nephews, Archie and Hamish, and Ethan whizz about the dance floor between us all, we all begin to chuckle, as they don't seem to be appreciating our heartfelt song. But I don't care. This is how it's meant to be.

This is our story. It's chaotic, unpredictable, and unique.

When the song comes to an end, Eva swoops past me with the look of wickedness across her angelic face. "For you." She pops a key in my hand.

"What's this?" I'm puzzled.

"The key to Knox's private office."

"How the hell do you have that?" I gasp.

"Who cares?" Fraser grabs my hand. "Let's go."

"Three doors down on the left-hand side," Eva calls from behind us.

Dashing across the floor, I pull my skirt up on one side, being careful not to catch my sky-high heels in the delicate lace.

"Where are you two off to?" I hear someone call. An instant dance of laughter breaks out.

How embarrassing.

Snicking the lock behind us, Fraser pushes me against the door.

"You have to take this dress off. I can't even pull it up. It's tighter than your leather pants."

It's tighter since I bought it. He's not wrong. Happiness leads to eating.

He unzips my dress for me. He peels the delicate lace fabric from my body and it falls in a puddle around my feet.

"Holy shit, what do you have on?" He gapes as I step out of my dress.

I splurged on my underwear. Okay, maybe it was a step too far, costing almost as much as the dress, but it's beautiful, and I couldn't resist.

Multiple fine straps and eyelash lace, it features a peekaboo, barely there bra and a suspender belt, and my panties are so small you need a microscope.

"You like?" I give him my best flirty wink.

"Oh, Bella, you have no idea," he groans.

I think I do.

Walking backward, he eyes me up and down as I sashay my way across Knox's office.

"You should wear heels more often. In fact, I'm making a new house rule. I only get to fuck you in heels." He pulls in a breath as he bites his bottom lip with his teeth.

"Okay." Although we both know that's not gonna happen because we can never keep our hands off one another, especially at three o'clock in the morning. I don't know why that is, but it's our new thing.

"Fuck, did I pick a sexy woman. You are *fine*, girl." He licks his lips in appreciation.

I watch as Fraser sits down on the leather couch, then pulls his black coat, waistcoat, shirt, and tie off, leaving him with only his kilt on, naked from the waist up. He looks like a sexy Roman gladiator. This is what dreams are made of.

I move closer and slowly straddle him. With hooded eyes, his sinful mouth takes mine.

I rock back and forth over his hard clothed cock.

"You're gonna give him carpet burns if you keep grinding against me; I am a true Scotsman after all," he breathes against my lips.

I slowly begin to move the coarse fabric of his kilt out of way until my wet lace touches his dripping cock.

He pulls my soaked panties to the side, and I glide the tip of his cock up and down my swollen lips.

Watching him move over my pussy, he grows harder and longer. Our eyes connect and he grants me the most shockingly beautiful smile, making my panties melt. He hooks his hand on the top of my shoulder before pulling me in for a kiss.

Teasing him, I put his tip in slightly, then slide him up my pussy lips again. I do this over and over before he's moaning loudly into my mouth, until he can't take my teasing anymore. Possessively, he grabs my hips, plunging himself into me. Arching my back, my eyes roll back into my head, and I cry out with unexpected pleasure.

Using his hard, athletic chest for leverage, circling and filling myself up with him.

He sucks my nipple, and I about come undone as he lashes at it relentlessly.

The sound of our slapping skin and wet excitement rends the air as he fills me to the hilt with his length.

I'm loud, he's loud. We need release, to brand us officially as husband and wife.

Over and over, I fuck him with everything I have. He grabs my ass with his strong, gigantic hands, coaxing me to go faster.

His breathing quickens and I know he's close. Flicking my heels off, I lay my feet flat against the couch and squat like I've never squatted before.

"Aw, fuuuucckkkk," Fraser groans.

And all he can do is grip my hips and ass as I ride him to pleasure.

Abruptly, he sits forward. At this angle, he teases my sweet spot inside and within a few hard pumps, the ecstasy building within me hits with such force I come, crying out his name like I'm wearing it as a badge of honor. Clenching all around him, he pistons me faster until I feel him hold himself deeper inside my body. He comes hard, breathlessly mumbling words of desire, telling me he loves me and how hard he comes for me. I can't take my eyes off him as the moonlight floods through the windows. His endless muscles look like they're dancing just for me.

Easing out of our haze of pleasure, Fraser wraps his arms around me, then kisses me as if I'm the most precious human being in the world.

"I love you, Mrs. Farmer," his whispers tickle my mouth.

"I've waited so long to hear you call me that."

"Me too." He blazes a smile.

"We have to get back to our guests."

"Let's leave. I want you in our bed, at home, and I wanna

stay inside you all night. I'm not going to be able to think about anything else but you in this sexy gear you have on."

He's not lying either. He keeps telling me we have years' worth of making out, dating, making love, and kissing to make up for.

"We have the rest of our lives to do that. But we spent a lot of money for this big shindig today, so we have to go and entertain our guests."

He rubs my back and all of a sudden, I feel exhausted.

"I'm so tired, tired of peopling," he says as if he can read my thoughts.

"I'm tired too. It's been an eventful few months."

"But we did it."

We did.

We clean up. Putting ourselves right again.

Shimmying back into my dress, Fraser slowly zips it back up. Smoothing it down, I wander over to the curved window overlooking the cove, the moon sparkling over the coal-black sea.

His warm, strong arms embrace me from behind.

"Do you remember the night in the fire exit stairs? The Championship Winner's Ball? You told me you loved me. I didn't believe you," I whisper.

He turns me around, not letting me move from his arms.

"I will never forget it. You were wearing a sexy black silk dress." He tucks a lock of hair behind my ear. "Your hair was draped over your shoulders and when you danced under the spotlight you were like an angel. You were glowing. I knew I had to sort my life out to be with you."

From nowhere, a tiny little white feather floats down between us. We follow its path through the air as it rests between our chests.

"You know, they say feathers are more than a symbol of guardian angels and protection?" I whisper.

"Oh, yeah?"

"Yeah." I nod. "They say feathers are a gift from the sky and symbolize freedom."

"Really? Like us. We are..."

"...free to love," we say in unison.

Finally.

Looking up into the inky night sky, as the stars twinkle above, I know he's right.

The stars weren't always aligned for us, but we made our own constellation.

And it's bright, shiny, and full of possibilities.

CHAPTER THIRTY-TWO

Ella

Surrounded by electric turquoise water, I lay back against the lounge chair and bathe in the dazzling sunshine.

Suspended in our private villa above the sea, my only decision today is, what should I have for lunch?

Our honeymoon in The Maldives has been divine.

Dipping my sunglasses down my nose, I peer across them as Fraser pulls himself out of the water. I will never grow tired of that view. His deep, sun-darkened skin highlights his even blonder hair. He's gone extremely fair in the sun. As soon as his electric blue eyes, that match the surrounding sea, connect with mine, our invisible charge that runs between us crackles through the hot air.

Like a wet dream, he's all bronzed skin, magnificent washboard abs, and naked. *Wow, so much nakedness.* The benefits of having your own private beach area, and money, you need vast amounts of green to have a luxurious five-star vacation.

Something Fraser keeps telling me we have lots of.

Fraser divulged every piece of information he had on

Nate Miller, hence where all his money came from. He's been returned what was rightfully his. Plus, he's modeling for a few exclusive designer brands, as well as his television network tell-all story fee too; it's mounting up.

Although between the house, honeymoon, and our wedding, it's been flowing out as quickly as it poured in.

To repay Fraser back for as she says, *looking after her and Ethan*, Anna gifted Fraser a ten percent share of her company, AJN Holdings.

Fraser had to blow into a paper bag to regulate his breathing when he opened the email. Anna has picked up the business in super-quick time and apparently, she's a natural born leader. She definitely takes after her grandfather, it would appear.

Fraser was also approached by a sports charity located in America to become an ambassador for them. The charity fights for upcoming young athletes, ensuring they are paid fairly, checking contracts. Educating them to empower them, so they know legal jargon, percentages, sponsorship deals, and how to negotiate, *and* how not to fall for a douchebag like Nate Miller. There's even talk of him overseeing the setup of the charity across the United Kingdom and beyond.

"Hey, baby, you look edible in this tiny leopard print bikini." Leaning down to kiss me, sprinkling cool water across my hot skin, he pings the string of my bottoms. "You could just as well not have it on. These three tiny wedges of material barely cover anything."

He's right. It's illicit.

I chuckle. "It's in case they drop off new towels again, like they said they would." I pop my sunglasses on top of my head.

"Fair point." Wrapping a giant soft white towel around

his waist, Fraser sits down beside me on the edge of my lounger.

"Nothing to do and all day to do it," he grins.

"I was thinking of having a massage later."

"Oh, because it's just so stressful here, you need something to help you unwind." He rolls his eyes.

"It's a very stressful thing deciding what you're going to have to eat each day. It's causing me copious amounts of tension."

He laughs, then tickles my ribs.

Next thing I know, I'm straddled across his lap as he grabs me like I'm a featherweight. I quickly lock my feet around his back, lacing my arms around his neck.

"Back to reality in a few days. Christmas as soon as we get back, too. I'm glad we are having dinner at your mom and dad's this year. Then after Christmas, you'll have lots of decisions to make. We need to finish Ethan's bedroom for his stay next month and then think about what you want to do with the three other spare rooms."

Anna and Lucas decided they wanted to spend their first Christmas alone together as a new family. Fraser is saddened he won't be there to share Ethan's special day, but Fraser understands his place now and knows he has to start stepping back to enable Lucas to be the father he deserves to be.

Ethan still calls all the time though, and I know how grateful Fraser is that Lucas and Anna allow him to do that. Fraser loves that boy so much.

"I think we should let Ethan decide how to decorate his room. I want to turn one into a dressing room. Like you see in the movies. Eden has one. I would love to have all my clothes color-coordinated and organized." That makes me feel excited.

"So, when you say color-coordinated, you mean rows of black, then?" he pokes fun at me.

"I have some colorful clothes." I try to rack my brain and come up short. "I think I do."

"You don't."

He steals a kiss.

"When you were asleep this morning, I was doing some thinking and decision-making of my own." His eyes hold mine. "I was thinking when I return to work, maybe I won't compete in so many golf tournaments, a bit like Hunter."

Well, this is new.

"Would you be happy, Fraser? I know how much you love to play and compete."

"I do, but my priorities have changed, and we've already spent so much time apart, touring means weeks, sometimes months away from you."

"But I could travel with you?" I put the feelers out because what I say next may decide for him.

"I don't think I want that life for us. It's great, don't get me wrong, but I love our new home. I miss our naughty, fun-loving scoundrels."

Our dogs are great fun. I miss them too. They've been staying with my mom and dad while we are on our honeymoon, no doubt being spoiled to the max and loving it.

"Okay, well, I'll be happy either way. For now, though, I am gonna call to see if I can get a massage. But I've been waiting for them to call me back to check which ones are safe for me to have."

Fraser's brows knit together. "What do you mean?"

"Well, sometimes it's not advised to have a deep tissue massage, say, for instance, if you've had a bad injury or an infection."

"Right? I don't follow."

"It's the same with pregnancy. I wanted to be safe."

Fraser's eyes bug out. "Eh?"

"We're having a baby, Fraser," I whisper.

He pauses, looking shocked. "We're having a baby?"

"Yes."

"I'm gonna be a dad, for real?"

I nod.

"But how do you know? We've been here for two weeks." His voice is laced with concern.

"I bought a pregnancy test yesterday from the little pharmacy. Five, actually. I cleared the shelf—all positive. I've been so busy I didn't realize I missed my little friend last month, and then this month again. I did the math and bingo."

Fraser stares at me. I don't know what he's thinking, but maybe it's not the right time and maybe he wanted to wait. So did I, but surprise!

"So what are you, like six or seven weeks, you reckon?"

I nod again.

"Is it too soon?" I ask as nerves ripple low in my stomach. "Even with the shot, it's not one hundred percent safe, and I know we didn't plan th..."

He cuts me off by sealing his lips with mine.

"It couldn't be more perfect." Fraser attacks my lips again. "We'll have a beautiful baby. I know it. And we'll be great parents. Our baby will be loved beyond measure. A mini me or you. Made from love."

I start chuckling when he gets excited.

"I couldn't be happier. I'm finally getting everything I wanted, with you."

His face turns serious. "You aren't going for a massage. Is it safe for you to fly? You'll need to be careful with certain foods. Have you looked it up? And oh my God, we need to go home now and start the nursery." "Fraser, calm down." I grab his face, smoothing my thumbs across his blond scruff.

"Calm down? What if it's triplets? We need to see a doctor today." He pales. "You and this law of attraction thing and everything's better in threes. No way, uh-uh. I've watched Hunter and Eden with three newborns. No, siree, not happening. Pass me your phone. I'm calling reception to arrange a doctor. They'll have to sail us to the next available island doctor. I am not waiting until we return home."

"We won't have a choice if it's three." I giggle.

"This is no laughing matter, Mrs. Farmer."

And I know he's joking.

"We're having a baby," he whispers.

"Yeah."

"This is the best honeymoon I've ever been on."

"I hope it's the only one you'll ever go on."

He gives a throaty laugh.

I watch my super protective man give strict instructions to the resort manager over the phone about how we need to see an ob-gyn today.

And we do get seen straightaway, where the local doctor confirms with an ultrasound scan that I am, in fact, pregnant, but with just one healthy baby bean.

"We have to call our boys back home to let them know they are going to have a little brother or sister," Fraser says as we sway back and forth in the hammock of our private deck. I swear Fraser loves our dogs more than me. He's totally smitten.

"I can't wait to tell everyone. But it's still a little early." I give his hand a quick squeeze.

"Little bean was meant to be. Everything is going to be just fine. I can feel it," he whispers.

I turn into him. Cradling his gorgeous face in my hands, his eyes mirror mine—full of love and possibility.

My hummingbird flits in my heart.

"I love you, Fraser."

"Forever and eternity."

I wished for my soul mate to find me in my journal. It happened. I won't be lonely this Christmas. Instead, in three days time, I'll be spending it with the love of my life.

We fought.

We conquered together.

He was right.

We were inevitable.

The End

EPILOGUE

Fraser - Six years later

"Where are you?" Ella pants heavily through the phone.

"Hello to you too. I'm on my way back from the airport. I'm close."

"So am I. How far away are you?"

"About four minutes? Why?"

"I need you."

"Okaaaayyyyy. Ella, what are doing?"

"I, I, uh…"

"You better not have that fucking glass unicorn dick out again."

"Better hurry home then." Her breathing becomes a moan.

"Shit. Don't you dare come without me. Do you hear me? I'm like three minutes away now." I look out of the window to check my surroundings.

"Ooooooh, Fraser."

"Can you drive faster, please?" I roll the privacy divider down between myself and the driver.

"Two minutes, Bella," I groan. I'm already hard and ready for her. "Are you still with me?"

"Yes!"

"I'm coming up the driveway. Stop what you're doing right now, Mrs. Farmer."

Nothing. She's hung up on me.

Fuck.

Unable to wait for the driver to escort me out, I dive out the car door, covering my throbbing hard-on with my jacket. "Can you dump all of my stuff in the front room, please? My wife needs me. It's, uh, an emergency." I slap a tip into my driver's hand. "Thanks. See you next week."

He chuckles.

"See you then, Mr. Farmer." He tips his hat.

Running through the door, I dart up the stairs two at a time, fling the door open, and growl at the sight of my beautiful, ready for me, pregnant wife lying spread-eagle on the bed. She's fucking herself with her stupid dildo. I'm throwing the thing out again. But that's pointless. She'll just buy a new one.

Pulling my top off quickly, then unbuckling my belt, her hooded eyes lock with mine as I stalk across the room.

"Hey, Mr. Farmer. I've missed you." Her eyes are full of lust for me.

She's beautiful.

"I'm so horny. Why did you have to go away when I am pregnant? You can't go away next week. I've decided." She continues to move that pink glass dildo in and out of herself, panting as she's on the edge of ecstasy. Spellbound, I can't take my eyes off her.

She's six months pregnant with our second child, horny as hell, and she can't get enough of me.

"You took too long," she gasps.

"You're going to give him friction burns, and I've only been away for three days. He needed the rest," I tease.

"Oh, Fraser." She arches her back off the bed.

I whip my pants and boxers off, hopping out of them, my cock bobbing up and down.

Holy shit.

Grabbing her unicorn friend out of her hand, I fling it across the room. It lands with a loud clatter against the wooden floor.

"Noooo, you'll break it."

"That's the plan."

"I need you now, Fraser."

Leaping onto the bed, I spread her knees wide, mine too, and carefully slide inside her wet heat, watching her unfold in front of me with her striking platinum hair fanned over the black bedding. She's the contrast I need in my life. Sweet and sexy, innocent and a deviant too. I love it.

"Ooooooooh, Fraser, I'm gonna come."

I tip her enticing hips ever so slightly and she comes all over my aching cock at lightning speed, her swollen belly tightening from the intensity. Milking me with her tight little pussy, she grabs my ass, pushing my full length into her, digging her sharp nails into my skin. And I know what happens next. Multiple fucking orgasms of epic proportions.

When she's pregnant, something happens to her body, making her more sensitive, and I'm totally here for it. Back-to-back, her orgasm keeps on dipping and rising repeatedly. Watching her is the most sensational thing I've ever witnessed. She's so goddamn sexy and unapologetic about her desire for sex, and for me.

"Oh, Fraser, come for me, babe; fill me up."

That familiar tingling sensation weaves its way up my spine, into my balls, and for a brief moment, I can't think straight as the tip of my cock becomes hypersensitive. Euphoria fires through me as I fuck her hard, pushing her up the mattress, coming furiously as I roar her name.

Together we are so in tune with each other and I've no idea how it's possible, but I fall deeper in love with her with every passing day.

"Welcome home," she smirks.

Sliding out of her, I rest sideways on the bed, wrapping her legs around me.

"Best welcome home ever." My breathing finally steadies itself. "When is Mason home from school?"

"He has after-school club today."

"Golf?"

"Yup, golf, just like his daddy."

Our blond, blue-eyed son, Mason, is adorable, super sporty and athletic, but he's quiet and such a beautiful soul. He may excel at all the different sports, but he loves nothing better than reading for hours or drawing. He's creative and active, the best of both worlds.

"I wonder what this little princess will be like?" I smooth my hand over Ella's swollen stomach.

We're having a girl. I've already implemented a no boy ban, not on my watch, and I'll be watching. You can count on that.

"Who cares, as long as she's happy?" Ella strokes my cheek.

"True."

"How was your meeting with Play and Pay Fair in London?"

"Great. They want me to speak at their charity event next month, but I'm not sure if I will have the time. I have tournaments in Georgia and Florida next month, and also Ethan is visiting too."

It surprises me that Ethan still wants to come stay, with us, but he's not exactly enamored with his two new little sisters Anna and Lucas had. He says all they do is play with dolls and dress up. He wanted brothers, hence why he enjoys coming to visit Mason.

And I kept on playing golf. It's the other one of the great loves of my life. I play all the major events for me to hold on to my tour card. One of the perks of being a pro, I can pick and choose. I never did get to number one position in the world rankings, but I don't care. My priority is my family. I do have a few commitments this coming month, but I'm hoping Ella and Mason come with me, like they normally do during school vacations.

"I'm limited for time, plus I have to keep satisfying my wife. She is a demon in the bedroom at the moment. I need a holiday," I groan.

Ella giggles. She does that a lot around me. She loves me. I feel it bouncing off her all the time. Ditto, I'm obsessed with her.

"I'm so happy you didn't give up as many golf championships as you thought you might. I know you love it all, really."

She knows me so well. "I do," I grin.

"Have you been managing the dance classes?"

"Yeah, I've been okay, actually. I don't want to start my maternity leave too soon. I would miss dancing and teaching too much. But the new building is causing us lots of stress."

"Oh, yeah?"

The girls moved their dance school to yet another, even bigger new building with multiple studios. They are about to be accredited and become a full-fledged dance school, offering scholarships and full-time classes. There's even mention of singing and acting classes too.

"They installed the wrong lighting in three of the studios, then the downstairs toilets flooded, and *then* they smashed six of the mirrors when they fixed them to the walls of the studios." She rolls her eyes. "I'm glad it wasn't me who did that. I don't want seven years of bad luck. I already had several years without you, and that was painful enough."

"That's never going to happen again, Bella."

"I know, we're forever."

We sure are.

The sounds of twelve little feet, jangling collars, and panting breaths enter our bedroom. Treacle, Toffee, and Trey are older now, but still as active and crazy as ever.

A loud knocking sound against the floor alarms me to the fact they've found something heavy on the floor.

Oh shit, I hope it's not my phone.

I sit up quickly to discover Trey has Ella's glass unicorn friend in his mouth.

"Well, that guarantees you won't be using it again."

I help Ella sit up.

"Ew. That's going in the bin."

I punch the air. "Finally. Good boy, Trey." He wags his stubby tail, all pleased as punch with himself as he dashes out of the room.

The front door suddenly slams. "Hey, it's me. After-school golf was canceled today, so I brought Mason home to save you. I was at the school for Hamish, anyway."

Eva.

I can hear Mason talking to the dog. "Oh, what's that you've got, Trey? Is that a new toy?" he coos.

I look at Ella, who's sitting in shock, then mouths a silent oh my God at me.

"Oh please, Mason, don't touch that."

"What is it?"

"It's eh, a, a..."

"It looks like a penis."

"It's not a penis; it's a, oh please, don't touch it Mason. Let Trey keep ahold of it."

"Oh, Trey is playing a game. I'm going to catch him." His innocent, sweet voice echoes with glee through the hall.

"Mason," Eva calls after him. "Oh, screw it. You two can explain what that goddamn thing is," she shouts up the stairs.

We both burst out laughing.

"I know what you're up to in the bedroom, you filthy pair. I'm off."

"Bye, and thank you," Ella bellows down the stairs, then we hear Eva exiting.

"We need to get dressed quickly, c'mon." I pop my hand out to help her roll off the bed. "And I wanna see my boy. I've missed him."

My son.

Pulling her into my arms, I steal a kiss. I want to touch her all the time.

"Why don't you take Mason for a golf lesson out in the garden? I'll make dinner and we can watch a movie tonight."

Sounds like the best Friday night on record to me.

She nestles into my neck, and I hold her as tightly as humanly possible.

I let out a sigh of contentment.

I love my life. My boy. My unborn child. My wife.

Since the day my eyes caught hers across the dining hall

at school, she's the only one I could see myself living my life with.

I'm living my dream.

As I hold her here, I realize it may have taken us too long to rekindle our flame, but it's made me appreciate her all the more. She's my forever.

Forever and Eternity.

Fraser & Ella.

F & E.

THE TRIPLE TROUBLE SERIES CONTINUES... Turn the page to read a sneak peek of Unexpected Eva...

Eva's Story: mybook.to/unexpectedeva (Book 3)

In case you haven't read Book 1 in the series:
Eden's Story: mybook.to/huntingeden_VHNicolson

SNEAK PEEK: UNEXPECTED EVA
CHAPTER ONE & TWO

Eva

Curving my body around the never-ending circular tables littered throughout the extraordinary ballroom, I'm on a mission to make it to my seat without being noticed.

I'm surrounded by hundreds of cheerful people.

Cheerful people I can*not* be bothered speaking to this evening.

Hitching my floor-length ball gown up at one side, being careful not to snag the delicate ink-blue silk on my towering gold heels, I'm suddenly stopped in my tracks. *Shoot.* Too late, didn't make it... And what's her name again?

Eh, oh, crap, hmm, think Eva, think.

"Hello dear, it's so wonderful to see you. How are you?" The cheery silver-haired woman smiles brightly.

"Evening. I'm great, thank you; how are you and the family?" I try my best to hide my confusion and flustered appearance, deep down hoping she does, in fact, have a family. A tiny smidge of memory slides in. I know her name; it's on the tip of my tongue. Is it Carol? Something beginning with *C*, I know it.

"Oh, they are wonderful, darling. Thomas is a top criminal lawyer now, and his wife, Matilda, is simply divine. She's also a lawyer. They've bought one of the Victorian mansion houses down Cherry Gardens Lane. You know the ones?" She raises her voice over the chitter-chatter around us, glancing to her left and right to see if anyone heard her momentary boast. She clearly wants everyone to know how successful her son is.

Cecilia? Is that her name?

Nope, that's not it either.

I'm at a loss.

"Yes, I know those homes. They are beautiful at that end of town."

The nineteenth century mansions down Cherry Gardens Lane are stunning. There are ten in total. Each one is unique, otherworldly, and big—dream goals big. Many of them can't be seen from the curbside because they're heavily guarded by surrounding trees, high stone walls, and solid wooden gates.

Our little town of Castleview Cove may be small, where everyone knows everyone, but those homeowners are a mystery to me and most of the residents of Castleview.

Owned by affluent businesspeople and celebrity types, they float into town for the weekend and then drift back like ghosts to their high-powered city jobs during the week.

The old-timers of the town do not approve of them at all, nicknaming the new town people *incomers*. Silly stuck-in-a-time-warp fuddy-duddies.

A couple of the homes have been inherited from townspeople of old, passed down from generation to generation. When that happens, the remodeling begins.

It's wonderful to see the old decrepit mansions

undergoing renovations, giving them a new lease on life, injecting new blood into our unique little community.

Rumor has it two pro golfers have purchased homes down Cherry Gardens Lane, but I'm yet to catch a glimpse of one in town. And my brother-in-law, Hunter King, also a pro golfer, doesn't count. He and my sister, Eden, built a brand-new all-glass home that sits up high on the hill overlooking Castleview Cove. Sometimes I just happen to be *passing by*. Any excuse to kick back on their deck, a hot steaming cup of tea in hand, and lazily drink in the view. It's beautiful and a far cry from the playpark I can see from the upper window of my little three-bedroom townhouse.

From Eden's house, though, you can see the entire town. The castle that sits prominently on top of the hill keeping watch, and the golf courses that span for miles, blanketing the landscape.

Our tiny Scottish town feels magical, like it's breathing in the sea salt air, exhaling spellbound particles, casting us under her charm.

It's a truly captivating place, one I have lived in my entire life, save from when I attended dance school to become a dancer. It's littered with ancient ruins and buildings; some date as far back as the eleventh century. Every twist, nook, and cranny is another discovery waiting to be uncovered. It really is something special.

Those homes down Cherry Gardens Lane, though, they are special. Intriguing.

I've always wanted a little sneak peek or tour of one. It's a shame I don't know anyone that lives down that road, apart from my father's friend, Knox Black, but I would *never* ask him. He's strictly off-limits. *Although I wish he wasn't.*

A sudden whoosh of recollection hits me.

Ah, got it!

The woman standing in front of me is Christie. Christie Burns. I knew it began with a *C*.

They live in the next town over. She ran the local Sewing Bee group with my mom when I was around eight years old. Thomas, her son, always tagged along with her; pulling my pigtails was his favorite pastime. He always did have the ability to wind me up something stupid. He's no longer a silly little boy, but a lawyer, no less. Thomas has done well for himself.

Pointing toward the stage, informing Christie the charity auction is about to begin, I shift around the dainty woman.

"Oh, it was lovely to see you, Eden. Please tell your mother I'm asking about her."

I bite my tongue and fake a smile.

It's Eva, you silly woman, not Eden.

One thing that annoys me about being a triplet—people mix us up. Although my sisters, Ella, Eden, and I are not identical, it has been known on occasion, like now, for people to get us muddled. We are fraternal triplets, like vanilla ice cream with different toppings.

Yes, we all have blond hair and yes, we look similar but we are very different in terms of styles and height. Eden is a continuous bundle of youth and laughter, while Ella is our sassy sexy platinum goddess then there's me. The homemaker. I'm the tallest in our trio and my style is more eclectic than them both combined. While Eden loves nothing better than a trip to the shops to buy more Disney apparel and Ella loves the whole biker chic, leather pant look, I'm more bohemian in style and love a mooch around a vintage clothing store. And it's normally a quick in and out, unlike Eden, I'm not a fan of shopping around dozens of clothes shops.

Also, Eden is only five foot two and I'm five foot ten. Clearly, not identical triplets.

Goodness knows how Christie thinks I am Eden.

Finally breaking away from Christie, I mosey over to my designated table. Politely greeting everyone with a small hello, I slide into my seat for the evening and make myself comfortable.

I'm relieved to be taking the weight off my feet for the day. They are already throbbing and the night hasn't even started yet. I'm wearing what my sisters call sitting shoes—too uncomfortable to walk or dance in, simply sit in and look pretty, although even that is too painful.

I push the sky-high gold heels off my feet and give my aching toes a wiggle in the cool air beneath the table.

Enjoying the welcomed calm in contrast to my busy day of school runs, teaching dance classes, cooking, cleaning, and washing, I relax into my chair.

I ferried my two boys off to my parents' for a sleepover for the entire weekend.

I do not know what I will do with myself for one whole day and night tomorrow. It's been months since I had any downtime. Although my ironing pile is massive, I'm pretty sure it was waving at me earlier, trying to grab my attention.

Sipping my crisp glass of champagne, I sneak a glance around the room in awe. No matter how many times I've been in this ballroom, it never ceases to amaze me.

It's stunning, decorated in luminous white with a contrasting navy-painted ceiling. Recessed into the ceiling are hundreds of fairy-style lights. It's dazzling and makes the ceiling look like a clear, starry night. White furnishings cover every inch of the room. Elegant white chairs, white flowers, white table covers, white everything, even the floor, which I thought was a brave choice. However, given the five-star hotel's clientele, it's not as if they have rowdy hen parties here every week. No sirree.

The Sanctuary Hotel and Spa is luxurious. Breathtaking. Expensive. Designed for the elite. When the golf championships are in town, this is where all the celebrities stay. You can't get within an inch of the security gate without being frisked.

When Ewan and I were planning our wedding, I had always dreamed of entertaining my wedding guests here, but it was a way out of our budget. Instead, we rented a large pavilion-style tent within the grounds of my parents' sports retreat. It was beautiful, but a far cry from the extravagance of this magnificent space.

The over-the-top auction items up for grabs this evening mirror the extravagance of the ballroom. Those items draw people in from near and far for tonight's yearly pissing contest—er, charity auction—and seated around the table, I only recognize half the people to the left and right of me. This could be a long night.

Me, Eden, and Ella literally pulled straws to decide who would represent our dance school, The 3 Sisters Dance School, or as we like to call it, *T3SDS*.

I lost.

Having recently decided to move our studio to bigger premises, we agreed only one of us would attend this year as we are saving like crazy to make that happen.

It will most likely be a few years before we can afford to move, but we've set our intentions. Therefore, sacrifices need to be made, and at two and a half grand a ticket for tonight's event, even one ticket was pushing it. Although it is all going to charity. How can I get annoyed with that?

Hours later, I've relaxed into the evening; surprisingly I'm enjoying it. I've made polite conversation with an older gentleman to my left, who I have learned is named Edward. He hasn't said a single word to his wife next to him since I sat down; the poor woman looks bored to tears. In between my new elbow buddy's never-ending sea of words, I've listened to the auctioneer's noisy chanting and hammering.

With each auction item, the bids, mainly from the men, get more and more elaborate. As I said, a pissing contest. Next, they'll be whipping out their dicks to compare who has the biggest.

"Going once, going twice, sold! To the gentleman at the back." The auctioneer slams his gavel down hard against the wooden podium, then points his oversized, battered wooden hammer toward him. "Number thirty-eight. Congratulations. You just won yourself a luxury all-inclusive week, right here, at The Sanctuary Hotel and Spa, courtesy of the owner, Knox Black," the auctioneer's nasally voice chants across the ballroom.

Not caring who won the item, I remain facing toward the stage area and softly clap.

I zone out, daydreaming.

Every year my little Scottish hometown hosts this charity auction in aid of the local children's hospital, Lily's, which supports children with life-shortening illnesses.

I love everything the auction stands for, its purpose and the incredible cause the money raised goes toward, but I miss being at home snuggled up with my sons.

A smile breaks free from my lips momentarily at the thought of them. Hamish and Archie. I thank my lucky stars and feel a wave of gratefulness; they are both happy and healthy.

They've both gotten so big this past year. Archie, who's seven, is going to be tall, just like his daddy, but with ice-blond hair like me when I was younger. He's shot up another three inches in height, and I've yet again had to restock his wardrobe.

Archie's a cocksure little lad, an infuriating little monkey at times. He knows what he wants, and he knows exactly how to get it. Negotiating and bartering are Archie's strengths. That's where my weakness lies, and he knows it. It's exhausting. I reckon he's going to be on the debating team at school someday. I can feel it. God help us all. Although he could maybe help me argue a case to pass a law for all upcoming divorcing moms to receive six months off, like a sabbatical, but paid to give us time to reevaluate our lives and heal.

I need that.

Then there's my little Hamish. He's my darling three-year-old boy who's utterly adorable, loveable, and playful. He giggles endlessly and smothers me in kisses daily. He's a mirror image of his father—dark-haired with big brown eyes. He loves playing in the mud and would eat worms for breakfast if he could. No matter how hard I try to dress him, he won't have any of it. He's fiercely independent and thinks he knows best when it comes to dressing himself.

I failed to stifle my giggles when he ventured down the stairs the other morning, not dressed in the outfit I laid out for him, but dressed in a pair of frog-green rubber boots on the wrong feet, red shorts on back to front, a bright-yellow sweater, and to complete the look, a pair of swimming goggles, and matching blue-and-orange swimming float. He wore it proudly, like he was modeling the finest waistcoat. Classic Hamish and oh so beautifully innocent. My boy.

There is no way I would have survived the last twelve months without their distraction, their love, and their cuddles. My two boys are my everything.

Although I'm not sure I've been the best mom,

struggling to keep my frustration and tiredness levels hidden. Snippy and shouty is what Archie has started to call me. I thought it would make a good name for a cartoon show. When I suggested that to Archie, he rolled his eyes, informing me how uncool I am.

Since my husband, Ewan, and I agreed to separate—well, I asked him to move out and then finally persuaded him we should divorce—I've been a cranky bitch.

My sisters can vouch for that too. I wasn't exactly myself earlier this year when Ella and Fraser, her husband to be, needed me. I was selfish and self-centered in their time of need. I have apologized profusely. Fraser understood and explained how divorce can make you feel and act out of character. He gets it. And Ella being Ella, she was forgiving and loves me unconditionally. It's just as well because I have needed them more than ever recently.

I've also been helping Eden and Hunter out with their new triplet baby boys too. Mainly out of guilt to show my sisters I am here for them and truly sorry for my recently mood swings. Separation and divorce has brought out the worst in me at times. But I'm trying to be more level-headed. As time has gone by I seem to be getting my moods under control and no longer feel like I'm on an emotional roller coaster

I'm still mad though.

Mad at myself.

Mad as a hatter at myself for not spotting Ewan's need for help with his alcohol dependency earlier. And mad at myself for not being able to save our marriage.

I failed.

Failed at marriage.

Failed to keep our little family together.

Filing for divorce at twenty-eight years old, a broken

marriage under my belt before the age of thirty, was *never* a future goal for me. I'm high up the failed marriages leaderboard. *Score.*

Now it's just me and my two boys, and even though I feel disappointed at myself that I couldn't make my marriage work, for the first time in a long time I feel happy. I'd almost forgotten what that felt like.

My mom said I should give myself a pat on the back.

I survived separation; I survived the lawyer meetings; I survived Ewan flipping out when I produced our divorce papers. He's still yet to sign them, but I survived.

I made it.

I did also shed an ocean of tears.

For losing my childhood friend.

Said farewell to our love.

Waved goodbye to our marriage.

But it made me question everything once we finally separated.

I'm not sure we were ever as tight as I thought we were.

Within three weeks of us separating, Ewan found someone new and started dating Ruby Thomas from five doors down the street.

Was he loyal and faithful to me?

Were they together before? With us living so close together?

Probably. I may never know, and I'm too proud to ask Ewan. I actually don't want to know if he cheated on me. That would be a step too far for me after he broke my heart the way he did.

Maybe that's why he stopped having sex with me. He was getting it from someone else. Or maybe it was the alcohol. Because he always chose that over me and our boys.

I don't feel jealous or upset that he's already moved on.

I feel... fine.

It seems like such a nondescript word, but I am fine.

I'm good and finally getting back on my feet.

I'm tired though, as my two boys, running a business, and teaching extra dance classes to cover Ella's unexpected time off and Eden's maternity leave, are taking its toll. I need a vacation. Stat.

Hence why I didn't want to come here tonight. I'm here to represent the business, nothing else. But I need more sleep and sunshine. Oh God, yeah, now that does sound lush. Maybe I should book a vacation? My boys would love a water park somewhere warm. Mentally, I make a note to ask my sisters when that would suit them for me to have a week off. A gentle buzz of excitement thrums through me at the prospect of a vacation with my boys. It's exactly what we all need.

An enormous *bang* from the auctioneer's gavel startles me, instantly pulling me from my thoughts. I jump, throwing my hand to my heart. I let out a small yelp and a flutter of laughter drifts around our table.

"Sorry, I was lost in my own little world there." I shake my head. Reaching out, I clasp my champagne flute and take another little sip of the sparkling liquid. This is only my second glass tonight. I don't want to waste my day off tomorrow by nursing a hangover. Being honest, I could take or leave a drink.

"Up last," the auctioneer bellows. "Twelve kizomba dance lessons for two people. Privately tutored by none other than our own local expert dance teacher, Eva Wallace. Who I believe is with us this evening." I clench for a moment at the use of my maiden name. That may take some time to get used to again. I reverted to it before my divorce is final. It's not legal yet, but it will be.

I watch the auctioneer curve his hands above his eyebrows, seeking me out in the crowd.

Making my presence known, I wave my hand in the air.

"Ah, there's the exceptionally talented Eva from the world famous T3SDS. Eva and her sisters really have taken social media by storm. Ask Eva for her autograph while you can because those girls are changing the face of dance, ladies and gentlemen." He claps a semicircle around himself, indicating others to join in.

Well, this is embarrassing. Although he's not wrong. Social media has been the best thing to happen to us. Dance routines are totally our bag and we have grown a massive following online.

A gentle wave of appreciation echoes across the ballroom as my ears catch some complimentary comments. *Their parents must be so proud. We should book private lessons, Geoffrey. Look at her figure. Has she not recently separated from her husband?*

Ouch.

Ignoring the last comment, I sit up a little straighter in my seat, push my shoulders back, and hold my head high, all while displaying a dazzling smile.

I'm always the businesswoman.

"Ladies and gentlemen, to get this underway, I'm starting the bids at one hundred pounds. Who will give me one hundred?" The auctioneer's brows shoot up.

And that's it, the bids go up by tens. Before I know it, those twelve intimate kizomba lessons are sitting at five hundred pounds.

"C'mon, ladies. You know you want these lessons. Kizomba is considered being *the* sexiest dance in the world. We all want to know how to move our hips, now don't we?"

A faint titter of laughter breaks out.

"Six hundred," someone shouts, and that's it. The bids go higher yet again.

What the hell? People are crazy here tonight.

Urging the bidders on, the auctioneer's chanting becomes more frantic. "C'mon, we are up to one thousand pounds. Who wants to learn a fusion of dance steps and how to synchronize those hips, baby, with the beautiful Eva here." Everyone bursts out laughing, including me. He's a great salesman; I'll give him that.

Kizomba is such a sexy dance. It's one of my favorites. Sultry, erotic, elegant. It combines many dance styles; like the auctioneer says, it's a fusion of footwork and flirting. I have always thought if I got the *right* dance partner, then I'm pretty sure I would orgasm on the dance floor from this dance alone.

It connects you together like no other type of dance. It's sensual and provocative; it creates tension with every smooth wave of your hips.

I hope I get to teach a couple who love each other and want to connect on a new level. I've watched so many couples eye-fuck each other to this erotic dance, then watch as they run off the dance floor to fuck each other's brains out; it's that powerful. The ultimate foreplay.

The bids rise again. Wow.

"Two thousand pounds. Are we done? Going once, twi—"

"Ten thousand."

A loud audible gasp ripples through the seated guests.

Aw, shit, I know that voice.

The auctioneer stalls.

"Did I hear that correctly?" His eyebrows pull together. "Ten thousand pounds?"

"Yes," the voice calls all the way from the back of the grand room.

A low hum of hushed tones gasp, gossip, and conspire all at once. All eyes in the room turn to the voice that makes my stomach loop the loop.

Every. Single. Time.

I slowly turn in my seat to face the infamous man that has flooded my dreams for the last couple of months. My eyes lock on his dark orbs.

Knox Black.

***

CHAPTER 2

Eva

Knox's eye color matches his name.

Black.

And they're looking right at me.

He's so handsome, suave, and sophisticated.

Dark.

He oozes power and dominance like no other man on the planet. It's unnerving. Sexy. Commanding.

He extraordinary and always manages to make me feel on edge. He has the ability to make me feel like I belong to him. I can't explain it.

For a moment, it feels like it's only us. His dark eyes never leave mine as he confirms his bid again, making my heart pound in my chest. "Ten thousand pounds."

From the left of me I hear a faint whisper. "He must have a new woman in his life. I wonder who the lucky lady is."

Oh, well, isn't that just perfect? Teaching him. Watching

him eye-fuck someone else under my instruction is *not* what I had planned when I donated the lessons.

"Right," the auctioneer bellows across the microphone, startling me yet again. Knox's gaze doesn't let up. It's me who finally breaks our trance. I look back at the auctioneer. "Ten thousand pounds, it is. Going once, twi—"

"Twelve thousand," a jovial voice I also recognize calls out from the other side of the elegant room.

Snapping my head back around, I see Knox's son, Lincoln, with his hand raised in the air, the other casually tucked into the pocket of his dress pants as he leans lazily against the back wall.

Eh, excuse me?

Whispered words dance across the vast space once more.

Knox instantly retaliates with his counter bid of thirteen, and then the two of them ping-pong incomprehensible amounts of money back and forth.

My brain can't accept what's happening.

Captivated along with everyone else in the room, we all bounce our heads between the two most handsome dark-haired men I have ever seen in my life, watching on as father and son play a virtual game of power tennis.

The auctioneer struggles to keep up with them as the bid reaches twenty-five thousand.

Twenty-five thousand!

But Knox doesn't stop there. "Thirty thousand plus another fifty to help toward the construction of the new ward for the hospital. Done." His deep velvet voice sends warm ripples down my spine.

His words are final. Lincoln shakes his head, blazing a knockout smile across his lips in my direction. He knows he lost, but he doesn't care. It's almost as if Lincoln was trying to prove a point to his father. About what, I don't know, but I intend to find out.

"Good gracious," the auctioneer stutters. "Eighty thousand pounds. Sold." *Slam* goes his gavel. "To Knox Black. What a way to end the evening."

A tremendous roar of claps, whistles, and whoops begins and all I can do is simply sit there stunned with my mouth gaping open like a fish out of water.

Eighty thousand pounds.

What just happened?

Nervously, I capture my bottom lip between my teeth, flitting my eyes around the room. Lincoln's eyes find mine. He smiles, then throws me a cheeky wink. Pushing his back away from the wall, Lincoln struts toward his father.

Where Knox is dark and quiet, Lincoln is bright and playful. He is only three years younger than me and I remember him from high school and the beach parties we local kids used to have in the bowl of the cove on warm summer evenings.

Knox and his ex-wife were teenagers when they had Lincoln. Lincoln's mother is no longer in the picture and I've never thought to ask what happened to her. I wonder if my father knows.

I watch both Knox and Lincoln exit the ballroom together.

Unsure of what to do, I quickly tuck my feet back into my uncomfortable heels, accept the looks of gobsmacked congratulations around the table for raising so much money on my auction item, then excuse myself.

Making my way to the exit door, I feel hundreds of sets of eyes on my every move.

Looking braver than I feel, I flip my long caramel locks over my shoulders. With my head held high, I exit the grand room and exhale a deep breath as I almost throw myself into the corridor.

Holy cow, that was intense.

Distracted now by the familiar raised voices along the corridor, carefully teetering on my heels, I follow them.

"What the hell do you think you were doing, Linc?"

Knox.

"Do you like her, Dad? I like her. *Really* like her. Be honest with me."

Knox does like me. I know this already. Knox disclosed his feelings for me last year, when I was still married, instantly following up his confession with an over-the-top apology, informing me he had overstepped the mark. He didn't make any advances on me. He was respectful and has kept his distance since then.

But Lincoln likes me too?

What the hell?

Did Knox bid to have dance lessons from me so he could get close to me? Eighty thousand pounds seems extreme.

"No. We've discussed this, Linc; she's off-limits to me. Now drop it, son."

"No way. You bid eighty thousand pounds to have private lessons with her." Lincoln laughs. "You need to explain."

I continue toward them.

"And you just bid twenty-five thousand."

"I wanted to see what you would do, if you would push. You did. I've seen you checking her out."

"It's for the hospital."

"Is it? I personally would like to get to know her better. *Do* you like her? You should admit it if you do. Now that Ewan's no longer in the picture, she's fair game. And what about Tabit—"

Words leave my mouth before I can stop them. "Why are

you two talking about me like I can be bought? You may have paid eighty thousand pounds, but I have never felt so cheap in all of my life." They both jump at my unexpected presence.

"Shit." Knox sighs under his breath.

Lincoln welcomes me with yet another wide smile. Gosh, he's handsome.

But when Knox swivels on his feet to face me, his eyes fixed on mine, my insides liquefy, and a tornado of flutters batter wildly in my lower stomach. He's even more captivating.

Knox creates strange emotions I have no control over. I have never felt this way, with anyone, including my husband, er, ex-husband to be.

"I'm sorry, Eva," Knox apologizes. "I never want you to feel like that. Please forgive the crassness of our conversation."

"You bid eighty thousand pounds for twelve dance lessons that cost only five hundred pounds. I'm confused. What was that about exactly?"

I point back in the room's direction. My eyes dance between the two of them.

"I think he's staking his claim." Lincoln grins.

"Enough now, Linc." Knox scowls through a tight jaw.

Staking his claim?

"Huh?" I pinch my brows.

"Go, Linc," Knox instructs.

"I hope to see you around, Eva." Lincoln bounces past me jauntily with his trademark cheeky smile. That guy is annoyingly cheerful twenty-four seven.

"So?" I bug my eyes out, waiting for an answer.

Silence. I watch Knox's throat bob up, then down.

Gosh, he's so, just so, *masculine.*

"I got carried away. I'm sorry. I didn't mean to offend you. I do genuinely want to learn how to dance. That dance in particular." He looks nervous as he loosens the top button of his crisp white shirt.

"You want to learn how to dance the kizomba? Since when?"

I genuinely want to know.

He's thinking.

"I've watched you before. I've seen you teach it."

Watched me.

"When?"

"When I've visited your father at his sports retreat. When we meet at the back entrance sometimes, next to your dance studio. Then."

"Oh."

"I'm always captivated."

"Oh."

"By you." A smirk pulls his mouth to the side.

I lick my lips, my mouth suddenly parched. "Could you not have booked lessons with me directly, instead of paying eighty thousand pounds for them? Or forty thousand per person, depending on which way you look at it. Who are you bringing?"

"It's for the hospital. And it will be me. No partner."

"Oh." I'm lost for words. Oh seems to be the only one I can sound out.

Just him.

I audibly gulp.

"Your father tells me you're now divorced."

His change in subject throws me. "Eh, yeah, well, not yet, but I will be soon."

"Are you okay?"

"Yeah." I faintly smile. "I'm slowly getting used to the feeling of being happy again."

He nods.

"How are your boys?"

"Fine. They'll be fine." I squeeze my tiny evening purse in my hand.

"Where are they tonight?"

Why is he asking? "Staying all weekend with Mom and Dad."

Knox bobs his head. I notice then exactly how close he is to me. Did he move or did I move? I don't know. What I do know is that he is only a foot away from me now.

"You look beautiful tonight, Sunshine." His deep voice rumbles low in his chest as he examines me, sweeping his eyes across, over, up, and down. I feel his gaze flood every inch of my body.

"Sunshine?"

He nods. "You light up every room you're in. You're like sunshine in human form."

That's beautiful. Thoughtful. "Oh."

I don't think I've ever had such a long conversation with Knox in my life. He's quiet most of the time, an onlooker. He watches everything. He doesn't waste words and makes every one count when he does speak. He doesn't suffer fools gladly, nor does he have time for idle chitchat. I would call him broody, but I think he's more thoughtful and profound.

"You never called me about the business proposition I have for you, Eva." I shudder as he draws out my short name through a soft exhale.

Ella and I bumped into Knox on the beach a few months ago while he was walking his dog, Sam. He said I was to call the hotel reception and book an appointment to discuss a business proposal. I had forgotten all about it.

"I've been busy. Sorry."

"I'll make it worth your while. The dance school, that is." Beneath hooded eyes, he zones in on my lips.

I clear my throat.

"I'll remember to call you." I breathe out, increasingly aware he's now mere inches from me. My chest heaves up and down with expectation. Of what, I don't know.

"You light up my soul, Sunshine. It's like a fucking blazing inferno burns inside of me when I'm near you." His confessions rolls off his lips.

Knox leans in unexpectedly. He runs his nose up the side of my neck, into the curtain of my caramel locks; his lips lightly ghost my ear.

I've dreamed about this moment.

I close my eyes as my resistance to him fades away.

"What are you doing?" I gasp, feeling every hard inch of him beneath my thin, silky dress when he presses his firm body against mine.

"Something I've wanted to do for a very long time. I told you last year. I want you," he growls into my neck. "You smell like heaven."

Oh God.

My skin flushes and my heart beats like a drum. He was as serious back then as he is now. His confession of longing to taste me has never changed.

Last year at the Spring Fling Ball, he expressed his desire for me. It was yet another event Ewan couldn't be trusted to attend, especially with a free bar, so I went with my sisters and friends.

Knox doesn't dance with anyone. But he asked *me* to dance. Pressed flush together, he threw a curveball. As we drifted across the dance floor, he confessed to me how I was the most beautiful woman in the room. How he wanted to taste me, but I was forbidden fruit. His forbidden desire. None of his words shocked me. He's always watching. Watching *me*.

He's never subtle, not to me. To everyone else I think he is, but I sense him everywhere.

"If you were mine, everyone in that room would know it. You come to these events by yourself. Ewan never appreciated you. Or your body. Your beautiful body fucking speaks to me, calls my name. I feel you everywhere in my veins. When you're around, I can't fucking think straight. You're an intoxicating goddess and a terrible distraction. I have bad thoughts about you, ones I shouldn't have, and I make stupid decisions when you're around."

I whimper at his admission. I don't think I'm intoxicating; I think it's the other way around.

"Like bidding eighty thousand pounds to dance with me?" I gasp.

"Best fucking money I've ever spent, if it means getting closer to you." His hot breath surfs across my goose-bumped skin before he pushes me up against the wall behind.

Well, this evening is not what I expected. It's way better.

"Eva. Tell me. Do you think about me?"

I can't deny it. "Yes. I dream about you sometimes."

Crap, I think they laced my champagne with truth serum.

"That right?"

"Yeah." I pant like a bitch in heat.

"Do you want me as much as I want you?"

"Yes." I'm not playing games. Screw it. If anything, the past year has taught me that life is too damn short.

"I know you do. I see it. I see *you*. The way your skin flushes around me. I know you want me. Your mind might deny it, but I can read this fucking sexy body of yours and it wants mine."

"It does. I do." I moan.

"Do you care that I'm fifteen years older than you?" he mumbles against my skin. I want him to kiss me.

"No, and it's only fourteen. I'll be twenty-nine in a few months. Forty-three isn't old. You've not long turned forty-three, right?"

Although that's not what I told Ella all those months ago on the beach. I told her he was too old for me. I was denying what my body desires, but I do want him.

"You pay attention. Good girl." He plants a soft kiss on my nape. "You should be with Lincoln; he's closer to your age," he says as if he's mumbling reasons we shouldn't be together to himself.

I shudder. "I don't want him."

"He'll hate me." He thrusts his hips into mine. I can feel how hard he is for me. His thick length is undeniable. He's big—bigger than, well, Ewan. That's all I have to compare him to.

"I don't want to cause trouble between you two."

"I'm a shitty dad." He kisses my neck again. "Fuck, I can't resist you."

"Then don't."

"I'm also your father's friend."

"He never needs to know."

"It's wrong." But he doesn't move away from me.

"I don't care."

"I'm a bad man for wanting you."

"I want you to be bad, Knox. I'm always the good girl. I want to be bad with you."

"Fuck," he exhales against my skin.

I'm clearly not thinking straight this evening. I think my deep desire for intimacy is doing the talking for me.

Knox lays a path of gentle kisses across my nape, toward my delectable spot behind my ear. It's another of my weaknesses.

I let out a frustrated groan as he flicks his rough tongue again and again over my sensitive skin, biting, kissing, licking, soaking my panties in the process. Warmth spreads between my legs and I'm aching for him to touch me *there*.

I let out another loud moan.

"Shhhhh. This is a classy hotel." A deep chuckle leaves his throat. I don't think I've ever heard Knox laugh before, and I kind of like it.

His hand drifts across my clavicle, gently stroking the silk of my dress as he heads south, between my cleavage. Skirting across my stomach, he goes lower.

He stops, teasing me, before he slips his hand inside the thigh-high slit of my dress and skims his large hand over the thin, now-soaked lace of my panties, then traces his fingers across my throbbing pussy.

I groan, feeling his powerful erotic touch. He surely must feel how wet I am for him.

"Oh God, Knox, I need you." It's been so long since anyone has shown me any affection; my body needs the release, and I want him to be the one to do it. I want him to shake off the last year. I want to feel free and desired once more, to feel joy and to be fucked right, like I know Knox will. He'll look after me.

"Stay with me tonight, Eva."

I snap my eyes open to find him staring back at me with deep, apprehensive eyes.

"Okay."

He gifts me a rare knockout smile and I practically melt into him.

He's gorgeous.

I want him.

For one night only.

That's all I need.

No one ever needs to know.

It's just one night.

Right?

OUT NOW: mybook.to/unexpectedeva

ACKNOWLEDGMENTS

Wow, what a ride huh? Book Two – who would have thought it? I can't actually believe I wrote a second book. To say the last year has been a huge learning curve for me is an understatement and I would like to take this opportunity to thank the huge party of people that helped me co-ordinate Eva and Fraser's story.

To my incredibly supportive husband, thank you for your never-ending belief in me. To my son who taught me everything I needed to know about TikTok (he still has more followers that me!). My boys cheered me on from the sidelines, urging me on to keep on going, to keep believing and to put the hours in to make this book happen.

Thank you to Kimberly, my editor, who put up with all of my strange queries converting British English to American English – I am still learning. I adore having you on my team.

To my mum, dad, and sister... yet again, thanks for all the little messages of encouragement and sharing.

A massive shout out and thank you to the most incredible mentor and Queen of all Swans, TL Swan, who without, I would never have written another book. When Tee formed a special group of girls over lockdown, I wasn't sure if my idea for my first book would even see the light of day, but I did it, I published it and here we are again. Tee told us girls to keep chasing our dreams, to stand in our power, follow our own path and to write the book we wanted to read. Without her stream of knowledge and without that group of beautiful Cygnets I would not be here now writing the acknowledgement for my second book. I will forever be grateful to Tee and all you talented Cygnets for your guidance, advice, sharing, cheerleading, and virtual hugs.

To Laura and Sadie, there are not enough words to thank you for always being there when I need you most. I love you girls.

Rosie, Carolann, Sarah, Sorrel, and Alison... my extraordinary beta readers... thank you for taking the time out of your days and nights to read for me. Your constant messages of encouragement, feedback and excitement gave me the energy to keep on writing every single day. You are a huge part of this journey and I love having each and every one of you in my world.

And to you, the spicy book reader, thank you for taking a leap of faith on a new author, you have no idea how much that means to me, I am eternally grateful. THANK YOU! Mwah x

ALSO BY VH NICOLSON

The Triple Trouble Series

Hunting Eden - The Triple Trouble Series (Book 1):
mybook.to/huntingeden_VHNicolson

Unexpected Eva - The Triple Trouble Series (Book 3):
mybook.to/unexpectedeva

The Boys of Castleview Cove

Lincoln - The Boys of Castleview Cove (Book 1):

mybook.to/LincolnVHNicolson

Jacob - The Boys of Castleview Cove (Book 2):

mybook.to/Jacob_VHNicolson

Owen - The Boys of Castleview Cove (Book 3):

mybook.to/OwenVHNicolson

COMING SPRING 2023

ABOUT THE AUTHOR

Since writing her first contemporary romance novel over lockdown, Vicki is now completely smitten with writing love stories with happily ever afters. VH Nicolson was born and raised along the breathtaking coastline in North East Fife in Scotland. For more than two decades she's worked throughout the UK and abroad within the creative marketing and design industry, as a branding strategist and stylist, editor of a magazine and sub-editor of a newspaper. Married to her soul mate, they have one son. She has a weakness for buying too many quirky sparkly jumpers, eating Belgium buns, and walking the endless beaches that surround her beautiful Scottish hometown she's now moved back to.

Website: vhnicolsonauthor.com
Facebook Group:
bit.ly/VHNicolsonFacebookReaderGroup

Printed in Great Britain
by Amazon